A FORGED HEARTS NOVEL

BLACK WAVE

L. RENÉE RICHARD

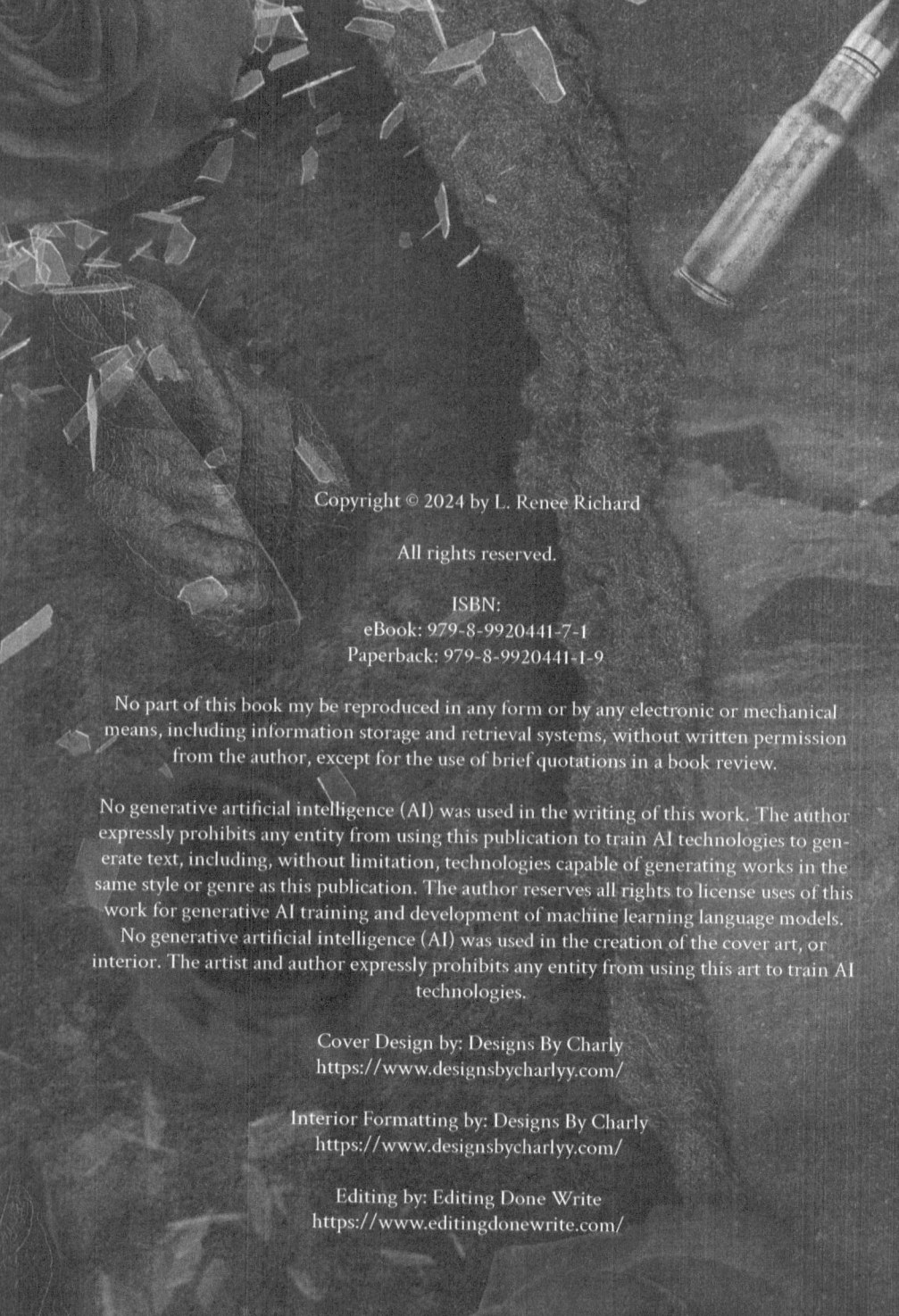

Cover Design by: Designs By Charly
https://www.designsbycharlyy.com/

Interior Formatting by: Designs By Charly
https://www.designsbycharlyy.com/

Editing by: Editing Done Write
https://www.editingdonewrite.com/

PLAYLIST

"Darkness at the Heart of My Love"—Ghost
"Nowhere to Go"—Bad Omens
"Heart Shaped Box"—Nirvana
"From the Pinnacle to the Pit"—Ghost
"Lonely Day"—System of a Down
"I Know How to Hex You"—Twin Temple
"Say it Ain't So"—Wheezer
"It's No Good"—Depeche Mode
"Never Gonna Give You Up"—Rick Astley
"Willow"—Taylor Swift
"Paint it Black"—Hidden Citizens
"Bad at Love"—Halsey
"Church Bells"—Carrie Underwood
"Hot in Herre"—Nelly
"Best of You"—The Foofighters
"Warning"—Morgan Wallen
"Voices in My Head"—Falling in Reverse
"Ghouls Night Out"—Misfits
"Kaiserion"—Ghost
"Square Hammer"—Ghost
"Still Into You"—Paramore

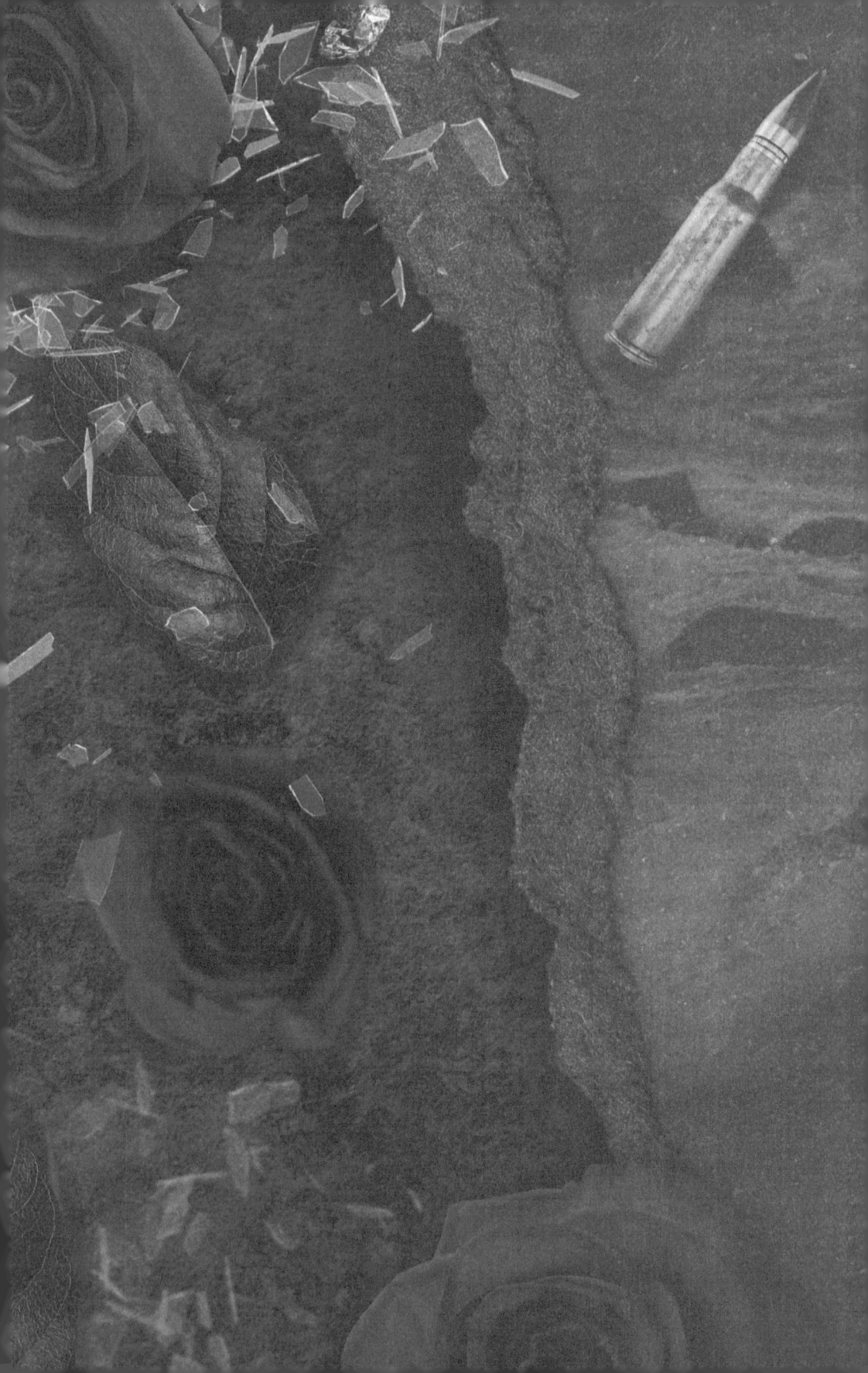

BLACK WAVE

BOOK 1 OF THE FORGED HEARTS NOVEL

He saw me. He had me. But he won't break me.
What should have been the beginning of my life felt more like a death
sentence–an all-encompassing blackness.
Evie, my twin sister and best friend, is no longer here. Now alone, I've
become as dark as the man who tries to imprison me. Julian.
He thinks he is all I have left in this world.
His to toy with.
To manipulate.
To fear.
But that woman died along with her family that night, and a stronger
woman rose from those battered waves, breathing in a newfound
purpose–to take revenge and reclaim my life.
I am waiting on a black wave, biding my time, until a powerful wave rises
in the aftermath of a storm, unexpectedly leaving casualties in its wake,
ensuring I will once again be free.

CONTENT WARNING

When the summer dies
Severing the ties
I'm with you always, always
Will you walk the line?
My path serpentine
Remember always
That love is all you need
Tell me who you wanna be
And I will set you free.

-Ghost

Songwriters: Salem Al Fakir / Tobias Forge / Vincent Pontare
Darkness At The Heart Of My Love lyrics © BMG Rights Management

PROLOGUE

Sitting in my designated alphabetized seating, I barely pay attention to the valedictorian's speech. I hear words carried away in the stifling breeze, along with my hopes and dreams. At this point, that's precisely what they are. I vaguely hear about the promise of a brighter future because I now live in an all-encompassing eternal darkness.

That's right. I was once a cheerleader, a daughter, and a sister. I look to my side, expecting to see anything but an empty seat. The chair should have been occupied by Evie, my twin sister. I touch the tattoo we had inked on our birthday. Something special for us both, a reminder that we would forever be tied together in this life.

What once was a bright future was taken from us in what the police are calling a horrific, unfortunate accident. Now left alone, I am as dark as the man who tries to imprison me. He thinks he is all I have left in this world. Only his to toy with, to manipulate, to fear.

He may have taken everything from me, but he will regret the day he tried to kill my spirit. I will see him dead, if it's the last thing I do. It will mimic the already dead look in my eyes. I have to play the part, play along with the ruse.

BLACK WAVE

The commencement speeches come to a close. We toss our caps in the air in a final good-bye to our last year of high school. I walk away, not bothering to retrieve my cap from the ground.

A hand reaches for me and tugs me backward. Goose bumps on my arms rise in recognition of *his* touch—every nerve-ending screams in protest. I fight the urge to recoil or pull away. I instantly calm my features in a well-practiced act, until I turn around to meet his dark-colored eyes. Julian.

He looks down at me with a wicked grin. I can't believe I never saw it before.

"Emma. How are you holding up?"

The false concern in his voice unsettles me. An average person wouldn't detect this, but I know Julian.

I give him my best attempt at a smile. "Better than I thought on a day like this." I shrug, trying to downplay my tempestuous feelings.

He pulls me into a hug.

I feel the bile rise in my throat as I fight the revulsion his mere presence brings about. I lift my hands mechanically and return his embrace.

He kisses my forehead as any dotting boyfriend would in the public eye.

I sigh. "At least I have you." I get these words out in one forced breath, disguising each spoken word's bite.

My words appear to please him.

He stares down at me and grabs my chin more roughly than I anticipated, lifting it so I am forced to look straight up at his tall stature.

"You will always have me, Emma."

I swallow hard as I verbalize this known truth from my lips. "I know, Julian."

He grabs my arm and drags me to a black SUV with equally dark tinted windows. A man exits the driver's seat to open the back door for us. I get in without hesitation.

What can I do at this point? Not a damn thing.

He gets in after me, and we drive off. There is no one waiting for me. No one I'm leaving behind. I look out the window, seeing the greenery and scattering of bluebonnets along the roadside. I say a silent good-bye to my previous life.

I won't be coming back. Not now. That girl died along with her family that night. Yet, a stronger woman rose from those battered waves, breathing in a new life. The gale force winds gathered all my broken pieces and rearranged them into a stronger and more punishing life-force.

I am waiting on a black wave, biding my time. Until a powerful wave rises in the aftermath of a storm, unexpectedly leaving casualties in its wake, ensuring I will once again be free.

CHAPTER ONE

EMMA

ONE MONTH BEFORE GRADUATION...

I glance at the clock for the third time this hour in anticipation of hanging out with Evie. I never get a chance to see her anymore. In thirty minutes, I am officially off the clock for the rest of the day. She made us a special appointment for our birthday. She thinks I don't know what it is, but I have my suspicions. She's always been terrible at keeping secrets, while I am the master of secrecy. I've been racking them up like crippling debt over the past few months.

I have her present in my bag, and I can't wait to give it to her. Thinking about it makes me smile. I can't wait to see her face when she opens the gift. Another trip around the sun with my sister always by my side. Nineteen, to be exact, and I wouldn't have it any other way.

I am all grins when the door chimes alert me to the arrival of a customer. I turn around. "Hi, what can I..." I trail off mid-sentence as I stare into the blackest eyes. I try to keep the smile from leaving my face as I hide the disappointment at what his visit could only mean.

"Julian." I grab the cleaning rag to wipe the already sparkling counters. "I didn't expect to see you today." *He can't see the truth if he doesn't look into my eyes.*

Fear.

Shame.

Regret.

"Emma." He pauses just enough to make me hate the sound of my name. "Do I need a reason to see my girlfriend? I just thought I could show you how much you mean to me."

He moves closer to me, and I step back involuntarily. I look around, but there isn't anyone around. My shift is almost over, and then we are closed.

"I miss you, Emma. I won't see you for the rest of the day and I can't get my fill of you."

I move back out of sight from the people passing along the sidewalk, peering in through the windows. I turn to walk away, headed for the back hallway, but he moves quicker and always seems one step ahead. I feel a push at my back as he directs me to the supply room. I enter through the doorway and hear the click of the door closing behind me, but I don't turn around. I stand there frozen. He steps closer to me, and I feel the hard outline of his erection pressing into my back.

"Emma, you didn't think I would forget your birthday, did you?" His words are whispered in my ear, and then I feel his tongue lick from my ear down to my mouth.

I attempt a weak reply. "Julian, you don't have to plan anything. I know you are swamped today and have a business meeting later."

I would try anything to stop his attempt at whatever he wants to do to me now. I only hear his zipper being pulled down as a reply. He turns my head around midway to gain access to my mouth. He kisses me forcefully, biting my lip when I deny him entry into my mouth, drawing blood. He sucks my bottom lip and drives his tongue in. I hear him growl in frustration at the complexity of my multi-buttoned pants. Finally, he unbuttons them and forces them down my legs along with my panties. They pool at my ankles, restricting my movement.

He moves us forward by the shelves and pushes my head down to rest on one as he pushes himself inside me. He sets a punishing pace. He palms my breast greedily as I try to move slightly to steady myself.

"Guess what, Emma?" He slows his pace as he speaks softly into my ear.

I don't bother answering because he doesn't actually want me to. This is just a powerplay for him, allowing me to think I have any say in this.

"I'm going to let you come today because it's your birthday. How does that sound, love?"

"Oh god," is all I get out because, even though I don't love him, my traitorous body reacts to his commands, even the ones I want to control the most.

He reaches his hand around and rubs my clit in circles, gathering the moisture that is instinctually collecting from his languid assault on my body. *I can't believe I used to enjoy this with him. When did he change?* He pulls out almost all the way and slams back in, causing a wave of pleasure that shoots through my abdomen.

"No, no, no," I chant, and I can't help the orgasm that is starting to build from his ministrations.

He pinches my clit and thrusts in over and over until I am a quivering mess. As quickly as the orgasm comes, I am jerked around and simultaneously pushed onto the tiled floor.

"Open," is the only thing Julian says as he forces his cock down my throat. He fists my hair and fucks my mouth until I gag. I can tell when he is close to coming because his breathing has picked up. He forces his cock so far down my throat that I think I will puke. I don't have to endure this much longer as he comes shortly after, holding me to him. I feel it, but I don't taste his release until he pulls it out, along with the saliva dripping down my chin. I gasp for air and look up at him through blurry eyes.

He grabs my chin and holds my stare. "Happy Birthday, Emma. I'll be back tomorrow."

With that, he walks away, and I hear the door chiming, letting me know he has left. I pick myself up like always, vowing that tomorrow will be different. Maybe one day, I'll get away from him. I can't let this continue. I make my way to the employee bathroom and clean up. When I look more presentable, I return to the cafe entrance and see my sister sitting on one of the chairs, waiting for me. I stop in my tracks, immediately self-conscious of my appearance.

"Hey, Evie. I'm just finishing up here. We can leave in a minute." I flip the open sign on the door to closed, and as I walk back, I grab my stuff from the back.

Evie stops me and pulls me into a hug. "I saw Julian leave as I was coming in. He had a smug look, and I knew he had won something. Are you okay?"

I return the hug, trying to convey to her all the emotions I am feeling with just my body language. "I love you, Evie. I'll be okay." *Lie.* It isn't the truth, but what else can I say?

She pulls back from our embrace and holds me at arm's length, looking into my eyes. "You know that you can tell me anything, Emma, right? I'll be here to listen and help you with whatever you need. We can figure it out together. You are not alone."

I nod in acknowledgment and release her. "Let me grab my purse, and let's get out of here, shall we?"

Moments later, Evie and I walk arm-in-arm down the sidewalk. "So, you aren't going to give me a hint about the appointment you booked for us today?" I say jokingly because I am almost sure that we are having matching tattoos inked today. We have discussed doing this for years now. Since we got into high school, we thought this was a great way to show our twin bond on the outside too. Even though we have been adults for almost a year now, this is where the real road to adulthood starts: after graduation.

Sure enough, we stop outside of Dark Tide Tattoo Studio. "I knew it!" I shout while jumping up and down, holding onto Evie's arm. "I knew we were getting tattoos today."

Evie chuckles. "Yeah, you guessed it. Was I that obvious?"

"Well, we have only talked about this day for about four years now. It wasn't hard to guess. Are you ready to get this done?"

"Definitely."

I gather my sister's hand in mine, and we walk into the tattoo studio, ready to ink our souls together.

"Hi, ladies. Just fill out this form on the screen and let me know if you have any questions. I'll need your driver's license too." Lalo, the big biker who will tattoo us, disappears down the hall.

We are just about done signing the required documentation about informed consent that tells you what to expect afterward and the obvious that this is permanent, when Lalo returns, holding a sketch out to Evie.

"I know you showed me the Pinterest picture of the heart for you and your sister, but I modified it and made you something more original if you don't mind looking at it." Lalo hands Evie the sketch, and I move toward her to look at the results.

"Wow, this is beautiful," we chime in unison. I grab the sketch from Evie's grasp to study it further. The original twisted hearts theme is there, but it is in more detail, with our initials in the entwined hearts and our date of birth underneath. To say we like the sketch is an understatement.

Lalo claps his hands together. "Okay, ladies, who is going first? Follow me."

Knowing I might chicken out, I volunteer to get mine first.

"Let's print your aftercare instructions so you can take them home if you need to refer to proper hygiene." Lalo places the clear bandage over Evie's wrist and then leads us to the front of the studio to collect our paperwork. After settling our bill, we leave the studio feeling carefree, as all nineteen-year-old girls should.

We continue our walk downtown and I ask, "Evie, do you want to get any ice cream? I thought we could get some and exchange gifts at the park across the street?"

"I think that is a great idea. I want the usual mint chocolate chunk, please." She walks off to secure a table for two as I am left to order our ice cream. I get my usual bubble gum flavor and place them on the table with napkins and spoons.

Evie takes a massive scoop of hers and groans. "This is orgasmic."

I frown as this reminds me of Julian's gift a while ago. Evie stops midway to her mouth, withholding the next ice cream orgasm, and looks at me before placing the scoop down. "What's wrong, Emma? Is it the ice cream? I'd have that face, too, if I got *that* ice cream." She points at it as if its mere presence offends her. "The bubble gum in there is rock hard. You're going to crack a tooth, babe."

I look at her and attempt a weak laugh. Trying to change the subject, I reach into my bag and pull out her birthday present. I place it in front of her, and this time, my smile reaches my eyes. Seeing Evie happy, in turn, makes me happy. It heals my soul and rights everything wrong in my life right now. She picks up the gift and tugs at the strings holding the box. She removes the top and picks up another box in there.

"You are such a joker, Emma." She undoes the other box and stops when she sees what's inside. She looks at me, smiling with tears in her eyes. "I love it," she says in a hushed voice. She picks up the ring and slides it on her finger. "It's a perfect fit too."

I had it made at a local jeweler. Dave's castings provide quality work and create unique pieces for clients. He starts with the design, beginning with a wax mold. If you like it, then he will proceed with making the jewelry. Like our newly-inked tattoos, I had a twisted heart entwined together to remind us of our sisterly bond–and because she likes them so much.

Evie reaches into her bag, pulls out an envelope for me, and hands it over. "This is your gift, Emma." She clasps her hands together on the table, waiting for my reaction.

I look at it quizzically and then at her. "What is it?"

"Just open it, Emma." Evie shifts uncomfortably in her chair as she resumes eating her now liquid ice cream.

I pick up the envelope and pull out the sheet of paper. I read it aloud, "One month of Krav Maga classes?" This comes out as a question, and I stare at her for clarification.

Evie puts her ice cream aside and moves her hands up and down her pant legs, then places them in a contemplative gesture in front of her mouth.

"Emma, I am just going to come out and say it. I know that you are in an abusive relationship with Julian. I want you to be able to protect yourself. Remember, I know what it is like not to have control over oneself and feel vulnerable."

I wince at the recollection of Evie's trauma. It's hard for my sister to remember when she was almost assaulted in an alleyway. If not for the help of a Good Samaritan, the outcome could have been a lot different.

"I was only able to move on from that with the help of my therapist and the power I took back when I was able to defend myself."

I look at Evie, and I know this is our turning point. I have to tell her what has been happening with Julian and find a way to rid myself of his restraining persona. I *need* to break up with him once and for all.

Evie looks at me, hoping that this will be the day I confide in her and tell her what she already knows. The problem is that she has no idea what I have been through. I shift uncomfortably in my seat and look away. I hear Evie sigh.

I straighten my back. When I look back at her, it is with a new determination. "Evie, I need to tell you something, and need help."

CHAPTER TWO

EMMA

I sit there and tell Evie everything. I see her flinch when I tell her how I suffer at the hands of Julian and how I'm scared for my life. I'm afraid I can never be truly free of his firm hold on me. She listens without interruption. I purge myself until I deflate in a slump, feeling the weight on my shoulders lift. Finally, someone else knows what I have been going through, but is it enough? Can Evie help me escape Julian?

Evie speaks after what feels like an eternity, and I wait with bated breath to hear anything, any advice that she can give.

"I think we need to tell Mom and Dad, Emma." She sits up straighter and shifts closer to me. "I think this is a much bigger problem than we can handle alone." She pulls me in for a hug, and I hug her back, taking comfort in her love for me. She kisses the top of my head in a motherly gesture, and I almost lose myself in the tears that threaten to spill out of my misty eyes.

"I know. You are right. I hoped not to have to tell them and thought I could handle this alone, but I didn't see a way of making him forget about me. I think he is obsessed with me for some reason. It's not love, I know that, but I fear he won't let his favorite possession go, Evie."

I notice Evie's eyes widen, then narrow in anger. "Don't worry, Emma. We will find a way to fix this, but first, we must devise a plan to tell Mom and Dad. They need to know what we are dealing with. This way, you won't be blindsided by anything he may do to prevent you from leaving him."

I feel my sister's love for me, and I am so thankful that she is with me in this. "Okay, Evie. Let's do it. Let's tell Mom and Dad and remove this monster from my life. It might take some time, but I will be strong and leave him."

Evie stands and holds out her hand for me to take. I gladly do, as she helps me stand up in more ways than one. I hope I don't regret what I am about to do.

We take the long way home and chat about plans for our future. Seeing that most of my life revolves around Julian, I wasn't motivated to plan for this before. I feel a nudge on my shoulder. I see Evie looking at me expectantly, awaiting my response. She had asked me a question. "Sorry, repeat that, Evie?"

"I said, what do you want to go to school for, Emma? As a career?"

I smile at her and reply without hesitation. "A nurse. I want to be a nurse like Mom and help people. I will always have a job and could travel anytime I want to take a leave." I smile at her, seeing the same face looking back at me. It's uncanny how similar we look at times like this. Even for me. "What about you, Evie?"

"I want to help people too, but I'm unsure how. Maybe with therapy or just killing the bastards that hurt the ones I love."

I start laughing and hit her arm. "Stop that. You are ridiculous." I look over at her, but she isn't laughing. She looks like she is telling the truth and aspires to be some sort of vigilante. "Um, Evie, you are joking, right?"

She stares straight ahead and replies, "Mostly, but I would do it if I could. Take out the fuckers that cause pain and prey off weaker people. Who feed off of their insecurities and vulnerabilities. Scum of the earth that don't deserve to breathe the same air that we do."

"Woah, okay, Evie, this is getting dark. I would hate for anything to happen to you, and I don't think I could survive this world if you weren't in it. So enough talk about this stuff, okay?"

"Of course, Em. I am mostly joking, as if that would never happen. Maybe a therapist is more up my alley, huh?"

I nod in agreement. "Yep, I knew you weren't serious. You are about as harmless as a fly but with the potential to kick ass from all your self-defense classes. You are seriously one badass bitch." I look over at her and see her laughing. She snorts and pulls me closer, linking our arms as we walk the last block toward home.

Ultimately, we decided to wait another week to tell our parents about Julian. We want to plan how we will do it and the most appropriate time to do so. It will have to be when Julian isn't around, my parents are home, and we won't be interrupted.

I remember Julian mentioning that he will be out of town next weekend, and I decide to ask Mom and Dad if Evie and I can make a family dinner that night. This is when we will come clean, and with the help of my sister, I will tell our parents what has been happening to me and what Julian threatened me with to tie me to him.

Time flies by in a blur of last week's events. The final bell of the day rings and students rush out, anxious to leave the building. I take my time because I don't feel this way about leaving. I'd rather stay where I am if it means not seeing him. Julian will be waiting outside for me while he returns phone calls. He usually picks me up, and I know that since he is going out of town and won't see me for a while, he will want to have sex with me. The thought makes me recoil, but it's almost over, and then I will be free of him. Evie and I are planning to tell our parents tonight, and honestly, this has been the longest week of my life.

I have my yearbook in hand and tuck it into my bag along with some books for this week's upcoming finals. I zip up my bag and reluctantly leave through the school's front doors. I spot Julian's black SUV parked off to the side and make sure not to spark a conversation with anyone before I leave. I don't want him asking any questions about anyone I talk to. Most guys know I am with Julian and steer clear of me, showing that he is one scary motherfucker, and I am justified for having the thoughts I do.

As I approach the SUV, the driver steps out and opens the door for me, nodding in greeting. "Time to put on my game face," I mutter as I step in, and the door quickly closes behind me. I grab my seat belt, but my hand meets his. I let go of the seat belt as he tugs me closer and straps me into the middle seat closest to him. He puts his arm around my shoulders, smothering me with the bulk of his frame, and grabs my face and pulls me in for a kiss. I kiss him with as much enthusiasm as I can muster so I don't raise any suspicions.

He lets me go and stares into my eyes. "How was school, Emma?" he asks with such concern that I could almost think he might be interested in my day, but I know that he's really just trying to see if he can catch me in a lie or to reveal anything about my day that he doesn't already know about. I doubt there is much he doesn't know about my life. His dad runs this town, and his affluent family has so much reach and political affiliations that Julian is following in his father's footsteps.

"Good," I say in return. "I just have a few more finals to take, and then that's it. I can't believe I am graduating already," I say earnestly.

He nods and grunts, "Good, I am happy about that too. It seems like we are on the same page then."

I straighten in my seat. "Um, what page is that, Julian? I just want to be clear."

He studies me momentarily to see if I will say anything else. When he can see that I'm not offering any other information, he speaks again.

"Moving in with me. It seems like the logical step in our relationship."

I sit there dumbfounded because what do I say to that? No? How about a hell no? Instead, I stare at him, debating what to say next. I decide to just go for it. "What about college? I might want to go." I shift uncomfortably in my seat but try to remain confident.

He chuckles under his breath. "Maybe we could compromise, my little pet."

I look up at him and see in his eyes that he has no intention of compromising. It has always been his way only in this relationship. I mean dictatorship. "Okay, Julian."

He studies me to see if I will continue this conversation, but instead, he says, "You will move in with me after graduation."

This time, I can't hide the annoyance in his commands over my life. "What if I don't want to move in with you, Julian? I don't want to leave my sister." I immediately regret showing my emotions and love for my sister, even though he knows we are close. I have never expressed how much being away from her would hurt me.

He turns his body toward mine and grabs my face harshly. "Need I remind you what would happen to your parents' jobs if you disagree with my wishes? What about your sister? Do you want to continue a relationship with her, because I have been very accommodating with your love for your family. I believe in that, Emma. I, too, am a family man, and you are part of mine now."

I sink into myself and think before I speak this time. "Of course, Julian.

I am your family now, but please don't hurt my family."

"I won't hurt your family, Emma. You know that it doesn't have to be this way." He gently kisses my mouth and licks across my lips, demanding access.

I open my mouth, and he takes the kiss further. He unbuckles my seat belt and pulls me onto him, my skirt fanning above his trousers. I feel his erection pushing through the fabric of my panties. He lifts me, unfastening his belt and unzipping his pants. He pulls his cock out and fists it several times. He pushes my panties aside and lowers me before shoving his cock through my entrance swiftly.

I gasp at the intrusion of his dick. He fucks me in the back seat of his SUV with his driver hearing his grunts, not attempting to hide the fact that he is getting off. He brings me closer to kiss him, but when I turn my head, he bites my neck as he comes in a couple of jerky movements. He pulls me off him and again places me on the seat.

I go to grab the seat belt, and he stops me. I look up at him, and he smiles at me. "Are you forgetting something, Emma?"

I look at him and wrinkle my nose in confusion. "No," is all I can say.

He tsks at me. "You forgot to clean me off, Emma." He looks at his now semi-flaccid dick, and then, to be clear, he says, "With your mouth, Emma."

He grabs my head and pushes me down toward his cock. I sigh, resigned to the task, and gently hold his dick. I proceed to lick him up and clean up his mess. When satisfied with my job, he pulls my mouth off with a pop. My head rests back on the seat, and he buckles me back in. He pulls me in and kisses my forehead, appearing to care about me.

Soon enough, we are in front of my parents' house. The driver parks, and Julian reminds me that he will be gone again this weekend but will call me when he returns. The driver quickly opens the door. I can't meet his eyes, mortified by what I just did with him sitting in the front seat acting like he didn't hear Julian fuck me and how I provided his aftercare with my fucking mouth. Ugh. I jump out of the car and walk to the front door without looking back. I step through that door, determined to end this relationship with Julian, and know that things will never be the same after tonight.

CHAPTER THREE

EMMA

I pace the living room, waiting for Evie to get home. I grab my Airpods, and "Nowhere To Go" by Bad Omens plays. I walk back and forth, waiting for the door to swing open, showing the face of my salvation on the other end. In what seems like days, she walks through the front door as I run up to her—ripping the Airpods that I had been using as a distraction out of my ears. She hears my quick footsteps on the tiled floor and looks up, surprised I am running her way.

"Oh, Evie. I can't take it anymore." The tears I had been holding spring free and cascade down my cheeks.

"Shhh, Emma." She drops her bags on the floor with a thunk and strokes my head. She tries to whisper reassuring words of comfort, but there is no stopping the long-overdue tears that are free-flowing without abatement anytime soon. "It will be okay. I promise you, Emma."

"You don't know that, Evie. Please don't make promises you can't keep." I sniffle and try my best to stop the tears. Evie pulls me closer and moves the hair sticking to my drying tears away from my face.

"Emma, we will tell Mom and Dad when they get home. I can't watch you lose yourself to this guy. He's such an abusive piece of shit."

I snort and remark, "That's an understatement," as I try to sit up straighter on the couch.

"Come on. Let's clean you up before Mom and Dad get home from work. I have a feeling it's going to be a long night."

With that, we go upstairs. I change my clothes, wash my face, and brush my teeth, removing any reminder of Julian from my mouth. Evie and I sit and plan to bring this up to our parents. Ultimately, we decide on a straightforward approach to let them know the severity of my situation.

An hour has gone by, and I'm sitting across from Evie, who is sitting on the bed twirling the twisted heart ring I gave her, when the sound of the door opening and closing interrupts me from my thoughts.

Shortly after, I hear my mom's usual call of, "Evie. Emma. We're home. You girls there?" alerting us they are both home from work. The familiarity of it makes me smile, if only for a minute.

I quickly sit up ramrod straight in bed. I know it's showtime, but I am nervous about my parents' reaction to my situation. Will they blame me for allowing this? I blamed myself for not being strong enough to handle this situation alone.

Sensing my thoughts of impending doom, Evie extends her hand to comfort my racing mind as we walk downstairs together in a unified front. It's time for me to tell them about my relationship with Julian. I just hope they can help.

My mom starts crying. She doesn't even say anything, just starts bawling her eyes out, and that's when I know it's worse than I thought.

"Mom, are you okay?" I go to touch her shoulder, and she jumps up from her seat on the couch and wraps herself around me.

"I'm so sorry, Emma. I didn't realize you had been going through all this alone. I should have seen it. I should have known. I'm your mother. I should have protected you. With you now, and with E-vie then..." she cries, referring to the attempted sexual assault on my sister four years ago.

"Mom, you couldn't have prevented that attack and certainly didn't know about Julian." I am comforting her now, and the irony isn't lost on me. I've had months to process the situation, whereas she just learned about it today.

"I had the means to protect you girls, and I thought I was doing the right thing, but…" she trails off and looks at my dad, who doesn't appear in any better shape than her. Honestly, he seems worse, just sitting there looking utterly defeated.

Evie walks toward my mom. "What do you mean you had the resources to protect us, Mom?" I can't help but notice the look of annoyance on Evie's face, which is shocking, since she is always the voice of reason in this house, but something changed in her that night at the hospital–the worst night of her life. She left that hospital room determined never to be a victim again.

Mom looks over at my dad, and he nods. An unspoken permission is given as my mom begins telling us about her life growing up in Mexico, only a short distance from where we are now. I had suspicions, but Mom verifies everything I thought and remembered as a young girl visiting my family there.

I fondly remember spending time with my cousins and Uncle Andrés in Mexico. It seems like a lifetime ago. Because of my family's corrupt business dealings with the cartel in the small bordering towns of Matamoros, she kept us away from them. Despite the loss of contact, they were still her family. Although she moved to another country, she was only a few miles apart, separated by a literal wall. When I explained the situation to them, they were enraged at the monster that was Julian.

"Your grandfather was in the Mexican cartel. My brother, your Uncle Andrés, is now head of the organization." She pauses, twisting her hands around her lap and contemplating her next words.

She looked at Dad briefly. "Your father and I thought it best once you girls started to get older, teenagers specifically, to remove you from that life. We saw things starting to happen, and I just wanted something different for you. I met your father in college, and we married. I knew then that I had started separating from my family and needed to cut ties to deter you girls from the mafia life."

"What made you decide this? Is that why we've never gone back, Mom?"

She glances down at the necklace I still wear religiously around my neck. The one given to me as a present for my twelfth birthday—a promise for a future date. A date that never happened. I touch it instinctively, and it clicks.

I finish the sentence I know she is going to say. "You didn't want me to date Eduardo." I feel a stab of anger that hits me straight in the heart.

"I didn't want you to date Eduardo," she confirms aloud. "I knew that you would be involved in the cartel life forever, and that wasn't the life I wanted for you. I want you to have a normal life. One filled with a future where you aren't in danger. It seems I failed you, regardless of wanting something different for you both. Despite wanting to keep you girls away, my family is now the only one to help and keep you safe. To keep us safe."

"What happened to Eduardo, Mom?" I can't help but wonder at the boy who wasn't only my friend back then, but who had my heart too.

"I'm not too sure, Emma." She sighs but continues rubbing her hand down her face in frustration. "Last I heard, he had moved to Houston and owned a nightclub and a couple of other businesses there." She starts to pace.

"Well, it looks like he is a successful businessman then, huh?"

She scoffs. "Sure. Suppose you can call money laundering successful. Those businesses hide Eduardo's family's illegal activity, Emma. Don't be a fool."

I visibly flinch at her harsh words. Never has Mom used that tone with me, but since I've risked everyone's lives, this is the treatment I deserve. "You don't know that for sure, Mom. They could be legit." I feel protective of Eduardo. I try to make myself believe this. Believe in the boy who was so sweet and kind to me—the one who started to look at me differently that last year.

Evie stands and walks to my mom. "What about my assault? Did that have anything to do with the cartel?"

She speaks with a controlled tone, but her stance doesn't portray the sound of her voice. Her fists clenched at her side and the tic of her jaw tells of the rage buried deep inside her about being a victim that night—something she swore never to become again.

"I'm not sure," she says as she waves her hands back and forth through the air. "I do know that they are the ones who stopped the attack. The Good Samaritan that killed the man wasn't a random act of kindness by a stranger, if you can call it that. It was one of my brother's security details."

"Oh my god," we both say in unison, much like we commonly do, being twins. This time, we don't find it amusing as we usually do. "I knew it," Evie says. "It was too coincidental for a random Good Samaritan to shoot the killer and then leave without a statement." The fire in Evie's eyes ignites, fueling a rage that resides in her, one she rarely lets anyone see.

I nod in agreement. "If that is true, then do they know about Julian? Are they watching me, too?" I start to get a glimmer of hope that maybe the situation isn't that bad. Maybe there is hope after all, but my mom's following words kill that sentiment.

"No. I blamed them for the attack on Evie. I thought it was because of our ties to the Mexican cartel that you were targeted. I asked them to back off, and they did."

I slump in my chair, deflated at the thought that I'm alone. Evie clears her throat.

"What about Emma? Is Julian so invested in her because he knows about her ties to the cartel? I suspect his family is as corrupt as they come, and a union with them would be most beneficial in the political side of things."

I shake my head back and forth quickly. "No. That can't be right. Mom?" I look to her for confirmation, but I don't get that either.

"I have my suspicions that that is the case, too, Evie. I don't know, but he became so interested in Emma, and I just don't know anymore. The fact that I couldn't say anything about him being older because you were already eighteen when you started seeing him was bad enough.

"Before you can ask, no, there isn't a reason for you girls being held back a year. That was strictly a decision your dad and I made about your age and progression that year. You guys were held back in kindergarten. We needed child care, and you guys just started a little before you were supposed to. It was easier if we all went to school together, instead of me working different hours than your father."

Evie and I look at each other, relieved that there isn't anything else. We aren't missing any other information or truths in our lives that now seem to have been turned upside down with the revelation about our past.

My dad finally speaks, which shocks us briefly because he has stayed quiet, letting our mom talk this whole time without interruption. "I think it's time, honey, to call your brother."

He stands up and walks over to me and Evie.

"I am so sorry, girls. We thought we were doing the right thing for you. Sometimes, parents make mistakes. This was one of them. All we wanted to do was keep you girls safe, and we have failed miserably. We knew that when we married and decided to have a family we would have to make a choice. We chose wrong, but it was unforeseeable. We just hope you know we had your best interest at heart."

He takes us both in a strong embrace when he looks back at us, there are tears in his eyes. "Can you both forgive me? Forgive us?"

My resolve crumbles, and I hug him back, along with my sister. My mom comes in to join us, and we start to heal. Heal as a family whose life has been turned upside down with situations out of our control, but not anymore. We are going to take back control.

BLACK WAVE

Mom looks up at us and grabs our chins softly. "I love you, girls. Never forget that. Now, I need to make a phone call."

With that, she walks away, and we stay in the living room, waiting for her to tell us what the next weeks bring.

CHAPTER FOUR

EMMA

ONE WEEK BEFORE GRADUATION...

We sit there waiting for what seems like an eternity for Mom to return from our parents' shared office space. She had undoubtedly been on the phone with her family, letting them know about the danger I put them in. It was hard to tell my parents all that Julian had threatened me with, how they would both lose their jobs, how his father would ensure that they wouldn't be able to secure employment in the surrounding areas outside of Brownsville. We would lose our home and friends, ruining us in any way possible. All because he wanted me.

I hear the door click shut to the office and my mother's footsteps heading our way. My dad, who was outside smoking a cigarette, which we hadn't seen him do since we were little kids, also returns when he sees my mom standing before us. He stands alongside us, and we wait for her to speak.

"I spoke to my brother, Andrés, and informed him of the situation," she begins. She rubs her temples to ward off the impending migraine she usually gets under anxiety-provoking circumstances.

I'd say that this predicament fits the bill. The frequent feeling of doom sets in with each passing second, sinking its claws into my skin as I patiently wait for her to elaborate. Sweat begins to run down my back, and I feel like I might pass out.

"He is going to come up with a plan. He is going to help us." She looks at my father, and he seems like he might cry.

He releases a sob of relief and covers his face momentarily. "That is such good news to hear."

"Agreed." Mom nods, running over to his side, where they embrace.

I fall to the couch and hold my head in my hands. I start to shake from the surge of catecholamines racing through my body in a flight-or-fight response, something I've grown accustomed to since Julian revealed his true colors months into our dating. Relief floods my system, knowing that if anyone can help me, it is someone stronger than Julian, someone more dangerous who happens to be on my side—my Uncle Andrés. Mom comes over to hug me, pulling me into her.

"I'm so sorry, sweet girl, that this happened to you. I wish you had confided in me sooner so I could have helped you." She looks over at Evie, who has still not said a word.

"Please continue acting like we don't know about this and continue the ruse. Pretend we have no idea what is happening, until Uncle Andrés comes up with a plan, and we can ensure you are safe–that we are all safe."

"Does this mean I will have to leave?" I shift back and forth on my feet, unsure of the future, and now I have no plans I know of. While other students my age are moving to go off to college, I am planning my escape from an abusive relationship. How did I get here? To this point, I have jeopardized everything and everyone I love.

"I don't know, but I'll have more to tell you this week. Uncle Andrés said to give him a couple of days to formulate a plan and get a hold of some people to move across the border, mobilize his security detail to help."

"Okay, so just act like nothing is up around him. I can do that." This week is the last week of finals before school ends anyway. We don't have much longer remaining before graduation. I can do it. I mentally prepare for what will seem like the most brutal week of my life, waiting in anticipation for my freedom.

The weekend passes by without a word from my uncle. I try not to think about when he will call, but it seems almost impossible when it's my life–my family's life–in his hands. I stay busy studying for finals, as does Evie. This Wednesday is our last final, and we finish high school. Graduation is Saturday, and I am anxious to get it over with. I hear a ding on my phone and check the text message.

Julian: I just returned from my business trip on my way over.

I look at the phone and frown. "Like I have a choice," I say out loud before typing my reply. With a snort, I promptly reply.

Emma: Okay. I'm here.

A few minutes later, Julian is pulling up out front. My parents and Evie are not home, and it's no surprise that Julian picked this time to stop by. It's almost as if he knows when they are here and when they are not. I hear a knock and go to answer the door.

He enters the house and looks around, scanning the living room. I answered his unasked question. "No one is home."

He smiles and pulls me in for a quick kiss. "Did you miss me, baby?"

I still my emotions, plastering on a fake smile as best I can. "Of course. You were gone all weekend."

"I like to hear that, Emma darling. I have plans for us this Friday before you graduate. I want to take you out to dinner with my parents. We are looking forward to your graduation."

"Oh." I look down and begin to fiddle nervously with my hands. Julian sees this and stills my hands for me. I gaze up at him, and he motions to move to the kitchen with his head.

"Why don't you get us a couple of waters? You look like you could use one, and I am thirsty anyway."

I go to the kitchen, looking over my shoulder. "Okay, I'll be right back then." I disappear and get us the water. When I return with our beverages, I find him walking toward the door.

"Julian? Where are you going? I thought you wanted water?" I say, extending my arms out, holding the two glasses.

He smirks at me and opens the door. "I need to go. Behave, Emma. Good luck with your finals, and I'll see you Friday."

With that, he leaves me in the living room holding the two glasses, wondering what the fuck that was about.

There is still time left in the two-hour allotted time frame when the school bell rings, alerting us that if we are finished, we can leave. I collect my things and exit the classroom for the last time as a student at this school. I'm curious if Evie is done, too.

> Emma: Hey! All done. I'll be waiting for you near the car.

I leave the school, and the students hanging out by the doors look at me, giving me the sense they are talking about me. Luckily, I have other more important things to think about right now, so fuck them.

I walk to my car and place my bag in the back seat while waiting for Evie to text me back. Another thirty minutes go by before my phone begins to vibrate. Expecting it to be Evie, I look down and see that it is Julian.

> Julian: How did it go? Does my special girl deserve a reward for all her hard work?

"I don't want anything from you," I say aloud, trying to be brave, knowing he can't hear me and I am safe from his cruelty.

> Emma: I am all finished. Yes.

That is all I reply to his text message. I look up to see Evie walking my way. She is texting someone. I look at my phone and don't see a response to my message, so I know it isn't me she is talking to.

I run up to her and give her a big hug. "School's finished, sister. Finally. Aren't you excited?"

She hugs me back with less enthusiasm. She quickly puts her phone away and throws her bag into the car's back seat beside mine.

"Yes, but I am also unsure about what the future holds for us, you know? It's hard to get excited with so many unknowns."

I nod in agreement. "Yeah, but I am trying not to think about it. I am too scared. What if the plan doesn't work? Uncle Andrés hasn't told us about what is going on." I chew my nails pensively, praying that he can keep us safe.

She gives me a small smile. "I am sure it will all eventually work out. I just want you to know that I don't blame you for anything. I love you so much, Emma, and no matter what, I'll never leave you. Even if you think I am not around, a part of my soul will always be with you."

She brings my hand up to her mouth and kisses the inside of my wrist, where we got our matching tattoos.

My eyes water at the sentiment, and I promise the same to her in return. Evie makes me promise to be strong, take the gift certificate she gave me for my birthday and learn self-defense classes. "I promise, Evie. I will learn to defend myself."

She accepts this and places her arm around me. "Come on, let's go home, graduate."

We get into the car and drive out of the school parking lot for the last time before our graduation ceremony.

When we get home, our parents are already there waiting for us. All our schedules have been a bit off lately, with finals going on and ultimately finishing this week. Mom comes to us with a smile and what looks like good news.

"Uncle Andrés called. He plans to get us all out of here and away from Julian and his father's political stronghold."

"Really?" I do a little jump from excitement. "Mom, are we leaving? All of us?"

She nods eagerly. "Yes, we are all leaving together. We will go to Mexico and remain safe there under their protection. Julian can't get to you there, and he'll forget about you soon enough. You can even go to school there in Mexico if you'd like. If that is still your goal, they have nursing programs you can apply to."

"Yes, yes. That is amazing. When do we leave? What do you think, Evie?" I look her way, and she doesn't say anything, just shrugs. She's been acting weird today. I won't let her mood deter me from asking questions. "What's the plan, Mom?"

She looks over at my dad. "Well, Uncle Andrés is going to come for us after graduation. Then we all load up into a car and leave everything behind. Just disappear."

I let out a sigh, grabbing my hair in frustration. "I am supposed to go to dinner with Julian and his family Friday evening. Is this something I should still do?"

I look over to my mom and dad. They decide that, yes, I should continue to act what Julian considers to be normal. Okay. Then that is what I will do.

BLACK WAVE

Julian mentioned that I should dress up since the restaurant that we are going to is a bit fancy. I apply my red lipstick like Julian likes and blot it with a napkin. I get a message from him when I pick my phone up to check the time.

Julian: I'm here.

Emma: Be right out.

I make sure not to take too long and kiss my parents. My sister isn't home, but my mom said she should be back any minute. A minute is something I don't have.

I grab my purse and shut the door behind me with a little pep, knowing this is almost done. Just one more day, and I'll be in Mexico after graduation.

CHAPTER FIVE

EMMA

I approach the SUV, and the driver opens the door for me. When I get in, I notice a girl I didn't know was in the car, too. The door shuts behind me, and I take my seat, looking at the scene before me, unsure of what is happening. The girl is kneeling in front of Julian. That's when I realize what is going on. His pants are around his hips, and he is thrusting into this girl's mouth. He doesn't even spare me a glance as he pushes this poor girl's mouth onto his cock, forcing her to take more of him. I hear her gag, and he sets a punishing pace fucking her face and using her like a random hole to fuck. I try to look away, but he grabs my chin.

"Look, Emma, look at how far she takes me in."

I hear the girl whimper as his movements become sporadic and his breathing picks up. This is his telltale sign that he is about to come. Another thrust, and he finishes, sending his load down her throat.

He pushes her off him, removes his handkerchief from his pocket, and cleans up before tucking himself back into his trousers. He tosses the used material to the girl kneeling on the SUV floor. She begins to wipe saliva, cum, and tears from her face. I look at the girl, not commenting on the situation but thankful that I didn't have to please him before I saw his parents tonight at dinner.

"Pull over," he says to the driver, and the SUV stops alongside an unfamiliar side street. "Get out." He looks at the girl and moves his head toward the door.

I looked at him because I initially thought he was talking to me. He looks at the woman and tilts his head toward the door again, indicating that her ride is over.

She protests, but the driver opens the door and removes her from the vehicle. She is unceremoniously discarded from the car like a piece of trash. I hear the door close, and the driver returns to the SUV and drives off, leaving the girl in who-knows-where Brownsville.

I look over to Julian, and he just slides his finger down my cheek in a gentle caress as if I didn't just witness my boyfriend getting head from a stranger in the SUV he picked me up in to go and have dinner with his parents. What a fucking head case.

"I didn't want to ruin your beautiful makeup tonight when we are having dinner with my parents. I did that for you, Emma. She means nothing to me, just like the woman I fucked yesterday on my business trip. I won't keep any of them, just you."

I want to rage and scream at him about how fucked up this all sounds, but what do I care. I will be out of this situation tomorrow, so with that, I will give my Academy Award-winning performance. He must believe me because he kisses me lightly on the lips and goes to lift my skirt. He moves his fingers up my legs and onto the slit on my pussy where he rubs his finger back and forth along the fabric.

"Take these off, Emma." I do and hold them in my lap. He takes them from me and puts them in his pocket.

I didn't even realize we had come to a stop. As the door opens, Julian helps me out of the SUV. He holds my hand as we walk into the restaurant. My only consolation is knowing my life will change forever when I leave here tonight.

We are dropped off in front of the swanky Argentinian steakhouse adjacent to the canals. Julian holds the door open and guides me to the hostess station with his hand on my lower back. The restaurant is busy, but when the hostess sees him, she smiles and greets him by name.

"Hello, Mr. Martinez." She blushes and tucks an imaginary strand of hair behind her ear.

I look over at her and laugh to myself. Yeah, I thought the same thing too. She just continues to stare, and I clear my throat. This makes her snap out of it as she looks my way.

"Right, sorry. I believe your parents are here, seated by the window overlooking the water. I'll take you to them. Right this way, Mr. Martinez."

"Perfect. My Emma loves looking at the water, don't you, love?"

I nod, acknowledging his comment. Keep it up for another day, I think to myself.

The hostess doesn't spare me a glance, and I enjoy the invisibility. She walks off, and we follow. I keep my head down while Julian drags me in my too-high heels. She stops at the table where his parents are seated and places two additional menus on the empty seats that belong to us before leaving. Julian pulls my chair out for me, and his mom beams with her delusional smile. His father looks at me dismissively as Julian sits across from him. I smile politely at his parents, waiting for this night to end.

The food looks fantastic, but I can't taste anything. I sit there and wonder when it will happen, constantly envisioning my new life and the happiness I long for away from this monster. I feel a squeeze in my hands. I look up and see Julian with an assessing stare.

"Are you okay, Emma? You look..." He stops, waving his hand around as if trying to find the correct word. "Preoccupied," he says and tilts his head to the side as if he can read further into my thoughts.

I look at him and then at his parents, who have similar expressions, except his father is staring at me with disgust.

I gulp, attempting to find my words under such scrutiny. "I apologize. I am just so excited to be finishing school and graduating tomorrow."

His mom smiles at me. His dad spares a glance at his son and picks up the rest of his drink, lifting his hand upward, indicating he needs another to the waiter passing by.

"Have you thought about what you will do after graduation, Emma?" His mother takes a long swig of her wine and winks at me.

I feel Julian squeeze my hand under the table, and I wince at the pain. "Um, no, not really." I look over at Julian and shrug. "The jury is still out, but I hope to have an idea soon."

His mother looks at her son. "Well, don't worry. I'm sure Julian will be happy to have you around more."

She beams up at her son, and he gives her his megawatt smile. "Maybe," she continues, "we will have a wedding soon? Hmm?"

I shift in my seat awkwardly. *Over my dead body.*

"Maybe, Mom." Julian grabs my hand and brings it to his lips. "You never know what can happen overnight."

I tense at his words, wondering what he means by that. I find that with Julian, there is always a hidden meaning to his words. My palms sweat as I think about just one more day, and this will all be over. I will be away from him.

"Emma?"

I hear his mom calling my name, and I shake away the thoughts that his words provoked. "Yes, Mrs. Martinez?"

"Are you okay, dear? You look pale all of a sudden."

His dad looks at his son, and I catch an upturn of his lip as he speaks. "Julian, maybe you should take Emma home, huh?"

I hear the rattling of ice cubes in Julian's drink as he finishes the last of his whisky. "I think that is a good idea, Dad. She has a big day tomorrow."

With that, he helps me to my feet, and we make our way out of the restaurant and to his car. The driver exits his door and holds the rear passenger door open, swiftly closing it behind Julian. We sit in silence that stretches out as we drive back to my house. Julian doesn't speak to me. I look out the window and count down the minutes to freedom. As we turn down the street that leads to my house, I notice a bunch of lights and a policeman who stops us mid-way. Julian's window rolls down as an officer puts his head near to speak with us.

"What's going on, officer?"

The officer acknowledges Julian and points his finger at the lights. "Sorry, Mr. Martinez, we can't let anyone down there. There's been an explosion, and we are actively trying to extinguish the fire."

I sit up and look where he's pointing, feeling dread. "What number did you say the house that caught fire is?" *Please, God, no. Please, no,* I chant to myself, hoping my greatest fear didn't come true.

"Oh, it's number 1322. The Taylor house," the officer states nonchalantly.

My stomach drops out as I realize he is talking about *my* house. I rip open the door—by some miracle, it is unlocked–and I run down the street.

"Wait, miss, stop. You can't go down there."

I hear the fading voice of the police officer as I throw my heels off and run toward my home. I stop, blending in with the surrounding crowd gathered around the chaos. My house is destroyed. My life is destroyed.

"Mom, Dad, Evie?" I scream out, my hand shaking, cradling my face. Julian catches up to me and grabs hold of me.

"Let's find out what happened, Emma." He holds me as he stops a firefighter coming out from around the back of the smoldering home. "Hey, can you tell me what happened? My girlfriend lives here." He points over at me, and the firefighter looks on with sympathy.

"I'm sorry, miss, but three people were in the house when the explosion occurred. They didn't survive."

I crumple to the ground, holding my face. A scream releases from my throat, but I can't control it. I can't control the sound that escapes me. I feel Julian's hands reach around and pick me up off the ground, and I move. He holds me against his chest as we return to the car. The door opens, and he places me inside the vehicle. I'm shaking from the shock. My mom. My dad. My sister. My everything. All gone.

I rock back and forth, willing myself to wake from this nightmare that is now my life. Julian hands me a drink.

"Here, Emma. Drink this. It will help calm your nerves."

I accept the drink and look at the liquid in the glass. Wishing I had died in the fire with my family, I drink the remaining contents, welcoming the burn that the amber liquid provides as it slides down my throat and into my stomach. Its warm and intoxicating effects suddenly make me feel sleepy. I drop the glass as it slowly slips through my fingers, which are now tingling. I look up at Julian to find him watching me. He pulls me closer to him.

"Sleep, Emma. When you wake up tomorrow, it will be a new day full of new beginnings." He whispers a lullaby into my ear.

To me, it is just the beginning of a nightmare. I go to respond but find that no words come out. I rest my head on his lap as he pulls me close, tangling his fingers in my hair. I try to stay awake, but it is futile.

"Evie," I try to call out. Her face is the last thing I envision as a black wave pulls me into the abyss.

CHAPTER SIX

EMMA

GRADUATION DAY...

I jolt awake. I try to stand but feel a wave of nausea and dizziness set in. Everything is black. I grab the bed I rose from to steady myself as sweat dampens my skin.

My eyes try to clear away the fog as I attempt to make out my surroundings. Slowly, things come into focus. I'm in a bed that I don't recognize. I feel myself start to hyperventilate.

I go to the door, but it doesn't open. I go to the window and pull back the drapes to see that it overlooks an expansive garden with decorative topiaries. I know this garden.

Then it hits me like a tsunami. My parents. Evie. The fire. No. No. No, it can't be. I thought it was a dream—a nightmare. I go to the door again and start to pound on it. I hear heavy footsteps make their way toward my door. I step back just in time to see it swing open.

"Emma, calm down. You are safe." Julian goes to approach me, and I can't hide my distaste for him this time. I pull back on reflex, and he notices my shift in demeanor. I've never done this before, but now I can't help it.

He steps back to assess me, like I'm a crazed woman escaping from a psychiatric lockdown unit depicted in movies.

"Emma, I suggest you calm down, or I will force you to miss your graduation today."

"My graduation?" I say slowly. I place my hand over my mouth to stifle my expression.

"Yes, Emma, your graduation. I have someone making your breakfast so you can eat something to shake off the residual effects of the sedative we had to give you."

"The drink." I look up at him to see him sneer.

I knew there was something off about the taste, and then I don't remember coming here or getting into the house, even less changing into these pajamas. Why does he have pajamas for me? That is freaking weird. I guess I should expect nothing less of this psychopath.

"Julian, I can't go to my graduation today. My fam…" I trail off, breaking out in a gut-wrenching sob that almost takes my breath away as I collapse onto the carpet.

Julian bends over to grab my chin and makes me look up at him. Anger radiates from his eyes.

"You can and you will, Emma. I am taking you, and we will go over to make funeral arrangements afterward for your parents." He stands again, grabbing me by one arm and lifting me.

"And my sister…" I touch the tattoos we got recently, and I feel my heart breaking. I go to speak, but he cuts me off. I look up at him and notice his expression changes only briefly. His mask is back in place.

"Don't worry about the money, Emma. I will take care of it. I will take care of everything for you from now on."

His penetrating stare makes me want to run as far away and as fast as possible, but I know it doesn't matter. If I run, he will chase me and bring me back. I don't want to be on the receiving end of his temper.

My uncle never did make it to us. Instead, they all died because of me. A wave of guilt crashes through me, attempting to consume me. My choices killed my family, and now I must live with that.

I finish my breakfast and decide to do as Julian says. He expects that, and

I won't disappoint him or else suffer the consequences. As I pull my chair back from the table, his mom enters the kitchen and sees me.

"Good morning, Emma. I hope you slept well."

My body goes stiff. *Is this lady for real?* This whole family is whacked. I decide on honesty.

"Actually, no, I didn't. You see, my family died in a fire last night." My fists clench at my side, and I fight the tears that threaten to fall.

She moves over to me. "Oh, Emma. Of course, you didn't sleep well. What was I thinking? Don't worry, dear, you are part of this family, and Julian will take care of everything." She taps my shoulder as she walks off.

I take some deep breaths to steady my heart's erratic beating that feels like it is shattering into a million tiny pieces. I envision my happy place, waves crashing on the beach, the smell of salt water, and a boy who held my hand–my heart.

I am pulled out of my trance when I hear voices in the hall. I make my way over to listen. I can hear Julian and his father talking in whispered tones.

"I take it you have everything under control, Julian. I don't want this to come back to bite us in the ass and screw up my re-election campaign. Even the smallest amount of questions can be detrimental to winning, despite me being the incumbent."

"Yes, Father. You have nothing to worry about. All bases are covered, and no one will ever find out about the details of the fire."

I cover my mouth before I let out a gasp. Fresh tears spring from my eyes, and I feel like I will throw up my breakfast. I hold it in to listen to the rest of the conversation but hear footsteps coming this way.

I pretend to be running from the kitchen and fall right into Julian. I brace myself against his chest as he grabs onto me to prevent me from falling back. "Julian," I say, burying my face into his chest to hide my expression.

He pulls me back and looks at me. "What's wrong, Emma?"

Let me think about that. *You killed my parents and sister, for starters, assfuck.*

"I'm just missing my family so much right now. Evie was supposed to graduate with me, and my parents won't be there." I don't realize how much I mean those words until they come out of my mouth. Even though he didn't directly commit the crime, he is responsible, somehow, for their deaths. Being with him last night, with his parents at the restaurant, gave him the perfect alibi for the perfect murder.

43

BLACK WAVE

Sitting in my designated alphabetized seating, I barely pay attention to the valedictorian's speech. I hear words carried away on the stifling breeze, along with my hopes and dreams. At this point, that's precisely what they are. I vaguely hear about the promise of a brighter future because I now live in eternal darkness—an all-encompassing blackness.

That's right. I was once a cheerleader, a daughter, and a sister. I look to my side, expecting to see anything but an empty seat. The chair should have been occupied by Evie, my twin sister. I touch the tattoo we had inked on our birthday. Something special for us both, reminding us that we would forever be tied together in this life.

We had a bright future, all taken from us in one horrific accident. That's what the police are calling it—an unfortunate accident.

Now left alone, I am as dark as the man who tries to imprison me. He thinks he is all I have left in this world. Only his to toy with, to manipulate, to fear him.

He may have taken everything from me, but he will regret the day he tried to kill my spirit. I will see him dead, if it's the last thing I do. It will mimic the already dead look in my eye. I just have to play the part, play along with the ruse.

The commencement speeches come to a close. We toss our caps in the air in a final good-bye to our last year of high school. I walk away, not bothering to retrieve my cap from the ground.

A hand reaches for me and tugs me back. Goose bumps on my arm rise in recognition of *his* touch—every nerve-ending screams in protest. I fight the urge to recoil or pull away and instantly calm my features in a well-practiced act, until I turn around to meet his jet-black eyes. Eyes that grasp onto your soul and whisper their sinister intentions through their penetrating stare—Julian.

He looks down at me with a wicked grin. I can't believe I never saw it before.

"Emma. How are you holding up?"

The false concern in his voice unsettles me. An average person wouldn't detect this, but I know Julian.

I give him my best attempt at a smile. "Better than I thought on a day like this." I shrug, trying to downplay my tempestuous feelings.

He pulls me into a hug.

I feel the bile rise in my throat as I fight the revulsion his mere presence brings about. I lift my hands mechanically and return his embrace.

He kisses my forehead, appearing as any doting boyfriend would in the public eye.

I sigh. "At least I have you." I get these words out in one forced breath, disguising each spoken word's bite.

This seems to please him.

He stares down at me and grabs my chin more roughly than I anticipated, lifting it, his stature forcing me to look straight up.

"You will always have me, Emma."

I swallow hard as I verbalize this known truth from my lips. "I know, Julian."

He grabs my arm and drags me away to a black SUV with equally dark tinted windows. A man exits the driver's seat to open the back door for us. I get in without hesitation.

What can I do at this point? Not a damn thing.

He gets in after me, and we drive off. There is no one waiting for me. No one I'm leaving behind. I look out the window, seeing the greenery and scattering of bluebonnets along the roadside. I say a silent good-bye to my previous life.

I won't be coming back. Not now. That girl died along with her family that night. Yet a stronger woman rose from those battered waves, breathing in a newfound purpose. The gale force winds gathered all my broken pieces and rearranged them into a stronger and more punishing life-force.

I am waiting on a black wave, biding my time, until a powerful wave rises in the aftermath of a storm, unexpectedly leaving casualties in its wake, ensuring I will once again be free.

Julian arranged everything at the funeral home in preparation for tomorrow's services. There is a small service at the gravesite without the funeral mass or typical rosary the day before. I look down at where my family is buried together in a row. They now reside under a large and beautiful Mexican white oak tree. I'm glad the tree will provide shade for them and keep them cool. The thoughts swirling in my head aren't logical at the moment. I know how things sound, but I can't help the way my brain is working, trying to process that my parents are no longer alive to feel the Texas heat and my sister is no longer alive to... I don't get to finish that thought.

"Where will you stay, dear." Mrs. Mendoza, my English teacher, interrupts my pensive trance, sincerity and sadness lacing her question.

The rumor going around town is that his family feels terrible about my circumstances, and Julian foot the bill for my parents' and sister's burial services.

Before I can answer her question, Julian cuts in.

"She will stay with my family. She will be taken care of."

I close my mouth and fight back the frown forming on my lips. I always seem to be fighting my emotions around Julian.

Mrs. Mendoza looks at me, and as if reading my thoughts, she places a hand on my shoulder and pats it. "It will all work out, dear." She looks back at Julian, puts her head down, and hurries away.

This seemed to anger him, and he pursed his lips. Not everyone is susceptible to his charm. His grip on my waist tightens, and I bite my lip until I taste the bitter flavor of copper on my tongue.

I won't make a sound. I won't let him know that he is hurting me. Besides, he knows he is, and he likes it. There is nothing that surprises me about him now that I understand the complete depravity of this character.

I feel another person taking my hand in theirs. The firm grip wakes me from my trance. "I am sorry for your loss."

"Thank you." I must say this a hundred times more, or maybe it just feels that way. There is a large turnout, since my parents worked at the school. Many people still come over to speak with me and offer more of their condolences. They talk about my parents in the past tense, which doesn't seem real. Another half hour goes by, and I can finally see the end of the line. The last person approaches me; the face is familiar, but I can't recognize where I know them from.

"I'm sorry for your loss, ma'am," the stranger says. He leans over to hug me, but instead, I hear him whisper, "Be ready tonight, Emma." With that, he walks off without looking back.

I glance at Julian, who seems oblivious to my interaction with this man. Noticing that there isn't anyone around, he lets me say good-bye to my family at the gravesite for the last time before we walk back to the car.

It was a beautiful ceremony. Julian was the ever-attentive boyfriend in front of people, with a punishing hand that left bruises around the small of my back when no one was looking. Maybe they saw but looked the other way for fear of garnering his attention. Everyone expressed their condolences and praised Julian and his parents for their generosity.

As we drive off, the song "Heart Shaped Box" by Nirvana is playing on the radio. The smooth lyrics of Curt Cobain ring out as I touch the tattoo on my arm and think about how my heart will always be locked away in a heart-shaped box. I am in a lifeless, loveless, and abusive relationship. I just hope someone can hear my silent pleas to save me.

CHAPTER SEVEN

EMMA

I told Julian I wasn't hungry and asked to be excused from dinner. I was glad to be changed out of that horrible black dress. Donning a pair of leggings, a hoodie, and sneakers, I just want to spend time alone to mourn my family, although I would never tell him that. I enter my new prison and sit on the bed, moving my hand back and forth along the luxurious duvet. I think about the past year with so much regret.

I wish I could undo the day I met Julian. I wouldn't have waited on him and taken his coffee order. Hell, I would have called out sick and missed work that day. I was so smitten with this handsome, wealthy guy who seemed fixated on me. He kept showing up, and I was so excited when he asked me out.

I remember going home and telling my sister about this amazing and handsome older guy that I had gained the attention of. I was eighteen already and graduating that year, so why not? A million telltale signs about his behavior should have alerted me. Unfortunately, I didn't listen or heed the multitude of red flags. I was head over heels and over the moon about anything Julian.

I stopped seeing my friends one by one and only hung around with him. He stopped asking about what I wanted to do and even ordered off the menu for me in restaurants of his choosing. My opinions ceased to matter, and it was too late when I noticed what had happened.

Even when we had sex, I rarely got off. It was all about Julian. Sometimes, he would come home so angry and would push me on my knees to suck him off. I was forced to comply as he fisted my hair and I gagged on the punishing thrusts of his cock. The possessive side I found so hot was now abusive because it wasn't about love. It was only about control.

I think about my sister Evie. My twin sister was an artist. She saw the beauty in everything, except Julian. She knew he was inherently evil. I just wished I had heeded her warning.

Evie suffered her trauma when she was attacked at age fifteen. She was almost sexually assaulted, but someone had heard her muffled scream and struggle attempts. A Good Samaritan killed the men, and the cops arrived shortly after.

The Good Samaritan, my grandfather's private security detail, as we later found out, didn't stay when the cops arrived, but at that point, nothing could be done to make my sister talk. After she reclaimed her life through the help of therapy and self-defense classes, she became highly intuitive to people with ill intentions. She could almost sense their predatory nature and was always on guard, determined never to become another victim. Her last present to me was a gift certificate to Krav Maga classes. In memory of Evie, I promise myself that I will take those damn classes and become strong like she was.

The night of the fire that killed my parents and sister, Evie pleaded with me not to go out with Julian and his parents to the restaurant, not knowing how I had tried not to. It was only one more night, and then we would leave Texas. I go through scenarios in my head trying to answer questions that would yield different outcomes from the current one I am forced to live in. Would he have continued to threaten me by attacking my family's livelihood? Would having money and crooked political ties ensure those threats were carried out? Would my parents really have lost their jobs and my family be homeless? Whatever the outcome, I know he would do his best to ruin our lives. I had laid all my cards on the table when I finally came clean. They ultimately decided I was more important. I wish they thought I wasn't; maybe I would still have my parents and Evie around.

It's surreal how in just one day everything can change. They had planned to get us out of there and send me away. Julian must have found out. I also suspected that he had watched me. The tingling of the hairs on my neck was always the telltale sign he was nearby. It was almost as though I felt the evil close by. The sensation that your body warns you to move. That your life is in danger. The intuition that something is just not right.

That cost them their lives. I cost them their lives. The fire happened so fast, they were trapped inside, and it left their bodies unidentifiable. Now, penniless and familyless, I am utterly dependent on Julian, just how he wanted it.

Julian had told me in the car that the fire was being investigated. The preliminary report blamed the cause of the fire on faulty electrical wiring– the fire chief was paid to say that. I wouldn't put it past Julian's family to falsify a report.

I start to think about my mom's family and wonder when they will come and get me. He didn't count on my mom's estranged brother from Mexico coming to my rescue. Uncle Andrés is 'the Mexican cartel,' albeit a rival adversary. He took over from my grandfather. I can't even imagine Grandpops as a ruthless cartel leader. My mom left that life behind when she married my father, a teacher at the local high school. This is why Julian is unaware that her family is a problem for him and his plans.

I loved hearing stories about when my parents met in college in Denton, Texas. They both found jobs in Brownsville and worked together at the same high school. It wasn't a coincidence they could gain employment at the same facility. It is sometimes hard to retain teachers and staff nowadays. That was one of the motivating factors for relocating to the Valley, as the locals called it. My mom was a school nurse who sparked my initial interest in healthcare. That had been my career path–that is, until I had no path.

I lie back on the bed and extend my arms out. What was the turning point for my mother? I suppose hearing about how Julian threatened me made her see red. The mafia life never left her.

I haven't heard anything from Uncle Andrés, but I suspect I will hear from him soon, especially given the visitor I had at the cemetery. I know they were strategizing and didn't want to wait too long before moving to my rescue. That wouldn't surprise me. Time is of the essence. Perhaps Julian will underestimate him. That's what happens when you're an entitled, narcissistic prick, after all.

What does surprise me is the note I receive under my door, pulling me out of my memories. I get off the bed and bend down to retrieve it. It's my uncle. My heart rate kicks up, beating with anticipation. The note says, *"I'm coming now."* This time, I will be ready. I don't have anything to prepare. All I have is me along with my determination to be free. I don't have time to process this. Something flashes up ahead, and I blink as the realization sets in.

Seconds later, I hear a commotion from downstairs and loud footsteps approaching my door. The door flies open, and I see my cousin. "Come on, Emma. We have to hurry," I hear Adrian say.

"Well, if you're not a sight for sore eyes, Adrian."

"Cute, Emma, but we'll catch up later, huh?"

We get outside, hop onto an ATV, and rush out from the property. Adrian must know this area well because shortly after, we are dropping into a tunnel below. He reaches his hand back, grabs my wrist tightly, and pulls me forward.

"Hurry, Emma."

"I'm trying, Adrian." I trip on my Converse as we whip around the corner at max speed. I quickly regain my composure as he looks back at me.

"Almost there. Pick it up." His voice carries on the hot, sticky air.

My lungs are screaming for air, and my hair is plastered around my face, slicked with sweat. It must be one hundred-plus degrees down here. I can barely see in the dimly lit tunnel. Yet I trust my cousin completely. Besides, I would already be dead inside if it wasn't for him and my uncle risking their lives to get me out of Julian's imprisonment. I was constantly being watched and restricted in my outings now, more so since I was staying at his house; I barely had time to react before my family's plan was implemented.

I can't hear anyone following us, but that doesn't mean they have given up trying to find me. I doubt Julian will ever give up until one of us ceases to exist. As we speak, Julian is losing his shit at the thought of losing his favorite possession. That's exactly what I am to him—a possession. He is a spoiled sociopath with a narcissistic personality to boot. He is the eldest son of a revered politician and our city mayor. His family is as crooked as they come. His father seems to have several elected positions in town in his back pocket, as well as other influential organizations due to generous contributions which were only made to serve his agenda.

I see the light ahead, and my cousin's encouraging words pull me out of my memories. We come to an abrupt halt, dust kicking up around us. He grabs two bags and hands me one. I immediately fling it around my back, securing it around my waist. He racks back a Glock forty caliber and gives it to me. I take it from him and place it in my back pants waistband.

He knocks three times and opens the hatch-like door just as we hear the sound of a vehicle's ignition starting close by. He jumps out quickly, and his hand goes back down through the hatch to help me out of the tunnel. A van is idling as we haphazardly throw our items in through the back door.

"Come on, Emma," he says again, offering me his hand to push me in first.

I get in, barely situating myself, as he follows behind me.

Before we can think of closing the door, the vehicle lurches forward, and we take off through the brush into the night, leaving a trail of dust and caliche behind us.

I sit back and take some deep breaths to calm myself.

Adrian closes the doors and then spins around, facing me. He looks me up and down, quickly assessing for injuries. He doesn't realize that most of them can't be seen. That was Julian's MO. He'd leave bruises occasionally, but nothing screamed abuse, unlike the emotional ones he inflicted daily.

"You're all right, Emma."

It comes out more like a question. Adrian is eyeing me with skepticism. I won't show him any weakness.

"I'm good, Adrian."

I repeat this to myself as I am used to saying it. I move the backpack over and place it by my feet. Then I remove the Glock from my back waistband and put it on my leg facing the door.

All my training when I was younger comes back on instinct. The summers I spent with my family in Mexico were among my cousins, who were all taught survival tactics through playful scenarios. My dad was against us shooting guns when they wanted to start at such a young age. Prior to Evie's assault, we didn't continue with self-defense classes either.

Ultimately, keeping us away from the cartel life didn't help my mom. They all died in that fire. They left a life they wanted no part of and kept Evie and me away because they feared what it would do to us—put us in possible danger.

It didn't work out for any of us in the end, but maybe that is my fault. I'm the one who put us in danger. Is there really anyone else to blame? Could there be? Shaking my head at the thought of it being anyone else's fault but mine, I wipe the sweat off my brow with my sleeve. I gather up my long, blond hair and put it up in a high ponytail, finally getting it out of my face. I was never allowed to put my hair up with Julian. This act, albeit small, feels like a big FU in regaining my independence.

All these random thoughts go through my mind. I must have been singing one of my favorite songs, "From the Pinnacle to the Pit" by Ghost. Talk about fucking inspiration right there.

That's when I notice my cousin's eyes assessing me.

I stop singing and quickly feel awkward at the exchange. I look briefly at Adrian and glance around, avoiding a conversation now; however, he doesn't comment on what he sees, and I am thankful for the silence. When it becomes too much to bear, I feel the need to fill it. I rub my sweaty hand up and down my pant legs, rocking my gun back and forth.

"I am just glad that it is over," I say and peek over at Adrian when he doesn't respond.

He tilts his head as if trying to decipher if I am joking about our situation.

I hold his stare. "What is it?"

He shakes his head. "Oh, my sweet cousin. "This"—he lifts his hand with a dramatic flair—"is just the beginning."

CHAPTER EIGHT

EMMA

The lull of the rough terrain takes my mind off my cousin's words. I can't believe I didn't realize it. Julian will never stop trying to get me back. This is my life now. I just hope Uncle Andrés has a plan. I can't be retaken by him. I'd rather die.

In what seems like an eternity, the sound of brush swiping along the van's sides is no longer heard, nor is the feeling of being thrown about in the truck along the bumpy path. The van moves around a curve, and the road smoothes underneath the tires. We stop momentarily to hear an electric gate opening automatically as we proceed down a lengthy driveway. I might not be able to see where we are going, but I have been around rural Texas enough to know what the landscape looks like without having to see it.

The surrounding ranches have been owned by the same families for generations. Some were offered land grants when Texas was being settled and was still a part of Mexico. Although we are in a different country now,

BLACK WAVE

I don't feel far from home. Maybe it's because I'm not.

There is no light leading the way. This is a private road that only people familiar with it know how to navigate. After driving another few minutes or so, we start to slow down. I hear the driver and another person speaking in Spanish. I wish I could look out, but the van boasts no view from back here.

I hear the sound of boots on the ground as the doors to the van open. I am staring at a man dressed in tactical gear. He surveys the back of the van and nods at Adrian. He closes the van door and taps it twice. The van continues through the iron gates, where we once again stop.

This time, when the door opens, I am helped out of the van by more armed men. I stand and immediately catalog my surroundings. The fountain in the middle of the circular drive is out of place. The easy fall of the water cascading down into the clear pool provides a displaced sense of tranquility.

Adrian jumps out of the van with our backpacks and throws one at me, returning my thoughts to the gravity of my situation. "Come on, cousin. Let's get you settled in."

I follow Adrian's steps to a spectacular Spanish colonial that boasts a beautiful balcony off the second floor with two considerably large additions. The stucco exterior and the clay-tiled roof have an earthy look that suits the desert-like climate of Mexico. The stucco exterior with cinder block framing provides a cooling element that helps insulate the house from the sun's relentless rays. It truly is breathtaking.

We open the grand doors and take in the expanse of saltillo tiles encompassing the entire home, sealed in a traditional, high-polished finish. So much careful attention was paid to every nook and cranny in this home, and it is apparent, even at first glance, the care someone took to make this a home. I should know because it isn't my first time in this house. Tia Cecilia died from cancer several years ago, but her memory still lingers in the home through her decor. Portraits on the walls tell a story of our family throughout the years—some I have missed out on because of my parents' choices.

I grab the necklace around my neck, a gift for my twelfth birthday, remembering my first love again—a wave in a circle with my birthstone, an emerald. As I touch it, I reflect on the boy who promised me a future. We were both young and still filled with the innocence of adolescence. The wave reminds me that I can change the course and fight any challenges in my life. My birthstone evokes themes of rebirth and renewal. Like the changing tides, the emerald is a reminder that as the flowers bloom in the spring, they are reborn again, new and perfect. He also stared into my eyes, the color of emeralds, and said the color was fitting. Goose bumps scatter around my neck and arms at the thoughts elicited about Eduardo, despite it being so many years ago.

Rubbing my arms back and forth, I shudder at the feeling of loss. Except this year, Evie won't be reborn. We won't celebrate a birthday together. Instead, this year reminds me of what was taken from me.

My twin.

My parents.

There isn't a day that I don't feel Evie with me. I thought that if she died, I would feel her absence, but it's as if she is still alive. She is protecting me, watching me.

I look up at the staircase that leads up to the bedrooms. I can hear children's voices—whispers of secrets between Evie and me as we slide down the banisters chased by Eduardo.

I always think about Eduardo, my first crush, and wonder what he is doing now. Is he still working for his family on the west coast of Mexico? When crime was at an all-time high within the cartel families, my mom decided to keep us away from her family out of an abundance of caution. But that wasn't the only reason. That was the last time I saw Eduardo. I guess he is in Houston now—a "business owner" of sorts.

He was a couple of years older than me, and I am sure my crush was all me. Still, I can't help but think that there could have been more if we had been around each other in our teenage years. Unfortunately, I never found out. I am sure he is married with many kids. I'm sure any woman would be happy to bear his children, if he grew into the man I suspect he did. Perhaps even an arranged marriage to benefit the organized crime families.

Our families were always together, especially our grandfathers, long-standing friends, or alliances formed between families. I didn't know the ins and outs of my grandfather and uncle's business, but I knew enough to understand that it wasn't strictly legal.

I knew much more than my parents suspected. Still, while I should have been frightened, I always felt safe and protected here. I knew that no one could ever hurt me because I was part of a well-connected family; nobody would dare to so much as attempt to harm a hair on my head without retribution from my uncle.

I felt the same way about Eduardo. I could see how he was so protective of me from a young age. I thought he was like an older brother I never had, but that year, on my twelfth birthday, I started to feel something different for him when he looked at me. When he gifted me that necklace, I had more confirmation of it. He promised me that we would go out on many dates one day. I laughed at the absurdity of that thought. He was going into high school soon, and the idea of him waiting for me was laughable.

"Welcome home, Mija."

I turn to the voice that startles me from my stroll down memory lane. "Tio," I answer back in greeting. I smile for the first time in months.

I make my way over to meet Uncle Andrés as he descends the stairs. He looks refined in his fitted trousers and dress shirt. The sleeves rolled up like he was busy working all day at the office. Despite his widow status, he never remarried, claiming he found his true love once, which was all he could ever hope for.

He pulls me into an embrace, and I hug him back. I feel him kiss the top of my head and breathe in his scent of whiskey and cigars. I hug him tighter and fight the tears threatening to fall.

He pulls me back to look at him face-to-face. "Emma, we will get revenge on the ones who took my sister and niece away from me. I will protect you, and know that you will always have family and a physical home here with us."

I melt at his words and seek comfort in them—this formidable force of a man who promises to seek vengeance. Just as I am going to ask how we are going to get revenge, he speaks up.

"Emma, first, get settled."

He lifts his hand, stopping any further argument from leaving my lips.

He shakes his head, expecting a protest from me about how I'm not tired.

"You have had enough excitement for today. We will get you settled in, and you need rest." He nods to my cousin. "Adrian, show Emma where her room is, please."

With that, he touches my shoulder, squeezing it gently. He begins to walk away as I stare at his back, but he stops to face me again. "Tomorrow, we will talk."

He must have noticed that I needed to hear those words. I relax and believe the conviction of his promises about seeking revenge. Footsteps slowly disappear around the corner and down the hall, where a door closes. The room is quiet as his men return to their protective posts, clearing the space.

I turn toward Adrian. I shrug, and he holds his hand out for me to take. "Come, cousin. I'll take you to your room now."

As my free hand trails along the wrought iron banister, we slowly walk up the winding staircase. The railing feels hard and cold under my touch. We continue up to the second floor and along the corridor to get to where I'm told is my room. Adrian pulls out a key from his pocket and opens the door. He turns and hands me the key.

"You're safe here, Emma, but this is the key that locks your room. It might make you feel safe..." he trails off. "Here."

He drops the cold metal key in my hand, and my fingers involuntarily clasps over the item meant to help me feel safe. The irony is not lost on me that I know how unsafe I truly am. I must rely on my uncle to protect me, praying that Julian doesn't find me. Or worse, make me return to his form of imprisonment. If he finds me this time, the punishment will be much worse.

Adrian opens the door to expose a splendidly furnished large bedroom decorated with soft feminine colors. He opens the double doors that lead to a veranda overlooking the property.

The warm breeze comes in, and I wince when I hear the sound of thunder. I walk in, following him out onto the veranda. I don't see anyone out there, but I know they are, just like the real threats that lurk in the dark, waiting for me to unknowingly walk into their trap.

The breeze picks up, and thunder and lightning erupt in the clouded sky, preventing the stars from shining through.

Adrian brings me back inside, closes the doors, and locks them behind him. He studies my face. I have no idea what he is looking for, but he won't find it there. I have learned to control my emotions and show people what I want them to see.

He smiles at me, and it isn't a happy one. It's filled with sadness and something far worse—pity.

He clears his throat.

"If you need something, please let us know, Emma. The bathroom has toiletries, and your closet is filled with suitable clothing."

He turns to leave, and I stop him.

"Adrian?"

He turns around, giving me his full attention. "Yeah, Em."

I bounce from foot to foot, feeling anxious about the uncertainty of my situation but grateful for the opportunity to be away from imminent danger. "Umm, thanks for everything."

He brings me in for a hug, kisses my forehead, and quickly releases me, turning to walk out the door.

I follow him and use the key he gave me to lock it. Once I hear the click, I slip out of my clothes and pull back the luxurious duvet. I turn the lights off and see lightning illuminating the night sky. I settle into bed as the heavens pour their tears down on me.

CHAPTER NINE

EMMA

I awaken to the sound of men talking outside in a familiar language. The morning light streams through the windows, and I can practically feel the morning dew steaming off the grass outside. We are well into summer here in Mexico, despite only being the end of May, and the temperature is hot. Hades hot. Luckily, I am in a climate-controlled house that camouflages the true feeling of summer.

I reluctantly get out of the most comfortable bed I have ever slept in and give myself a good stretch. My body feels unexpectedly well-rested. I open the closet doors and am immediately assaulted with a wardrobe for every occasion.

"Holy shit." I blow out a breath as I begin rummaging through the clothing, I settle on a pair of yoga pants, a mid-crop hoodie, and seamless undergarments, making my way toward a much-needed shower.

The bathroom is spacious, and the tiles feel cool under my bare feet. The colorful ceramic tiles in the shower are beautiful, and I ache to touch the bright-blue tile and trace the patterns I remember from when I was here last. The mosaic-looking tiles are a repeated theme throughout the house. The bright blues were a favorite of my aunt's.

I strip out of my clothes and turn the shower jets on. The steam fills the bathroom, and I immediately turn the temperature down, knowing it will feel good to be cool before I go outside to see my uncle. The scent of vanilla from the bath gel permeates the air, and I sigh in contentment.

After a most lavish shower, I dress quickly and put on a pair of Converse sneakers. I spread some tinted moisturizer on my face and apply minimal makeup. I won't need to do much today, since I am getting answers and learning about our revenge plan. Lastly, I put my hair into a messy bun and step out of my room, quickly locking the door behind me and pocketing the key for safekeeping.

I quickly take the steps to the lower level, fighting the sudden urge to slide down the banisters as I frequently did in my youth. I chuckle to myself, remembering all the suppressed memories of my time here. Resisting, I hop off the last step and walk toward the sounds of conversation coming from the back of the house. *Is my uncle still back there?*

I reach the kitchen and see many men outside on the hacienda-style courtyard terrace. I immediately notice that there is no female presence in sight.

Sure, I mumble to myself. It's not *a threatening vibe at all.*

It would feel *less* threatening if I'd at least recognized a few faces besides my uncle and cousin. I open the door to the covered patio, where a large spread of food covers the entirety of the table. The condensation drips from the carafes holding the breakfast beverages. The ceiling fans rotate, circulating the humid air that hangs in an oppressive blanket around us. It hasn't yet reached ninety degrees, a small blessing this morning. However, wait until noon.

"Sit and have some food, Mija." Uncle Andrés motions with his hand to the enormous food spread before us. I quickly take his advice, not needing to be told twice.

Adrian, reading my thoughts, smiles. "You didn't have to ask twice, huh, Dad? Some things don't change." Adrian chuckles at my vigor in stacking large quantities of fruit and Mexican confections on my plate.

I promptly sit on my chair and sprinkle a salt, lime, and chili mixture on my citrus fruits. Someone places a horchata on my right side, and I smile while beginning to eat. All my childhood foods are served, and I wonder if my uncle didn't plan this on purpose. Soon, someone clears their throat, and my bright-pink frosted cake is stilled midway to my mouth as I turn to the noise source.

"We should discuss what we must do about your situation, Emma." I hear my uncle talking, and I slowly place the cake back on my plate.

My uncle sees this and frowns at the action. I shake the crumbs off my napkin and pat the corners of my mouth, nodding in agreement.

"You're right, Tio."

I lift my glass of water, placing the condensation against my forehead. Gulping the entire glass of water, I set it on the table and face my body toward my uncle, giving him my full attention.

"Do you have a plan, or do you have any questions for me, Tio?"

He nods. "I have plenty, Emma. Though, why don't you start at the beginning."

And I do. I tell Tio how I met Julian and how he relentlessly pursued me, isolating me from all my friends until I was only with him. I tell him about confiding in my sister about everything I went through with Julian and the intervention of my parents and Evie, all leading up to the plan to run. It was supposed to all work, until it didn't, and they were killed.

"We didn't expect that either, Emma." Uncle Andrés stands from his chair and paces back and forth.

Adrian and I look at each other.

"How did it happen, Tio? I thought we were safe?"

He shakes his head. Regret and sadness are etched on his face before he conceals it.

"I suspect a listening device was hidden in your house, allowing him to hear about your plans. This gave him the heads-up he needed to eliminate the threat. I don't think he knew about us because my call was secure. He must have only heard one side, so he did not know who or what was said, only what your mother was saying. We never use names. She grew up in this life. She knew better."

I think about this and wonder if he bugged my house when we were dating and I initially trusted him in my home. Then it hits me. "When he asked for water, I went to the kitchen. When I returned with the water, he walked out the door, never drinking it. He was downstairs planting listening devices in my house." I shake my head and place my hand over my face. "How could I have not realized it?"

"We will never know now, Emma, since the evidence is non-existent. Everything was destroyed in that fire."

A tear escapes my eye, and I attempt to wipe it away quickly, but Uncle

Andrés and Adrian notice it, although they don't comment.

Keep it together, keep it together, I chant in my head, refusing to show weakness in front of my family.

This life doesn't allow for weakness, and I want to prove to my uncle that I can be strong and face whatever happens next. Except I am not strong. Evie was the strong one. I have to be strong like Evie, I think to myself.

"Does that mean I am safe for now, Uncle?" I take my thumb to bite my nail. It is a nervous tic I have had since I was a child.

Tio Andrés looks at me and nods. "For now, you are. It would be stupid for Julian to come across the border into my town and try to kidnap you. No one would be stupid enough to get involved and help him now."

I let out a breath I didn't know I was holding. "Well, at least that makes me feel a little better." I smile weakly at my uncle.

He frowns and then continues to tell me the truth. "You are safe for now, Emma, but not forever. Do I think he will forget about you and fixate on something or someone else? Not likely. His ego is bruised, and nothing is worse than a narcissist with a hurt ego. No, he will always be after you, but we must be smarter this time. Always be a step ahead."

"Uncle, that doesn't make me feel better." I run a hand over my face and chuckle nervously. "So what's the plan then?"

"We lay low for a while and let things settle." He shares a look with Adrian. I don't know what it means, but I don't like it.

"What's that look for, Tio?" I glance between them both, letting them know that I saw that awkward-as-fuck interaction and I want answers.

Uncle Andrés tugs at his goatee, rubbing the hairs between his fingers, contemplating his answer. I patiently wait, but I am starting to get nervous.

"What do you want to do with yourself now that you are done with high school?"

Well, that wasn't what I thought he would say at all. I laugh out loud because surely he must be joking, right? When I see that he isn't kidding, I stop and think about it.

"Before this happened, I wanted to attend college to be a nurse, like Mom, but I can't foresee that happening now. If I leave here, I must worry constantly about Julian and can't return home. He will find me and force himself on me. Besides, I don't have a home there anymore."

I hang my head down and hear the scraping of a chair before it topples over.

At my words, Uncle Andrés gets up abruptly with fists clenched at his side, walking over to me. "That motherfucker will never retake you and force himself on you against your will, you hear me? I will end his life, and consequences be damned, Emma."

I startle at the outburst but know that my uncle has a bad temper, and I am lucky never to have been on the receiving end of it. I am his beloved niece, after all. "So what do you suggest, Tío?"

He touches my cheek and kisses the top of my head. He motions to Adrian, and he walks over to his father. "I will find a way to make your wish come true. We will wait it out, find a way for you to get your degree, and ensure your safety." Just as quickly as he got up, he heads out of the patio with Adrian on his heels.

No one is around now, and I am left alone to my thoughts. *Did Uncle Andrés mean what he said?* I thought my college plans would be squashed now that I had this problem, but he seemed confident I could. Wow, to be a nurse was a dream, and now that my mom is gone, it would connect me with her to follow in her footsteps. *Would she be proud of me?*

I stand up, gather my pink frosted Mexican pastel and an empanada, and place them in a napkin for later. I see two men coming out of the brush toward the house, catching me off guard. *Will I ever get used to this life?* I understand why my mom kept us from it, but I can't help but think this would have been normal if I had continued to stay here over the summers.

I decide to go back to my room and rest up, think about what my uncle said and if it is possible. I take the key out of my pocket and unlock my door. I close the door, and the click echoes through the hallway. I lock up again and replace the key in my pocket. I put my pastels on the table by my bed and take off my sneakers.

My hoodie crop top hides my tattoo, and the bright red of the colors catches my eye. I lift my sleeve to expose the tattoo and trace the pattern. Evie saw one Marilyn Manson had and showed me something similar. It was corny as fuck, but we laughed, and it was so us because we were always together as one in utero and in this life. Just like the ones on our forearms, forged hearts as she had called them, we stuck together.

The irony is not lost on me that my family died in a fire that night. Evie once said what is forged in all of us can only be created through fire. When something bad happens and causes everything you once believed in and loved to burn, I'd like to think that our spirits rise with an unbreakable strength amid the flames. The newfound strength helps to heal you during these intense periods of pain you feel because you miss them so much.

Our pain becomes a black wave—unrelenting. You become grateful for the pain, welcoming it because at least it is an emotion that makes you feel something again when you were once incapable of feeling anything else. With that, you learn to free yourself from the life-sucking hold it has and everything else that has cut you to the bone.

Perhaps it will give us peace when we know that even in the darkest of nights, when we cannot see our way out of the pain, we can trust that the love we shared is forging something stronger in our hearts, healing us. Something that cannot be broken by anyone who tries to hurt us, no matter how desperately they may try to do so.

My sister. My best friend. The ache in my heart intensifies when I think about all that Julian took from me. I just hope that he can feel what it's like someday to lose it all, and I will watch him burn.

CHAPTER TEN

EMMA

The following month goes by in a blur. I made good on my promise to Evie about taking self-defense classes. It helps to keep my mind off things and allows me an outlet to fight the demons that threaten to consume any remaining goodness I have left in my heart.

"Lonely Day" by System of a Down filters in through the surround sound speakers in the gym. I say gym, but it is more of a training facility that most staff use to keep in tip-top shape. Given the nature of our job, fitness is a must. It has become my job, too, because I am becoming quickly acclimated to the mafia life. I love the family that I was kept away from. There is a fierce loyalty present in this type of environment, where you rely upon one another to keep you safe and are willing to sacrifice yourself to save your family at all costs. I realize that it was always there—engrained in every fiber of my being. The ease that I fell back into the life I grew up in and have now returned to was never really far away. It was always a rolling wave—the familiarity there breaks in a stable, unrelenting pattern.

BLACK WAVE

The song finishes with the last line's screaming lyrics, and I realize that for the past month or two since Evie has been gone, I am finally allowing myself to feel the crippling guilt. I caused her death. Julian may have executed his plan, but that was why they died that night. It has taken some time to feel like I wish I didn't die in that fire with them.

After my workout, I decide to get on the treadmill and vent my anger. It is the healthiest way I can grieve. I've been depressed, and I didn't want to eat. I realize now that Evie wouldn't want that life for me—punishing myself. Her ordeal when she was almost assaulted showed me how strong she was. She begged me to become stronger, too. I chose to seek help instead of getting strong, and that backfired. I won't allow myself the same fate as before. When I meet Julian again, and I know that I will because he will never stop looking for me, I will be ready.

I see the door open in my periphery, and I stop the treadmill abruptly. I take out my AirPods and see my cousin walking toward me with a smile. "Looking good, cousin." Adrian comes over and peeks around on my treadmill mile count.

"I just started," I tell him to justify my one-and-a-half-mile log.

He chuckles and raises his hands in the air. "Hey, I believe you. No judgment here. I just came to tell you that my dad wants to talk to you in the courtyard."

I nod and grab the towel that is slung on the bar of the treadmill. I wipe the sweat off my face and around my neck and chest. I wipe down the equipment and stroll out of the gym, pleased with myself and the effort I am putting into getting stronger, not just in my body but also in my mind. I must have both faculties if I plan on fighting off Julian.

I walk to the courtyard and see Uncle Andrés sitting on the bench across from the water fountain. He has his legs crossed and a drink in his hand. I sit next to him and stare at the water cascading out of the fountain. The calming effects of the water dripping and cascading down the triple tiers make a bubbling sound in the otherwise quiet area. This is my favorite part of the house because it is enclosed and offers security in the hacienda-style home. I hear the rattle of his ice, and he brings the last of the liquid up to his mouth and tosses back the remaining amber fluid in his tumbler. I feel him look my way, and I turn to meet his stare. His lip quirks up.

"How has your training been?" He shakes his ice around, trying to loosen any drops of his whiskey.

I turn my body to face him. "Good. I could use more, but it has been a good therapy. An outlet to release some of my anger and try to ease the thoughts of my family's death that constantly plague my mind. It also keeps me busy, so what can I say."

He seems to think before he responds. "I'm glad to hear that. I thought it was about time to implement some of your plans."

Hearing this perks me up, and I stand abruptly. "You mean it's time to act and fight against Julian?"

He shakes his head. "No, Emma. It is too early, and they will be expecting it. I am talking about you returning to school and fulfilling some of your dreams of becoming a nurse."

I open my mouth to speak and then shut it. After a minute, I find my words. "You mean that? I can go to school to study nursing? College?" I am in shock because I thought that was just a dream. I didn't know I would be able to go to school.

"Well, not right away. I thought you could do your classes here, in Mexico, and then apply to nursing school in another town away from here. Maybe back across the border. He stands up and paces a bit. As he explains the plan, I can see the wheels turning in his head.

"Tio, I can't go back to Brownsville." My voice creeps up an octave as I become worried about being close to Julian again. I wipe the sweat that coats my forehead. I am not sweating from the workout at this point, but from the anxiety. He grabs ahold of his goatee, running his fingers up and down, as he usually does when he is deep in concentration. I don't know if he is aware that he even does it. I certainly am not going to bring it up.

"What do you think about Corpus Christi? It's not Brownsville. It's farther up the coast, and I think we could hide you, and Julian won't expect you to be there. You can go to a community college there. It has an outstanding nursing program, from what I hear. Just take everything here and apply to the associate degree program. It's up to you though."

I walk over to my uncle and embrace him. He chuckles and holds on to me, bringing a kiss to the top of my head. "So, is that a yes, Emma?"

"Thank you, Tio. I appreciate this more than you know. The chance at a degree that I can use to support myself later. That is a big yes."

He releases his embrace to regard me, and I can feel there is something he wants to say but doesn't continue. Instead, he nods and walks off. I look at his retreating form and wonder what it could have been that he wasn't saying. I try not to dwell on it and focus on the fact that I am going to college. I'll have a career. *One step closer to being independent,* I whisper to myself.

I lay back on the lounger and look up at the stars. It is so peaceful out here, and the stars are so bright. I used to do this often, but I wasn't alone. I remember one time I was out riding with Eduardo. We would take the truck. Since we weren't leaving the property, just riding through the acreage, avoiding the country roads, I sat close to him, feeling so carefree. My mom saw me and was upset about how I presented myself. It was no way for a lady to be acting. I thought nothing of it back then, taking off with a boy at night. The boy that was my friend until he wasn't. The man who never gave me my first kiss under a blanket of stars.

"Emma, you are hogging all the covers." He tugs at the blankets, and I hold on tight. I giggle when he tries to tickle me to let go.

"Eduardo, stop. I ate way too much. I think I could throw up," I stammer as he lets go to see the seriousness of my scrunched-up face.

"Okay, fine. Take the blankets, but just know you are a little thief, Emma."

I laugh and turn to face the boy who gets all my smiles. "Why do you always call me that?"

"Call you what?" he says with a smirk.

"Call me a little thief." He stares intently at me, so I blush, looking away and quickly changing the subject.

"It's so beautiful out here. I wish I could stay out all night and look up at the stars...with you." I say this last part in a whisper, but it doesn't get past Eduardo.

He grabs my hand, and I refuse to look at him. This moment feels different from the boy who would play football with us and push me down into the dirt face-first without remorse.

I swallow down the lump of anxiety in my throat. "It's so beautiful. I could get lost in this."

He runs his fingers up and down my forearm with the slightest contact. It feels like my skin is on fire from his touch, making my hands sweat.

"Me too, Emma. I wish I could stay like this forever, my little thief."

Suddenly, I am afraid we aren't talking about the stars anymore. When I can no longer resist, I turn and see Eduardo staring at me. I swallow down saliva that has lodged, forming a lump in my throat.

I see something cross my line of sight. "Look! A shooting star." I point with excitement at the streak across the sky. My giddiness is coming off in waves. I close my eyes and concentrate.

"What did you wish for Emma?"

Shaking my head out of the dream, I reflect on all my wishes. I would wish for a new bike when I was younger. Then, as I got older, I wished for an ATV to ride with my other cousins instead of riding with someone else.

That day, though, I wished for a boy I had crushed on to kiss me. Now, when I gaze at the stars, I wish for love. I know that my uncle and cousins love me, but it isn't the same. I miss my sister and my parents, but most of all, I miss being held and protected.

In Brownsville, the city lights obscured the stars, but out here... they are so brilliant and clear in the country. I see a shooting star and make a wish like I did back then. Maybe it's the little girl in me who used to look out at the colossal sky with hope and make a wish, but I wish on a star that someday I can find the fairy tale love that every little girl wishes for. Instead of Prince Charming, I want to wear the crown with that badass boyfriend who would give his life to protect his queen and would rather die than live without me.

CHAPTER ELEVEN

EDUARDO

She bobs her head up and down on my cock. Her red lipstick smudges all over her mouth and my dick. Her nickname is Cherry Pop. She always orders a rum and coke with cherries as her signature drink. That, along with the cherry-red lipstick, and you get the picture. The joke isn't lost on me that this is far from the first time Cherry was a virgin. Her saliva is pooling down her chin. I am almost about to come when she looks up at me with those big green eyes. *Fuck.* I shut my eyes and stop thrusting, pulling my cock out of her mouth as her teeth scrape the underside of it. I hiss in response. She immediately stands up and puts her hand on my chest.

"Eduardo, what's wrong, baby? You were about to come. I could feel it. Can I–"

I don't give her a second to finish her sentence as I turn her around facedown on my desk. I push her skirt and panties down as they remain stationary around her knees, restricting any further leg movement. I push my cock into her pussy without much warning. I mean, if she doesn't understand what is happening here, then she is dense.

Cherry grips the end of my desk and holds on for the ride. I lift her slightly by placing one arm under her hips. The position allows me to have a firm grip, keeping her in place. It also allows a better angle for me to fuck her. I fist her ponytail with the other hand and pull, causing her back to arch toward me. Cherry starts to groan, and I slow my thrusts, trying to get back to the feeling I had of almost coming before she looked at me. The familiar green eye color of a girl I've wanted to forget about—a girl I was told to forget about. If I did, she would be safe.

"Please, Eduardo, if you care about my daughter, you will forget about her. I don't want this life for her. You are going to start high school and meet girls your age. She's too young for you now anyway."

She looks at me, thinking I will say, sure, okay. I'll stay away from Emma. My little thief. "I'm sorry, Mrs. Ortiz, but I can't do that."

She quickly corrects me. Frowning, she replies, "It's Mrs. Taylor, Eduardo." *I know this, but she tries to forget where she came from, and I quickly remind her that she is just like me, as much as Mrs. Ortiz-Taylor doesn't want to admit it— born into the same life. The same rules. The same mafia-style family.*

"I figured you would say that." *She looks me up and down disapprovingly and walks away.*

When I returned the following summer to be close to Emma, she didn't return. Her uncle said that her parents broke ties with the family to give the girls what he quoted from her mother "A normal life." That was the last summer I saw Emma. My dad made me promise to respect the family's wishes, but the consequences be damned. My heart be damned. It wants what it wants, right?

High school came and went in a blur. I had my share of girls, but nothing in the form of a relationship. If I couldn't have the one girl I wanted, then I would go through it alone.

When I went to college, I moved to Houston, Texas. I was in a fraternity and made great friends who quickly became my frat brothers. Many of them I still talk to. I focused on the family businesses and, more importantly, made myself a name in the industry.

I own a few companies. One is a gym/fitness center, and the other is a nightclub—the one where I am supposed to blow my load into a bartender's red-lipped mouth. Instead, I had to turn her away from facing me because I was having flashbacks. Fucking triggers.

You know that saying you shouldn't eat where you shit? Well, I should take my advice, or it will come back to bite me in the ass.

I pick up my pace, and Cherry moans like a porn star. "Oh god, baby. Just like that. Harder. Faster."

I fight the urge not to roll my eyes and give the woman what she wants. Her breath turns into a high-pitched cry as her pussy quivers. My phone rings, and I stare at the name on the screen. Ramiro. Fabulous, what does my brother want now?

I pick up the phone mid-thrust, and the sound of skin slapping skin can be heard throughout the room. "Ram," I answer the call.

"Hey, dick," My brother responds. "What the..." he trails off.

Cherry's walls tighten around me, gripping my dick like a glove, and I come shortly after. Her breathing is all quick pants and then a moan in satisfaction as she falls on the desk with a grunt. She giggles.

"Baby, you fuck me so good."

I pull out of her and discard the condom in the trash. I pat her ass twice, letting her know the fun ride is over and please use the quickest exit line out the closest door. She stands still, looking over at me, and I move my head, tilting it toward the door. She gets the hint, tugs her panties upward, and pulls her skirt down. She goes to speak, but I cut her off, shaking my head. I point my finger at the door.

"Out, Cherry. Now." She nods and quickly exits. I hear my brother chuckle on the other line.

"You didn't have to pick up the phone, you know." He laughs into the receiver.

"Well, I knew you would just call back, so I was avoiding the hassle of having to hear the phone ring repeatedly."

"True, true," he quickly admits. "Cherry, huh?" His laugh intensifies.

I snort. "I know, right." He doesn't even have to comment further about the name. I've already heard it. "So, tell me, brother, what has you interrupting my nighttime club activities this late evening?"

He waits for a minute and clears his voice. His pause before speaking concerns me because my brother has no filter. The fact that he wants to choose his words has me quickly perking up with increasing paranoia.

"Ram, is everything okay? You sound serious." I worry because my brother is the biggest asshole to mostly everyone, except twin girls we both adored. Once upon a time, a long time ago. And, of course, our mother. "Is it Mom? Is Mom okay?" My voice rises as I try to calm the sound of panic rising in my throat. "Who do I have to kill?" I say in a low growl. It sounds like a joke, but I am far from joking.

He clears his throat. "I came upon some news today and reached out as soon as possible. I had to gather more details before I called you." His voice sounds different, sad even.

"Just spit it out already," I say, becoming more pissed off by the second. My anxiety skyrockets.

And he does. I just can't believe what he tells me. "Can you repeat that, Ram?"

"I talked to Dad today, and he informed me that the Ortiz family is mourning."

My stomach twists in knots. "Who died, Ram?"

"The Taylor Family," he says quickly, "but there was one survivor."

I wait for him to tell me what I pray is the one person I need to be okay. Please, God, I say in a silent prayer.

"Emma."

I let out a breath. "Emma is alive?" I ask quickly for confirmation. I grip the desk, hanging my head down. "Thank fuck. Thank fuck," I pant out in a whispered prayer to anyone who will listen. It is all I manage to get out before I can process the severity of the situation. "Tell me what you know."

We go back and forth on the phone, and Ram tells me that Emma's parents and sister, Evie, died in a house fire that destroyed everything. The house burned to the ground, with only one survivor. Emma was apparently out to dinner. She was spotted at a restaurant in town when the fire occurred. Talk about luck.

"What caused the fire, Ram?" I can hear his fingers drumming on the desk as he builds momentum—anticipation awaits his following words.

"That's just it, Eduardo. The fire chief reported it to be faulty wiring. It was an electrical fire, and it just spread too quickly. They were trapped inside and could not get out. They died of smoke inhalation before being rescued and passed out before being burned to ashes."

I cringe at the details of the accident. "They just couldn't get out? That seems all kinds of suspect if you ask me."

I can see Ram sitting at his desk thinking the same thing I am right now. Going through the scenario, it just doesn't add up. "The math isn't mathing."

"It was investigated though?" I need to know more details.

"Yep," he replies unconvincingly. "That's what they reported, but then the weird thing is that Emma just disappeared."

I sit up quickly upon hearing this. "What do you mean disappeared?" I try not to become upset because my brother is the messenger. Don't kill the messenger, right? But if I could reach into the phone and wring his fucking neck... He didn't do anything wrong. He didn't, but someone did.

"People are talking and saying that she is back in Mexico under the protection of her family, but no one has seen her.

I stand abruptly. "We have to find her!" I scream, slamming my fist against the desk. "We have to find Emma. We have to do something."

"Eduardo," he says, attempting to soothe me, "she doesn't want to be found. Her family doesn't want her to be found. Don't you get that?"

I run my hand down my face. "Emma's family is dead, Ram. How am I not supposed to worry about her." I feel my voice cracking.

"If you care about her, you will let her go, Eduardo." I can hear her mom speaking to me with determination. *"You will always be a part of this life. I want my daughter to have a normal life. One with school activities, prom, college, and a normal marriage with someone who helps her raise their kids. Someone who doesn't put a target on her back and put their family in danger. Risking their lives because of the life they were born into."*

I shake my head, not even trying to pretend that I will do this. "I'm sorry, Mrs. Taylor. I just can't let her go.

"I thought you might say that. But you see, you don't have a choice."

She leaves me there dumbfounded as she walks away, never to return to the house in Mexico again because I was dangerous. All because she thought I could get her killed.

The irony isn't lost on me that everything her mother tried to keep her away from was the one thing that could have saved her. I don't know what happened to get them killed, but it is clear that foul play was involved. I wouldn't be surprised to learn that the fire chief was paid off to falsify the report.

"Eduardo?" I hear Ram breaking through my thoughts as I try to make sense of this devastating news. "Are you still there? You are too quiet."

"Yeah, I'm still here. I'm just trying to wrap my head around the sequence of events. It seems fishy, but I don't know anything about it. I haven't talked to Emma in years, and now, how do I find her?"

I hear Ram let out a sigh on the other line. "We have to wait it out, brother. We wait and see what we can discover or hear from the families. If her uncle is protecting her, we will know sooner or later. That is, if they want us to know at all."

"Yeah, you're right." I agree with Ram because having him think I won't be a problem is best. I only want to find her and make sure she is okay.

"Besides," he continues, "you haven't even seen her in forever. You don't even know what she looks like anymore. How she is."

BLACK WAVE

The truth is almost on the tip of my tongue, trying to break free and announce that I stalked her. Well, I stalked her socials and even saw her once through the window of a coffee shop. Emma had just started working there. She turned into such a beautiful woman. What had me smitten was her infectious laugh. She threw her head back and laughed animatedly with her hands, throwing them left and right to accentuate her point when telling a story or rehashing an event. So full of energy, so alive. "Thank god she is alive," I whisper.

"Eduardo? Are you still there?"

His words snap me out of my memories. "True, Ram." I clear my throat, wanting to end this conversation already. "Will you keep me posted on anything you hear?"

"Of course. Be safe, Eduardo." With that, he hangs up, and I do the same.

I am standing there unblinking at the oddity of the situation. I place my hand on my desk and lean over. My breathing picks up as the anger starts to seep over. I see a wet spot on some papers, probably from where Cherry came on my desk as I fucked her from behind. Because I couldn't look her in the eyes. Eyes that reminded me too much of the emerald-green ones I stared at once long ago and couldn't get enough of.

Anger rushes through me, and I hurl all the items off my desk. They fall and crash on the floor in a thunderous clatter. Any items initially missed from that first pass, I sweep off my desk until it is free of anything, and my mind remains full of everything that is Emma.

CHAPTER TWELVE

EMMA

PRESENT DAY...

After a few more minutes, my best friend Liv will be here to relieve me from this shift. I am looking forward to hanging out with the girls tonight. It's too bad that Liv has to work the night shift and won't be going out with us. We are all giving one last hurrah to spring break on Padre Island.

Liv and I graduated nursing school together and have been inseparable ever since. I didn't know anyone when I moved here, and she immediately brought me into her circle of besties. Immediately, they treated me like I was part of their gang of friends. I gathered that they all knew each other from grade school or at least high school and were a close-knit group.

Liv and I attended a recruitment event hosted by the hospital and decided to accept the positions immediately. We took a sign-on bonus after graduating, which helped since we had not been working while we were in school full-time. I took the offered day shift, and Liv took the much despised night shift. She is going to school to finish her baccalaureate degree in nursing and is already accepted into a nurse practitioner program, pending graduation in a couple of months. I am beyond proud of that girl. I'd be even prouder if she got her ass in here and relieved me from this god-awful shift.

I would like nothing more than to take a scorching-hot shower and scrape this pestilence off my body. I still smell that poor man's rotting toes in my nose. The stench was overwhelming, and I tried not to let him know that I wanted to gag right then and there. I shiver at the thought.

Dr. Hall, the never-ending flirt, throws his arm around my shoulders and pulls me toward the clock, pointing at it jokingly. I know he mostly means nothing by the action, and I have told him repeatedly that I was not interested in dating him. Dating a coworker or someone in a higher position of power is always a recipe for disaster. They hold all the authority over you, and I never want to be in that situation again.

I frown, and Dr. Hall seems to notice. "Are you okay, Emma? You seemed upset just a second ago."

I immediately school my features, and my mask falls back into place. I smile radiantly at Dr. Hall while simultaneously scooting out from his claustrophobia-inducing side shoulder hug.

"Of course I am. Do you see the clock?" Now that I am free from his restrictive hold, I point animatedly at it, waving my hands. "I am almost out of here, Ethan."

He smiles at my use of his first name when answering him. I knew he would like that, and it was a good distraction from asking pointed questions about my previous mood.

"If you'll excuse me, sir, I must finish some last-minute things before my shift relief person arrives." I see him eye me hungrily at my use of the word sir before nodding and walking away. I laugh to myself. Men are so predictable sometimes.

Walking to the medication dispenser, I see a tall girl nod at me. She heads my way with her long, wavy hair bouncing along her shoulders and honey-brown eyes holding back laughter.

"There you are, girl. I am here to relieve you. I witnessed that encounter with you and Dr. Hall, by the way." She bounces back and forth on her toes in a playful manner, much like the cat that caught the canary.

I give her the biggest smile because she just made my night. Ignoring her quest for more information about Ethan, I deflect. "Thank god you're here.

It's been hell today."

Liv attempts to stifle a laugh but fails miserably. "You say that every shift, Emma."

"I only say that because it's true," I counter. I carefully finish counting the narcotics in the bin before closing it. "I hope your night is better, but looking at the stacks of pending charts…" I trail off, giving her a sympathetic frown.

"Judging by the waiting room as I entered this place, I think I'm forever and eternally fucked tonight." Liv brings her hand to her temple with what I think is a weak attempt to ward off an impending headache.

I fling my arm around my best friend, but it is more like around her back because, damn, that girl is tall. "Well, let's hope nothing memorable happens." I release her side and push my remaining charts into her hands. Liv groans.

"Come on, Liv, I'll give you a report on my patients. Room ten has some pain meds ordered, and I'll give her those before I leave. Can you reassess her pain in a bit?" I walk away with a little skip in my step, knowing my shift is almost done for the evening. "I'll be back in a few minutes to give you a report on the rest of my patients. The sooner I do, the sooner I can get my drink tonight."

I finish my last remaining task and go to find Liv again. I am finishing my sign-out when I realize she is only half listening. I stop mid-sentence, scanning her eyes for clues as to why she is so distracted. If I had to gamble money on it, I bet it would be about her on-and-off-again boyfriend, Brodie. Now there's a douche canoe if I ever met one. But, hey? What can I do but support my friend in her bad decisions? I am certainly not one to advise about the best choices, considering all I lost because of it. I quickly shut that thought down; instead, I refocus on Liv.

"You know that we will all miss you tonight, right? It's the last time for a long time that we can get together."

"You have no idea how jealous I am right now, Em." I put both arms out and up toward her much taller stature and pull my girl in for a big embrace.

Liv reminds me that she will see us tomorrow and to take plenty of pics so it will seem like she is there with us. "Of course, you know I will. I expect to meet up with the whole gang tonight and will send you a ton of pics." I remind her about going straight to bed after her shift because I am only giving her a few hours of sleep before I pick her up for the last days of spring break on Padre Island. I grab my stuff by slinging my tote around my shoulder.

"I expect a large iced coffee and a greasy breakfast burrito when you pick me up."

That cracks me up because as much as Liv eats, the girl doesn't gain an ounce of weight. Ugh.

"Naturally," I retort. "Only the breakfast of champions for my bestie." I wave my hands over my head in a good-bye as I exit.

I spare one last glance at Liv to witness Dr. Hall's attention on her. He sends me a playful wink. I roll my eyes, turning my head toward the revolving door. I put on my sunglasses and take a cleansing breath of fresh, salty air before I head out into the Texas sun.

I place my scrubs in the sanitizing cycle of the washer and walk naked into the bathroom to take a scalding-hot shower. The hot water does wonders to wake my body up after working a grueling twelve-hour shift and rid my body of the emergency department germs. I sigh in contentment as I step onto my bedroom's fluffy faux fur rug. The apartment is cool, and the scent of lavender in the infuser provides a sense of calm energy as I scan the contents of my closet for an outfit to wear tonight. I hear my phone sound with an incoming text.

Ainsley and Val: Hey, girl. Running a bit later. See you in an hour. *Kissing emoji.*

Emma: Alrighty.

I relax, knowing that I can count on the girls to never be here on time. I have a little longer to decompress. I make my way into the kitchen with a little skip in my step as I grab my favorite bottle of red and pour myself a glass of Freakshow wine.

I return to my closet and stare at the choices. I'm resolved to play some music. Walking over to my speaker, I hit my favorite song. Twin Temple's "I Know How to Hex You" blares out through the Bluetooth speaker. I sway back and forth to the rock and roll doo-wop sounds of Alexandra James's sultry voice.

I finish up my glass of wine and decide on a black romper with a fishnet-looking top. I braid each side of my hair and twist it back into a messy ponytail. I pair it with some black patent wedge loafers. I hate that my life has become shoes I could potentially run in, but better safe than sorry.

Looking down at the wedged heel, I wonder if maybe I should change into my Converse sneakers. Hm. What should I do? Fuck my life.

I resist the urge to channel my sensible side by pouring another glass of wine. As I place the glass on my bedside table out of sight, I notice the dark-purple lipstick residue lingers on the edge of it, and I go to the mirror to reapply more before I leave. I hear a knock at the door, and I quickly throw my lipstick in my purse before heading to answer it. I don't have to look to see who it is because Ainsley and Val are so loud.

I open the door with a flourish, and they come barging in. "Hey, Em!" they both say in unison, hugging me from each side. I lift my arms and gather them for a group hug, rocking each other back and forth.

"Are you ready to go?" Ainsley asks, releasing me as Val barrels toward the bathroom.

"Just gotta pee before we go," she yells, already shutting the door.

"I swear that girl has a squirrel bladder." Ainsley throws her hand over her forehead, shaking her head back and forth. She turns her attention to me. "You look nice."

She eyes my outfit, and I chuckle at her accusatory tone. They are both wearing flip-flops and tiny sundresses. It is the typical outfit here because it is so hot. I reserved that for my bathing suit at the beach. Of course, they just throw on little shorts and no shirt over their bikini top or wear it all day. Val comes back out, announcing she is ready, and that's all the motivation we need to have us heading for the door.

We all pile into the car and head out to The Surfboard Bar and Grill. This place is a hang-out that we frequent. It has good food, live music, dancing, and fabulous drinks. It is located on the water, so with luck, we will have a little breeze coming in or just some hot steam. One or the other, we will likely find out soon enough.

We pull into the bar parking lot, and by the looks of it, the place starts getting packed quickly. We notice a few cars belonging to our friends and look forward to seeing everyone. The music is loud on the outside deck, so we go there knowing that's where our friends will be. Sure enough, we see Zach, Brodie, and Crispin out here, along with Piper sandwiched in the middle. We move faster toward the tables and hug everyone in all our southern hospitality. Piper is throwing her hands up in the air along with her beer can, singing along to "Say It Ain't So" by Wheezer.

"I love this song!" she screams at us over the music. Piper returns her focus to the band.

"As if we couldn't guess that," I say jokingly, to no one in particular.

"R-ight." Brodie laughs at her dancing around. "She's not driving home tonight, is she, Zach?"

Zach shakes his head. "Definitely not."

We all laugh, knowing we are just getting started.

The night continues, as do the drinks. We take lots of shots, and I take pictures for Liv. I hope she knows that she is missed. One of the pictures is of our discarded shot glasses piled high on each other, resting on a napkin with the words, *I wish you were here,* written in Sharpie marker. Being a nurse requires always having a Sharpie marker in your possession.

I grab my clutch and excuse myself to go to the bathroom. When I turn the corner, I stop abruptly at what and who I see in front of me.

CHAPTER THIRTEEN

EMMA

I can't believe what I am seeing. That motherfucker. I quickly make a turn and head back around. I don't think he has seen me. I hurry back to our table toward Val and Ainsley. They are in a heated debate on whose turn it is to buy the next round. I tug on Val's sleeve, and she faces me.

"Emma, what do you think? Didn't I buy the last round?" She twists her lip up in a snarl at Ainsley. I throw my hands up at her face.

"Hey, Val! Focus. I need to show you something." I look at Ainsley and put my finger to my mouth to silence her from asking more questions. "Bring your phone and follow me," I say, dragging them by the hand to bear witness to the act. Their interest is now piqued, and they follow me eagerly. I slow down before we get to the corner, where I see that jerk. I halt, throwing my hand back and signaling them to stop. I turn around to face them.

"What is it, Emma?" they ask in unison.

BLACK WAVE

I bring them in closer as if he can hear us around the corner, despite the loud music infiltrating through the open patio and the multitude of voices carrying over from the crowd gathered here tonight.

"I have just seen Brodie making out with some girl around this corner." I hear a gasp from Val as she puts her hand up to her mouth.

"No way!" She looks over to Ainsley, who looks back and forth at us, waiting to see if I am joking. I am, in fact, not joking.

"I swear, guys, it's him. I was so shocked. I headed to the bathrooms, rounded the corner, and he had some girl he was making out with and groping her against the wall for everyone to see."

"What should we do?' Ainsley asks.

Val shakes her head in question. "Should we confront him?"

I contemplate the best form of action at this point. "I think we need proof—proof to show Liv once and for all that he is a lying, cheating scumbag. If we just tell her, she may not believe it. I think we should video it, and then she can determine whether or not she wants to pursue this"— signaling air quotes—"relationship." This whole long-distance relationship is making her more unhappy due to the uncertainty of their situation. Are they together or not? From what I saw, I think not.

Val nods in agreement. She turns the corner with her video ready to record. I hold Aisley back because I don't want to draw any other attention to us, and I want to ensure we get this on tape for Liv. After only thirty seconds, but what seems like an hour, Val faces us with a look of disgust on her face.

"Come on, girls, I think I got enough footage. We need to watch this." She pulls us outside onto the deck that is a bit quieter and away from where the band is playing. We head outside, and she shows us her phone, hitting play. We all lean in to look at the scene on her recorded video.

The video zooms in on Brodie off in the corner by the bathrooms. He has a girl with long black hair pushed up against the wall. One of his hands is on her thigh as he holds her leg around his waist. She has a short black skirt with a purple halter top. Her breasts are smashed against his chest. They are grinding against each other to the music, and his face devours the side of her neck. Her head is thrown back in ecstasy, and his other hand is locked onto her very prominent, most-likely silicon, boob.

A guy begins to walk across the screen as we look away, not needing to see any more. Val shuts the video off. She sends the footage to Ainsley and me to have as copies in case one gets deleted.

"What should I do, guys?" Val whines and stomps her foot. "I can't send it to Liv. It will devastate her."

I agree with Val about this. "But I do think she should know about Brodie," I interject.

Ainsley volunteers to send it, and we don't have a problem letting her take the reins on that one. Ainsley types something out, her thumb hovering over the send button as she looks at us for confirmation. We both nod in agreement, and then she hits send.

After that, the girls and I fight off a bout of melancholy at having to disclose this information to Liv. We decide to call it a night and go home. We return to our table of friends, tell everyone good-bye, and plan to meet by the pier in our usual spot tomorrow. We don't see Brodie after that, and when we go to the bathroom before leaving, he is no longer there with that girl. Scandalous.

The drive home is somber. I turn on the music to fill the silence, and "It's No Good" by Depeche Mode sounds throughout the car. The girls drop me off at my place first, and they wait until I make it into my apartment and turn on the light in my bedroom before they pull out of the complex.

I drop my bag on the chair and take my shoes off. I undress and put on a tank and sleep shorts. I unbraid my hair, throwing it into a messy bun before I head to the bathroom to wash my face and brush my teeth. After completing my nighttime ritual, I dive into my cooling sheets and lavender-infused pillow.

I hear my phone chime, and I read the messages from Ainsley, Val, and Liv. She asks who that is with Brodie, but we don't know. I reply that I am so sorry and ask if she is okay. Liv replies that she isn't sure, but she needs to get back to work and will chat with us about it tomorrow.

I punch my pillow, attempting to make it more comfortable, but I know that it has little to do with my pillow and more to do with the thoughts that lay heavily on my mind. I close my eyes and dream of my best friend crying and I blame myself for causing her so much sadness.

Before I know it, morning is here, and Val and Ainsley have returned to pick me up. We are on our way to Liv's apartment before heading out to the beach, and as promised, I arrive with her requested breakfast items. The weather is punishingly hot, and the air is sticky with humidity, ruining the best of hair days. We park next to Liv's jeep and start loading things into the open back area.

When we get to the door, Liv answers, and we stare at each other, not saying a word. I feel responsible and reach out to her first. "Oh, sweetie, I am so sorry. Are you okay? I brought you breakfast."

Ainsley enters and hugs her, too, as Liv shakes her head and holds back the tears. "Are you going to confront him today?' Ainsley asks. "If you do, I think you should do it sooner than later." We all agree with Ainsley, knowing about his problems with alcohol and drugs, not to mention Brodie's decreased coping skills.

Val goes in for a hug next, adding her thoughts. "I think you should ignore him. You are way too classy to make a scene, Liv." Luckily, Liv is a classy girl, and there is no way it would happen, and she confirms as much.

"Come on, guys. Let's go have some fun." We all pile into Liv's jeep and soon head to the causeway. We spot our favorite mile marker and see that our small click of friends has indeed saved us a spot. Crispin is waving his hands in the air like air traffic control. I hear him call out to Rhett. He and Zach spring up from their chairs and begin maneuvering things out of the way to accommodate yet another vehicle in our circle.

I stick my fingers in my mouth and let out a whistle. "Come on, boys. It's not going to unload itself." They all laugh at my brazenness, and I know that, secretly, the guys love it. I flash them a pearly smile, and they laugh. I push my sunglasses up on the bridge of my nose and fan myself with my hand dramatically.

"Anything for you, doll," Crispin retorts.

"Now, that's the Texas hospitality we love," Liv and I say in unison. We both laugh, and I am glad I can help alleviate her somber mood. I head over to the guys as they pick me up from the ground and carry me around as if I weigh nothing.

"Your chariot, milady." Crispin places me in one of the lounge chairs, and I am not unhappy about it.

I let out a contented sigh. I place my finger to my chin and do my best pensive stare. "Now, if I just had a beverage," I say to no one in particular.

Crispin picks up the not-so-subtle cue, snapping his fingers. He laughs, shaking his head. "Coming right up," he says as he grabs me something to drink.

I see Liv looking at Brodie. I brace myself to run interference if need be, but when I think she will approach him, she turns around and goes to the water. She stares at the Gulf waves rolling on the shore, and my heart breaks for her. *"Cheaters are the worst,"* I say under my breath.

Just then, I hear footsteps approaching. I turn my head just in time to accept the beverage from Crispin.

"Here you go." He drops a cold beer on my leg and several ice cubes.

"Yikes!" I jump up, screeching. "That's cold. Oh my god, you did that on purpose." I'm flinging residual ice that hadn't melted on contact with my skin off my body as I plop myself back into the chair. Crispin chuckles and walks off.

I notice Liv looking intently at someone and walking past our cars. I walk a little over to where she is heading, and that is when I see a tall guy sitting in a chair with sunglasses on. He has his leg propped up and an air cast encasing his ankle. He gets up from the chair and begins walking toward Liv. *Interesting.*

I intercept Liv before she reaches him. I have so many questions. "Who's that guy?" I ask in more of a playful tone.

"That's the guy," Liv says as if I should know who "the guy" is.

"Who?" I ask because I don't know.

"His name is Dax, and he is 'the' guy."

I laugh. "Girl, you have some explaining to do." I touch her shoulder, encouraging her to move along. I witness this exchange, until suddenly, I feel like someone is watching me. I immediately become uneasy. I rub my arms back and forth as the hairs begin to rise.

Thoughts rush through my head—Did Julian find me? Am I in danger? I have had such a good time so far that I am waiting for the other shoe to drop. I have let down some of my guard. I swear that I felt this odd sensation at the club yesterday but chalked it up to the situation with Brodie. The cheating got to me. Despite their complicated history, I felt angry at his disregard for their long-time relationship.

With Julian, I wasn't too upset about him cheating on me behind my back, but he did it in front of me, too. How I saw Brodie with that girl—he didn't care about her friends being there, possibly witnessing his infidelity. I take some deep breaths to calm the anger I can feel rising within me.

When I am more relaxed, my skin starts to tingle again with that same awareness of being watched. This time, when I open my eyes and look around, scanning for a threat, nothing seems out of the ordinary.

I look toward Liv and Dax when I see a blond-haired guy of similar stature staring intently at me. At first, I figure he must be looking at someone else, and I glance around to see if that's true. Nope. His smile increases, and I hear him laugh across the lot.

Well, this day just became more interesting.

CHAPTER FOURTEEN

EMMA

Liv is talking with Dax, and his friends have also come over to chat with us. The guy who was staring at me came over to introduce himself, and I felt a sense of familiarity with him. I don't know what it is about him, but I am relaxed and at ease.

He puts his hand out. "Hi, I'm Jameson." He continues to hold my hand.

"I'm Emma." I look over to Liv and then back at Jameson. "How do you guys know Liv?" I pull my hand out of his grasp, and he frowns at the loss of contact. My lip pulls up at seeing how adorable he is when he pouts. His full lips puff out like a toddler who has to part with his favorite new toy.

"Liv didn't tell you?" He looks over at Liv and Dax, who are deep in conversation, much like long-lost friends catching up on the past ten years of not seeing each other.

"No, she didn't," I say reluctantly. "Although, she didn't have much time since she worked last night and..." I trail off, not wanting to discuss Liv's problems with a stranger. I don't feel that mentioning this is appropriate.

I don't have to because when I look back, I see Brodie has pulled Liv aside and they are now in a heated discussion. That girl from the bar is here and is laughing, walking away after saying something over her shoulder at Liv. Anger heats my face, and my fist clenches at my side. Jameson must notice because he touches my shoulder, and I tense at the feel of his hand there.

I see Liv walk away. "Excuse me, Jameson. I have to go check on my girl," I say over my shoulder as I walk off, intently focused on Liv right now.

The sadness is etched on her facial features when I reach her. I know she has uttered the words that should have been said years ago. She held out hope for some reason, but waiting for someone to change is nothing but a life full of misery and disappointment.

Liv walks back toward us, and I catch up with her. "I take it you talked to Brodie about last night, Liv?"

"Oh, yes," she sniffs, barely holding back her tears. "Brodie told her it was a mistake. I overheard their conversation. She also told me to enjoy her leftovers or something to that effect. I don't remember her exact words because I was trying to make my brain catch up with what was happening."

"Whoa," is all I manage to get out. "That's crazy, girl. What happened next?"

Liv shifts on her feet. "He told me he was 'drunk-impaired.'" She mockingly makes air quotes for emphasis.

I have to admit that I like this side of Liv. A side that finally makes me believe she has had enough of this shit relationship. I wish I could confide in her. I wish I could let my best friend know that I understand. But I can't. All I can do is be there for her. I feel like a fraud. I am a liar, but my selfishness has already put enough people in danger. I can't lose anyone else. I refuse to be responsible for someone else getting hurt or killed.

"Oh, using *that* excuse, is he?" I mutter the word 'asshole' under my breath.

"R-ight, Emma!" Liv begins to raise her voice. "Like drinking and wrong choices are a medical condition of his."

I change the direction of this conversation. "Do you think you could ever trust him again?"

Before I even finish this sentence, Liv is shaking her head back and forth. "No. I told him it was over."

"Well, hell. What about this Dax guy? A spring break fling then?" I want to know all about this spectacular specimen of a man who seemed hot and heavy for Liv. His friend, Jameson, isn't bad looking either.

"I'm not sure," Liv replies, but she bites her lower lip, which she does when telling a little lie.

I chuckle. "Dax's friend is hot," I admit, and Liv laughs. "Come on, Liv. Let's get back to the party." I throw my arm around her shoulders and then remember how short I am. I scowl and curse in anger. Liv laughs, and I swear I see tears of laughter leaking from her eyes.

"Are you making fun of me?" I can't help but laugh along with her.

"Here." She throws her arm around my shoulders and tugs me closer. "How's this?" I hook my arm around her waist, once again annoyed with my short stature. "Perfect, jerk face. Let's go."

"Real mature, Emma," she taunts as we return to the beginnings of a bonfire.

Let the festivities begin.

Before we know it, the night is upon us, and the bonfire has increased in intensity. Even though my friends surround me, I can't shake the feeling that someone is still watching me. I thought it was Jameson, but I have been talking to him, and the feeling will not subside. It's not the feeling I had when I noticed Jameson earlier. The tingling of my skin was different. This feeling is the hair on my arms standing up and a tightening in my stomach. It reminds me of when you are at the amusement park ride, and you get to the top of the roller coaster, hovering there, waiting for your stomach to drop out at the quick descent into the abyss. That is what I feel, as if my stomach is on the precipice of dropping out.

I scan through the flames and don't notice anyone in particular. I look around and still don't see anyone. Unfortunately, I have to pee. I saw a skid-o-can farther back behind the sand dunes. I shift back and forth on my feet.

"Emma?" I hear a voice call my name. I must have zoned out because Jameson is looking at me strangely.

"Do you have to pee or something? You can't keep still?" There is amusement on his face. I know this is the perfect opportunity to get him to escort me to the portable bathroom on the beach.

I laugh, looking at him. "What gave it away?" I reply with a big smile.

"Oh, I don't know. It looks like you have ants in your pants."

"Ha! I hope not. What do you think about escorting me to the bathrooms? I need to pee, but I also don't like that it's so secluded over there and..." I gulp for effect. "Dark."

"I'd be happy to escort you." He reaches for my hand and swings it back and forth in a playful manner. "Come on. Let's go."

We walk hand-in-hand to the stalls, and I thank him before going in.

"Do you want me to wait here?" he asks. "I'll give you some privacy."

"Nope, no privacy needed," I reply before stepping in. "Can you wait here?"

"Of course." He smiles, and I close the door. After the longest pee of my life, I am thankful for the hand gel and somewhat cleanliness of the portable bathroom as the door loudly shuts behind me. Jameson grabs my hand again, and we return to the crowd of partygoers.

Before we cut through the sand dune, Jameson stops and faces me. He looks at me intently, and I feel this longing that I thought was dormant for so long. My breath hitches as he places his hands on my cheeks. I look up at him as he moves closer to me. He stares down at me with desire. I swallow in anticipation of what he is going to do next.

He picks me up, and my legs go to wrap around him. I feel his thick, long erection on my stomach, and I gasp when I feel his cock twitch at the contact. He looks at me, with one arm around my ass, holding me up, and the other arm crossing my back. I lick my lips, and he smirks, moving in. Our lips touch, and he kisses me passionately. I open my mouth for him and... Nothing. I feel absolutely nothing.

Jameson must sense me withdrawing from the contact because he stops and looks at me. I remove my legs from around his hips and place them firmly on the ground. He touches his lips and then gives me a questioning look.

Not wanting to make him feel bad about the awkwardness of that kiss because maybe he felt more than I did, I clear my throat. "Umm, we should get back to the group. They will wonder where I am soon." I look away from him and glance back toward the crowd that doesn't seem to be wondering where I ran off to at all.

"Sure. I'll walk you back." He retakes my hand, and I let him. When we are back in a place where we are visible, I release his hand and pretend to be fixing my hair into another messy bun that probably looks just like it does now. I hope no one saw us leave and then return like this.

I notice Liv talking with Dax, looking our way. I don't get to school my features because a scream penetrates the air and makes me look around. That's when I hear, "Help! Someone help!" I see Liv and Dax jump up and take off, and Jameson and I run toward the source of the screaming.

I see Dax crouched over Brodie, lying limp and unconscious on the sand. Liv is hysterical, and Jameson and I are just trying to help somehow. Dax seems to take charge and asks if anyone called an ambulance.

"I called an ambulance as soon as it happened," Ainsley reports.

"What's the ETA of the ambulance?" I hear Dax bark out.

We hear the faint sound of sirens approaching and know that help isn't far away. Soon, the paramedics are here and taking Brodie away on a backboard. He still hasn't woken up, and I think Liv is in shock. The girls go to get her jeep and pack everything up quickly. Dax announces he is taking her to the hospital, yet Liv still doesn't move. I see Dax stroking her face and telling her this isn't her fault.

I look over at Jameson; he is already preparing the truck. I hand him Liv's purse, and he takes it from me. He wants to say more to me, but now isn't the time. Everyone quickly loads up to follow the ambulance that left about five minutes ago. I jump in the jeep along with Ainsley, Val, and Piper.

The drive to the hospital is quick and silent. No one wants to comment about what transpired or our thoughts about Brodie's prognosis. We head into an emergency department similar to what we left not too long ago. Shortly after the CT scan revealed spinal cord compression, he underwent surgery. We all move to the surgical waiting room and await the results of Brodie's surgery.

When the surgeon asks for Liv and tells her that Brodie is asking for her, she goes through the operating room doors without looking back. Dax, Jameson, and his other two friends stand up. Dax looks utterly defeated as he wipes his hand over his face. Jameson says something to him and pats his shoulder. They make their way toward the staircase, and Dax looks at the doors as if he expects Liv to come back through any second. Jameson grabs his arm and leads him out. He takes a moment to look around, and his gaze lingers on me. He smiles sadly and then turns to walk out the door with his friends in tow.

CHAPTER FIFTEEN

EMMA

It's been eight weeks since the accident. The night at the beach where Brodie attempted to do a backflip, landed wrong, and the injury left him paralyzed. Liv has been there for Brodie through it all. From the night of the surgery to Brodie's rehab and moving to Houston. He will live with his father and have full-time nursing care. Liv didn't go to her graduation and has been a shell of herself since the night of the accident. She blames herself, and I understand, without a doubt, what that feels like. I try to get her to talk to me, to open up about her feelings. I feel like a fraud. Here I am, trying to get her to open up when I won't do the same thing I am preaching about.

I should be taking my own advice, but I can't tell her about my problems and how I feel the same way. Living with the crippling guilt daily is hard, just like putting on a mask of happiness. Where everyone thinks they have no care in the world. I'm just living in the moment and, currently, not feeling much of anything. I wish I could confide in Liv, but that would be selfish.

BLACK WAVE

To tell her what happened with Julian would put her in danger. No, I have no one to talk to and no one to blame but myself for the loss of everyone I loved. I won't let him hurt anyone else just to ease my own conscience.

I finally get home after seeing Liv. She refused to let any of us stay with her, stating that she needed to be alone to process everything. After driving Liv's jeep back to her apartment and then Ubering home, I feel exhausted as the day's events weigh heavy on my mind.

I head to the shower to get the beach grit off my body. We tried to go to the beach, and it wasn't the same. The girl loved the beach, as did I, but it was too hard. We even went to a different mile marker to not have to be in the same area where the accident occurred. I hope that she can go back there one day. There were so many happy memories there, until there weren't. That one day changed it all for our small group of friends. I honestly just want to go to bed, but there is no way that I am getting sand all over the place.

I throw all my clothes in the hamper and jump into a cool shower. The tepid water feels good on my sensitive, sun-kissed skin. I don't bother with blow-drying my hair and decide on some mousse to hold in the light wave. I can almost see the sun setting on the horizon.

I close all the apartment's blinds, and the light-blocking window treatments are set to prevent the punishing rays from filling my bedroom until the sun sets around nine. I sigh in contentment as I pull the covers up to my head. I hear an incoming text message received on my phone as my mind shuts off. All my thoughts vanish, and I drift off into a deep sleep.

"Oh goodness," I mumble as I stretch out my limbs. I slept solidly last night. "What time is it?" I rub my hand over my face and twist my body to glance at my Alice in Wonderland clock on the bedside dresser. My uncle had it commissioned for me as a present when I graduated from nursing school. It was and continues to be one of my favorite books. I notice I slept the morning away, which is now reading noon on the rabbit's white-gloved hands. I lay in bed for a few minutes, staring at the ceiling and contemplating calling Liv to see how she is holding up, but then I think better of it.

I pick up my phone and see a text message from an unknown number. It is a video with a message underneath it.

Unknown number: 'Watch until the end.'

My finger hovers over the video as I hesitate to hit play. I'm sure it's nothing. Rick Astley's "Never Gonna Give You Up" will probably come on shortly after; I chuckle out loud. I click on the video, and a familiar scene appears on the screen. I see Val, Ainsley, and me around the corner of the bathroom while we recorded Brodie with that Alexis girl.

Someone was recording us. Mesmerized by the video from a couple of months ago, I continue to watch and remember the night we sent this to Liv. Instead of getting Rickrolled, I see a familiar face move across the screen. I can't believe what I am seeing.

"No. No. No," I chant. I drop my phone on the floor and sit on my bed, cradling my face with my hands. "Julian." I whisper his name as if conjuring an apparition. I pick up my phone and immediately dial my cousin Adrian.

He picks up after two rings. "Hey, prima. How—"

I cut him off before he can continue his salutations. "Adrian," I choke on a sob.

"Emma. What's the matter? What is it?"

"He's found me, Adrian. He was around when I was out one night. He was there." I walk in circles around my bedroom, biting on my nails. I feel light-headed, like I might pass out. "Oh, god. What am I going to do? He can't find me, please, Adrian."

"Em. I want you to take some deep breaths."

I do as he says and tell him about the video once I am calmer. "You know, Adrian, I felt like I was going crazy. I felt like I was being watched and thought it was just me being paranoid." I guess I had reason to be.

"What? When?" he asks, getting angrier with each question.

So I tell him about the times at the club and the beach. Even when I walked out of work, I felt someone was watching me. Luckily, security walked me out whenever I asked, claiming I was afraid after watching too many true crime shows and listening to podcasts on the way to work. Too bad I lived it.

"Where are you now?" he asks earnestly. "I want to ensure you are safe."

"I'm in my apartment. I am off today. Oh, Adrian, what do I do." I sink onto my knees on my bedroom floor.

He is talking to someone in the background—a woman. I hear a door close and a car starting sound shortly after. "Emma, I am on my way to my father's house. Stay put, and I will grab a bag and come to you. I should be there by tonight. Do not leave the house. Do you hear me? Do not leave the house."

I'm shaking my head, realizing he can't see me. Instead, I answer, "Okay.

I'll stay here and wait for you."

"Okay, I'll call you when I get close to town. Stay calm, prima." The line goes dead.

I sit up with my back against the bed and sob. I know that I am supposed to be strong, but I let myself have a false sense of security. And I almost had an everyday average life for a while, but that isn't in the cards for me. I will never have a normal life while Julian is alive. After I have plenty of time to feel sorry for myself, I start to get angry.

I ensure everything is locked and search all my belongings for anything that can be a potential bug or camera. When I feel that I have looked through everything satisfactorily, I sit on the couch and pull up social media feeds on my laptop. I no longer post on my account, but I decide to look for someone in particular. Someone I have put out of my memory for a long time.

I hit my Spotify playlist, and "Willow" by Taylor Swift plays on my Bluetooth speaker. I hesitate for a moment but then type in his name. *Eduardo Ruiz Houston Texas.* There are a few hits that are not him. Then, in one of the hits, I click on the profile.

Sure enough, I see the face of a boy who is now a man—and he is *all* man. I begin to Instagram stalk him. I see his club, and on the opening night he is so handsome in a suit. He was so stocky when he was little, but that stockiness turned to pure muscle. He is a vision standing in front of the club and inside under the lights all around, hitting him at different angles.

One picture in particular draws me in. I notice a tattoo curling up through his white shirt, escaping up onto his neck, but as mesmerizing as that is, that isn't what gets my attention. I enlarge the photo of his knuckles, where a word is tattooed across. I gasp when I see what it spells out. EMMA.

Oh, my. I stand up abruptly, and my laptop hits the carpet with a soft thunk. I grab my necklace and pace the small living room in my apartment, wearing a path back and forth. Taylor Swift continues with her song, the lyrics sounding out. Taylor Swift sings about wrecking plans and telling someone that he's her man. I think how true that is—the complexity that goes with loving someone.

I continue looking through social media post after post, until I hear my phone chime with an incoming message. It's Adrian.

"Oh, thank goodness," I say out loud because he is finally here. I must have been stalking him more than I thought, because the time flew by. I look out the window and see my cousin outside his truck, stretching as he slides out of the driver's seat.

I close the blinds and put away my computer. I hear a knock at the door, but I still check to ensure it's him. I look through the peephole and see Adrian smirking at me on the other side. I unlock the double bolts and let him in.

Adrian steps through and wraps me in a hug. He closes the door with his foot and locks it with one hand, not letting me go. I break down and cling to him like a lifeline. He holds me without saying anything and allows me to get out my emotions. After, I sniffle for what I hope is the last time.

He pushes me back. "Emma, it's going to be okay. I'm here to protect you, and we'll figure it out. My father is coming up with a plan as we speak. He told me to get here and he will call us tonight to let us know. Have you eaten?"

I shake my head no. "I could eat," I say, biting my lip.

His smile widens. "That's my cousin. Let's grab some food now that I am here, okay?"

"I'd like that." I put on my shoes, and we walk out of the house with an agenda.

We pull up to my favorite pizza place near my apartment, which is also close to my work, making it the perfect place for meeting up. They have a fantastic sourdough pizza crust with three hundred-plus microbrews on tap.

I walk through the door, and the bell jingles, letting the patrons and staff know about the incoming person, which so happens to be me and Adrian. I go to the table in the back, where I usually sit by myself with a book. This time, I have Adrian as my company.

Sumi immediately comes up to me and gives me a big hug. "Emma! I haven't seen you in a couple of months, girl. Where have you been?"

"I've been helping a friend through a rough time, and I've been otherwise working. I've missed you too, Sumi. Oh, this is my cousin Adrian."

She looks over at him and blushes. He puts his hand out for her to take, and she does but immediately pulls it back. The blush is now down into her neck and chest.

I save her from her embarrassment and order the usual. She takes one more look at Adrian and walks off. He chuckles when she leaves. I hit him on the shoulder. "Would you stop making my friends nervous? Geez, she was all flustered." I glance over at the bar and see her pouring us a beer. Poor Sumi. Maybe she should drink one.

For a while, I forget about my problems with Julian and enjoy the company of my family—what's left of it.

CHAPTER SIXTEEN

EDUARDO

At home, I finish reviewing contracts before it's time to leave for the gym. I stop by the kitchen area and make myself a latte to take with me on the road. The Breville state-of-the-art touchscreen espresso machine is top-notch, beckoning me to have a tasty caffeinated beverage despite not currently wanting one. Still, I'm glad I invested in this priceless piece of morning bliss machinery.

The latte infuses straight into a to-go mug. Picking it up along with my leather messenger bag, I close and lock the door behind me to leave my ultra-modern uptown apartment home near the Galleria. The exclusive penthouse level boasts terraces and a three-bedroom light-filled floor plan with a necessary wet bar and wine chiller. The twenty-four-hour concierge with a dedicated phone line is a game changer in my line of work, where I need security and a defensible location. I walk out to my garage with private access and enter my Bently SUV. I travel a short distance to my other business—my gym.

BLACK WAVE

This morning, I had an early meeting with the contractors. The project helped with branching out with a legitimate business portfolio. It is all a front, but I do enjoy the non-criminal side. Sometimes, I forget the business I am involved in—my family's business and one I love more than I'd care to admit.

We opened this gym this past year, and it has done incredibly well. We place suggestion boxes at the entrance to improve our business and take the customers' suggestions to heart. Helena is the front desk person, but she is also my manager. I trust her implicitly, and she sorts through the comments, looking for improvements that we can add to the betterment of this establishment.

After much feedback from the members, we have decided to accommodate their request for a nutrition station and cafe. I can't deny that this gym would be almost perfect with that addition. I say almost perfect because I believe there is always room for improvement. Complacency is the death of any corporation; in my line of business, it could be the difference between life and death.

The gym is state-of-the-art with an indoor pool, sauna, indoor track, and all the standard gym working parts. Members will come to exercise in the morning before work and leave suggestions stating that it would be great to grab a protein shake, smoothie, or matcha before they go to work for the day. Bougie as fuck, but when you make this type of place in a prime location, the clientele demands a certain level of accommodations. I can charge up the ass for services, and they won't even flinch in paying for it.

In fact, they tell their friends about it, and more people sign up for the membership. We are almost at max capacity and will soon offer a waiting list spot only. Fuck. When there is a waiting list, it only fuels the consumer to desire a membership here more than ever. They feel that they are missing out, and we exploit that. I am in the profession to deliver on these requests. The more services and amenities, the more their fees increase, and so forth.

Equally important to the drinks is the need for lunch. Some patrons like to work out on their lunch break. Go figure. Now, that's dedication—something I can admire. After listening to my manager, Helena's, suggestions, I hired someone to rent the space from us. Businesses bid for the spot, and we have much interest, but we are looking for something hot and upcoming. It needs to be perfect. It's not the usual juice bar, vegan protein type of place.

We are holding interviews for the various small business owners vying for a chance to rent this space at one of the most popular gyms in the metro area. The lead runner-up is a small business specializing in poke bowls, superfruit bowls, smoothies, fresh pressed juices, coffee, and shots. It would meet the criteria that the gym members are looking for and the nutritional standards of serving members of a gym with high expectations such as ours. I also sample the goods and am impressed with the Hawaiian food flare. I order an ahi tuna poke bowl over white rice with avocado, cucumbers, carrots, edamame, and fresh ginger. They give me a twenty-ounce cold brew with Laird superfood brewed in-house. It is fucking amazing.

As I go over the space with another contractor and paperwork that requires my signature, I approach the front desk at the same time a woman approaches me. Initially, I notice that she has a body made for sin as I continue to peruse her voluptuous figure. She sees me appreciating her fine form and smiles seductively at me. She touches my arm with her long, pointed, manicured fingertips and trails it down my bicep and forearm. I raise my eyebrow in question to her bold moves as she leans in closer.

"I was wondering if you could show me where the locker rooms are." She looks down at my cock and then back up at my eyes.

I look her in the eye and run my tongue over my teeth. Contemplating the offer, I turn my head to the side. This isn't something unusual for me. She has noticed my appearance and probably my expensive watch and clothing. Gold-digging much?

Her breath hitches in anticipation of where this could go. I turn to look at the front desk. She follows the path my gaze has traveled, waiting for my next move. She probably expects me to tell Helena to cover for me so I can show her to the locker rooms.

"Helena?" The girl at the front desk looks up from her book as if she is guilty of doing something. "Would you mind showing this lady where the locker rooms are, please?" She puts her book down and walks our way. I stop her as she walks past me and whisper, "Maybe you should calm your reading down on the spicy romance books."

She snorts. "Yeah, that won't happen, Boss." Having quickly regained her regular coloring, she looks at the woman and walks past her. I don't give her another glance.

"Follow me."

The woman follows Helena but shoots a look back at me and shakes her head back and forth before following Helena to the locker room. I am willing to bet that she knows exactly where they are. Luckily for me, that is no concern of mine. There is only one person on my mind these days, and I hope to find her.

BLACK WAVE

I go to my office and pull up my social media page. I advertise the gym and the updates on the food and cafe space. We have a comment right away about the excitement over the cafe. Then, I look to my club and post updates to the various DJs headlining on the upcoming weekends. This will surely fulfill the excitement recipe for any coming-of-age raver.

Influencers and elite society compete against other VIPs to gain entrance into my club. We spare no expense to provide a thrilling environment. It offers a rollercoaster of emotions, from excitement to fear of the unknown and endless pleasure. It's no secret that my club boasts endless drugs to satisfy every vice the patron desires. They only need to know the secret codes to access these substances and obtain access to a bathroom to partake in the ecstasy this atmosphere enables. As long as it is discrete, we don't care, which helps with the other side of my profession—the illegal one that is the backbone of our family's revenue.

After completing my work posts, I started to go the personal route. I don't post much on my personal page, but I keep it updated. I have a close group of friends from when I was in college and maintain good relationships with my frat brothers. We had so much fun then and stayed in touch. We get together quite often, but work prevents me from hanging out with them as much as I would like. I allow them access to my VIP area with exceptional bottle service whenever they want. It's a perk of being the boss. I can still work and then spend some time with them if they can come to party at my establishment. They also don't mind being granted access to one of the finest clubs in the city with VIP service.

I decide to pull up the social media for Emma and am not surprised when I see nothing recent. The last time she updated anything was a couple of years ago. It has pictures of her and her sister. I zoom in on the one picture of her and Evie. I almost stop breathing when I zoom in on the image and see Emma up close. It isn't her beauty that catches my breath, but the necklace around her neck. The chain that I gave her about a decade ago. She still wears it. The thrill that racks my body is intense, and my possessive side that has been fighting the urge to claim her rages. I knew it. I slam my fist on the table, and my laptop jumps. Fuck. Her mother kept me away, but I hadn't considered Emma's feelings.

Does she still think of me? Does she still want me? Is she waiting for me? These are all questions that I will get the answers to. She still wears my necklace, a telltale sign that she remembers me. Now, I just need to recreate our past and make her remember me in the present tense.

We are both of legal age now, and unfortunately, we never got to explore the possibility of more because of her parents. I respected their wishes, but I know they aren't around. She has no immediate family, and I'll find her, despite what her uncle wants, and I will protect her. I'll be the family she needs. If she will have me, that is. And if she won't, I'll have to convince her otherwise. I know I won't give up easily like I did last time, thinking I was doing the right thing. I am doing this for me and Emma—for our future.

Without considering it, I pick up the phone and call my brother, Ram. He finally picks up as I am about ready to hang up. "Hey, fucker, why did it take you so long?" I am annoyed, but the humor in my voice is still present.

"What the fuck, asshole? I was busy." I hear a woman in the background laugh as he discreetly tries telling his fiancée that it's me and he has to take the call.

"Is that Anna?" I say mostly to annoy him.

"Of course it's Anna," he growls into the phone. I hear my future sister-in-law's voice in the background and her telling me hi.

"Hello," I say into the phone.

"Yeah, just a second." I hear him kiss her, and the door closes. "Okay, I'm back."

"Wow," I mock. "Someone is pussy-whipped."

He laughs. "Damn straight. You're just jealous."

He isn't wrong, but I hate to admit that. I gather up the courage to ask him about what I called for. "Hey, I was hoping you could help me with something?" He doesn't comment; he just waits for more pieces of information. "So, I was looking through my social media stuff and came across Emma's profile."

He laughs at this. "Just fell into the profile, did you? Just stumbled across it, or did you type in her name and Insta-stalk her."

Not wanting to lie, I go with the truth. "I Insta-stalked her. What was more unsettling was that she was wearing my necklace in a picture. I gave her that about ten years ago."

"No shit," he says.

"No shit, brother," I echo his words. "I was wondering if maybe we could look for her. See where she is. I know her parents died in that sketchy-ass fire, but perhaps it is nearby?" He stays silent, but I know that he has listened to me and is absorbing it all, devising a plan.

"I think we could do that if that is what you want?"

I don't hesitate to reply. "That's most definitely what I want."

CHAPTER SEVENTEEN

EMMA

After consuming our weight in pizza and beer, I'm slightly buzzed as Adrian helps me back to my apartment. He brings his duffle bag and throws it on the couch. He begins to get out his toiletry bag and sleep pants.

"Hey. I'm going to use your bathroom for a second, okay? I'll be right back." He disappears into the bathroom, and I sit on the couch, twirling my hair, something I do out of habit when profoundly thinking about a problem.

Adrian emerges shortly after changing to get ready for bed. I stand and go to my room, returning with bedding for the couch. I hate that he has to sleep there after driving all this way. Soon, I'll be able to buy my house or become more settled, where I'll have a spare bedroom for guests.

I start to make up the couch with my bedding, and Adrian grabs a side of the fitted sheet and pulls it over the pillowed cushioned seats. I apologize to Adrian for the accommodations, but he just blows it off. He is too kind to comment about having to sleep on a sucky couch.

"So, cousin, what do you think of the plan?" He tugs on the last side of the sheet, and we drape the other top sheet and blanket, placing a couple of down pillows on top.

I actually love the plan because I have other feelings about it. Feelings I have yet to say aloud. Liv is also my best friend, and it seems like the right choice to help her. "I love it. Houston sounds like the right move." I instantly touch my necklace, and Adrian notices right away.

"Emma?" he asks. "Is there something more I should know about you wanting to go to Houston?" He motions with his chin, nodding at my necklace.

I look over at Adrian to see him frowning as he observes me, waiting for my reply.

I realize I'm still holding the necklace and drop it quickly. I cannot lie to my cousin. First, he would see right through it because we grew up together. Second, I find that I don't want to lie to him. I am at a time in my life when I have no one to confide in, and it scares me. I used to have my sister, and she is gone. I live with that realization every day, so I decide to be honest.

I sigh in resignation. "Maybe." It's all I can give him, and I shrug his concerns away.

His eyebrows shoot up into his hairline in a dramatic fashion, much like a cartoon character does when he hears shocking news. "Oh boy. This should be good. Should I sit down?" my cousin asks, but doesn't require an answer. He immediately plops onto the couch, grabbing one of the pillows and tucking one foot under his leg. He pats the seat next to him. "Sit and tell me all about it."

And I do. I start with me stalking Eduardo's social media. I bring my laptop over and show him everything I found about Eduardo and what he is doing.

"You know…" Adrian clears his throat, almost hesitant to bring this up, but continues despite his reservations. "He came looking for you the next summer back then. He expected to see you there, and when he couldn't find you, he had this look on his face. You had left, and we knew you weren't coming after your mom's speech about wanting to leave the restrictive confines of the mafia life."

He rolls his eyes. "She said it was both a blessing and a curse. She wanted to keep you guys away from growing up in that lifestyle. He told us she had approached him to leave you alone, but he said no. He stayed looking out the backfield with his hand in his pockets. Then, without another word, he turned around and walked out the front door. He didn't return the next day or the following summer."

I place my hand to my mouth. "I can't believe Mom told Eduardo all that, and he still came looking for me." I shake my head in disbelief.

Adrian clears his throat. "My dad spoke with him and told him that it was your parents' wish for you to have a life without corruption. He strongly requested that Eduardo not seek you out. If he cared for you, he would allow you to be free."

I don't know if it is just the topic or if I am sad about the friendship cut short and the potential for more. I think about all that could have been. I would have been promised to Eduardo. I would not have met Julian. I would be safe, happy, and have my family alive with me.

But that wouldn't be right, would it? My mom was the reason that this happened between Eduardo and me. I still would have been protected if we had my extended family. We were isolated and free, but there is something about being free. Sometimes, you make the wrong choices and suffer the consequences of your actions. Free will isn't really free.

I look at Adrian, and he gives me a sad face. "I have to go to work early tomorrow, but after work, I'll go to Liv and see how she is. I'll put my two-week notice in at work. I'll let her know that we are leaving for Houston together."

The following day, Adrian drives me to work. I told my nursing supervisor that I would be moving to Houston for family reasons, and I am officially putting in my two-week notice. It isn't untrue because I consider Liv my family, and she needs me too. I have my reasons for leaving, but no one can know about Julian. The corruption of his father's reach is an unknown factor to me. The fact that Julian has found me scares me. I escaped him for a while, but now he knows I'm in the States, so he has a better advantage.

My uncle wanted me to come back home, but I refused to. I can't leave Liv and don't want to live like that. Once I get to Houston and secure a location, Adrian will stick around until he can guarantee my safety. My uncle doesn't tell me if I have anyone around for security, and I don't want to make it apparent, so I don't. I thought I was safe, but maybe I never will be.

After the longest shift, I walk out with security to Adrian's truck. I wave to Todd and thank him. He smiles and returns to the ER doors.

Adrian looks over at me. "How was work? Did you put your notice in?" He pulls out of the parking lot.

"Hey, Adrian. Instead of going to my apartment, can you go by Liv's? I want to talk to her and tell her about the move."

He nods. "Where to?"

"Here." I pull it up on Apple Maps and connect it to his Bluetooth before answering his initial questions. "Today was good but long. I thought the nursing supervisor was literally going to cry after I told her I was putting my two-week notice in. One girl went out on maternity leave, and Liv and I are leaving, making the department down three nurses this month." I wave my hand around.

We pull up at Liv's apartment, and I see a light is on in her place. I look over at Adrian, and he gives me a reassuring smile. "Go, Emma. I'll be here waiting for you, cousin."

I smile at him affectionately. "How are you still single?" I open the door, and I hear him laughing.

"It's by choice, Em. Trust me, I have a variety of prospects."

"Yuck." I stick out my tongue at him playfully, much like when we were children. "I'll be right back." I go up to Liv's door and knock. "She better answer," I mutter under my breath.

After the third knock, I hear her approach the door and then the turning sound of her unlocking the double bolts. She opens the door, and I take in her appearance. She looks tired and sad. I push my way in, and she stands there for a second before closing the door and letting out a sigh.

Once Liv turns around, I rush in for a hug. "Hey, girl. How are you?"

She releases me without commenting and walks toward the table, retrieving the glass of wine she had been drinking before I arrived. "Did Brodie make it to Houston okay?" She takes a big gulf of wine.

"Thanks for thinking of me, and I don't know." She turns to look at me. "Did you want a glass?" She drains the rest of her glass and pours me one. She must see the concerned look in my eyes because she shakes her head. Her eyes are pleading *don't ask.*

"Just thought I'd come in and check on you after I got out of work." We sit at the table. "Have you heard from Dax?"

Liv stops mid-pour. "Not since the last text he sent the week after the accident." She doesn't comment further on this, but I know she didn't reply to his message.

"Liv, you know this isn't yours or Dax's fault, right? Brodie made those choices—to cheat on you, get drunk, and do a backflip drunk when he knew he shouldn't. You can't blame yourself for another person's bad choices. I won't let you. Those events were always his bad choices." Except I understand it—the guilt I feel. It was a wrong choice that caused my family's death. My bad decision. I was involved with a monster, and that relationship caused my life and everything I cared about to crumble.

Changing the subject, I look around the apartment. "How's the packing going?"

Liv also looks around at the chaos of her imminent move to Houston. "Slow."

She gets up to move another box, and before I can stop myself, I blurt out, "How would you like a roommate in Houston?" She stops mid-walk.

"What?" Liv stutters like she didn't hear me the first time, glancing back.

"You heard me. I was thinking about taking a travel assignment and just doing it. I figured now would be as good a time as any. And then we could stay together."

I look at her, waiting for a response, and see Liv's now turned in my direction, giving me her full attention. Her eyes brim with excitement, and for the first time in months, she smiles. "I would really like that," she stammers.

"Good." I stand up to embrace my friend. "I already called the recruiter for the travel agency in Houston and gave my two-week notice at the hospital today. It's a done deal. You're stuck with me again."

"Are you sure, Emma?" Liv looks nervously at me.

I don't want to give too much away, but I have learned there should always be some truth when omitting details. That way, the omission is believable, and the lie is easy to remember. So, I go for a partial truth. "I stayed here for too long and have to leave anyway." I laugh, which sounds bitter with resentment. "I was getting too comfortable." I wave my hand in my usual fashion and feel my lips pursing in discontent. I try to school my features, but it is too late.

Liv notices but doesn't comment. Her eyes squint, as if trying to see through the hidden meaning of my words.

"I'll call my job placement and make sure they can secure a place for two bedrooms. It shouldn't be a problem, and it will allow us to look for a place we can both like living in once we get there."

We say our good-byes and promise to chat later. I walk up to the truck, and Adrian unlocks the door. I jump in and almost miss the seat. I hear him stifle a laugh. "Not funny, asswipe." He full-on laughs now, not bothering to hide his amusement. I close the door and buckle up.

"You are just tiny with those little legs." He pulls the truck away, and we start the drive to my place.

"I don't have short legs. I told you I'm proportional." I shake my head and look out the window. "Anyway. I told Liv, and we are all set for the move. Now, we just need to get through these next two weeks before we leave."

CHAPTER EIGHTEEN

EDUARDO

ONE YEAR LATER...

I'm sitting in my office at eleven p.m., and the club is getting packed. This is when I do most of my work, choosing to stay away from the crowds and the patrons who try to access my club and, worse, the women who try to gain access to my heart. They are fucking deluded if they think that I could give them what they want. A first date, gifts, marriage. Fuck that. I have a business to run.

My father has been down my throat with the prospects of women who would make a suitable match for the son of a don. Many have tried and failed. They pretend they don't know who I am or don't see the money I have and want to get their gold-digging claws sunk in. I've seen it all. My dad wants heirs, and my mom wants me to find happiness in the comfort of a woman who will provide the stability my life probably needs, but a home isn't just having someone there waiting for you to satisfy the duties of the house. I want to look forward to coming home to someone. To see my kids in the likeliness of their mother, them greeting me and welcoming me to *our* home. I can't have that and have thought over and over about the fantasy of it all. I see my brother and how his eyes light up when he sees his fiancée. My hand rubs over the stubble on my face contemplating the possibility someday.

I'm pulled out of these daydreams when I get a call. I answer, pissed off from allowing myself to have these thoughts when I have work to do.

"Boss?" the voice of one of my bouncers calls. I know this can't be good if they are bothering me.

"Yes," I bellow into the phone. "What the fuck is it?" The door opens without anyone knocking.

I don't get the answer because Gustavo is holding his hand. I see the cloth covering it that is saturated in blood. A tiny drop falls to the floor and I growl. "Fuck."

I look at him up and down and signal him with my hand to come in.

"If you're calling to tell me about Gus, he is in my office, and I can see what has happened. Is there anything else I need to do about the situation?"

"No, Boss. It's been handled."

We hang up, and I turn my attention to my security detail.

"What the fuck happened?"

"That waitress Cherry is what fucking happened." He shakes his non-injured hand at me. "Her boyfriend came over here looking for you. She bragged to one of her friends about your 'attention' toward her. That fucker found out and came here to settle a score."

I scoff at this. "Cherry? Where is she?" I look at him, and my anger is barely contained at such a nuisance happening in my club and so early in the night at that.

"Escorted out with her boyfriend. She was hysterical about what happened, saying she loves you and for him to leave."

I bring my hand down my face. "Enough of this shit. Fire Cherry and ban them both from the premises."

"Already done, Boss."

"Good." I shake my head in agreement. "Now, on to more important things. Your hand? How is it? Do you need treatment?"

He nods his head yes.

"Okay then, I'll accompany you."

Gus tries to protest. "Boss, you don't have to do that. I know you are busy here. I can get one of the other security personnel to take me. I'll be fine." He starts to walk to the door.

"Gus, you are not just hired help. You're my friend. I've known you my whole life, and I said I will take you." I pat his shoulder as we walk out.

We walk into the emergency department, and it is a fucking zoo. As we walk to registration, someone is vomiting into a bucket. The clerk is kind, despite the craziness of this place on a Friday night. She looks at the blood dripping from his hand and frowns.

"He was stabbed, and the wound is deep," I tell her. "It hasn't stopped bleeding." She looks a little queasy, and I think that perhaps this isn't the best job for her, but I keep my thoughts to myself. "We might need some more…" I pause to look over at Gus. "Gauze, maybe?" He nods without saying anything, looking back at the lady.

She visibly gulps and nods. "I think maybe I'll put you in one of the rooms in the back, but let me get you to the triage nurse so they can look at you and make that determination. Just a second." She gets up and walks away.

As she does this, a lady in cuffs with a police escort falls back and hits her head on the floor. The 'thwack' that sounds across the room makes others gasp, and one child who witnessed the fall starts screaming. We stare at this clusterfuck and shake our heads.

"Yep, a fucking zoo," I comment aloud. Gus grunts in agreement.

Staff come out from behind the locked door and gather the woman in cuffs onto a backboard. One of the nurses yells at the officer to take the cuffs off. I have to admire these nurses. They have probably seen it all. It takes a special kind of person to have to deal with this level of shit on a daily basis. A couple of people place her on a stretcher and wheel her in through the doors, followed by the annoyed-looking police officer.

A man who must be the triage nurse tells me to come through a locked door displaying a green light as he holds his badge up to it, allowing us entry. We get up and proceed to follow him through the door. Once we get in there, he notices a trail of blood coming from the door to the chair he asked Gus to sit in.

"Fuck me," he mutters as he runs his hand through his hair. "Follow me," he mumbles in resignation. "No need to have you bleeding all over the place, and I need to unwrap that anyway."

"Fucking perfect," I say in agreement.

We follow the tall nurse into one of the bays that is big enough to fix a few stab wounds to the hand or other body parts tonight.

"I'll give this to the nurse assigned to this area"—he smiles maliciously as he continues speaking—"who'll be in soon. If you think you'll pass out, come get someone." He glances my way before leaving.

Gus nods also, but we know that won't happen. This isn't our first rodeo, and it's not as if he was shot in the chest. I think we are both remembering that time when only an inch over for the gunshot wound that went through his chest could have killed him. Luckily, the bullet happened to miss important structures and vessels. Otherwise, it would have been a very different scenario, and likely that we wouldn't be here today. Getting his hand stitched is nothing in comparison, but no one needs to know that.

About ten minutes later, the nurse comes into the trauma bay with what I assume is Gus's chart and, without looking at us, announces that her name is Emma, and she will be the nurse caring for him. She halts when she finally turns and looks in our direction. She looks right at me and drops the chart along with whatever she was going to say. One hand goes to cover her mouth as she gasps in shock, while I notice the other hand goes to the necklace I gave her a decade ago before she vanished from my life, but there she is, a vision from every dream I've had over the years made flesh and now standing before me.

Gus watches this exchange but doesn't comment. I stand and walk around the equipment to get to her. She stays where she is, and I look at her hand holding her necklace. I tower over her, and I realize how little she is. She looks up at me with those striking green eyes I have pictured in my mind over the years. The mental pictures that haunt my every thought and when I try to sleep at night stay with me in my dreams.

She sees me looking at her, holding my necklace. I break the silence. "Is that the necklace I gave you? You still wear it?"

She realizes she is holding it and lets it go. Her eyes are a little teary, and I instinctively want to keep her and wipe away the heartache about to spill from her eyes.

She swallows. "I never took it off. I've worn it since you gave it to me and held on to it when I never saw you again."

She looks down, and I grab her chin and raise it to look at me again. I always want her to look at me so I can get lost in those emerald-colored eyes. I need her to look at me so she can see the truth.

"I tried to return to you, but I had to honor our family's wishes—your family's wishes, too. I thought it was what you wanted. Had I known, I would have come to you sooner. I would have reached out to you after your high school graduation."

She steps back and turns around, not looking at me. I walk over and grab onto her, spinning her around. "What is it, Emma? Is there something wrong? I heard about your parents..." I let my words trail off.

She looks up at me. "Yes, but first, let's fix your friend here."

I don't like the redirection of this conversation, but I'll play along for now. "How do you know he is my friend, not my employee?" I want to know this girl's thoughts and how her mind works. She's all grown up now.

She laughs. A hint of humor touches her eyes as she looks at me and over at Gus, who still hasn't said a word, just staring at what I am sure is an amusing and conflicting exchange between Emma and me.

"Well," she continues, "if he was just your employee, then I bet you wouldn't be standing here personally seeing to his medical care." She raises an eyebrow, challenging me to deny it.

I laugh, and so does Gustavo at this. Gus finally pipes up. "She knows you, Boss. Is that good?" He looks at me in all seriousness.

I keep my focus on Emma only. "Yes, that's very good indeed." Emma blushes and turns her back toward us, gathering some supplies from the cabinet.

"All right." She looks at Gus. "Let's see what we've got here." She starts to unwrap his hand.

Gus pulls it back a little. "You're not queasy, are you, Emma? Of a little blood?"

I can't tell if he is testing her or seriously concerned after how the lady at the check-in desk reacted to his injury. He doesn't show much emotion, so it's hard to gauge his line of questioning. Emma just snorts.

"Please," she says. "I've seen it all my life." She must realize what she has said because she stops to look at me and then at Gus. Now, it's time for Gus to raise an eyebrow in question. She looks at me and smiles widely, displaying her perfectly straight white teeth. I can't help but return the smile. Gus watches the exchange.

"I think I'm getting the full picture now, Eduardo." He extends his hand for her to treat.

When she smiles at me like that, I imagine coming home from our line of work and seeing her welcoming me. I envision her pregnant with my child, her hand on her round belly, looking at me with that smile and a... future? Could that be in the cards for me after all? I'm unsure, but I know I'm not giving up on her again.

She unwraps the bandages and looks at the wound, frowning. "I need to clean this up to see what I'm looking at."

She puts Gus on a monitor and has him lie on the stretcher, which makes Gus grumpy, but he doesn't dare say a thing to her because he must sense that Emma is mine, and he won't disrespect her like that—friend or not. *Definitely not as an employee*, I think to myself. It dawns on me that I have now thought of Emma as mine for the first time in years.

After she cleans it up, she tells us that she'll be right back but needs to get the doctor to look at it. "Can you do it?" I ask her before she leaves.

She nods, then says, "I can't do it here because my license doesn't allow me to do this."

I smile at her. "Perfect," I announce and see Gus's recognition of my question dawning on him. Not only is Emma the perfect girl for me, but she can also help when I need to trust someone, and discretion is imperative. He nods in silent agreement.

She returns momentarily with a doctor in tow, and I frown because he seems too comfortable talking to my future wife. *Well,* I think to myself, *that escalated quickly.*

CHAPTER NINETEEN

EMMA

I despise doing the night shift, but one of my friends asked if I could please work it for her because she had a wedding to go to. Well, at least I have the day off tomorrow because I'll be sleeping most of it away. I make a mental note to set my alarm for noon to shop. Then I have light plans to meet up with some people from work. I'll have to get Liv to come out with me. I have a ton of preparation to get done for the girls' visit to Houston. They've always treated me like one of them, and I can't wait to see them.

As soon as I walk through the door of this place, there is one emergency situation after another, and it's only going to get worse after midnight. My parents used to remind me that nothing good ever happens after midnight, and as I look around this hellhole, I tend to agree with their assessment and stance on the issue. Nothing is good in this place.

I sigh in resignation as I take a much-needed sip of my coffee, looking around the forty-five-bed ER from the inner core nurses' area. The music in the nurses' station plays "Paint it Black" by Hidden Citizens. Rånya's chilling vocals just add to the vibe.

Everything that is harmful or evil seems to live in this place. The sounds of pain and crying combined with the sight of vomit and blood harden my emotions to when someone comes in mostly dead and we have to act quickly to save their life. I don't know how Liv did this god-forsaken shift all those years while attending school. This graveyard shift is a fitting name, and it royally sucks ass. I have a new appreciation for anyone who works the night shift because it is pure hell.

I'm pulled from my thoughts as the devil himself sets his gaze on me heading out of the triage room.

Lucifer, Satan, Beelzebub, or as we call him here at work, Brett, walks up to me with a purpose, and I fight the urge to roll my eyes at him. He is so condescending and full of himself. He thinks he is so good-looking, flexing his muscles. It just doesn't do it for me, which irks him to the max. Imagine a woman not throwing themselves at his feet—the horror.

"Em-ma," he calls my name using two-syllables, making me instantly annoyed. He brings his cupped hands forming a funnel appearance around his mouth back down after calling my name. He's such a jerk. He can't call me short, and he says my name like this because he thinks I am slow to hear things. You know, since I am short, the words have to travel down until I hear them. I get the meaning of his act; it's just not funny. I once tried to tell him that I knew I was short and could hear just fine. He smiled, knowing that he got to me, so he kept doing it every so often. To other people, it doesn't look like anything when he does things like this, but I know what he's implying. I decide not to react to his childish behavior. He knows how I feel when people call me short. Schooling my features to Lucifer, I smile brightly at him.

"Yes, Brett." I look up at him. He tries to stand too close to me as a means of intimidation. He doesn't realize I am thinking about punching him in the balls—one benefit of being vertically challenged.

As I look back up, I realize that I may not be throwing my best poker face on because he smirks at me. Ugh, he must be interpreting this all wrong. *I wasn't looking at your balls. I was thinking about punching you in the balls.* I shake my head to obliterate the appalling mental image from my mind.

"What is it, Brett?"

He hands me a chart. "Here. Your next patient is over in trauma bay four."

Brett is so smug, and I bet he thinks he is upsetting me by giving me a more complex patient, but it would take more than this to rile me up. I quickly glance over the chart and see his narrowed eyes focused on me.

"Is the knife or object still lodged in the wound?" I ask.

"No, it's not," he replies quickly.

"Pity," I say and give him a once-over before I walk toward bay four.

"Whatever," is all I hear as he walks back to triage.

I decide to get this over with and assess the damage to the hand wound. I step through the curtains into trauma bay four and announce myself like I do whenever I come into a room. Except this time, I am astonished. It's not the patient or their presenting trauma that makes me feel this way, but the man standing with the patient.

I instinctively grab my necklace and see when he notices what I am holding on to. The look in his eyes is cataclysmic. His nostrils flare with what I can sense as anger, although I don't feel it directed at me. Because when he looks back at me, his eyes soften.

"Is that the necklace I gave you?" He waits for my answer, and I want to deny it.

I am so overwhelmed by the feelings that come at me with the impetus of a tidal wave, making a flood of emotions pour over me. I know my eyes are beginning to water, and I can no longer look at him. It isn't just the thought of him leaving me but the realization that I don't have anyone in my corner anymore. Except for Uncle Andrés and my cousin Adrian. I am so grateful for everything they've done for me and how they stepped up to rescue me, putting themselves in danger. A potential danger I have seemed to cause everyone around me. Eduardo didn't abandon me but didn't come to find me either. I look down so he doesn't witness the barrage of conflicting emotions.

He raises my chin to look at him. I swallow, giving him the answer he already knows. "I never took it off. I've worn it since you gave it to me and held on to it even when I never saw you again."

He stares at me and I imagine he sees the sincerity displayed on my face. This time, he swallows before answering me. "I tried." Regret radiating from each spoken word. He stops and restarts with more conviction. "I tried to return to you, but I had to honor your family's wishes. My family's ultimata were clearly explained when your uncle called my father to ensure I didn't *bother* you." He says that word as if it sickens him. "I thought it was what you wanted. Had I known, I would have come to you sooner. I would have reached out to you after your high school graduation."

I know he can see the pain that crosses my face at the mention of my family and the sea of emotions that surge through me. He must sense that. I know he can still somehow read me like a book. I turn around so he doesn't see me. My guilt, my sadness, the mask that momentarily feels like it fell, exposing my truths, my secrets. Can he know? About Julian? I doubt it. If he did, he would have found me sooner, right? I have no idea. I bite my lip to stifle the cry that threatens to escape my lips.

He grabs my shoulders, spinning me around to face him. "What is it, Emma? Is something wrong? I heard about your parents..." his words trail off.

I look up at him. "Yes," I say, not wanting to have this conversation that should happen in private. Words that need to be spoken only where the chance of Julian not hearing is imperative. Am I being overly cautious? Yes, but I was wrong once and won't repeat that mistake. I continue, "But first, let's fix your friend here." He seems not to like or want the redirection of this conversation but doesn't push it along for now.

"Emma," he all but growls my name.

I touch his chest and look at him. "Later, Eduardo. This time, we will have our later, okay?" His eyes soften, and he grabs my hand.

"Okay, baby." He brings my hand to his lips, giving it a soft, wet kiss that makes me melt and my center throb. He releases my hand and steps away.

I now focus my attention on the actual bleeding patient. "Sorry about that, Gus." I laugh, but Gus still holds his bleeding hand, perplexed at our exchange.

I lay the patient, Gus, as Eduardo refers to him, onto the stretcher and attach him to our monitors. I just want to ensure his vital signs are stable and he hasn't lost too much blood. I doubt this type of man would admit to feeling faint because it would make him appear weak. Believe me, I know the type all too well. Like my whole life, to be exact.

Eduardo asks me if I can fix Gus, and I know what he is really asking. "Yes, but I can't here. My license doesn't allow me to do it." He smiles, and I leave to get the ER doctor working here tonight.

I return shortly with Dr. Hernandez in tow. He looks at the wound and asks if it was a knife wound. Gus nods, and Eduardo speaks for him.

"It was a fight at my club." He doesn't elaborate, and Dr. Hernandez waits for him to continue. When he doesn't, he looks over at Gus.

"Is that true?"

Gus nods but doesn't answer. I almost giggle at this exchange. Dr. Hernandez might think he is the top dog in this ER, but he doesn't understand the hierarchy in this room.

"Okay, then. Let's fix this. Emma, can you get some antibiotics? It says he has no allergies, so how about two grams of Ancef IM."

"Sure, no problems. Here is the suture tray and numbing medicine. I'll be right back." I step away, and Dr. Hernandez grabs my arm to stop me.

"I'm buying the staff food tonight. I couldn't find you earlier, so I ordered your usual order from the day shift. I hope that's okay?"

I look over to Eduardo, whose gaze is fixed on where Dr. Hernandez is still holding my arm. Eduardo's nostrils are flaring, and I see the tick in his jaw that lets me know he is very displeased at seeing another man touching me. Gus is tensed on the stretcher, anticipating a full-out loss of control on Eduardo's part, and is waiting to see what happens.

I remove my arm from his embrace, and Dr. Hernandez looks at me when I glance over at Eduardo, shaking my head at him. This seems to confuse him, and he looks back and forth at Eduardo and me, sensing a familiarity between us. Luckily for the good doctor, he isn't an idiot and picks up on social cues because he clears his throat and focuses back on Gus.

"That sounds perfect, Dr. Hernandez, thank you." I leave the room but turn back to see that Eduardo still fixates on me as I walk away. I mouth the word "behave" at him. He smiles brightly at me. As I walk off, I shake my head and hear Gus snort at the exchange.

I return with the antibiotic in a syringe and assist Dr. Hernandez where needed. Pretty soon, the wound is closed, and Dr. Hernandez stands. He gives Gus instructions about keeping the sutures clean and dry. I add some antibacterial ointment to the site and dress it.

"You'll need to get the sutures removed in ten days," he instructs.

Eduardo looks at me and tells the doctor they have that covered. I already know what that means, and I nod after Dr. Hernandez has turned around and walked out. "I need to give you this shot, Gus. Drop your pants," I say with a smirk, knowing how this will go. Eduardo stands, and the chair falls back, knocking over at the hastiness of his stance. Gus looks over at Eduardo.

"Oh, hell. Fuck that."

He walks over to me, and I can't help but wait for the reaction I provoked. "Over my dead body will you ever say that to any other man. Do you understand me, Emma?"

"Yes, sir," I mock him and wink.

His mouth twitches in delight. He steps closer into my space. He raises his hand to my cheek in a soft embrace and trails it down my neck, leaning forward to whisper in my ear, "You can call me that anytime, baby." His breath tickles and heats down my neck, and I shudder in response. He kisses the side of my mouth quickly, not hitting the area I want him to kiss. He pulls away. "Now, give Gus the shot in his arm, and we must be on our way."

I pull Gus's shirt down to expose his deltoid muscle and clean it with alcohol. "Are you sure you want it here? I could give it to you by injecting it into a leg muscle."

"For fuck's sake. Do you want to get me killed? I'll have to take my pants down."

I purse my lips. "Okay, if you insist." I give Gus the intramuscular injection, and he grimaces." I rub the spot. "It was too much medication for that muscle, but what do I know? I'm just a nurse." I place a *Frozen* princess bandage on it and pull his shirt up. "There. All done."

I hand them their discharge instructions.

"Okay, I'm going to need your information now, Emma."

I pretend to think this over. "Hmm, I guess I could do that." I write my number on the paper and hand it over to him.

"I need all the information, Emma." I must look puzzled because he points at the paper and hands it back. "Address too."

I blush but add it to the sheet and hand it back.

They start walking to the door. "What time do you leave here, and how are you getting home?"

"My shift ends at seven in the morning, and I drive here."

He nods. "Someone will be here to follow you home, and, Emma?"

"Yes?" I ask nervously.

"That will be the last time you drive to work alone. I'll be in touch this afternoon." With that, he walks away and leaves me here at a loss for words and, for the first time, a feeling of security.

CHAPTER TWENTY

EDUARDO

We leave the emergency department, and I can't think straight until I escape this cesspool of disease and pestilence. I am no germaphobe, but even I can appreciate the nastiness that coats every inch of that place. There is no way Emma is going to continue working there after we have kids. She'll bring that crap home. I shudder at the thought.

Gus and I walk together side by side, and patients and staff part for us, sensing the dangerous vibes we ooze from our pores. It's the confidence that comes with being the top dog, or maybe it's the amount of ink that adorns our bodies. Each tattoo represents or acknowledges our different memories or special moments in our lives.

Did Emma see the tattoo I had of her name on my knuckles? If she did, she didn't let on. I remember that day I got the tattoo. I had a tattoo completed of a tidal wave with a mermaid underneath. A mermaid that had a striking resemblance to Emma with her emerald-green eyes. She had my heart in her hand, like it had been pulled from my chest, and was weeping blood and tears.

I don't know what possessed me to do that vivid tattoo with an anatomical-looking heart covering where my actual heart resides–where it ceased to beat for anyone else. Maybe I was drunk, but it was true that Emma owned my ripped heart and held it in her hands.

We were more friends the day I was told I couldn't continue to see her. The feelings were there, but I was older than her. Geez, she was in junior high, and I was going to start high school. There is no way that I could pursue anything with her at that point. A couple of years at that age is like a decade in older years. I thought I had imagined it all and the feeling that might have made her seem much more of a goddess in my head, but after seeing her here today, I know that whatever feelings I had are real and never went away. If anything, they are stronger because she was always someone I confided in and trusted. I feel that is still true. She grew up and is even more beautiful than I would have thought.

She is short though, and that makes me chuckle. She always hated being so vertically challenged. Her sister, too, but I hadn't remembered her exact features. While their physical traits were similar, their personalities were vastly distinguishable. I had this fantasy in my mind that kept her there with us as little kids. Now? Well, now she is all woman. The curves of her body and the long blond hair that I itch to fist in my hand as I stare into those luminous green eyes and watch her mouth part, calling out my name as she comes. I'll kiss her, swallow all her cries, and lick away all her tears.

I wonder what all the tears she held back today were about. There is a story there. I sensed her sadness, but I don't know if it was about losing her family or if it was something else. I'll need to find out what has happened to her. Why was she left alone, and why did her parents die? It doesn't add up, but I want to make sure that she is safe, and until I can be reassured that my worries aren't justified, I will continue to keep her under my protection.

Gus remains silent as we walk to the car. He must sense that I am deep in my thoughts as he opens the door for me, despite his injured hand, and I get in. I start up the car, and he gets into the passenger seat. I turn to look at him.

"You didn't have to open my door, Gus. You're injured," I state the obvious, pointing to his hand.

He ignores this and gets to what he really wants to ask. "That's the woman from your tattoos?" He fixes his gaze on my knuckles and points to my chest.

I sigh. "Fuck. Yes, that's Emma." I rub my hands up and down my face, then reverse the car so we can finally leave.

He nods his head up and down and then drops it. He looks out the windows, deep in thought. I have my own issue instead of trying to determine what Gus is thinking.

I must return to the club and see what else has happened while away. Then, I need to consider digging into Emma's past to get a head start on what the woman is hiding from me. I sense there's quite a bit. I know just the person to unlock those secrets, too. Now, how much I want to piss off his fiancée is the real question because there is no way in hell that I will wait until tomorrow.

I enter the club, walk past my security, and enter my office. I shut the door and halt in my tracks when I see Cherry sitting in my chair. "What the actual fuck?"

Cherry startles at my anger toward her and immediately tries to soothe my temper. "Eduardo, baby. I am so sorry. We broke up, and he couldn't accept that I was in love with you. He came to try to win me back, but there is no one else but you."

I stare at her in utter shock because what the fuck is happening right now, and how did she get in here? She provocatively struts over to me and grabs my cock.

"Let me make it up to you, baby." She drops to her knees, undoing my zipper in one fluid movement. I immediately step away from her and zip my pants up.

"Are you out of your fucking mind," I snarl. I grab my phone and call Gus. "Send security in, Gus." I hang up. I look back at Cherry with venom that sprays forth from my mouth. I don't mince my words so that she understands I mean business when I say, "I *never* want to see you again in my club. Is that understood, Cherry?" She starts crying, but I continue reinforcing my point. "Use your words, Cherry. Say that you understand."

She nods and sobs out, "Yes, I understand."

"Good. You are not to return. If I so much as see you in my club again, you will regret it. Do I make myself clear?"

She nods just as two bouncers come barging in. I turn my anger on them.

"I thought I told you that she nor her boyfriend, ex-boyfriend, whatever the fuck he is, is not to be allowed in here ever again. So how is it that I returned from taking Gus to the ER after seeing *my* girlfriend there, and now walk into this." I point at Cherry to emphasize the 'this' point. "She is sitting in here alone on *my* chair in my office, huh?"

She gasps in shock, shaking her head back and forth. I can tell she wants to say something.

"Get her out of here!" I yell. "One more slip-up and I'll be finding and vetting new bouncers for my club."

They take a very tearful and shrieking Cherry Pop out of my office, and I slump in my chair. Fucking hell, what a night, and it's not over either.

I hit the phone number for my brother, Ram, and I know he'll pick up no matter what time it is. He answers, and I hear his fiancée ask who's calling. He tells her to go back to sleep, and I hear the sound of a door closing as he speaks.

"What the fuck do you want at this hour?" He is so grumpy at 3:00 in the morning.

"Please tell my future sister-in-law I'm sorry for the intrusion at this early hour, but I need to talk to you."

In hearing my sincerity, he speaks up. "What's up, brother? Everything okay?" Any anger he had at my phone call this early in the morning is quickly forgotten.

I run my hands through my hair. I swear I'm going to go bald like the old man. I'm beginning to understand how he lost his hair early in life.

"I had to take Gus to the emergency room tonight for a minor altercation at the club."

"Is he okay?" he asks.

"Yes, but that isn't why I called." I hesitate before I get the words out. "I found her." I wait for that statement to seep in.

"Found wh-o..." he trails off. "No way. Emma? You found Emma?" he asks for confirmation.

"Yeah. I did. Emma is working in the emergency department, Ram. It was such a coincidence seeing her there. Like it was meant to be, but something happened with her, and I need to find out what, and more importantly, I need to keep her safe. For me to do that, I need to understand what happened. Do you think I should talk to her uncle? Should I call him?"

Ram thinks this over. "Well, they weren't too keen on you wanting to pursue her, but honestly, I think it was her mom doing all that. Don't you? With her parents out of the picture, I think her uncle might be thankful to have you look after her."

That reassures me about what I have to do next. "I'll call Andrés, but first, can you find out what happened with her family in Brownsville? I need more information to see what is going on here. Is she in danger? A lot was weighing on her mind. I could sense it. I hope she will open up to me about it, but if not… then I intend to find out through any means necessary to keep her safe and protected."

"How is she?" he asks, sincerity pouring in every spoken word. We were all friends back then, when things were simpler.

"She's still short. I don't think she likes that, but I think it's cute as fuck." I laugh, trying to make light of the situation.

"You still care for her, don't you?" He waits for my answer, but it doesn't take long for me to reply.

"Of course. I've always loved Emma." Finally saying this out loud to another person feels good. It feels right. Now, I just have to tell her and hope that she feels the same way toward me. I don't think I can let her go a second time. I know I won't.

"I'll find out what you need. I'll be in touch, Eduardo. Be safe. Love you, bro."

He hangs up, and I ponder my choices while I sit at my desk. First things first. I call my main security detail, Philip, and have him come in.

A few moments later, Philip walks into my office. I will explain the reason why he is here. I need to make sure Emma is safe. He is her detail from now on, and I need him to keep me updated on her whereabouts and everything she does. I also ask him to order some red roses and deliver them to her address.

"I need you to give her access to the club at my office and put her name on the VIP list. Give her this card with the roses so she knows to come here." I hand him the access card for the club. He looks at me like I've lost my mind.

I know what it must look like. I have never cared for another woman in my life besides my mother, but Emma is not an ordinary woman. She's *my* woman, and there isn't anything I wouldn't do to protect what's mine.

CHAPTER TWENTY-ONE

EMMA

The girls are planning a visit to Houston. Val, Ainsley, and Piper are coming soon, and Liv and I look forward to the company. I send out a text to Liv.

> Emma: I'm picking up some things for the girls' upcoming visit. Do you want to come?

> Liv: YES

> Emma: Well, that was easy. I thought I was going to have to bribe you. I know how much you hate shopping for clothes.

Liv doesn't reply, so I go about my business and rush home. Even though I am off, I promised my favorite people at work that I would meet them this evening. I got off early today. Well, early this morning, and I slept until noon. Remind me never to work another night shift. Hell, that was rough, but it turned out to be a very good thing, I think to myself as I touch the beautiful floral arrangement Eduardo sent, now sitting pretty on my table. Only day shifts for me. That work-life balance keeps my sanity, unlike my bestie, Liv, who continues to burn her candle at both ends. I laugh at that idiomatic expression.

My mom used that saying often, and I think of her every time I use it. It physically hurts my heart to think about it, but I refuse to make myself forget about them by not talking about them or taking the time to remember the good moments with my family. Maybe I am a glutton for punishment, but I miss my parents and Evie so much. I try to carry their memories with me as if they are still around. I probably need an appointment with a therapist, but what do I say when I am interviewed? "Yes, my family was kind of killed, but my psycho boyfriend tried to keep me in a locked house to rely on only him. His dad has political affiliations with the mafia, but my mom's parents are the mafia, too." Yeah, that won't go over well. Instead, I am trying my best to cope with the grief and guilt that occupy my daily life.

I get dressed quickly and am ready to meet my friends at the sports bar near the hospital. It is a place we frequent for some pre-clubbing drinks. It's kind of like tailgating before the main event. Happy hour is usually packed with people behaving worse around seven p.m. I grab my keys and admire the roses that occupy most of the kitchen table. They are so aromatic, and as I touch them, I sigh, remembering our encounter from the other night. Staring down at my key fob, I decide against driving there. Instead I open the app settling for an Uber, and place my key back on the table.

I glimpse at my phone. "Five minutes until they get here. Gotta love this city," I mutter as I close the door behind me.

I enter through the door and look for my friends. I go around a few people and head toward the other side of the bar, seeing the group sitting by the bar at a side table. As I walk over, I see a guy approaching me with purpose, and I stop mid-stride, worried about Julian, until I recognize him—Jameson. The guy that I met with Liv and Dax on Padre Island over a year ago. Geez, crazy. He pulls me into a hug as if we are long-lost friends.

"Oh my god. Who are you with? What are you doing?" I exclaim, throwing my hands in the air like I can't believe it.

Jameson points over to the table he was sitting at. "I'm here with the guys from the beach when we all last hung out, when..." He doesn't finish that sentence because we all remember what happened that night before the accident. "I honestly didn't think I'd ever see you again." He throws me a megawatt smile, and I can't help but smile in return. "Come on and say hi to everyone." He pulls me over to the table where his friends are engaged in conversation, until they all stop to look at us.

"Hey, everyone. Do you remember Emma?" He goes through the introductions, but I remain focused on Dax. He looks at me until recognition dawns on him, and it's as if the poor guy wants to ask a million questions. "Dax, you remember Emma, right? Liv's friend?" He pulls me in for a hug, and I laugh.

"Well, gentleman, what a warm reception I'm getting this evening."

Theo and Eric wave at me in unison, like they are waving to the Queen of England. Jerks. "Well, the whole gang's here tonight." I quickly turn my gaze back to Jameson, and we begin to catch up on everything we have been up to in the past year. I enjoy how easy it is to talk to him. I can see Dax from the corner of my eye sitting on the edge of his seat, radiating excitement at the possibility of asking me questions about Liv. Instead, he turns to me and asks if I want a drink.

I raise an eyebrow at him, calling bullshit, and he chuckles in response. "Sure, I'll take a gimlet." I hear them all laugh at me. "What?" I reply, shrugging, not getting the joke.

"A gimlet? Isn't that what older people drink?" He pats my arm in a placating fashion.

"First of all, shame on you, Jameson, for age discrimination and...well, I guess I am just an old soul too. Lastly, it also helps when it is later on in the night, and I just end up getting soda water and lime, and everyone thinks I have the fastest elimination process for alcohol consumption."

Jameson snorts. "All right, smarty pants. One gimlet is coming up." He steps away, and I can feel Dax staring at me. I look over at him.

"Will you just ask me already?" I laugh because he is so predictable. He looks like a love-sick popular jock in high school crushing on the nerdy booktrovert.

Then he spews a verbal vomit of questions all about Liv. "Finally," I laugh. "I was waiting for that." I proceed to catch him up quickly on how Liv has been and the guilt that eats her up on a daily basis, but how she perseveres, continuing to work and attend school. Jameson comes back with my drink, and I take a big swallow of the clean-tasting beverage.

"I moved to Houston for her, you know. She was a wreck. I worried about her and told her I was ready to make a new life for myself. Start a new adventure." I can see Jameson perk up at these words. Little does he know that there is another reason for my move. Despite Julian finding me, I am still trying to live my life, until he either catches up to me or I cease to exist. He once told me that if he couldn't have me, then no one would. I absolutely believe him. "Honestly, I couldn't let her come here by herself. She didn't even go to her graduation."

Dax rubs his hands down his face. "I tried to reach out to her."

"Yeah, she told me. She seems to have put all her focus into school and this per diem job we both work at the hospital."

This piques his interest, and he sits up straighter in his chair, but before he can ask, I hold my hand up, refusing to tell him anything more about Liv.

"I don't want to tell you anything more because you both need to talk first—"

"I saw Liv today," he interrupts. "I was with some woman from work. We, um, work together."

I believe Dax, but I am also not naive enough to think it was a platonic relationship. At least not initially. Before ending this discussion, I give him one last piece of advice. "If you want to make a go with our girl, you will have to try harder. She fell for you that weekend. And it scares her. And she is living with so much guilt that it is suffocating her. If you care about her, then don't stop trying."

I look for my friends, and I can see that they are giving me the 'what the fuck look.' I tilt my head up in acknowledgment. I say my good-byes and head over to my friends.

After a couple of drinks, I decide to message Liv.

> Emma: You will never believe who I ran into at our after-work sports bar! Jameson from Spring Break, and he wasn't alone.

I don't elaborate on who he wasn't alone with. I expect to hear right back from her, questioning what I mean and who else was there, if it wasn't blatantly obvious. Instead, I get radio silence, so I call Liv. She answers quickly; I know she's probably at home by now. Did I catch her before she threw on her comfy PJs, and I can't get her to come out?

"Hey, girlie! What's up?" I don't give her a chance to reply. "Get dressed and meet me out. I need to dance, and you're coming now."

I hear her laughing on the phone, so I hope she will agree. "Yeah, I guess I could. Where are we meeting?"

And that's all I need. I got Liv to come out. That in itself is not a small feat.

We talk about what we are wearing, and I tell her to wear something cute and sexy. Liv bursts out laughing. "Okay, so something low cut and short," she states jokingly. "Got it."

I scream-shout my excitement on the line. "Call me when you pull up. It's a big club, and I'll come out to get you." I hang up before she can say anything else, fist-pumping the air. "Yes!" I say to no one in particular.

Liv shares her ETA with me, and I see her pull up, look at the long-ass line, and get into line at the back.

No, no, I think to myself, that just won't do. I'm waving at Liv, screaming her name, laughing at her look of shock. I see her walk over to me at the front of the line, getting ugly looks from the girls waiting in the queue. I'm talking about death stares now. I immediately wrap her up in a hug.

"How did you get up here? The line is crazy!" she yells at me over the crowd's noise and loud city nightlife scene. The bouncer lifts the rope, and we walk through the club doors.

"Come on. Let's get a drink."

I drag Liv through the crowds, not letting go of her hand once. We walk toward the bar.

"Let's do some shots." I place myself against the bar to get the bartender's attention. He smiles widely.

Liv agrees, and I order two each. She tries to pay, but the bartender points to someone at the end of the bar.

"You ladies are all set."

We take our first shot, and he immediately pours us our second one. He pushes the next shots at us, and we look at each other, shrugging.

"So. How did you get us in here?" Liv asks. I take my last shot, suck on the lime, and discard it into the now-empty shot glass on the bar.

"I took care of the guy that owns this place. Well, no, not him, but an employee. I can't tell you much more because of patient confidentiality. I've probably said too much as it is. Blame it on the alcohol." I shrug in a sorry-not-sorry manner. "He told me to come here and put me on the VIP list." Liv takes her second shot, and I ask the bartender if this is from the owner. He raises his eyebrows at my question.

"No, it wasn't him," he says as he collects the glasses. "It was someone else," his words fading away as he leaves.

I should tell Liv.

"It was Jameson, then," I say quickly, not wanting to hide it from Liv any longer. I see the look on her face as she tries to place that name from her memory when it hits, and her eyes widen in surprise.

"I ran into him at a sports bar before calling you. Our favorite sports bar, and, Liv? He wasn't alone."

She stares at me and realizes who he wasn't alone with.

Without further questions, I point to the dance floor. Liv points to the roped-off area leading to a floor above us.

"That's the VIP section. I am not sure I have access to that area or if it is just to enter by skipping the entrance line. I was allowed entry into the club with this card, but I have no idea if my name is on *'that'* list." I tuck the card away and we stare at the darkened VIP area as Liv hits my shoulder, then points behind her.

"Come on. I don't plan on getting off the dance floor anyway," Liv says.

"I agree." I lead her to the dance floor, where the sound systems blare EDM, pop, and other mesmerizing dance music. As we start to dance, I shout by her ear, "I don't plan on getting off the dance floor either anytime soon."

CHAPTER TWENTY-TWO

EDUARDO

I have watched Emma's every movement since she entered my club, The Viceroy. Philip told me that she was outside. He delivered the roses and, obviously, the access card for the club. I am glad she didn't waste any time coming to me tonight. I didn't want to have to send for her. I see her walking around with a tall girl. Then return to the bar to take some shots. Tequila.

"Interesting choice," I mumble to myself.

That's not all that is interesting. I see Jameson, my frat brother, fixated at the end of the bar with his gaze set on Emma. He motions to the bartender to get the girls another shot and hands him a card to set up a tab. He is with a few guys, and they go to the VIP room. I'll visit him and see how he knows my little thief.

Jameson is standing with another guy, and they stare at the dance floor, pointing to someone. I zoom in on what has them transfixed and sit up, my spine rigid at the fact that they are pointing to Emma and her friend.

They go to the dance floor, and I see the guy Jameson was with, dancing alongside the tall brunette. He is standing behind her with his body gyrating with hers in sync to the music. When the song ends, she turns around appearing shocked to see him staring intently at her. Her face goes through a series of emotions until it softens and he leans in to kiss her. I see Emma's face up close on my surveillance monitors, and, much to my displeasure, I see Jameson looking at her.

"Oh, fuck no." I get up and call Philip to bring them up to the VIP area where I will meet them.

I am on my way to intercept her when one of my security people stops me in the back hall.

"Boss, I think there is something I should tell you about." He looks over at the bouncer with him.

"Yes, what is it." My patience wears thin because, while I want to know about the operation of my club, I am only thinking about what Jameson is doing with my girlfriend.

"We caught one of the bartenders stealing money." He shifts uncomfortably on his feet.

"How much?" I spit out. I look at both of them, trying to get them to hurry up and give me an answer.

"Not much, Boss, just a couple of hundred bucks, but it's the principle, right?"

I nod in agreement. "Get the money out of him, and if he doesn't have it, take it from him in flesh." I start to walk away, and they stare at me. I usually prefer a more hands-on approach when things like this arise, but now I can't be bothered to deal with a thieving employee when I have to get to my own little thief. Except she didn't steal money; she stole something far more valuable.

"Oh, yeah, and before you fire him, in case that wasn't obvious, bring him to my 'hospitality room' so I can see him personally." I open the door hard, banging it off the wall as I walk out of the office with a purpose—to find her.

I finally go up to the VIP section, where that tall girl accompanying Emma tonight sits on Jameson's friend's lap. Jameson is very close to My Emma. I see a brunette, sidled up next to Jameson, get up angrily as he refuses to acknowledge her. Emma seems amused, but I'm sure they see it differently. Only I know her genuine emotions. That is, if they haven't changed. That is something I'll need to re-familiarize myself with.

Jameson calls the waitstaff over as I approach the table. I have a big smile on my face for Emma.

"Emma," I say her name seductively so they get the meaning of my intrusion.

"Hey there, Eduardo," she replies playfully, her eyes alight with humor. "Thanks so much for letting us into the club and setting us up tonight. That was so…" She thinks of the word for a second. "Hospit-able of you."

I catch the play on words as I only reconnected with her at the hospital earlier today. My lips twitch in amusement. I see the group watching our dialogue and the playful banter between us that I thought we were being sneaky at concealing.

"Liv and I are having such a great time," she continues.

I see Jameson visibly tense. I give him a once-over, trying to determine how much of a threat my frat brother is and if I like him enough to let him leave here with all his teeth.

I turn my attention back to Emma. "I'll be in touch. I must attend to some business, but please enjoy yourself and let me know if you need anything." I feel their eyes on me, but the only eyes I care about belong to a green-eyed vixen who stole my heart long ago.

"So, you thought you could steal from me." I pick his head up to look at me. Well, from what he can see of me from two eyes that seem to be swelling shut as we have this conversation. "I never want to see you in this club again. You should be leaving here minus a limb, but I felt pretty generous this evening and I am in good spirits. I also don't want to get my hands dirty, so to speak. Consider today your lucky day."

I have the bouncers escort him out of my room, and after they leave, I trail behind, returning to the VIP section. It's almost closing time, and I notice that Emma is intoxicated. Jameson is hovering like a vulture, and my blood pressure rises.

"Este vato." He is fucking dead, brother or not.

He hands her a cup, trying to get her to drink water. I can't believe she got this drunk. She sways back and forth. Jameson clings to her, and I see fucking red. He may be trying to help her, but his intentions aren't strictly honorable.

I call Philip and have him get the car ready to take Emma and her friend home. It looks like her friend has other plans though, so I go up to Emma when I can't take it anymore.

"Philip is taking you home. Get rid of Jameson, Emma. The only name you are going to be screaming tonight is mine."

Her eyes dilate, and she whispers in my ear, "I'll hold you to that, babe."

I touch her cheek, feeling Jameson watching us.

She walks over to him, and he asks her questions, looking at me. I walk off, not needing to deal with this exchange. I know who will be with whom later tonight. I see Jameson at Emma's side as she sways a bit, and he holds her. Philip brings the car up to the door and gets in after her. I see her drive away without me for the last time.

I pull up in my black Porsche 911 turbo at Emma's apartment complex. I quickly get out and hit the lock on my key fob. Philip told me he dropped Emma off about thirty minutes ago and took a very dejected-looking Jameson home right after she closed the door in his face. He tried to enter her apartment, but my girl sent him away. I know she is alone, and I plan to take advantage of this alone time with her.

I take the steps two at a time and barely reach the landing when she opens the door. She stares at me while sipping something from her Stanley cup. Her face is washed free of makeup, and she wears a cropped tank and sleep shorts. I look her up and down in a slow perusal. I have never seen her look more beautiful. It's so similar to when we were younger, and I swear I feel like a kid again. I was pining for a girl I had to let go of. If I had known when I gave her that necklace for her birthday, all those years ago, that it would be the last time I would see her, I would have taken more time with her. That's the thing about good-bye. Sometimes, you're not lucky enough to have one. Emma knows this more than I do, and my heart pains at her having to endure that hardship and more all alone.

She smiles brightly at me, opens the door wide, and heads back inside. I trail behind her like a love-sick puppy. She places her drink on the table next to where the roses I sent her are standing on full display.

"Nice roses," I say with a smirk playing at the corner of my mouth.

"Oh, do you like them?" she asks, quirking an eyebrow upward. "My boyfriend got them for me. I hope that's not a problem for you?"

"Definitely not a problem for me. Maybe for Jameson though?" I ask in question as I move toward her.

"He was rather upset when I sent him home." She pretends to be upset about his departure, casting her eyes toward the ground, pursed lips.

I move in quickly, catching her off guard, and she squirms with delight as I wrap my hands around her waist and pull her to me. My fingers dig into her waist, and she fights the urge to laugh. She's always been ticklish.

"Just in case you were wondering, Emma…" I pause as I bring my mouth to her neck, trailing light kisses up to her ear. "I don't give a fuck about Jameson," I say harshly.

She shudders as my breath lays heavy on her ear. I kiss my way over to her cheek and pull back slightly as I reach her mouth. I stare at her. "You are fucking mine." I smash my lips to hers, and she opens her mouth to allow entry. I suck on her tongue and deepen the kiss.

"Where is your bedroom?" I take off my jacket and drape it over the chair. I undo the cufflinks on my dress shirt and unbutton it, taking it off and draping it along with where my jacket resides.

She just watches me, making me smile to see how I affect her. Her eyes widen when I go for my belt buckle, undoing it and my pants as they fall to the floor in a swoop, pooling around my ankles.

I step out of them, and my socks and shoes are all discarded on the floor. I stand in my boxers with my hard cock sticking out the top, my tip glistening. She is zoned in on it and involuntarily licks her lips. My cock twitches, and the mirth in her eyes says she saw it.

"If you keep looking at me like that, Emma, I will fuck you for our first time on this carpet."

She walks up to me. Her one hand touches my cock, rubbing the precum around the tip, making me hiss at the contact of her fingers. "Maybe later," she says. "Tonight, I want you to fuck me properly in a bed." She sticks her finger in her mouth and sucks my arousal from it.

That does it. I lift her up as if she weighs nothing. She wraps her legs around my waist as I walk through the door she pointed to as her bedroom.

"All night…" she trails off as she brings her lips to mine, and I lose myself in an all-consuming kiss.

CHAPTER TWENTY-THREE

EMMA

He carries me into the bedroom. His cock is hard against my center, and I grind into it, feeling the heat of our bodies and the wetness that pools between my legs. I have never been so turned on in my life. I thought teenage Eduardo was hot, but this is so much better. He is all man, and I haven't even had a proper look at his cock.

He places me carefully on the bed, like a fragile treasure he doesn't want to break. I look up at him hovering over me, mesmerized by the heat in his eyes that's directed at me. He's barely containing himself, and I relish in the knowledge that I can turn him on this much.

"Be a good girl and take your shirt off for me, baby," he purrs, and my core tingles in anticipation of speeding this process up, but he has no intention of getting to it. He is going excruciatingly slow, and it's starting to bother me. I need him to touch me, expose me, and make me his in the physical sense—the primal act of taking me and ravishing my body. I crave him, and it is driving me mad with lust.

BLACK WAVE

I focus on him as I lift my tank top over my head and toss it to the floor, attempting to play his game. He pulls my bra down, making my boobs stick out over the top. He licks his finger and circles around one of my nipples, leaving wetness and goose bumps in its wake. He cups the other breast roughly with his hand, and I groan at the contact. He pushes me back on the bed and removes my sleeping shorts, finding I'm not wearing any panties. His nostrils flare, and he stares at my bare pussy. He looks at me with hooded eyes, and I arch my back up in response as if I am offering myself up to him—a silent permission to take me.

That must do the trick because his control snaps. I win. He drops to the ground, pulling me forward on the bed, and dives in to feast on my pussy. I cry out at the sudden intrusion. He is like an animal biting and sucking on my clit in tandem. I don't know what to feel. The pain mixed with the pleasure causes pressure to build rapidly. But whenever I feel an impending orgasm, he pulls back and then circles my clit slowly with his tongue, causing the tingles to subside.

I begin to whimper after he does this a couple of times, but then he adds a couple of fingers arching up toward my cervix while sucking on my clit until I feel it come on quickly, full force, and I cry out, my orgasm shattering throughout my body. He doesn't stop pumping in and out with his fingers until the pulsing starts to abate. He pulls his fingers out and licks them in front of me. I almost climax again. It's filthy and dirty, and I am so incredibly turned on by the sight of it.

I breathe in and out, my heart rate starting to slow down as if I've just run a marathon. My arm rests over my eyes and I suddenly feel spent. He stands and picks up my legs that have fallen open on the bed and rubs his warm, leaking cock up and through my folds, still slick from my arousal, to lubricate his shaft.

I lower my arm from my face and concentrate on his mouth, still wet with my juices. I look up into his eyes, and without breaking contact, he thrusts inside me, filling me completely. His hips are flush with mine, and he begins to move. He moves painstakingly slowly, and I almost can't take it. I meet each thrust with my own, and we have a rhythm that he decides to change up because he throws my legs over his shoulder and drives in hard. I cry out his name.

"Eduardo, fuck yes, harder, babe. Fuck me harder." I don't even know who I am right now.

The things coming out of my mouth should embarrass me, but this feels so good, so right that I can't stop the crudeness that leaves my lips. The porn star version of myself cries out so loudly that my neighbors will surely hear our lovemaking. The look I'll get from them… but I don't care. Nothing exists right now except the pounding of our hips and the thrust of his cock that hits my G-spot so deep that I start to orgasm again.

Eduardo's thrusts become more frantic as he starts to lose control. He is a beast, picking me up off the bed, knees bent, holding me close. He kisses me as he thrusts into me, pushing and pulling me onto his cock. My hips will be bruised from the tight grip he has on me.

I throw my head back, and he latches on to my boob, biting my nipple, and I swear I will climax again. He pounds relentlessly and pulls me into a searing kiss as if he is branding me. Finally, making me his. He sucks on my neck, leaving a bruise, crying out and throwing his head back. I look at him in the throes of passion. With his breath still labored, he brings his head back to look at me, and I smile at him.

He picks me up, still impaled on his cock, and the smile that graces his lips should be illegal. He leads us to my bathroom and starts the shower. He walks us in, and I feel him harden again. I look into his eyes, and he kisses me passionately as if he is making up for all the wasted years apart.

"About that all-night part?" he says as he leans me up against the wall and begins to move.

He comes into the bedroom with my Stanley Cup. "Here, baby, I want you to drink more water."

I take the cup from him and take a few more sips at his encouraging request. I know that I will be so thankful tomorrow, and after all the water and the ibuprofen I took before he got here, I should feel okay. Maybe that's wishful thinking because I know an imminent conversation we need to have will make me feel anything but okay.

"Emma," he says, and I sense that by the way he says my name, he wants to ask me something serious. I just wish it wasn't in the early morning hours before dawn.

"Yes." I look up at him and cup his cheek. I stare into his eyes and know that this will be the conversation I am not ready for, but it is necessary. If there is one person I can trust, it is him.

So I start at the beginning—with Julian. I see how his face hardens and the disgust that lingers in his features when I talk to him about the abuse I endured.

"Emma—" He halts his words, trying to remain calm. "Why the fuck didn't you say something sooner. Why did you let him treat you that way?"

"He threatened me and, more importantly, Eduardo, he threatened my parents. He told me there would be consequences if I tried to leave home. He would ensure my parents' careers were ruined, and we would lose our home and life as we knew it. I believed him because his dad is the mayor." He also is into some sketchy dealings, but I leave that part out for now. After hours of talking and crying, he holds me, and for once, I fall asleep without the fear of Julian.

CHAPTER TWENTY-FOUR

EDUARDO

Emma is sound asleep, and the thought of leaving her alone is agonizing. I get up and put my boxers on. I look for the rest of my clothes and realize that Emma, that little sex kitten, seduced me in the living room, and I left all of my clothes out there. I grab my watch from the bedside table and walk out to close the door to Emma's room behind me with a soft click.

I walk the short distance to the living room when I see Liv, Emma's roommate, drinking a glass of water. She was about to wave when she realized it wasn't who she thought it was. *Did she think it was Jameson? What the fuck?* I'm sure she will tell that guy she was with last night, whatever his name was—Jameson's friend—that I was here. I run a hand through my hair, giving her my best impression of an innocent look. Her eyes narrow, and I can tell she does not buy the innocent act. Oh, well, I tried.

"Hi?" Liv says in question. There is a reluctance to get near me. Maybe she senses danger when she looks at me. That wouldn't be wrong. Little does she know that I am not the real danger here. I am the closest thing to safety when it comes to Emma—and possibly her, since she is Emma's best friend.

I laugh at the thought. "Hi, Liv. I'll be out of your hair in a second," I tell her as I gather up my discarded items from last night's sexcapades.

"Just need to get dressed." I pick up my clothes, not bothering to change anywhere else. Fuck it. If she can't give a guy some privacy, she can see what a real man looks like. I grab my keys off the coffee table in the living room.

"I'll see you later. Have a good day." I throw her a wink before I walk out the front door. I just couldn't help myself. I almost laughed at her reaction.

After I leave Emma's apartment, I start to recall the truths she told me. I am reeling with anger. I know it took a lot for her to tell me about Julian, but I am glad she confided in me, and I vowed to protect her. I would keep her safe. The relief that flooded her face when I told her that shook me to my core. The fact that she had been out here alone, unprotected, killed me. I thought her uncle had someone following her, but I'll need more information.

I suspect she hid details that would anger me, but her parents and sister died. I couldn't say anything more after seeing the guilt surface in her expression after mentioning them. That she feels responsible for their deaths instead of blaming that monster she dated is ridiculous. When she also told me about overhearing a conversation between that scumbag and his father when she was imprisoned in their house right before her cousin came in to remove her from that place, it was suspicious as hell. I already suspected he had something to do with the fire that killed her family. After she overheard the conversation alluding to Julian's father having covered up the incident, it is obvious that there is more going on than just Julian's obsession with Emma, but it remains to be seen.

I won't let him anywhere near her. The only way I can do that is to provide her with twenty-four-seven security. I'll also need to tell my father and speak with her uncle about his plans so we can put forth a unified front. I won't have anything happen to her. Just the thought has me in a tailspin. If he found her in Padre Island, he would still be searching for her, and she probably won't escape him for long. I suspect he found her sooner than she realized, and he was about to execute another planned attempt at kidnapping her.

I get in the car and call Philip to meet me here. There is no way that I will allow her to be unguarded without me or someone looking after her. As I check my emails and catch up on returning messages, I notice Philip,

Emma's newly appointed security detail, pull up in the parking lot. I get out of the car and tell him what is at stake. After many assurances that he understands that Emma is not to leave his sight, I send a message to Emma before I leave the parking lot of her complex.

> Eduardo: Philip is outside your apartment and is keeping watch on you. DO NOT go anywhere without him.

I'm waiting for her to text me back. The minutes tick by, and I begin to feel unsettled as the city lights pass by in a blur of colors through my window. I tap my fingers on the steering wheel, trying to calm the anxiety I have radiating through my body. No other person can unsettle me like this—only Emma. A text message alert displays on my car screen. I hit play, and a female voice speaks Emma's message.

> Emma: Yes, sir.

I groan at the double entendre her comment insinuates. I speak into the car's voice assistant and send off a reply to her message.

> Eduardo: Are you trying to make me wreck? Miss you already.

This time her answer comes without delay.

> Emma: Please don't wreck.

> Emma: Miss you more. Chat later?

Her sincerity makes me smile. I love how much she cares, and I don't miss the hidden meaning of her comment.

> Eduardo: I'll never leave you again. More than chat later;)

Once those words enter the cyber air, I know truer words have never been said. I was forced to leave Emma, but nothing can come between us again. I snort aloud in the car for my use of a 'wink emoji.'

"What the fuck is wrong with me?" I utter to no one.

My brother would have a field day with these jokes at my expense. I have, for one, been busting his balls about his devotion to his fiancée. I'll have to do better when I see them, I suppose.

I pull into my parking spot and take the private elevator to my residence. My place has a separate key card for the keypad to get to my floor. It would be much easier to have Emma stay here. Then, I would not have to worry as much about her safety, not to mention the security system in my home is top-notch. That is a huge relief because I'll be able to keep an eye on her.

I just have to address her working schedule.

I don't care if she works. I fully support her independence, but not when a psychopath is stalking her. At least she has some safety measures in place there at the hospital. I'll just have to add to it. Contemplating how I will do all of this, I head to my office to make the calls that need to be made today.

"Eduardo. How are you, son?" I hear a door close as I suspect he is going to his office for a more private conversation. I rarely phone my father for a social call. I reserve those for my darling of a mother.

"Father, I need to talk with you about a girl."

I hear him getting out some glasses as if he thinks this is a call for celebration. He must think I am telling him about a marriage proposal or accidental pregnancy. Either of which would result in both, one way or the other. To be married with an heir. The click of ice confirms my suspicions.

"Continue. I can't wait—" He stops abruptly at the interruption.

"It's not simple." I know he can't possibly guess where I am going with this.

"Is she pregnant? Not a problem," he continues, as if it means nothing to him either way.

"Not yet, but it is someone you know." I clear my throat, contemplating how to give him all the news.

"Who is she, Eduardo? How do we know her?" I hear him take in a drink of alcohol as he blows a loud sigh into the phone.

"It's Emma." I pause for a bit when he doesn't speak. "It's always been Emma."

The glass, probably empty, hits the desk with a clunk. "What? Did I hear her parents died? The Ortiz family? What is going on, son?"

I told him what Emma told me, how we reunited in Houston, and how her safety was jeopardized. How I plan to take care of her, marry her.

"You can tell Mom the good news," I chide.

He snorts. "I hardly call this good news. Even telling your Catholic mother about an unplanned pregnancy is better than this." More ice clicks in a glass.

"Well, that is certainly a possibility now." I laugh so he knows I am mostly joking, but I wouldn't care if she gets pregnant with my child. That's the plan for later, anyway. I don't want to be the one to take away her choices though. She's had enough of that.

"I'm going to call her Uncle Andrés and see what he is doing to ensure her safety, and I hope I can count on you for support as your son and for your future daughter-in-law."

He sighs into the phone. "Of course, son. I just wish you hadn't picked the one woman you couldn't have. There are so many other options—"

"There are no other options," I growl. "And I wouldn't have to go through such a difficult time to be with the one person I love if it wasn't made this way. Things would have been so different if no one interfered. She'd be safe from so many unnecessary dangers."

"I'm sure you will discover that that isn't true, Eduardo, but I'll support you with anything you need. You can count on your family for that."

I hang up and can't help but reflect on the conversation with my father. What did he mean that it isn't true regarding unnecessary dangers? She wouldn't have met Julian if her mom hadn't stopped us from seeing each other. She would have been promised to me. That was always the plan, until it wasn't. Her parents would have been protected.

Alive.

I struggle to see how it could have turned out any different if she were mine.

I shower, hesitant to remove the imprint of Emma's smell on my skin. As I walk, I get a faint whiff of her scent and groan at the thought of last night. The anticipation of seeing her again is too much now. I must put her out of my mind if I intend to get any work done today.

I get out of the shower, needing to get to the gym and see how the new restaurant owners we selected for the space in our nourishment center are orchestrating, implementing the design, and advertising for their new customers. Before, they had a food truck-type establishment in the area, which would get them a guaranteed flow of customers who wouldn't hesitate to pay for a good product. This establishment is the type of place that could make them succeed and pin their name on the Houston middle- and upper-class demographic map. I, for one, am hooked and am glad to have a lovely family-run business in my gym catering to healthy food options for our patrons.

As I walk out the door, my phone rings, and I see it's my brother, Ram. I decide to make a coffee before leaving and prepare myself mentally for whatever he has to say. I am sure my father has already called him or, even worse, my mother.

I answer the phone without saying hello. It isn't needed because I already hear his voice coming through the phone.

"So, you told Dad that you are getting married?" I hear laughter coming out of the speaker along with a female voice.

"I am glad you are both laughing at my expense." I can't help but chuckle at his teasing. I had this coming.

"Let me ask this. Does Emma know she is getting married?" He starts laughing harder, a full belly laugh, wheezing as he tries to stop.

"Don't keel over without your inhaler," I reprimand him. "I'd hate to see you wheeze to death," I deadpan.

"Oh god, oh god. Okay, that was just too good to pass up. Mom called and told me the good news. Seriously though, does Emma know? Did you actually propose?"

I contemplate my words before I ask him. On the way home, I had thought about it but wasn't sure if it was a good idea. "Do you think I should ask her uncle for her hand in marriage?"

The line is quiet, and I swear I think Ram hung up or the line was disconnected. "You're serious, aren't you?" Ram's tone is quieter, and I hear a door close behind him.

"Yes. I have always loved Emma, and now...fuck, Ram. She is so alone, and I'm afraid something will happen to her. I left Philip with her as her protection when I am not there, but I didn't want to leave her side. I can't help but think about how things would have been different had we had the chance to be together."

Ram clears his throat. "I think you should call her uncle and see what's going on and get more details about this family. You know something is happening, and I bet it has more to do with Emma. Also, yes, you should ask her uncle for permission. I think he will be more than happy with the arrangement."

I nod and think about when I should call. "I guess I'll call sooner than later, bro. Thanks for the advice."

"Anytime, man." He hangs up, and the wave of uncertainty breaks, battering me with the fear that I could lose her again. I can't let that happen.

CHAPTER TWENTY-FIVE

EMMA

I finally get to spend a night with Liv. It seems like I never see her anymore. She has been spending all her time with her new hottie, Dax. I totally approve of that male specimen for her. I had to witness the emotional roller coaster of Brodie and Liv's relationship. After the accident, she seems to be coming more and more out of the personal guilt bubble she perpetually floats around in. The girl had a complicated history with that guy but also deserves happiness. The happiness that she currently has now with Dax.

I bite my lip. I understand how guilt can be all-consuming. I finally feel alive since reuniting with Eduardo. He has brought back so many happy memories from my childhood, and we frequently talk about everything we did when we were younger. Nostalgia is a bitch, and I welcome her with open arms. I wish those memories didn't have to end, where we had our separate lives without creating memories together, but we have this second chance to recreate new ones—our future together.

BLACK WAVE

I heard back from the girls in Texas about our upcoming girls' trip, so I decide to text Liv.

> Emma: Hey! The girls are coming to visit. It's gonna be hella fun.

Not waiting for a reply, I take a quick shower, and then we can plan our attack on the town. I just have to run the details by Eduardo. He doesn't ask because he wants to control me. He asks because he wants to keep me safe, and I love that about him. He is so different from the men I grew up with.

I shower quickly, not bothering to wash my hair. It's almost coming out of my messy bun. I flip my hair back, and that's when I see a message written in the foggy condensation on the mirror.

I really hate condensation, I think to myself. *Liv is such a trickster.* I anticipate her shouting, *"Emma, the condensation...Ohr Nor."* It was our thing while working in the ER on Padre Island when we would place our iced coffees in the cubby. Every time we picked the plastic cups up, water would drip off the bottom, and we'd reenact our favorite Australian-based show.

When I get closer to the mirror, my pulse spikes. I start to feel faint, and I think I might pass out. I grip onto the counter, trying to prevent myself from hyperventilating. Once again, I look at the mirror in disbelief. Tears threaten to fall from my eyes, and my vision becomes blurry. I blink them back effectively, clearing my sight. I begin slowing my breathing down and chant in my head.

Breathe in.

Breathe out.

Don't run from me Emma

I can't look at the writing anymore. I wrap the towel tighter around my body and quickly leave the bathroom to call Eduardo. I almost crash into the door when I see someone in my room.

I jump back quickly. "Oh dear god, I didn't hear you come in." I laugh and look at her. "Did you just get home from work?"

Liv looks over at me, and I know she wants to ask me questions—the ones I have repeatedly been vague about. I see the concern in her stare, and that guts me. I want so badly to share my secrets with her, to lessen my burden by confiding in my best friend, but that would be selfish of me. I was selfish before, and the price was losing my family. Julian killed them. My sister, my best friend. I won't let that happen to Liv, and to protect her, I have to keep my secrets and somehow convey that she means the world to me. I look away.

"Let me get changed," I tell her and shut the door, effectively shutting her out, as well as the conversation. I hear the door to my room close, signaling Liv's departure. I immediately pick up my phone and call Eduardo.

It goes straight to voicemail. "Great. I guess I'll call Philip," I say aloud.

He answers on the second ring. "Is everything okay?" I hear his voice increase in intensity.

"Umm, yes. I tried to call Eduardo, and he wasn't answering. Do you know where he is?" The line is silent for a minute, and Philip clears his throat.

"Business." He doesn't elaborate. "Do you need anything? Are you upset about something? Did something happen?" I hear the urgency in his voice increase with each question. I hear the sound of the door unlocking, and I am afraid he will barge in at any moment. That would take a lot of explaining that I don't think I could do at this point, with Liv already witnessing my weird behavior.

"No, I'm okay," I say quickly before he scares Liv and bursts in, further adding to the many secrets I am hiding.

I can sense Liv getting close to asking me. The mental questions show through on her scrunched-up eyebrows or her narrowing eyes—suspicions I tend to downplay or use distraction techniques to prevent the onslaught of her questioning things I cannot speak to her about.

"Can you tell Eduardo I have to talk with him?" I wait, thinking about bothering him. "But it isn't urgent."

I hear him sigh, almost in relief. He must be returning to his car. "Of course, Emma. I'm just outside if you need anything, okay?" He declares reassuringly.

I nod, even though he can't see me. "Okay, Philip. Thanks."

I decided not to make a big deal of it or worry anyone. Liv is here with me, and Philip is outside. I'm safe. I repeat the words in my head until I believe them to be true. I'll tell Eduardo when he calls me—no need to panic. I change into my sleep attire and go to find Liv, but first, I need some wine.

I search for Liv and see her watching me from the kitchen. She grabs a wine glass from the shelf, pours a chardonnay, and caps it with a top that keeps it fresh. I can feel Liv staring and watching my every movement. She lifts the glass in my direction, and I give her a subtle nod indicating that I'll take a glass too. She is using Jedi mind trick nursing skills to assess me. I almost snort. My face will remain blank. I am the master of secrets.

"Here," she says, handing me a glass of wine. "You look like you need this." She probably thinks the wine will loosen my lips and get me talking, but I hate to disappoint her if that is her objective. Maybe she thinks I need one, and I think the worst about my best friend's intentions. I have become the most distrusting person ever. She sits next to me, pulling her feet underneath her.

"How was your day?" I ask, taking a big pull from my wine glass. And back to those distraction techniques I am so good at.

"Good," Liv comments. "I saw Dax there," she states excitedly, and I can't help but smile. She loves talking about Dax. Seeing her happy again makes me happy.

"No way!" We sit on the couch with our wine glasses in hand. "Tell me everything." I grab her leg and squeal, genuinely excited to hear about Liv and her new man.

She tells me about her insecurities with her boyfriend but is happy they are together. He made it official that they were an item, and I'm sure it will spread throughout the hospital rumor mill.

Thinking I hear my phone ring, I run to my room, shouting that I will be right back. When I get there, it is just a group chat from work, and I roll my eyes. I throw my hair back up in a messy bun and walk out to rejoin Liv. I see that she has put on some music and is dancing to Halsey's "Bad at Love."

"That's my girl," I call out as I join her in screaming lyrics into a wine glass. We laugh hysterically, and I don't remember feeling so carefree. We fall onto the couch, and another song ends as we sip our wine.

Liv looks over to me and says, "So, will you tell me why I came home and saw Eduardo practically naked in his boxers, pulling up his pants in front of me before he left?"

I wince at the thought of her witnessing my man pull his pants up, but I can't help but put the visual in my head. Liv is watching me, expecting an answer, and I feel like a shit friend for constantly dodging a response to her questions, so instead, I go for honesty, or what little I can provide.

"I sent Jameson home, and Eduardo came over after he left. I didn't plan on anything happening between us, but it did, and that's all there is to it."

Liv looks at me in shock that I opened up to her. A slow smile spreads across her face, and I almost laugh at how much I needed this girl talk with her.

"How did you meet him?" She sits up straighter, hungry for information.

"And here it begins, the never-ending questions." I roll my eyes playfully. She smacks my leg with her hand. "Oh, you are not getting out of this one, Ems."

"Long story short, an employee of his was injured at the club, and I guess that was what brought him in. The triage nurse, the one I call Satan, took him into the trauma bay and handed me the chart. I entered the room to introduce myself and placed him on the monitors. I called the doctor—"

"Trauma bay?" Liv interjects, eyebrows raised in question.

I pause before speaking, taking another drink of my wine, not wanting to have this conversation. "Stab wound to the hand." I bite my lip, not wanting to elaborate.

"What?" Liv practically screams. "Stab wound to the hand?" She flicks her hand at me.

I try to downplay it as much as possible because it really was nothing life-threatening. "Oh, it was nothing. It needed some stitches and didn't hit anything important in the way of vessels. Weirdly, it looked more bloody than the wound was. Lucky, actually. You know how some things are more vascular, and the bleeding looks worse?" I pause, deciding how much I want to say. I'm sure it wasn't just his blood, but that's not for her to know.

Liv looks at me. "The hand is more vascular?" she asks, tilting her head sideways, questioning my medical knowledge.

"Whatever, let me finish the story." She puts her hand up, signaling for me to continue. "Eduardo showed up, said something to his employee, and sat in a chair, staring at me while I worked."

"And he sent you flowers?" She smiles at me, and I almost sigh.

"Yes, he did. Weren't they beautiful?" I gaze adoringly at the wilting floral arrangement.

"Definitely." Liv wants to say more but doesn't, instead opting out for a change. "So when are the girls coming?" she asks excitedly.

I immediately perk up at this. "In a few weeks!" I am vibrating with excited energy at this point.

"Well, we will have to plan a great outing for them and show them the town," Liv states, happy to be spending time with me. I nod in acknowledgment but become weary.

Liv grabs my hand. Her touch reassures me without prying for more information.

"We also have to go shopping for outfits," I tell her.

"Sounds like a good time, Emma, but I don't have much money to go shopping," Liv states matter-of-factly.

I grab Liv's hands, holding both in an embrace. I feel so many emotions flow through me as I hold onto her hands. The friend who had always been there for me. Who introduced me to her friends and made me feel welcome from day one.

"Don't worry about it, Liv, I got you, my boo," I say. "I got you covered, girl."

She nods. I feel sadness radiating off her, but also for myself. I swallow the lump forming in my throat.

Don't go.

I want to tell you everything.

If only it wouldn't get you killed.

Like my family.

Liv gets up from the couch, letting go of my hand. She tells me she has some things to do. I sit there and think about everything that Liv and I said, as well as the unspoken words. We both are in newish relationships, and I am terrified. I am so terrified of royally screwing it up.

I go back to my room and wait for Eduardo to call me. I decide to take one of my romance novels and begin reading about fated mates. I love this stuff. I read for an hour and feel my eyes become heavy with sleep. I tuck my Kindle under my pillow and prepare for a restless night when my phone rings.

I check the number and notice that Eduardo is calling. I answer the phone in earnest.

CHAPTER TWENTY-SIX

EDUARDO

I have to work tonight at the club as a few things require my attention. I didn't want to tell Emma, but I am meeting someone who may have information about Julian and the Martinez family. It's the perfect time for the meeting, since she isn't here with me, electing to spend some quality time with her friend, Liv. Although it won't be a late night, I miss having her here with me. The club is also a primary source of my income, as much as the other dealings that occur here, supplying a better compensation for my family's overall business endeavors.

Seth, one of my father's business associates, was in attendance. He seemed to remember the name of Julian's father and said he would do some digging around for me. I asked him to use discretion; he knew he owed me a favor. That's the thing about this business. We all have our secrets that we want to keep. The one thing our organization hates is associates who talk.

At the close of the meeting, he vowed to stay in touch, and I felt a small amount of relief in knowing that we might find out what really happened to her parents and sister and why Emma is still being pursued. All along, I've suspected there is more to the story than just Julian wanting Emma for himself.

My phone rings, tearing me away from my thoughts. I go upstairs to my office from the basement's back stairwell, where we usually conduct business. This area has a room for complete privacy and is soundproofed. It's also where we keep people who need questioning. I look down at my screen and see that it's Philip calling.

"Yes, Philip." I enter the office and loosen my tie.

"Boss, I'm sorry to bother you, but Emma was trying to reach you. She called me and sounded…off. I asked if she needed anything and was on my way up when she said no, but for you to call her."

My pulse quickens. "Have you seen anything? You are there at her apartment, correct?" I pour myself a drink and let the cool amber liquid settle me. He reassures me he is there and hasn't seen anything that appears suspicious. Liv is there with her, and she is fine. So why do I feel unsettled?

"Thanks. I'll call her now." I hang up and immediately call Emma. Fuck, I knew that I should have just brought her here. I hate that she is alone at night. Either she comes here with me or—

"Eduardo?" She sounds out of breath, and I am on alert.

"Baby, is everything okay? What's wrong?" I suddenly feel that there is most definitely something very, very wrong.

"Umm," she hesitates. "I'm okay. Liv is here, and Philip is outside, but…"

"Emma, spit it out," I almost yell into the phone, trying not to scream at her. It isn't her. It's my fear of losing her again. I'm scared that something might happen. I grab my keys and head out the door. "I'm going to get you. Stay there and pack a bag. No, better yet, pack a suitcase."

She's quiet on the other line for a minute, and I think she hung up. I look at the phone, and she is still there.

That's when I hear her say, "Okay, hurry." And I fucking do.

I speed all the way over there and think of all the ways to gut this prick slowly and painfully. I hate the number he did on Emma and is still trying to get to her. If he touches a hair on her head, he's dead. Honestly, he's dead anyway once I find him. I'm raging when I pull into her apartment complex parking lot. What was I thinking even allowing her to stay here? Without me?

I jump out of the car and see Philip run over to me.

"Is something wrong, Boss?" The concern in Philip's voice is palpable, and I look over to him.

"Emma called and sounded off, almost scared just like you said. I didn't give her time to explain and she told me to hurry. I'm going in to get her and bring her home with me." I almost say *where she belongs*, but I don't.

"Wait there, and then follow us to the penthouse," I bark as I race away, taking two steps at a time to Emma's door. I knock lightly and text her that I'm outside. She opens the door, slowly stepping away. I walk in and close the door behind me. I look her up and down, and she jumps into my arms.

"It's okay, baby. What is it?"

She breaks away and looks at me. "I have to show you." She grabs my hand and leads me into her room. I'm confused as hell and wonder what she is doing.

When we reach her room, she closes the door behind me. She saunters into the bathroom, almost hesitating, then starts the shower. She closes the door and returns to stand in front of me. Now, I am confused. I'm sure my bafflement is visible on my face. Where is she going with this? She looks at me, biting her lip. I arch an eyebrow at her and wait, not uttering a word. She clears her throat and averts her eyes.

"I came home and was looking forward to hanging out with Liv." She pauses and still hasn't made eye contact with me as she recounts the events. "I took a shower, and I…" She trails off, and her breathing is labored, as if what she is about to say pains her.

"What is it, Emma?" I am freaking out inside and don't want to scare her by yelling. "You can tell me. I'll fix it."

She lets out a small gasp, almost a cry, shaking her head back and forth. I am on high alert, not liking where this conversation is going. I want to shake her, make her tell me because I am freaking out. She looks me in the eye and says the words that are my undoing.

"Eduardo, he found me."

I see red. My nostrils flare, and I try to hide my anger. "What do you mean he found you?" I spit out. "Baby?"

She doesn't say anything. Instead, she grabs my hand and leads me into the steamy bathroom. She looks at me and then points to the mirror.

That's when I see it.

Don't run from me Emma.

I stare at it. My breathing is labored. I get my phone and make a call.

"Philip, we have a crisis here. Emma is in danger. We are going to my place. Have extra security sent. She won't be back here alone and definitely not to sleep. We will be out after she packs up her things."

I turn to her and pull her into a smothering hug. "Baby, I won't let him have you."

I think to myself and repeat it in my head, *You are mine.*

Mine to love.

Mine to protect.

"Now, let's get out of here."

I help Emma pack a bag for now so we can get the fuck out of here. She leaves Liv a note to tell her that I came over and persuaded her to stay at my place. She left the message in plain sight and wrote in a playful tone, so Liv thinks nothing of it. Little does she know the chaos brewing surrounding Emma's life.

We drive to my house in record time and enter my secure complex. I knew I should have brought Emma over here and insisted she stay with me, but I was trying to be considerate of her feelings and independence. I knew she was staying with Liv and came to Houston to help her deal with some issues. I also know that her reasons weren't entirely selfless. She was scared of Julian and tried hiding from him after saying he found her in Padre Island.

After I get her settled in my room, I leave her to ensure everyone knows that Emma is my number-one priority and she is to be watched at all times. I added another person to her security detail along with Philip to ensure she is protected with another set of fresh, watchful eyes. I also told them that if she wants to get a hold of me, she is to be immediately put through. If I am in a meeting, interrupt. I don't know how to make it any clearer.

I can't imagine if something had happened and she couldn't reach me. In fact, that is what happened. She had tried to contact me but couldn't. What if it was more serious? What if he was there? I shiver at the thought of her being helpless and taken from me. I won't let it happen. Maybe I can put a tracking device on her. We will get something for her tomorrow—a necklace or bracelet to let us know where she is, just in case. That will at least make me feel a little better when I don't have my own eyes on her.

I need to talk with Emma, so I return to our room and find her sitting on the bed. Her legs are crossed, and her head is in her hand. I close the door behind me and see her head swing up. Her emerald-green eyes are fixed on me. I immediately go over and sit on the bed next to her. I pick her up and sit her on my lap. She holds on to me and places her arms around my neck. Her scent envelopes me, and I kiss her head, saying soothing words I didn't think I was capable of. My life doesn't allow for this kind of talk, but with Emma, I find myself saying everything I've ever wanted to tell her.

Words I've thought about saying to her if I was given a second chance.

Words I would have said to her if this wasn't our second chance, but if we had stayed together all this time.

She leans into me and raises her head to look up at me. I bring my lips down to hers and kiss her passionately. I want to convey all my love to her, along with all my insecurities and fears. I try to tell her I can't lose her again, but I don't. Instead, I kiss her, letting my body show her what she means to me. I break the kiss reluctantly.

"Emma, we need to talk, and I want you to listen." She nods, and I am expecting more of a fight, but I guess when you have been hiding and fearing for your life, you have to explore all options.

I tell her about the addition to her necklace we will get soon. She agrees, and nothing will seem amiss since she already wears this necklace. I want to buy her something unique; this isn't exactly how I envisioned this going. At least it will serve a purpose and keep her safe.

The next piece of jewelry will be an engagement ring. That could be an option. If I marry her, then everyone will know she is mine. She will be safer, except this guy is unhinged. It will bring her into the spotlight, and she doesn't want that either. When I give her a ring, I want it to be because we want to be married, not for her to be forced into a marriage of convenience with me. I don't think she would see it as that, but that's how it would seem. She has had so many choices taken from her that I want her to choose me.

"Emma, I will have you stay here. We also need to figure out something with your work schedule. Do you want to continue to work?" I ask her because I don't want to take that choice away from her.

"Yes," she replies. "Do you think it's okay and safe for me to continue working at the hospital?"

I want to answer no, but I can't have her at the club with me all night. In the daylight, she is safer. Monsters come out to play at night. That is what Julian is—a monster.

"What if we change your shift to nights? Would that work? I would know where you are for those few days, and I can have extra security around for you without drawing suspicions. I pick you up from work, and you sleep at our place. We will be spending a lot of quality time together."

I smile at her and bring her hand up to my lips. I lightly press an open-mouthed kiss to her hand and bring her finger into my mouth. I suck on her finger and lightly bite her. She pulls her hand back and laughs.

"I like the plan," she says. "But right now, I'd like to not think about the plan." She smiles mischievously at me.

BLACK WAVE

I stand up and shrug off my jacket. "I agree. No more talking in general. Just you screaming my name." I lunge at her and bury my mouth in her neck. She shrieks with laughter, and a wave of happiness washes over me at hearing that sound. A sound I hope to hear for years to come.

CHAPTER TWENTY-SEVEN

EMMA

"Hey, sis, are you ready to go?" Evie jumps up on top of the counter with excitement.

I swat her ass with my cleaning rag. "Get off the counter. We have customers." I place my hand on my hip, and she laughs.

Evie looks around at the only customer in the corner of the cafe with Airpods on, typing away on a computer. She snorts. "Nice mom impression, Em. And you have, like, one customer. For real though. I'm starved, and I'm thinking…" She pauses as if there is anything to think about. "Street tacos?" She says this like it's a question, but we both know that she has her sights set on the Me Muero Por Los Tacos food truck. It literally translates to I'm dying for tacos. This spot, located across from the park, has become one of our favorite places to eat and is super inexpensive. The truck is run by a young couple who have quite the following. In the summer, they also go to the beach and do fruit cups, paletas, and liquadas. My mouth waters at the thought of the frozen sweetness on a hot Texan day.

"Hmm." I give my most pensive look, staring out into the vast emptiness of the cafe. The traffic from lunch ended as quickly as it started. "I suppose we could do street tacos." As I say this, my treacherous thoughts quickly go to craving some elote. Their street corn covered in crema and spices is orgasmic.

We hear the door's chime, alerting us to another person entering the store. We avert our gaze to see Jackson walking in, interrupting our heated debate about elote versus their spiced potato wedges.

He throws his bag behind the counter. "Ladies, looking ravishing as usual." He gives us a wink, and that causes Evie to laugh. He looks her way and eye fucks her slowly, and bites his lip to stifle a moan. I almost laugh at his playboy act. We all know Jackson is a fun guy. You just have to realize that there isn't more to him. If you are looking for a romp in the sack with nothing meaningful, then he's your guy. Many girls have tried to get him to commit, but he is upfront with them all. If they think they can change him, they will be sorely disappointed with the outcome.

Of course, Evie isn't falling for his womanizing tactics. She rolls her eyes. "Still not going out with you, Jackson." She looks him up and down, clearly not liking what she sees.

"Eves." He clutches his chest and band T-shirt with his hand. "You wound me with your cruelty." His hair falls into his face, and he brushes it back. I have seen this move hit its mark with the ladies, and I can't say that he doesn't have rizz. The boy is extraordinarily charming, and he knows it.

"Please," she counters, "that's why I saw you come out of the dressing room with Katrina wiping her mouth at The Naked Contessa boutique." She arches an eyebrow, begging him to deny it.

The look in his eye says he enjoyed that encounter very much. "You are too much, Eves, but it's time for me to clock in and for you guys to have some fun." He waggles his eyebrows as he walks off.

"That guy is a piece of work," Evie mutters.

I laugh. "I think you like him, Evie. I see the way you look at him. He is kind of hot." She doesn't deny it.

"Em, I don't mind sharing. I just don't want to share my men." She smirks and jumps off the counter. "You know what I mean?" She isn't looking at me but at Jackson, who stands there with his mouth open. He quickly closes it as I look between the two of them.

"I have no idea what that means." I toss the cleaning rag over the counter and grab my bag as Jackson rounds the corner. He recovers from whatever that expression was that flashed on his face, getting straight into work mode.

"Have a great day, ladies." He gives us a little wave but doesn't look back at us as Evie and I exit the shop. Weird.

We walk arm-in-arm laughing about what we did today. "Let's cut through here," *Evie says.* "I'm so hungry I could chew my arm off."

We cut through the alley instead of walking around the blocks to get to the food truck, electing to take a more direct route. We are so enveloped in our conversation as we reach the end of one alley to enter the next one that we don't notice them until we come face-to-face with two men. We recognize both, and I'm immediately frozen in place. I open my mouth to speak, but nothing comes out.

I feel a tug at my arm and hear my sister speak up. "What do you want, Julian?" *He takes his gaze off me, and I feel as though I can breathe again, if only momentarily.*

"This doesn't concern you, Evie. This is between Emma and me." *He steps closer to me while maintaining eye contact with my sister.*

"Of course, it concerns me," *she counters.* "Emma is my sister. My twin sister," *she states defensively. Julian just snorts.*

"Well, even that can be changed, Evie." *He nods at his driver, urging Marcus forward. Marcus grabs Evie's hand and tries to drag her away from me.*

"Marcus, what are you doing?" *I turn to try to help my sister.*

Julian grabs my arm. "Do not say another man's name in my presence ever again. Do you understand me, Emma?" *His fingers are digging into my arm and will surely leave bruises. I try my best to pretend he isn't hurting me, but I know he will just hurt me more until I make a sound alerting him that I am in pain. I let out a small whimper, and he disengages his grip slightly. He must feel that the hurt isn't enough if I am not showing I am hurting.*

"Emma," *Evie cries out.* "Are you okay?" *She tries to push Marcus away, but he is just too big for her to fight off.*

"Shut her up," *Julian barks at Marcus. He covers Evie's mouth.*

"Ouch!" *I hear Marucs say and yell expletives at Evie in Spanish.* "You stupid bitch." *I hear Marcus shout* "fuck" *as I hear the sound of a hit. I look to see Evie slumped over on the ground as Marcus bends over, holding his crotch. Evie is lying on the ground, a bruise already showing on her face.*

"Well, look at what you've done now, Emma." *He growls in anger at me.* "You made Marcus have to hurt your sister."

"Fucking bitch bit me and kicked me in the balls," *he snarls as he tries to stand upright.*

Julian pays no attention to his hurt driver. "You'll have to make that up to me, won't you, sweetheart?" *he says sweetly, as if he almost cares about me while he continues stroking my cheek. I want to throw up as the tears come rushing out and down my face. He holds me close, stroking my hair. "Shh, it's okay, honey, I'll make it better." I shake in his embrace. "Leave the sister there, Marcus. Let's go." He pulls me along.*

"No, Julian, stop." I try to escape from his hold. "We can't leave her there, Julian, please," I beg, yet he keeps moving. I look back at my sister slumped over on the floor. I break away from him and run over to Evie, dropping down by her side. I notice that she is still breathing. Julian picks me up, dragging me away. I see the SUV parked around the corner as he drags me to it.

"No, Julian, please, stop. We can't leave Evie. Evie!" I cry out. "Stop."

But he doesn't stop. He never will stop.

I feel someone shaking me. "Don't touch me!" I scream, and then I feel someone holding me. I cry out and try to escape. I open up my eyes, but I only see darkness. I feel someone stroking my head.

"Shh, baby. It's me, Eduardo. It's okay. I've got you. It's just a dream. You're safe."

I stifle a cry at his words. "I'm safe," I repeat.

He kisses my head, and my breathing starts to regulate from the fight-or-flight response I felt upon awakening from the nightmare. I'm sweating, but I also feel cold. Goose bumps gather along my body as I fight the twitches that threaten to take over.

Eduardo starts to rock me back and forth in a soothing manner, all the while whispering softly in my ear, repeatedly verbalizing that I am safe, that he loves me.

I grow stiff in his arms. I turn to him, and the soft moonlight illuminates his tan features. He is looking at me lovingly.

"You love me?" I ask in question.

He sighs, kissing my cheek. "Of course, I love you, Emma. I was given a second chance with you. I just regret that I didn't fight harder for you—for us. I thought I was doing what was right. I should have been there to protect you all along."

I look into his chocolate-brown eyes and see the truth there—the sincerity.

Hearing him say this is my undoing. All the emotions I have held back come bursting in a tsunami of tears. I cry for my family and mourn their death. I realize that I haven't let myself miss them since they passed away. My sister. My best friend. Eduardo holds me through it all, rubbing my back until there are no more tears to cry. Until all I have left are some hiccups.

I get the sleeve of his hoodie that he placed on me when we got to his house and bring it up to my nose. His smell—whisky and leather—lingers on it and reminds me of home. A home I had when I was younger around my family. When Eduardo was around wearing a leather jacket that made him devilishly handsome. A jacket he placed on me when we went outside, sneaking out to look at the stars.

I bring the sleeve over my hand and wipe away the tears that have crested and lay fallen, pooling along the neckline in their aftermath. The taste of my salty tears lingers, and I wipe the evidence away. Eduardo rises toward me, kisses my tear-stained face, and places soft, open-mouthed kisses all over. He holds my face in his hands and stares into my green eyes.

"Emma, I promise I will find this guy and end his life. I never want you to feel unsafe again, and I promise to keep you safe for as long as I walk this earth. You are my everything." He trails a finger down my cheek, and I shiver in the wake of his sensual touch.

My body is alight; he is the match, burning me from the inside out. I can no longer deny that we were always meant to be. Call it kismet. I know for sure that I am safe with him. While I can no longer help my family, I will make sure to help myself and seek the revenge my family should and will have.

I look him in the eyes. "You'll help me kill him?" I touch his face and keep my hand on his cheek.

He holds onto my hand. "Yes, baby. I will be there when you end his life. I want to witness you rise in a giant wave of destruction, taking out anyone who stands in your wake. Whoever stands in the way of getting your revenge. You are strong. You withstood so much and emerged stronger, a punishing force that will prevail. I promise you."

My chest rises and falls at his encouraging words.

He thinks I am strong.

He believes in me.

I will get my revenge.

I repeatedly tell myself this until I believe these unspoken words to be true. It's as if he has my heart in his hand and is physically mending the broken pieces together with a needle and sutures.

Friedrich Nietzsche once said, *"What doesn't kill you makes you stronger."* Songs were even written about it. My heart withstood the worst heartbreaks and suffering; through it all, I am reborn, resilient, and strong.

CHAPTER TWENTY-EIGHT

EDUARDO

I got Emma to change her schedule to night shifts, and I feel better knowing that she is in a somewhat secure building with video surveillance and many people who would notice her absence should it ever occur. I can tell she doesn't like the shift as much, but after several weeks, she has developed a routine. Even the nurse she calls Satan has backed off. All he needed was a little persuasion.

I laugh at how he almost pissed his pants when I confronted him. Serves him right. She is working peacefully, free of that dickwad's insulting behavior, and is able to be part of the much-needed ER team. Not to mention that she is also well-liked there. She has a fantastic personality, and she is hot. I hate that people ask her out or flirt with her, because it comes up when I get updates about her throughout the night. Luckily, I know that she is committed to me and that trust is something I have with her. We have history and a long-standing friendship, which are the makings of a strong future. A future that we will be able to have now.

BLACK WAVE

I hate the way things happened. She was forced to leave Brownsville, but I may have never had the chance to reunite with her if not for Julian's actions against her family and her meeting Liv in school. He is still after her, and that thought frightens me more than I care to admit. I have never had a weak spot, but now I do. I can be exploited, and they know I will do everything in my power to make sure she is safe and keep her with me always. Not from just Julian, but from the countless criminals that come into my life through our various business ventures. Enemies who wouldn't care about using my girlfriend or, later on, my wife and kids to get what they want. I'd like to let them know what that means to hurt what's mine.

My heart.

My life.

My future wife.

The thought brings a smile to my face.

"Eduardo? Did you hear what I said?" Helena has this shit-eating grin on her face.

"What, Helena?" I try my best to use an intimidating voice on her, but she isn't buying it.

"Well, well, well. What has Eddie all preoccupied this morning?" she sings-songs, and my teeth grind at admitting that I was daydreaming about Emma. A beautiful short, blond-haired goddess I left this morning in my bed to sleep off her work night.

I recall her coming home. She places her bag on the foyer floor and walked into the house, removing her hair from her bun. She runs her hand through her hair and massages her scalp with her long fingers. I stand there in the kitchen, enthralled, sipping my Americano, having very impure thoughts about my girlfriend.

As if sensing these thoughts, she looks up at me and smiles the most sensual smile as she saunters over to me. I put my coffee down, and the lust that coats every pore of my body leaks my scent of arousal. She sits across from me at the counter and licks her lips. I stop the groan that threatens to escape my lips as I look her over. "How was your night?" I ask. I always want to ask her about her work night.

She sighs. "Busy. I am glad it's over with." She yawns, and my heart melts.

"Are you tired, baby?"

She looks at me and gives me a slight nod. "I want to go to sleep, but I'm just so wired from our last patient. There was an accident, the patients almost died, and we barely saved their lives. It's such a good feeling, but the adrenaline rush, mixed in with the fatigue, just makes me jittery and tired at the same time. It's like I had three espresso martini shots right before bed, ya, know?"

I shake my head, understanding the feeling. Maybe it applies to terminating a life instead of saving one, but the feeling is still the same.

"I understand, baby. I think I can help you to relax." I walk toward her, relinquishing my firm grasp on my coffee.

"Eduardo, I am covered in gross hospital cooties." She tries to scoot away, but I hold her in place.

"Emma, you aren't even wearing the scrubs anymore."

"Well, that's because we change into some at work and back into our clothes before we leave. Most people do. Oh, except for Satan."

I snort because she won't let the grudge go. "I still need a shower, Eduardo. I don't want to make you late." Her expression is sincere. "I know you are busy, and I take up a lot of your time."

"Emma, don't ever feel that way. You come first, and I run my own businesses. That is the perk of being the top dog." I laugh, and she visibly calms. "Now, let me take care of you."

I pull down her joggers and panties, inching her bottom off the barstool. They hang around her ankles, touching the floor, and I quickly remove them and her Converse sneakers. I drop to my knees and look at her above me. I kiss her foot and move myself upward, leaving a trail of kisses on her calf as I hook one leg over my shoulder. I make my way to her center, blowing a stream of air onto her core. I feel her shiver, and I look into her eyes as I make my way to part her folds.

A groan escapes me as I see her glistening pink pussy spread out for me. Her scent that is purely Emma, fills the air, and I swipe my tongue along her center, eliciting a moan from her. She slumps down a bit, trying to bring her center to me, and I hold her down with one hand splayed across her abdomen.

With her folds parted, I fuck her with my tongue. I suck on her clit and pump my fingers in and out of her cunt while curling them upward, flicking them upward to find the spot that makes her cry out. I remove my fingers and use both hands to bring her forward as I bury my face in her pussy. I hold her in place while I suck on her clit and she screams my name, holding my head in place as her body convulses.

She starts to giggle and tries backing away, but I continue to lap at her, cleaning up every bit of her cum. Her arms fall to the side, and I stand up, seeing her eye me from her slouched position. I wipe my mouth and chin. The wetness coats the back of my hand. She gives one slow exhale. I smile knowing I succeed in relaxing her.

"Now, how do you feel? Do you think you can go to sleep."

She doesn't even speak, just nods.

"Good," I say as I pick her up, guiding her to the shower. I place her on the expansive bathroom counter and start the shower. "I'll be at the gym. I'll call you after lunch?" I ask, and she continues to nod. "I see I have rendered you speechless," I say jokingly, rubbing at my jaw and licking my lips that still very much taste *like my sweet Emma's pretty pussy. She strips and laughs, watching my pants tent in the process.*

"Love you," she says as she gets into the spray of the water.

"Love you too," I say as I take my hard-on and reluctantly leave.

I'm pulled away from my thought of Emma to the sound of laughter. "Eddie?" Helena shakes her head. "Someone sure is smitten." She waves at a customer coming in.

"Don't fucking call me Eddie," I say, rubbing my hand across my face. I get a faint scent of Emma and smile.

"I would have thought you would say, don't call me smitten," she counters, and I shrug. "I knew it. Good for you," she replies, sincerity lacing her words. "You need a good woman in your life."

"Well, I have one, so you don't need to worry about that anymore."

Her smile widens. "About time."

I look over at the cafe, noticing a line forming at the counter. "How's the cafe doing, Helena? Have you noticed a lot of activity there?"

She looks at me, knowing I changed the subject, but not commenting on it. "Besides today?" She gestures over to the cafe, waving her hand about. "Yes, actually, there has been quite a lot."

"That's good to hear. I am glad for us but also delighted for the owners. They are hard-working and might just need this opportunity to get their name out in this area. Their food is fantastic and fits our location perfectly. I already overheard one of our gym customers asking about catering an event at their workplace, and that makes me happy to hear. They have the potential to branch out." Just as I begin to ask Helena another question, I see a familiar face sitting at a table with a woman who is not Emma's friend, Liv.

"Excuse me, Helena, I have to chat with someone."

"Oh, boy," Helena counters. "That's never good." She turns around to help a customer coming up to the counter.

I chuckle, not disagreeing. I turn to walk toward Jameson's friend, Dax. Now, to see what this is about.

I observe Dax and this girl for a bit to pick up a feel for the vibe. Their body language suggests an awkward conversation. Dax is mimicking a defensive stance, and it appears he would wish to be anywhere than here at this moment.

I reach their table and notice that the attractive woman is angry. Well, that's interesting. "How's it going? Dax, right?" I extend my hand in what I hope is a non-threatening way.

He takes my hand, shaking it in a firm grip. I expected his hands to be soft, but surprisingly, they are calloused. Maybe from surfing?

"Eduardo, good to see you."

So he does remember my name.

"Thanks again for your generosity at the club the other night."

I nod, shifting my gaze between him and the woman currently giving him daggers. His body would be dismembered all over my gym floor, if her looks could kill.

"Eduardo, this is Tatiana, one of my work colleagues."

She purses her lips, and I know exactly what this is about. Meeting in a public place. This is the 'I am seeing someone else' type of discussion. This woman is beautiful but probably a complete psycho.

I turn to her and see her dainty, manicured hand extend to me. I, in turn, embrace it. Amusement lingers in my eyes at this awkward-as-fuck exchange. Dax is exuding major anxiety at this situation. No doubt, he thinks I will tell Emma all about it, and in turn, she will tell Liv. I have to think about that for a bit. "Good to make your acquaintance Tatiana."

Dax eyes me up and down, noticing my slacks and button-down shirt. I know what he is silently implying. What am I doing here? He watches me with suspicion, which is fucking ironic since I'm not the one here with another woman.

"So...you don't look like you were exercising here? What brings you over? Looking for a membership?"

I laugh at this comment because the guy is clueless. I shake my head. "No, I don't need one since I own this gym." I wave my hand, extending it to the gym in an exaggerated performance.

I see the shock and questions that run through Dax's mind. He swallows, and I give him a menacing smile. I see the recognition on his face that alerts him to the fact that I am a dangerous man. Good, I think to myself. He should be afraid. If he does anything to upset Emma, I'll have his balls. If that means making her friend Liv unhappy, and it just so happens to make Emma worry about her further, then I will take that personally. I may be a mafia guy, but my parents loved each other, and I hate a fucking cheater.

"I had no idea," he says, looking between Tatiana and me.

"Yeah," I admit. "I have my hands in a little bit of everything, I guess you could say." Changing the course of this conversation, I say, "Emma was telling me about the gala. Are you guys going?"

I hear Tatiana snort—a very unladylike snort at that. I smirk, knowing precisely what I am doing, getting the hoped-for response. I look at Dax, the mirth dancing in my eyes. He scowls, knowing and understanding setting in. Tatiana must have thought I was referring to her when I asked if 'they' are going. Dax knows I am referring to Liv.

"Well," she replies sluggishly, "I thought I was going, but it appears that I am out of a date," she retorts, practically snarling like a rabid dog at Dax.

The guy has the decency to look remorseful. I look over at the girl who is now out of a date. She is attractive, no doubt, and well put together. Any man would be happy to have her as a companion to that function. No doubt she would be dressed to the nines. Tatiana perks up at my perusal, but it is not what she presumes.

I scrutinize people, assessing, judging, and calculating to see if they are a threat to anyone I care about, which happens to be Emma. I don't want any retaliation that could affect my little thief. Emma would be very upset if Tatiania is resentful toward Dax and takes it out on Liv, since they all work at the same hospital. They both have had some terrible things happen in their past, and as for my Emma, well, some are beyond that.

"Well, that's a shame. A beautiful woman like you shouldn't be waiting on anyone that doesn't put you first." She seems to perk up, eyes alight. "Unfortunately, I am already promised to another or I would take you." I give her a sincere smile and a good-bye handshake, hoping she can be someone's everything one day and stop taking the offered scraps.

"It was nice talking to you, Dax. I thought you should know that the girls will show up at the club for a girl's night. If you understand my meaning, I have everything set to ensure they are well taken care of." He nods appreciatively. I ask anyway just to confirm. "You work that night, right?"

He runs his hand through his hair. "Yep, Liv mentioned it briefly but didn't go into details, but I know I work. I appreciate that, Eduardo." His expression softens at the mention of his woman, Liv.

I wave it off dismissively as I walk away from the clusterfuck of this conversation. I chuckle to myself. Poor guy almost shit himself watching me, and the look on his face when I told him I dabbled in a bit of this and that. Fucking priceless, I laugh to myself. Now I have to wait until noon to call Emma.

CHAPTER TWENTY-NINE

EMMA

Eduardo and I fall into a pattern of domesticity. I almost forgot that I have an unhinged stalker after me. He vows to keep me safe, and I feel the safest I have ever been. Since the day Julian revealed his true colors, I haven't been familiar with having someone care about me like this. Not since my family was alive.

It's not that I don't appreciate everything Uncle Andrés did for me, risking his life and that of his men to break me out of Julian's stronghold. Now, I have someone I talk to every day. We eat dinner together when I am off, and if I have to work at night, we have breakfast before he leaves for the gym, and I sleep after working a night shift in the ER while he is off working. It's, umm, nice? Normal? I have a family again.

I try not to let the memories of my past taint my day. After all, it is my day off, and I want to see Liv. We had been making plans with the girls coming up from Corpus Christi to visit us, and it's finally here. Eduardo encourages me to have fun with them, but I have to have security with me at all times. I honestly don't fight it. I feel better knowing that I have someone watching out for me where I can let my guard down a bit.

I sent a group text to Emma, Val, and Ainsley, letting them know I was going to the apartment Liv and I shared. We are all meeting there, and the girl should be making record time on the interstate if I know my besties and their problem with adhering to the speed limit on the open Texas highway.

I pull up to the apartment with Philip by my side. "I don't see anyone around." I look in the parking lot as Philip drives us around once again.

"I'll walk you up and check things out. If everything looks clear, I'll wait in the car to ensure you are okay." He looks over at me, and I smile.

"Thank you, Philip. I appreciate that." I haven't returned to this place since I saw the writing on the wall. Literally. I shudder at the thought of him being around my belongings. Did he touch my things, place anything there to allow him to watch me?

When Eduardo and a few of his men went to gather most of my essentials, they checked the room extensively and couldn't find anything, but it still wouldn't surprise me if there were. Julian is very resourceful, and that thought is the nightmare my dreams are made of.

While waiting, I make a cup of coffee and get my laptop out of my bag. I glance down at my watch and wonder what is taking so long. "They should have been here by now," I mumble under my breath as I search for articles in the Brownsville newspapers about anything related to Julian. I'm reading an article about Julian's father being re-elected when the door swings open. A very green-looking Liv walks in with the assistance of Ainsley and Val. I jump out of my chair.

"Liv, what's wrong?" I immediately think the worst. Did Julian do something to her?

She looks up at me, and some vomit is on the side of her mouth. I grab a rag and head over to wipe it away. "Hey, girls, make yourself at home. I should have something for vomiting." They look at each other, worried about schooling their features, but they bring their bags to the living room and sit on the couch, looking over at us.

Liv tries to downplay things as usual. "I have been exhausted from school and work in clinicals. I felt super dizzy today and must be dehydrated because I haven't been drinking enough water." She looks around at us, seeing if we are buying the lies that she is selling.

I narrow my eyes at her, and she continues.

"You know how it is?"

I shake my head. "I think I have some medication to help with that.

Come on, let's get you cleaned up and find something to wear." I grab a water bottle from the fridge and hold her hand, leading her to her bedroom.

Once we get into Liv's bedroom, I close the door and turn around, hands on my hip. The annoyance is displayed in my features. "What the fuck, Liv?"

She looks like I slapped her. Okay, that may be too harsh. Her eyes narrow back at me.

"I could ask you the same. What the fuck is up with you, Emma?" she retorts as we stand there, not allowing any secrets we may have to be spoken between us.

"Are you pregnant?" I grab her boob and twist it.

"Ouch." She grabs her boob, rubbing it. "What are we, twelve-year-old boys?" She is angry with me but is hiding it or in denial. The vomiting, the dizziness, the missed periods perhaps?

"You need to take a pregnancy test." She nods in agreement, and I get her some medication from her drawer where she keeps her headache and anti-nausea medicines in a bag for emergencies.

"I have an upcoming appointment with Planned Parenthood to refill my birth control," she says, rubbing her forehead.

I go over to her. "You know I love you to the moon and back, right?" She returns the embrace.

She has tears in her eyes when I pull away. Let her keep her secrets. I can't disclose mine and wouldn't want to put her in any more danger than I would have if I had continued to live here.

Opting for a change of conversation, I clear my throat. "Let's get ready, shall we?" I turn on Carrie Underwood's "Church Bells," and we laugh at the crazy memories. It was a favorite song we frequently played on the old-fashioned jukebox in this dive bar during our nursing school years.

"For old time's sake," I say, hitting play on my phone, and the girls laugh. Soon, we are all dressed and ready for a much-needed night out.

We elect for an Uber, or at least that is what the girls think. Instead, Philip drives us to the club. The club is packed, and the girls are excited. My besties are wrapped up in short dresses and mini skirts, ready to break hearts.

I lead them to the front of the line, smiling at the bouncer. He nods at me and opens the rope, allowing us entry. By this time, everyone knows me or is made aware of who I am. I turn around to make sure everyone makes it through and grab onto Liv to keep her close to me. Yes, I am hovering like a mother hen, but she is my best friend, my ride-or-die.

We go to the VIP section and walk up the stairs single file. The bouncer at the entry to our VIP area stays with us, standing by our table. He is replaced by another person, allowing access into this secluded space. A nervous-looking waitress comes over to take our order.

"I really missed you guys," Val and Ainsley say in unison, exchanging excited squeals at the opportunity of having us all here together again.

The petite waitress comes back with our bottle service. The security guard comes over, and before she can pour us anything, he stops her and they exchange a look. She stops what she is doing as he picks up the tray's contents and makes himself a drink. The girls watch with curiosity, and he takes a large swig and nods at her. She continues to pour us drinks and leaves after we all have one in our hands.

I don't know how to make this seem normal, but I try to take their concern away from that weird exchange. "I guess he is making sure it isn't diluted." I shrug. "I think that has been happening. Call it quality control." The girls seem to buy it and pick up their drinks. I see them looking at someone, and I turn to see what has gathered their attention.

My man is walking this way, looking dangerously handsome. His tattoos are visible past his sleeves and reaching up toward his neck. The one I had my tongue over earlier today.

The girls thank him for letting us skip the line, but his attention is always on me. He leans over to tell the security guard something, and the security guard tenses. He nods and looks over at me. I squint my eyes, wondering what he said. Before I can ask, Eduardo leans over and kisses the top of my head.

"Behave," he says with a playful wink. He walks away to the other bouncer at the stairs and looks back at our table. He pats the guy on the shoulder and leaves the area through the back stairs.

Needing a distraction from my worry, I pick up the liquor and pour us some shots. "Come on, girls, let's take some shots and go dance."

We dance for a couple of songs, and when "It's Getting Hot in Here" by Nelly comes on, the girls scream in excitement.

"Yay, who doesn't like a little 2000 throwback!" I laugh, throwing my hands in the air and my head back. I am feeling the temperature rise as more people pack into the small space to dance around us.

I see security around us, and they are talking into their headset. The sight makes me nervous, and I look around apprehensively. I see one motion over to the other side of the dance floor with his hand, and I am on high alert, no longer feeling so carefree.

A big, muscular guy comes over wearing a tight-fitted Henly shirt with tattoos in similar places to Eduardo, but it isn't Eduardo, and I don't like how he looks at me. He starts to grind against me, and a small commotion occurs on the dance floor. I see security approaching us and tapping the guy on the shoulder. A very pissed-off Eduardo tells the guy something in his ear while looking at me. I look over at the guy, and he nods, recognition of his misstep clearly visible in his facial expression.

Eduardo grabs my hand to lead me off the dance floor. I was starting to get creeped out anyway, and I am relieved that he has me in his embrace. I look back to see if the girls are following me and notice Liv. She is leaning over a barstool, and I run over to her, yanking my hand away from Eduardo. This shocks him, and he follows me, waving security over.

"Pick her up and take her to my office." Eduardo has security over in seconds as they take a now very passed-out Liv upstairs.

I grab a cool compress and place it over her forehead, and she stirs. "There you are, Liv." I am thankful she is coming to, but I am no less scared of what happened to her. "You made us all so worried."

She tries to sit up but seems to think better of it, placing one foot on the floor to steady herself, I assume to stop the vertigo. I hear Eduardo talking on his phone, saying to let him in and to bring him up around the back to his office. Moments later, a distraught Dax comes in to scoop Liv up in an embrace. When she has difficulty standing, Eduardo offers to help him to get her into his car.

Eduardo comes back in, and the girls and I are still trying to figure out what to do. I decide to make the most of the time with them, and we return to the VIP area with our hearts a little less intact, missing the girl who completes our circle of friends.

CHAPTER THIRTY

EDUARDO

I had to get on the phone and call Dax to tell him about his girlfriend lying passed out on the sofa in my office. People pass out occasionally in my club, but no one has ever been brought up here. Emma had hovered over her best friend, clearly upset. She doesn't need any more shit in her life. I understand her concern for her friend, but I am more concerned with the fact that someone was touching my girlfriend and, even worse, the thought that he was used as a distraction for someone to get to her. If Liv hadn't passed out, Julian could have gotten to her. After they left and Emma returned to salvage the rest of the night with her friends, I had to confirm whether we needed to be worried now.

I had let my staff and security know in a meeting before the girls got to the club that there was a person of interest, a man who posed a threat to my girlfriend. I showed them the picture and made everyone aware that if, for any reason, questions or suspicions came up, or worse, if this person was near Emma, I was to be notified immediately. No call was to be taken lightly and no question considered stupid.

I was glad we had the insight to have this meeting beforehand because I received a call from someone who met the criteria for such an occurrence. That put everyone on high alert, and we thought we had the person in our sights when the incident with the guy getting handsy with Emma happened, and then Liv passing out added to the debacle, making us lose sight of him in the crowd where he later vanished.

I sit in my office watching Emma on surveillance, surrounded by her friends, some discreet and some not-so-discreet security in the area, all watching. I doubt anything will happen now, but I won't take any chances, and the thought of her going back out there with her friends was hard to let her do. I have the face magnified on my security monitor and a few men around me. I ask for Philip to be brought in as well. He walks in, shutting the door behind him.

"Boss, you wanted to see me?" Philip, my most trusted friend and Emma's personal security detail, stands before my desk, looking around the cluster of men in my office. I motion for him to come around to my side of the desk so that he may get a better look at the face I will show him.

"Philip, have you seen this man?"

He takes a look, leaning in closer, and lets out a breath slowly. He nods. "Yeah, I have. I've seen him a couple of times. I thought it was a coincidence..." Philip trails off.

I stand from my chair abruptly and it topples over. One of my men comes in to right it.

"You thought it was a coincidence?" The anger in my voice rises steadily, as does the anger radiating throughout my body. Repeating his words slowly, I say, "A...couple...of...times?" My fists are clenched, and I try to calm my anger. "Where? When?" I pace the room, walking back and forth to give myself a purpose other than punching my most trusted security personnel—dare I say, friend.

Philip goes to sit on the couch, placing his head in his hands. Looking up at me, he rubs his hand over his face, steepling his hands together under his chin. Philip stands and begins pacing just as I had been. He stops and turns toward me. "I know I saw him in the coffee place by the hospital that Emma likes to go to. He was on his computer with headphones on. Not the Airpods, but like Beats or something like that."

He looks away as if trying to remember more. "I noticed him..." He pauses and looks back at me. "In the hospital waiting room." He has the decency to flinch as he continues to fear my unexpected outbursts. "He was reading a book, and I thought he was just a patient. Maybe he lived around the area. Now, I know it wasn't, Boss. I am so sorry."

I stand, staring at Philip with barely controlled anger overtaking my body. My nostrils are flaring as I try to unclench my fists. "Men, leave us now."

The guys look at one another and then at Philip with a sad look—a look that says good-bye, nice knowing you.

Philip stares at me and pays no one else a second glance. Once the door closes, I go to lock it. I sit at my desk and motion for him to sit.

"So now that that show is done, I have a job for you." I smirk at him, and he lifts his eyebrow in confusion.

"I don't understand. When you texted me with 'impromptu acting needed,' I tried, but I have no idea what you are getting at. You already knew the times I spotted Julian when I told you, but somehow, you made me look incompetent, and I want to know why?"

"Oh, yes. I like the extra commentary about the Beats, not Airpods." I wave my hand around my ear. "Very believable, by the way."

He throws his arm out in a theatrical half-bow. "Of course, but what's the plan? I know you have one, and for some reason, I think I am in fake trouble?" He poses this like it's a question.

"Yes, I think there is someone giving information to Julian. He seems to know when Emma will be somewhere and about her party tonight with the girls. I will let everyone think that you will be punished and appoint someone else to be around Emma as a driver. You will still watch her, but without anyone else knowing. No one will be allowed to see you."

He shakes his head, seeming to follow the plan. "So, are you going to kill me? Is that how everyone else will believe I am no longer around as Emma's security detail?"

I look at him, nodding in confirmation. "Well, fake kill you, but yeah." I let that sink in a bit

He grabs his chin, pondering the idea a bit. "Ok, so what next?"

"I will call the guys in and have them escort you to the basement. You'll be held there, and I will let you out through the back door. I'll need to call my computer geek to come over and help me scrub the video, in case anyone else sees it, but I'm not too happy with him these days." I roll my eyes. Philip snorts.

He stands abruptly. "I have an idea that may work, but you must hear me out."

I narrow my eyes in suspicion. "Spit it out already. I know I'm not going to like it."

He laughs harder. "Oh, you will hate it, but it might work, Eduardo."

He proceeds to tell me the plan, and I abso-fucking-lutely hate it. I can't deny it's good though, and it might just work. I make the phone call reluctantly, all while Philip gives me mock words of encouragement. I should kill him after this, if he weren't such a good friend. He's lucky I don't have many friends, and I am currently not accepting any applications to fill his spot. It's too hard to make friends at our age. The fact that we were once all friends in college surprises the hell out of me.

An hour later, Jameson is at the door, and a very suspicious Eli eyes Philip up and down with disgust. I look at Eli, and he nods, closing the door behind him. I see his retreating form on the camera outside my office and look at Jameson. He eyes me with concern and mistrust.

"Jameson, good to see you, brother. I am glad that you were able to get here so soon. Like I said earlier, it's important." He sits forward in his chair.

"You mentioned important and Emma's name in the same sentence, which is why I am here so fast," he clarifies, and it makes me furious as fuck, but I have to think about what's more important—Emma.

My Emma, I almost growl in my possessiveness over the girl I have loved first and only.

"Right," I say in what is probably a sarcastic rebuttal. Jameson visibly straightens and stares at me. I get up from behind my desk that I was initially sitting at and move over to the front, feeling more relaxed with my feet crossed, extended out in front of me. My arms are pulled back on my desk. I want to get in his face and for him to understand what I am doing and what needs to be done to keep Emma safe.

"Jameson, I called you here because I know that you care about Emma, and I need your help. What I am about to disclose to you is to stay between us in this room and no one else. It is about her safety, and I can't jeopardize that." He sits up, looking at me and then Philip. Concern etches his features, and I reluctantly wait for his acknowledgment.

"I understand," he says. "What can I do to help? Is she in trouble?"

I pause because I don't want to tell him, but I have to do it to keep her safe, even if he may be in love with her. Believe me, man, I know the feeling. "I don't know the history between you two..." I pause to see if he will elaborate, but he doesn't. That fucker. "Yeah, well, I have known Emma for most of my life." He seems confused about this, and I tell him about our families being business associates and up to a point about us reconnecting. I explain the abusive relationship with Julian, minus the details and how we think he and his family are responsible for her parents' and twin sister's death.

He looks up. "Twin sister?"

I shake my head. "Yes, she had a twin sister named Evie, who was her best friend. She misses her terribly and blames herself for their deaths."

He stands up and looks as furious as I feel. "This guy is still after her? He was here tonight?"

I nod in confirmation. "I need your help looking at the security feed to see if I missed anything, and I also need you to wipe it a little bit." He looks at me, confused. "Well, since you installed it, you know more about it than anyone else would, right? You are the super geek of the bunch?" I laugh when I say this because it has always been a joke about how brilliant the guy is. There are worse things to be called and known for—like a mafia criminal. I shrug as I think this through.

"Why do you need it wiped?"

I look over to Philip and then at Jameson. "Philip here has to die, and I don't want there to be evidence."

Philip snorts, and Jameson seems to want to be anywhere but here. "You're fucking joking, right?"

"Mostly," I say, trying to rile Jameson up. He may be a tough guy, but he isn't a killer and surely not a part of this life. I decide to put him out of his misery. "I need it to look like I killed Philip, but he will stay hidden and keep an eye on Emma—from the shadows. With everyone thinking he is dead, that will give us the upper hand so that he can go unnoticed. People won't suspect he is secretly watching out for the person giving Julian information if he is thought to be dead. We need to find that out before he gets to Emma."

Jameson looks over at Philip and then at me.

"Okay. I'm in."

After Philip is presumed dead and the surveillance feed is wiped, I invite Jameson back up to my office for another chat. This one is between us. "I want to know what happened between you and Emma. I know that you have feelings for her." I leave it there and wait for him to tell me what I have had suspicions about. If he slept with her, I don't know if I could contain my rage, but it was before we reconnected. I had meaningless sex, too, and... I can't even think about it anymore. It just kills me inside.

He is looking at me and blows out a long breath. "Nothing." He stops trying to decide how this will go if he tells me something I don't want to hear. I have been known for having a bad temper and losing it. "We met on Padre Island while on Spring Break. That's when Dax met Liv. He was a patient in the ER and met up at that beach the next day. We shared a moment, and then that was it. I was hoping for more, but then we came here, and she saw you. I don't know."

My breathing has increased, and I can't get the idea or unthink that he fucked my girlfriend, future wife, and future mother of my children. I just can't let it go, and I have to know.

"A moment?" He shakes his head yes.

"Did you fuck my girlfriend?" I come out and say it, laced with the most controlled anger I can muster.

He looks at me and shakes his head. "No," he says quietly. "We had an awkward kiss, and that's it. I think Dax and Liv thought there was more between us, and I wanted there to be, but now she is with you."

"Awkward kiss?" I ask, waiting for more details. He rubs the back of his neck.

"Yes, awkward as fuck. It felt like I was kissing my fucking sister, despite being super attracted to her." I snort. "I can't explain it, but I feel super protective of her, too."

"Okay, sister fucker."

He laughs, and that breaks the ice a little. "You have nothing to worry about. I care about Emma, but if she is happy with you, I just want her to be happy." He shrugs noncommittally.

I get up and pat him on the back. "I'm glad to hear that. Now, I need your help with a tracker for Emma."

CHAPTER THIRTY-ONE

EDUARDO

I get Eli to drive us home and drop the girls off at Liv's and Emma's old apartment. The girls say their good-byes, and I drag a reluctant Emma back to my place. I help her tiredly walk to the bedroom, where she quickly washes her face and gets into her pajamas. She gives me a quick peck on the lips and dives on top of the bed. Before I can tell her good night, I hear her soft snores. I kiss the top of her head, pulling the covers over her body. Now, it's time to make a long overdue call.

I turn the light on in my home office and stare at the phone for what seems like an eternity. "Here goes nothing."

"Hello," the familiar voice picks up the phone.

I cringe at the same voice that told me to stop seeing Emma. If I loved her, I would let her go.

I haven't heard this voice in about a decade, but anger bursts through me at the memory of our last exchange. Things went differently then, when he told me I should respect Emma's parents' decision. I went looking for

Emma the following summer, but her mother held true to her word in not returning with the girls to her brother's house.

"Andrés? This is Eduardo Ruiz." I let that sink in for a bit and wait to see what he will say in the introduction.

"Eduardo." He pauses in what I am sure is confusion mixed with what I hope is also some regret, but I highly doubt it. Andrés Ortiz doesn't feel bad about his decisions or have regrets.

"To what do I owe the pleasure of this call?" He's curt but not unpleasant.

I know we have the same goal in mind—to keep Emma safe, or at least that's what I remind myself when proceeding with this exchange.

"I am calling about Emma. I just wanted you to know that we have reconnected, and I am keeping her safe."

I hear Adrian, her cousin, in the background.

"I'm putting you on speaker, Eduardo. Adrian, my son, is here."

I respect the disclosure, but it isn't needed. I'm not the same kid I was back then, and I won't be walking away, no matter the cost.

"Hello, Adrian," I say in greeting, which he reciprocates.

"Gentlemen, it has come to my attention that Emma is in danger. I have moved her in with me after a scare at her apartment." I hear a chair topple over.

"What the fuck happened?" Adrian is upset. Not knowing about another issue with Julian before this conversation looks equally bad since they are supposed to have someone watching Emma; however, their piss-poor job is ridiculous.

"Julian Martinez is a dead man. I am currently gathering information about his family and should have some idea what their obsession with Emma is. He was in her apartment and left her a message in the bathroom mirror. He is fucking with her, and I am not at the liberty of him toying with my girlfriend." I hear a series of expletives leave Andrés's mouth.

"What do you mean your girlfriend, Eduardo?" He isn't very gracious in concealing his feelings about Emma and me rekindling our courtship.

"Is that all you got out of that?" I applaud his reaction. At least I am keeping her safe, unlike these fuckwads. Instead, I continue as if this doesn't phase me.

"Well, that is also the reason for my call. I appreciate that you have been helping Emma, but I feel I can assist and be there for her. I know her parents are not around and—"

"Let me guess," he interrupts. "Do you think you can date Emma now that her parents aren't around to prevent you from being together? Eduardo,

I was never against it, but…" He seems to rethink what he was going to say. "How does Emma feel about it?"

"That is part of the reason I am calling. We have been given a second chance, and I never want to lose her again. As her next of kin, I'm calling you as a courtesy, and as her next of kin, to ask for her hand in marriage officially." I hear a drink being poured, and I understand the sentiment. "Is that a celebratory drink I hear you pouring?"

He sighs, and when I think I will have to marry her without their approval, he finally acquiesces. "I know that you love her and will keep her safe. My niece has lost so much. If you can bring her joy and provide a home, then you have my blessing."

Adrian verbally agrees in the background.

"I appreciate your approval. I will keep you posted on what our sources find out. I will also update you on our wedding announcements when I propose to Emma. That is, if she accepts it, of course."

I hear Adrian scoff as if he has moved closer to the speaker. "I will keep you posted as well."

Andrés counters, "I, for one, haven't been able to find out anything. You, being on the other side in the US, might be more successful."

We hang up on a consensus. I feel more relaxed knowing that Emma is mine and I only need her to agree to my marriage proposal. Now to think of how to get the girl.

Julian seems to slip away and hasn't been seen in a few months, but that doesn't mean he isn't plotting or planning to abduct Emma. Emma questioned where Philip was, and I told her he had a family emergency to take care of. Everyone else thinks he is dead, but I won't tell her the same story. She won't discover what I said to other people because my men wouldn't dare tell Emma I killed her bodyguard because of a mistake. I've had her watched at work, so I know Julian hasn't shown up again in the waiting room or at the coffee shop she likes to frequent.

Today, I have a surprise for my girl. I spent the whole day at the gym tying up loose ends when Helena started talking about a concert she was going to buy tickets for. The girl is always going to some heavy metal venue, and I only half listen, but when she mentioned her Ghost concert tickets, I perked right up.

"Excuse me, what band?" I ask, but this time, I listen thoroughly to her ramblings.

"Oh, so n-ow you are paying attention to me?" she snorts, typing data into the patient account on the computer.

"Sorry, but this band you mentioned is… Ghost? Are they the ones who wear the masks, and the lead singer dresses up as a satanic pope?" I look at her with exaggerated interest.

"Yes." She narrows her eyes on me. "He doesn't just dress up. It's part of the lore," she replies, annoyed at my lack of Ghost band knowledge. "Why do you ask?"

I can tell she thinks I'm going to make fun of her, but I'm asking because Emma loves that band so much. She is obsessed with the Ghouls and even wears little bracelets made of beads with letters spelling out 'little sunshine.'

"Emma loves that band, and I want to take her to the concert." Obsessed might not even cut it with the way she sings all the songs and has the two little stuffed dolls of the lead singer. The little doll is creepy as fuck too.

"Hmm." She seems hesitant to give me more information. "Well, I doubt there are more pit tickets, but you can at least get her some VIP experience tickets to the ritual."

"The ritual?"

She just shakes her head. "Never mind." There are still a bunch of options. "There." She starts typing into the computer screen. "Here are the seats left. See? Take a look for yourself," she says as she turns the screen my way.

Ultimately, I purchase two VIP tickets that allow us early access to the venue, a better parking option up close, and free merch. I think she'll like it. Needing reassurance, I decide to ask a fan. I really do want to make her happy.

"Do you think she'll like it, Helena?"

I see her tilt her head to look at me, and what she sees makes her eyes soften and she smiles. "I think she is going to love it. I bet she will be super excited to go." She gives me a little side hug. "You did good, Boss." She squeezes my shoulders once more and walks off.

I feel good about the surprise and hope my plan to keep her safe won't backfire.

I finish at the gym and walk out the door a little earlier to pick up Emma at our home. She works later tonight, and we now have a routine going. I never thought I'd be a guy who likes the mundane routine of domesticity, but I do. I might be enjoying it a little too much. Maybe it is just because it is with Emma.

I pick her up and we head through the Starbies drive thru line per Emma's request. I order her an iced matcha latte, and espresso for me. As we pull out into traffic, I hear her favorite band play on Spotify and laugh when she asks about attending the concert. Little does she know that she'll be getting the full VIP experience soon.

I hate to admit that I always like having her with me, and dropping her off at work is always hard. Seeing her walk away through the doors and the possibility that it could be the last time I ever see her again guts me. This threat with Julian has to stop, and I won't let these thoughts take up space in my head any longer. I am becoming that clingy motherfucker that everyone laughs about. I laugh, thinking about the time during our family's last Christmas conversation when Jasmine, my future sister-in-law, explained her favorite romance trope–omegaverse–to us. The alpha obsessed with his omega.

I have a little skip in my step thinking about Emma and how she will lose her shit, and I can't wait to tell her about it. I place my messenger bag on the table, along with the food she wanted to get before work tonight, when I hear her phone ring. She sees who is calling and answers it, talking with Liv on speakerphone.

"Hey, girl, how are you feeling?"

She has her back to me and hasn't noticed that I am standing there listening. I would usually go about my business, but something has me standing there. Her bubbly demeanor radiates sparkles and rainbows down the line. And I am captivated by it. This is the happy woman I always wanted to see.

"I am feeling better. This is just my first obstetrician appointment."

Emma rubs at her temples, and I imagine her trying to ward off an impending headache.

"So, it's true then, Liv? You're pregnant?"

I nod, even though I'm not part of this conversation, but after the way she acted at the club, it was pretty apparent that was the case.

Her words echo back Emma's. "I am pregnant with Dax's baby." She lets that sink in before replying to Liv's answer.

"Are you happy, Liv?" She looks sad, and I watch her wanting to come over and hug her. Tell her she isn't alone, and I will always hold her when she needs me to, for better or worse.

Liv answers with more conviction, and I believe her when she says that she is indeed happy about the news and about her and Dax starting a family.

She continues, "I know it's weird to say, but I feel I was destined to be his since I met him. The way he makes me feel and the way he touches me. It seems familiar, like I was already his, and he was mine."

Emma stays silent for a moment and then breathes before speaking. She grabs at the necklace I gave her, and my heart stops. "Yeah, I understand that. Sometimes, you can't fight who you end up with. Sometimes, it's just the way things are meant to be."

They end the call, and Emma turns around, releasing a slew of expletives as she clutches her chest. "You scared the crap out of me, babe." She walks over to me and kisses me on the lips. Before she can let go, I pull her in with my hand firmly planted on her ass as I let her feel the effect she has on me. My cock is rock-hard, but that will have to wait.

"I have a surprise for you," I say as I pepper kisses lightly down her neck.

"I hate to break it to you, babe, but your monster cock is no surprise." She laughs, her eyes alight with humor as she grabs my dick.

I laugh and grab her hand. "You keep grabbing me like that and the surprise I got you will have to wait."

She removes her hand reluctantly. "So the surprise isn't you feeding me your cock?" She raises her eyebrows, and I groan.

Now she has me all worked up. Maybe we could fuck, and then I'll give her her present. I decide on the latter and take my phone out of my pocket. She eyes me suspiciously, and I can't help the smile that forms on my lips, despite trying to remain stoic. I can see her getting agitated that I am on my phone and pushing her hand away from my cock. She thinks I am blowing her off as if I would prefer anything on my phone than to her touching me.

I forward her the proof of purchase for the "Imperium" VIP experience Ghost concert tickets. Her phone dings with an incoming message, and she opens it eyeing me suspiciously as I place my phone back in my pocket. Her eyes widen, and I can tell she is looking at the tickets, and a smile that melts my dark heart begins to blossom on her face. She looks over at me and unexpectedly throws herself into my arms, but I catch her. I'll always catch her.

"Now let me thank that cock of yours," she says.

I kiss her, and she drops to her knees. The look in her eyes is something I will remember until my dying days.

CHAPTER THIRTY-TWO

EMMA

I am getting dressed when Eduardo comes in. It's a bit cooler today, and even though the holidays are right around the corner, Texas doesn't have many temperature changes, but when it does get colder? Holy mother, it's cold.

I put on some leggings and my favorite hoodie by my favorite band. I scream internally. I still can't believe I will see Ghost in concert soon. I have been riding that high all week. I wish it were sooner, but what's a few months, right?

"Hey, baby." He bends over to kiss me quickly, breaking me from my Ghost-lust-filled trance.

"Hey yourself," I say, looking up at him like he hung the moon and stars. The same moon and stars that we gazed at together when we were younger, making plans when we thought we had a future. All the time in the world, but we both learned how precious those moments are and how they can all be taken away in the blink of an eye.

"I got you a present," he states matter-of-factly.

I stop applying my mascara and look over at him. An involuntary smile pulls from my lips, and I swear he blushes.

"Eduardo? Did my big bad, mafia boyfriend just blush?" I question playfully, and he grabs the back of his neck, rubbing at an imaginary spot.

He shakes his head and looks at me. Amusement lines his face, and I love that look on him. It's as if I am staring at the boyish Eduardo who first stole my heart, except he is no longer a boy. He is all man. My man. He sits on the edge of the bed, and I drop down to my hands and knees, crawling to him. His pupils dilate, and his breathing picks up.

"Emma? What are you doing?" he asks. I go up to his legs and plant my hands over his thick, muscular thighs, rubbing my way up to his cock.

"I already had this present this morning, but do you want to give it to me again? In my mouth this time?" I lick my lips for added effect and wish I hadn't put my mascara on yet since it will probably run down my face in another minute, but I think that is his favorite look on me. Thinking about this makes me smile.

He holds my hand on his cock. "Emma, as much as I'd like your mouth on my cock, I do actually have a present for you." He pulls out a wrapped package, and my heart melts at seeing the vulnerability in his eyes. I squeal at the thought of getting a present. It has been a while since anyone bought me a gift, and I love that he put some thought into it. He puts his hand up to my cheek and strokes it gently.

"If you still want to suck my cock in thanks after you open your present, well, I won't turn the offer down," he counters.

I laugh, shaking my head. "You got it, baby." I wink and lean over to kiss his cock through his pants. I see it jump in response to my affection, and I chuckle.

"Goddamn tease," he says playfully as he readjusts himself.

I get up and sit on the edge of our bed, holding the box in my hand.

"Go on. Open it, babe," he encourages.

I look at him and nod with a smile that spreads from ear to ear. I unwrap the gift to see a velvet box. I place the golden wrapping paper off to the side and open the box carefully. It's an earring, bracelet, and matching pendant set—a starburst earring in white gold with emeralds and diamonds. The pendant matches the earrings, and I am in awe.

"This…" I swallow, trying not to cry. "Is so beautiful, Eduardo. Thank you." I veer around to hug him, and he pulls me into his arms just a few inches away from his face.

"The stars remind me of us, gazing up at the stars. I remember you saying how they look like diamonds in the sky. The green reminds me of the color of your eyes. It's your name that falls from my lips when I see a shooting star, making a wish. It's your name forever on my lips." He gives me a kiss that is soft and lingering. It lets me feel all the emotions we convey and all the ones we don't say. How time is precious, and this time is ours. He pulls away.

"One more thing." He clears his throat. "I had a tracker put into the necklace." He points at the large pendant. "I didn't want to mess with your pendant I gave you when we were kids, but I thought you could wear both on your necklace. Or put that one on the bracelet.

I look over at him. "How romantic," I deadpan.

Eduardo looks at me. "Emma, I just want to keep you safe."

"I know. I was only kidding. But honestly, thank you, Eduardo. I love it."

"Here, let me help you put it on. I put on the earrings, the bracelet, and the necklace."

"It is perfect." I touch the pendant, knowing that it is my lifeline to Eduardo.

"There is a button on it. If you depress the star, it will send an SOS to my phone and my security team with your location. The device will let us track you, in case that is ever needed. I hope we never need it, Emma, but I am unwilling to risk the chance."

I nod in agreement. I'm sad that this happy moment has turned into talking about my safety once again. I can't wait for the day that this is a distant memory. To live life in peace without fear of someone trying to kidnap me. When you are married to a mafioso, things like this are always possible, but I trust Eduardo to keep me and our future children safe.

I speak the words that we are both thinking, but always afraid to voice aloud. "Do you think we will always have to worry like this?"

He cocks his head to the side, trying to read my expression. "About danger?" he asks. I nod once. He rubs his chin.

"I'm not going to lie to you, Emma. Our life together may always have the potential for danger, but I vow to keep you safe. Always." He grips my chin for me to look at him.

"What about our kids?" I counter.

His lips twitch. "Definitely. But first, I need you to marry me." His playful expression is gone, and now all I see is determination.

I place my hand up to his face and stroke his cheek. "Well, love," I say, placing a chaste kiss on his lips, "I guess you are going to have to ask me first to find out my answer."

He grabs my face and kisses me. His mouth desperately seeks possession over me, and I open for him. He fucks my mouth like he fucks my pussy, dominant and commanding. I feel all the emotions that Eduardo places into it: protection, adoration, control, dominance, and most of all, love. I feel it to the tips of my toes. I could never be loved like this again. If living a life of danger with him is all I could ever have, then I'll take my chances in this life. The life that my parents tried to keep me from.

He lifts me into bed and places me on the pillow at the head of the bed. He straddles my body with both of us clothed. He places my gifts on the bedside table and returns his gaze to me. He lifts my arms in the air and removes my dress over my head, discarding it on the floor. He stares at my breasts, kneading them through the soft lace bra. He shoves the bra down, pushing my tits out, then tweaks the nipples with his fingers, making them pebble in anticipation of his mouth on them. He looks at me longingly, his gaze roaming the entirety of my body down to my thong, soaked with my desire. He leans over and buries his face in my drenched panties, inhaling deeply.

I feel the wetness leaking around the pantyline seam. Eduardo notices this and licks at the side of my panties, pushing back the material, moaning as he buries his face in the scent of my underwear, rubbing his face in it as if I'm marking him with my scent. It is filthy and erotic, and I am so undeniably wet for him.

He rips them off my body and throws the torn material to the floor. He begins to unbuckle his pants to free himself of their confines. Pushing his pants down, he drags them past his ankles and kicks them off with his boxers. His dick is beautiful, long, thick, leaking precum beading at the tip. I lick my lips, wanting to taste him, intentionally leaning forward to catch the moisture with my tongue. Eduardo leans forward and drags the end of his penis along my lips, coating them in his arousal. I dart my tongue out and flick it over his cock, feeling it twitch and harden further, with my tongue tracing a figure-eight pattern over the tip. I lap and suck, causing him to groan.

This must snap whatever restraint Eduardo has because he parts my lips with his finger and holds my mouth open as he thrusts his cock inside. I feel him hiss as his cock scrapes my teeth. He grabs my head, lifting it up as he straddles my chest. He hangs one arm over the headboard as leverage and starts to thrust in and out. His moans become louder as he fucks my face. I love seeing him come undone, and he moans and grunts in approval, calling me his fucking star. He shoves his cock so far down my throat that I think I'm going to gag, and he holds me there, shuddering. He pumps in and out deeply with small movements, holding me down on his cock. I think he is about to come, but he pulls out abruptly, cursing.

"Fuck, Emma. You take my cock so well." He lifts me up. "Come on, baby. On all fours."

I quickly get up and lean over with my face down on the bed and ass up in the air. He kneads my ass, parting the cheeks as he bends over, licking from my clit to my ass. I almost come on the spot. He slides his cock through my wet pussy lips and lines himself up. He thrust in in one push, all the way to the hilt. He grabs my hair, picking me up from the bed with my back arched up, taking every inch of his long girth. He sets a punishing pace, and it has my toes curling in just a minute's time.

He sits me up, and I am upright on his cock, straddling him reverse cowgirl. He bounces me up and down on his cock forcefully, the curve hitting my cervix with each thrust. He pinches my nipple hard with each hit. The sounds echo with the slap of our bodies as the scent of sex permeates the air in our bedroom. He licks up my neck, whispering filthy words in my ear as he sucks my earlobe into his mouth.

"I'm coming, Eduardo," I announce. "Keep going. That feels so good," I cry out as my orgasm hits, and my walls clamp down on him.

He keeps going through the spasm, pushing me forward, placing me back on the pillow, face down, and holding my ass up in the air. He lets go and entwines our hands, pushing me farther into the pillow. His balls slap my ass, and the sound of wetness fills the room as he fucks me.

After a few more thrusts, he comes with a loud "Fucking feels so good" as his hot cum shoots into me. He lays across my back, still holding my hands down as I slump flat onto the bed, totally spent.

He pulls out of me, grabbing my fingers forcefully. He pulls me over so that I am now laying chest down on top of him as he runs his fingers through my long hair. He holds me close, telling me how much he loves me. How I am his, and he is mine. Then he asks, "So what do you say, Emma?"

I look over at the questions lingering in his eyes. He brings my hand up to his mouth and kisses me.

"About what, Eduardo?" I ask as I rub my fingers across his lips.

He nods his chin at my finger, and that's when I see the massive rock on my hand. I sit straight up and look at it. He sits up and joins me.

"Will you marry me, Emma?"

CHAPTER THIRTY-THREE

EMMA

"Will you marry me, Emma?" He looks at me, waiting for my answer. I stare at the sizable emerald-cut solitaire occupying a large portion of my finger in disbelief. I don't think I have ever been this excited in my life, but I still haven't answered. My heart races, and I feel like I may throw up. I frown. I feel a hand caress my cheek, and I look up to his face. Tears begin to fall when I realize I don't have anyone to walk me down the aisle or give me away.

As if sensing my thoughts, Eduardo clears his throat. "I hope you don't mind, but I reached out to your uncle and asked him for your hand in marriage. It wasn't exactly permission because anyone who tries to tell me this time that I can't have you or attempts to tell us we can't be together can get fucked." He wipes my tears with his finger. "He said he would give you away," Eduardo says in almost a whisper, "if you'll have me."

I place my hand on his cheek. "Yes. I would love to be your wife. The answer is always yes."

He looks at me with a fierce protectiveness. "Not just my wife, Emma. My partner in this life and the next. My everything."

I kiss him, showing how much I love him. We stare at each other, and I wonder how things would have been if we would have stayed together. I am so scared of what the future holds because of the uncertainty of Julian, my stalker. I won't entertain bringing a child into this world as long as he is alive.

He shocks me with the next question. "How would you feel about us visiting with your family for Christmas in Mexico?"

I look up at him, blinking. "Umm, like next month?"

He laughs. "Yes, next month. We will have a quiet Thanksgiving here. I know you have to work that night, and we can't do much, but you have the week of Christmas off, right? I remember you telling me this because Liv's getting married?"

I can't help but laugh. "Well, she doesn't know she is getting married yet. I mean, they just got engaged, but with the baby coming, Dax wanted to whisk her away for the holidays somewhere tropical, and he was going to have the venue all ready for them. He knows she will say yes while they are there."

I was confident she would be okay with it when he asked me about it. I told him I would like to get her something because I know her mom probably couldn't afford it. I had to be all stealth-like in claiming that I had to get her measurements for the gala dress in case we needed it altered. I mean, of course, we would need to do this. As her belly grew, so would the need for the dresses to accommodate the increased girth of pregnancy, but we could always get another. I got her a beautiful dress for her wedding and some Christian Louboutin shoes with blue embellishments. Her something blue. I can't wait to hear all about it. I can't wait to share the news with her.

Shaking myself from these memories, I blink and smile up at Eduardo. "Yes, let's go." I squeal a little in my excitement, and Eduardo kisses my forehead.

"Perfect," he says as he rolls over. I look at my ring again and smile.

Realizing he is getting up, I ask, "Where are you going?"

He looks back at me. "To make the arrangements, of course." He smiles and leaves me in the room, and I fall back onto the bed.

I can't remember when I have been this happy. I haven't seen my family in a while, and I miss my uncle and cousin terribly, not to mention the rest of the bunch. It will be good to see everyone and have a Christmas with family after all these years.

I am pulled from my thoughts when my phone rings. I retrieve it from my pocketbook and see that Liv is calling. "Hey, girl? What's up?" I can't wait to tell her my news, but I hear her sniffle. Immediately thinking something is wrong with the baby, I straighten my body, preparing for the worst. "Liv, what the hell happened? Is the baby okay?"

She stammers out, "Yes, it's..."

I release the tension and figure it must be Brodie.

"What did the fucker do now, Liv. I swear he is asking for it." I feel for the guy after everything he has been through, but he is still selfish as fuck.

"I told him about the pregnancy and moving in with Dax. He saw my engagement ring, and it was just too much. He told me to get out and he needed time to process everything. He doesn't want to talk to me." She is crying, and I am not there to console her.

"Do you need me to go over, Liv? I can be there soon," I tell her, already packing up to go over.

"No, Dax will be home soon, and I just wanted to talk to my best friend. You are the only one I tell everything to. My ride or die, right?"

I shake my head back and forth. The guilt of this being a one-way street is too much sometimes. "Right, Liv. Your ride or die forever. I love you, honey. Are you sure about not needing me to go over?" I hesitate and look at myself in the mirror. The fraud and lies I tell myself daily stare back at me, and I hate what I see.

Liv continues. "He said he needed time through the holidays to be alone and not talk to me." She blows her nose, and it sounds so squeaky.

"Honey, you are making yourself sick. Think about the baby. You need to take care of yourself, okay? This is good. Maybe he just needs time. You've always been there for him. You sacrificed your own happiness long enough."

She blows out a breath on the phone. "You're right," she relents and blows out a long, audible breath through the phone as she stops crying.

"Of course I'm right, Liv." I hope she takes my advice. I worry about the girl. Dax is so good for her, and I just hope she takes this time to enjoy herself away from the mindfuck that is Brodie.

We hang up, and I sit on my chair at the vanity looking at myself in the mirror. Eduardo walks in and sees me upset.

"What's wrong, baby? When I left you a few moments ago, you were happy. Did you change your mind about marrying me?" I see the joke Eduardo is making. I think there is some uncertainty swimming in there.

"Of course, I haven't changed my mind about you. You are the one constant thing in my life, and I will never feel anything other than wanting to spend the rest of my life with you."

He smiles at me and kisses me. "Okay, so what's this about then?" he asks. The concern on his face overwhelms me. I have someone in my corner, and I love that he is here.

"It's Liv." I hesitate. "Her usual Brodie drama."

He whistles. "Still?"

"Yep," I reply. "He found out about the baby, Dax's proposing, and her moving in with him and said that he needs to be alone and have time to process everything. Liv is upset because he doesn't want to speak with her, and maybe after the holidays, they can talk about everything then." I get it all out and blow upward, causing my hair to rise off my forehead. "That guy is selfish as fuck."

Eduardo rubs his chin, thinking it over. "I understand that I don't know the full story, only what you've told me, but, Emma..." He pauses, thinking about how to formulate his response, and I can tell that I'm not going to like or agree with what he says. "The guy is in a wheelchair, and he lost his girl, friends, and life as he knows it. He doesn't even have a family who cares about him. He needs to talk to someone about it all."

I think about what Eduardo said and realize that Liv is the only constant in his life, and now he is losing that, too. Sure, he cheated on her, and no one likes a cheater, but he has more than suffered.

Laying my head in my hands, I groan. "Ugh, I hate when you're right, Eduardo."

"I know, babe. It's going to happen more than you care to admit. I just see things from a different perspective. I love that you are fiercely protective of your friends." He ruffles my hair like a little kid. "Now come on, I want to show you what I booked for us."

With that, he leads me to his office, and I stop thinking about Liv and how our friendship seems one-sided. I'm doing this to protect her, I tell myself. I say it so much that I start to believe my lies.

Eduardo and I went all out for Thanksgiving. We had it catered for us. After it was all set up, the caterers left us to eat alone. We had no one over, and we spent a quiet day alone until I had to go to work, which meant I couldn't even have any wine with our early dinner. Adulting is so hard sometimes, but I am looking forward to spending the holidays with my family in Mexico and maybe reliving some childhood memories.

I thought it would be an excellent idea to go shopping with Liv and both of us could get some things for our trip together. Dax finally asked her if they could get away for the holidays. He told her about going to the Caribbean for Christmas, and I couldn't agree more. She has her mind on Brodie, and the fact that they are not talking lays heavy on her mind. She's worried about him. She's worried about his mental health. The guy has a lot going on, and few people who were in this corner championed him through this rough time in his life that changed everything he once knew. We can all see how depressed he is, and he needs to fix that. I hope that he gets the help he needs.

I can't tell her I already knew about her island trip and that Dax intends to marry her there. He wants to be married when the baby is born. It was a romantic gesture, sweeping her away and getting married. If I thought that Liv would have said no, I would have told the guy no or that she isn't ready, but she loves him so much, and this is their second chance. I know how important second chances are too.

When he asked me if I wanted to contribute anything to Liv's special day, I was glad to be able to. Since we can't be there, I want her to have something special, something that will remind her of me for the rest of her life. She is the one person in my life I can count on. Even though I feel I can't tell her everything. It's because I care about her so much that I can never tell her, but I can show her. I can show her my support and happiness about her special day by giving her the dress and something blue for tradition.

Dax asked her mother for her hand in marriage, and I contacted her to let her know that I would happily buy her dress for her. I think her mother was relieved about that, and she could maybe not pick up so many shifts to help Liv.

We haven't spent much time together. Liv moved in with Dax, and I knew Eduardo would spend time with me at my old apartment, but since Julian left that message, I feel safe and less violated staying at his place. Seeing my reflection in that mirror reminds me he could get to me anytime, and I am still very much in danger.

Liv and I decided to meet up to do some shopping in the River Oaks District in Houston. Eli parks my car in the garage, and I can't wait to meet Liv. We will shop and then eat at my favorite French cafe on the corner. It boasts beautiful outdoor covered seating and is a perfect spot for a late lunch. Not to mention, their drinks are superb. I could go for Chanel No. 6 martinis as well.

I walk up ahead, and I know Eli is following. I miss Philip so much, but he had a family emergency that couldn't be helped. When I asked Eli if Philip would return soon, his eyes narrowed, and he said "doubtful." Whatever that means. It isn't my business, I guess. I try not to ask too many questions. I know it's a waste of time, and I won't get a straight answer anyway.

I round the corner and see Liv walking toward me. I run a bit to reach her sooner and hug her tightly. I put my hand on her expanding belly. "Hey, beautiful, Auntie is here."

Liv laughs. "Best auntie ever," she agrees. "Come on, let's do this."

We walk up the sidewalk arm in arm and find a store we both want to enter. The lady in the boutique greets us and asks us to let her know if we need anything. I see the moment she catches our engagement rings, and her smile beams a bit brighter.

Right, I think to myself. She knows we have money to spend.

Liv is shuffling through the racks. "I feel bad about using Dax's credit card to buy stuff," she says in a whiny voice.

"Yeah, sounds rough," I deadpan. "I wouldn't. He wants you to have some nice things for the trip, and let's face it, Liv, you need some clothes you can wear in a few months, so let's get to it. Chop. Chop." I mimic clapping my hands with each word. She side-eyes me and grumbles something intelligible.

We both try on some outfits, and the salesperson rings us up gleefully. I bought a bit too much and saw her look at my ring again. I wonder if Liv will notice. I planned on telling her that night when she called me crying, but she was so upset about Brodie that I thought it wasn't the right time. I wanted to see her in person to tell her my good news anyway, hence the reservations at the French cafe.

As we are walking out, I see a woman walk in with oversized black Chanel sunglasses covering most of her face. She looks expensively dressed and wearing a plaid wool-blend beret. After all that, that's not what stands out. It is her glossy red lipstick that matches her unnaturally red hair. She stops and looks me up and down. Her lips turn upward in disgust.

"Do you have a problem?" I question the woman.

She turns to me and scoffs. "No, I just don't know what they see in you." She turns and walks off. I'm left there stunned.

"What the fuck," I hear Liv say, and I look at her.

"You heard that, right?" I ask to make sure I didn't get it wrong.

She looks at me, confused as well. "Yep. What was that about?" Liv asks.

I shrug. "I have no idea, but let's get out of here before I get arrested."

Liv snorts, and we walk out hand in hand, mostly Liv pulling me out of the store reluctantly.

CHAPTER THIRTY-FOUR

EMMA

We round the corner of the restaurant where we have our upcoming reservations. I approach the lady at the hostess station who seems busy looking at her computer screen. "Hi," I tell the woman, trying to get her attention. She doesn't look up. "We have reservations for two under Emma Taylor, please."

The hostess notices me, smiles, and looks through her list. "Sorry, but we don't have a reservation under Emma Taylor," she replies, sounding sad but not actually being sad about saying it.

I put my finger to my chin, wondering if the reservation could be under another name. I look at Liv, shrugging. "Eduardo made the reservations, and I have no idea what he put the name under."

Liv shrugs as well, offering up some suggestions. "Did he put them under another name or his name, maybe?"

I think about it. It seems logical. The hostess looks annoyed as we go back and forth with it, trying to figure it out.

"Are you sure he made it here?" she asks, and I nod a yes.

"I know it is. I asked him, and he said he did it. "Is it under Emma Ortiz Taylor or no Taylor at the end?"

She looks again. I see a frown cross her lips as she looks back at me and my ring finger. The one that currently houses my engagement ring. Liv still hasn't seen it. I hide it a little because I want to tell Liv about it over lunch.

Liv goes on. "Do you think he put it under his name, Emma? Under Eduardo Ruiz?"

This makes the girl cough as we both look over at her. "Are you married to Eduardo Ruiz? The one who owns the gym uptown and the nightclub?"

I look at her without answering. My eyes narrow, and I am about to speak when Liv interjects.

"Is it under Emma Ruiz?"

The lady looks at the reservation and then at us, nodding. "Ladies, let me show you to your table." She turns abruptly without looking back to see if we are following.

Liv mouths, "What the fuck."

I just shrug, shaking my head and trying to catch up to the hostess. Liv isn't usually one to make a scene, and I don't want to have this conversation about it here. I can guarantee that Eduardo and I will have this conversation when I get home.

Why would he do that, and why here?

Did it have something to do with the hostess out there?

So many questions, and I better get the answers. I feel the jealousy and redness creeping up my neck as my cheeks begin to flush.

We sit at the table where she places down two menus, telling us to enjoy our lunch, and leaves without another glance our way. We sit, and a waiter comes up to us right away. It gives me the opportunity to cool off. My anger subsides for that moment.

"Good afternoon, ladies. Have you been here before?" We both nod, and he smiles. "Okay then, can I get you something to drink?" He looks at us patiently.

I already know I want a French martini, and the one here comes with champagne. I need it now. "I'll have the Channel No. 6 martini, please," I say before Liv gets in a word.

She just shakes her head, laughing silently.

"Of course, and for you, miss?" He looks Liv's way, and she just shrugs.

"Sparkling water with a lemon twist, please."

"Great, I'll be right back with those. In the meantime, here are some lunch specials for today and a special dessert made by the pastry chef." He hands us the daily menu on a sheet of paper and walks away.

Liv immediately dives in with the inquisition. "Okay, what was up with that hostess? Why would she ask that?"

I shake my head, also feeling perplexed. "It beats me, but it is clear that she slept with Eduardo or wanted to. Maybe they were...dating?" I look up at Liv, grabbing my necklace without thinking, tugging at it. I take a swig of my nasty table water, waiting for the fluorinated taste to hit, but it doesn't. "Thank god. I thought it was going to taste like pool water."

Liv laughs. "We are at a nice restaurant, Emma. I doubt it tastes like pool water here. Now, tell me why you think that." Liv must sense when I am trying to change the subject. She's had years of this with me and is well practiced, so she is familiar with my tactics and plays along.

"I know, I forgot, but I always prepare myself for that first sip, you know?"

She laughs. The waiter comes over with our drinks, and we place our orders. The martini couldn't have come sooner. I also order another martini with my food, since I know I will need more alcohol to deal with this amount of shit in my life.

Liv places her hand on her belly. "I look forward to a drink when this little one is born." She keeps her hand on her stomach, now displaying a progressing pregnancy.

Soon, there will be a baby, and I long for the day I can have a family with Eduardo.

"Are you happy, Liv?" I look at my friend, and I can see when she looks at me that she is in love and happy, whereas that look wasn't there before.

"The happiest I have ever been. I thought I loved Brodie and he was it for me, but I realized we were just comfortable with each other. We didn't have the connection that Dax and I have. I just wish things could have been different and the accident never would have happened."

I grab her hands from across the table. She has made such progress in therapy and talking to someone about the guilt that she carries.

"Liv, you know that isn't any of your fault. He made a terrible choice that had terrible consequences. Sometimes, people make mistakes that cause harm to other people they love, and it can't be undone. We think, what could we have done differently? If I didn't do this, then this wouldn't have happened. But it did, and all we can do is try to move on. Learn from it and try to forgive. Otherwise, the guilt will kill you."

She squeezes my hand and smiles. That is when she sees my ring. "What the heck is that, Emma?" She points at my engagement ring.

I smirk. "Took you long enough," I say, wiggling my finger at her. "That's why I asked you here for lunch. I knew you wouldn't notice, and I was trying my damnedest to hide it from you, but now it seems like the time to flaunt it."

She touches it and brings her hands to her face. Liv exits her chair and walks over to me, leaning down to hug me. She rocks us back and forth. "I am so happy for you, Emma. Please tell me all the details."

She moves back to her side of the table, and I tell her the clean version of how Eduardo proposed and that we don't have plans for the wedding to take place anytime soon. I ask about her wedding plans, and she says the same. No plans yet, but maybe before the baby is born. I smile, knowing that she will be married by the end of the year, which is only a few short weeks from now.

"What do you make of that woman out front?"

I shake my head. I knew she wouldn't forget about that. "The hostess? I assume that she knows Eduardo. A lot of women do. He is a very wealthy and successful man, but he's all mine. We have our past, Liv, but that's not important. What's important is that he chose me, and we are moving forward. We can't change anything we did, but I am his, and he is mine." I want to tell her more. I want to say to her he has been mine for as long as I can remember. He was always supposed to be mine.

Our food comes, and we order a crème brûlée. It has a dark berry gel with orange crystals served with lemon gelato. Liv orders the mille-feuille with fresh red berries. Delicious is the only word I can use to describe the food. I am so full right now and am so glad that we went shopping first on an empty stomach. I might not have been able to fit into anything, but I didn't want to feel this stuffed. We signal the waiter over, and he asks if we need anything else.

"I'll pay this, Liv." Before she can protest, the server holds his hand up.

"The bill has been paid for, and the gratuity as well. Thank you, ladies, for coming to dine with us and for your generosity." He pulls our chairs out for us, and we stand, perplexed as we leave the dining area.

We are passing the hostess station in front, and Liv looks into her purse for her keys before we go outside the restaurant—typical thing for living in a big city. Always have your keys ready with panic button mode, or as my mom taught me, use your keys as a weapon, intertwining them in your fingers to punch or stab an eye. I internally laugh, remembering when she taught my sister and me that technique. It scared us for a couple of days, but we recognized the importance of it.

"Liv, we can give you a ride to your car. In fact, I insist." She shakes her head.

"Emma, you have done enough. Eduardo paid for that whole meal, didn't he?"

I hear the hostess from earlier snort. I turn around and look at her, remembering we have an audience.

"Do you have something to say? If you do, then I suggest you say it."

She looks at me like I'm beneath her. Little does the hostess know who I am and who my family is. Eduardo and I are the same. I may not have been in this life all along, but I was born into it, and my uncle is too, also passed down from my grandfather, of course.

"What do you have that I don't have?"

I look at her, walking up slowly to her station. She senses the danger, backing up a little, and maybe I am dangerous. I have a dangerous family and a dangerous fiancé.

"I have his heart," I say, lifting my flashing diamond to her face, "and his ring, if you count material items. I have many material items if you want to get technical. Even before him." With that, we leave, and I don't bother further acknowledging someone like that.

We give Liv a ride to her car, and I am fuming over the audacity of those two women—first the red-haired one and then the one at the restaurant. I am sure that Eduardo slept his way through the greater Houston area, but I just wish I didn't have to deal with his conquests breathing down my neck.

Eli helps me with my bags, carrying them into the apartment, and I thank him for his help. It feels odd that Liv and I both live with our fiancés and still have an apartment of which we still continue to pay for the lease. The lease contract is not up until next year. We didn't expect to both be engaged. I am sure that if you asked us last year where we saw ourselves now, it would not have consisted of Liv being engaged and expecting a baby and me engaged as well. It is strange how things work out sometimes. Eduardo wanted me to keep the lease contract so if there is more activity with Julian, they could catch him there instead of at our home. We are still trying to track his whereabouts, but he remains untraceable.

I am putting my stuff away when Eduardo comes in looking scrumptious in his workout gear. He came straight from work at his gym today. As I take him in, I am glad to be off tonight. He looks at me with his deep-brown eyes and tousled hair. Curls just hanging a little over his right eye. He walks toward me and gives me a hug and kiss. He places his chin on top of my head.

"Did you have a good day out shopping with Liv?" He pulls back to look at me, and I tuck a piece of hair behind my ear. He searches my eyes, and I look away, stepping back.

"Yes. We did."

He cocks an eyebrow at me. "Why am I sensing a 'but' here, Emma?"

"*But*," I begin again with emphasis on the 'but' mimicking him, "I was verbally harassed by two women today when Liv and I were out."

He moves in closer. "What do you mean harassed?"

And I begin to explain. "Well, the waitress was shocked at the restaurant when she saw my engagement ring. Thanks for making the reservation under 'Emma Ruiz,' by the way." I say that with supreme sarcasm to ensure he understands further questioning is coming from that separate topic. "She said, and I quote, '*What do you have that I don't have?*'" I spare a glance at him, and he looks furious.

"Well, you have had me, Emma, from day one. We lost each other once, but I swear I will make it up to you."

I hug him, and I never want to let go. "The other girl was equally psycho. She all but bit me like a rabid dog. I had no idea who she was, but she knew me."

I see his head tilt to the side. "What do you mean she knew you? What did she look like?" I feel his fingers tense protectively around my shoulders.

I attempt to remember. "I'm not sure because her face was hidden behind a large pair of sunglasses, but she had an unnatural shade of red-colored hair and red glossy lipstick to match. Definitely well-off."

I feel Eduardo stiffen in my embrace, and I look up at him. "What's wrong, Eduardo? Do you know who that is?"

CHAPTER THIRTY-FIVE

EDUARDO

I walk to my soundproofed office and quickly call Philip. I know Emma will have questions, but I need to check this out first. It never occurred to me that Cherry could pose a threat to Emma, but I have a suspicion, and my intuition is rarely wrong. There can be no mistakes regarding Emma's safety. Philip picks up on his usual second ring.

"Hey, Boss, what's up?" I clear my throat.

"Philip, we have a problem I need you to check out. Remember that server, Cherry, from the club?"

He scoffs into the phone. "Yeah, the girl you hooked up with?"

I cringe at the memory. I must tell Emma, but I don't want her to know that. She knows I slept with women, but I don't want them to come to light. It looks like I am a little late for that, but I want her to know that there has been no one since that last night with Cherry in my office. Since I found out about her, I went for what I truly wanted. Her, just her.

"Eduardo, are you still there?"

I stop myself from having these thoughts. "Yes, unfortunately, that's her. Emma was shopping today with Liv and ran into Cherry at River Oaks. She was dressed in expensive clothing and shopping at high-end stores."

"Interesting." That is all Philip says.

"She also said that Cherry confronted her, saying 'I don't know what 'they' see in you' to Emma in the store." That makes the hair on the back of my neck rise. This must also trigger something in Philip because he immediately confirms my exact thoughts.

"What do you mean she said 'they see in you'?" he asks.

"I honestly don't know, but it is an odd choice of words. Also, Cherry was a server with a loser boyfriend. He could barely keep a job, so she picked up extra shifts. I assume it was also to be close to me. When I met her, she was money-hungry and broke. Her boyfriend was a bit possessive and held a job, but not by any means rich." Replaying Philip's and my questions in my head, the intrusive thoughts resurface that this could be something more.

I blow out a breath and brace myself for the words leaving my mouth. "Do you think when he said 'they' that she meant me and..." I pause, not even wanting to speak his name and have my suspicions confirmed.

"Julian?" Philip finishes my thoughts for me. "Yeah, Boss. It's very possible. You said Emma relayed the fact that she was dressed in designer clothes and shopping at luxury stores. He must be. Possibly even buying her off, or worse, leading her on as if he wants Cherry. That girl screamed for attention and was drawn to rich, powerful men. She must not realize how dangerous Julian is."

"Do you think that she is the one giving Julian information? Maybe she still has access to the club? Do we know for sure that she isn't around there anymore? Maybe, somehow, she is still able to or is helping Julian to track Emma's movement?" Each question makes me want to vomit. My involvement with Cherry could cause Emma harm. I am starting to sweat. If I am responsible for Julian getting to Emma, I don't think I could live with that. I won't let him have her. I start to pace the room, thinking of a way to stop this once and for all.

"Philip, I need you to be vigilant and see if you can track Cherry's movements. See what she is up to. Maybe through her, we can finally find out where Julian is hiding." I don't know where to begin. My thoughts are muddled as I try to make sense of this fucked-up situation. We are leaving in a little more than a week to Mexico to see her uncle and spend our first Christmas together there with her family. I will think of a plan by then and let the family know. Perhaps together, we can devise something to end this once and for all.

I end the call with Philip, and he promises to stay hidden and see what he can find out about Cherry and Julian. If anyone can, I know that Philip will pull through. He is trustworthy and someone I can call a true friend. With Jameson helping, we can track him down sooner.

I need to go and discuss this with Emma before she jumps to conclusions about Cherry. I am sure she has figured it out, but I don't want to have to tell her about my suspicions that Cherry, my previous hook-up, is the one telling Julian about my girl's movements. That would only scare her and not help the situation.

I leave my office and mutter under my breath, *"Well, here goes nothing."*

I find Emma curled up on the couch with a glass of wine and her Kindle. She has her hair in a messy bun, fuzzy socks, and wait, are those glasses?

"Since when do you wear glasses?"

She quirks her head to the side, assessing me. I am sure she can sense the stalling.

"They are blue light glasses to prevent a headache." She doesn't say anything else. Just stares at me.

"What are you reading?" I ask her, further stalling the conversation about Cherry.

"Mafia romance, of course. What else?" She shrugs. She is still watching me.

I would laugh if I didn't know she grew up in the mafia life, but I know she did, making this much more amusing. She is using the same techniques against me, and I wonder if she even knows what that is—using silence, not answering, allowing the other person to feel uncomfortable so that they need to fill the silence and end up giving themselves away. This girl? She could wait forever, just watching me. Since this is my Emma, I stare right back at her.

She lifts an eyebrow at me. "Cut the crap, Eduardo. Who were the women?"

I start to hesitate and then sigh. She waits patiently for my response. Knowing she won't like what I have to say, I sigh again, rubbing my hand over the stubble on my face. Still, she waits, just looking at me, devoid of emotion. She has learned to school her features, and I hate that she has to do this with me. I want to be the only one who always sees her genuine, unabashed emotions. I look up at her and can't help but wince. I know that she has shut down, and it guts me. How many times has my girl had to do this before?

I inch closer to Emma and gently hold onto her face, stroking her cheek. Still, she doesn't change her expression.

"The woman from the restaurant is a customer at the gym. She hit on me before when applying for a gym membership. I can't remember the exact details, but she was agitated when I pawned her off to someone else to show her the 'locker room.' I knew her intentions and I wasn't interested. It might have even been Helena who had shown her around, but I'm not sure at this point.

"I remember she listed that place of employment as a hostess on her application when I was punching the demographic information into the computer. I remember that scenario because I was afraid she would come back and tell me something at a later time. I looked over her account just in case, and it stuck out. When I made the reservation, I don't think she realized I was the one who called to place it for you, but I thought it would send a big FU to her. She came in again recently, and I told her I was engaged. I thought that was the end of it. That is nothing compared to what I have to tell you." I get up off the chair and pace around. Emma continues to sit and just looks at me.

"The other girl was a waitress at my club. Her name is Cherry." At this, Emma snorts, and I see the anger begin in her eyes as she slows her breathing. "I hooked up with her a few times." I wait and look for Emma's reaction, and she sits there, fists clenched at her sides. I will myself to continue. "One time, her boyfriend came to start shit at my club and found out she had been cheating on him. I, of course, had no idea, nor did I care because I was not interested in a relationship with her. It was something we did at work only."

Emma stood up at this. "So you fucked her in your office or some shady part of the club." She starts to walk off, and I run to her. I grab her hand and spin her around.

"Emma. This all happened before you, and I swear it would not have happened if we were together. I stopped hooking up with her when I learned your parents had passed away."

She looks up at me, trying to control tears that threaten to fall.

"When was the last time you were with her, Eduardo?"

I cringe at the memory and don't want to tell Emma, but I won't lie. "Cherry and I were together that night when Ram called to tell me." I look at her and grab her tight, burying my head in her neck and breathing in her scent. She smells like my bath soap. The one she uses because she loves it so much—to remind her of me. "Look, Emma, I love you, and once I learned what happened to your parents, I haven't been with anyone else since, even after all those months from when Cherry and I were last together until I saw you in the ER that night."

I feel her tremble against me. "Does she still work there?" I shake my head and push her back to look at me.

"I fired her even before I reconnected with you again. Like I said, her boyfriend caused a scene, and she came in proclaiming how she told him she was in love with me, and he couldn't handle that. I didn't even know she had a boyfriend, Emma." I look up at her and place kisses along her face. "I told her I didn't feel the same, and she could no longer work there, especially with the scene her boyfriend–or ex-boyfriend–caused."

I kiss her on her lips, pressing hard, trying to convey how much I love her. How much I want only her. "Emma, if you see this woman again, I want you to tell me, okay? I want to make sure she isn't a threat to you."

Emma doesn't seem to get it because she says, "I'm not scared of her, Eduardo. She can't hurt me."

I almost tell her about what I think is her involvement with Julian, but I don't want to alarm her, so I keep these thoughts to myself. At least until I know for sure that Philip has confirmed such things to be truly accurate. Until then, it's all just speculation, and it would cause her to worry unnecessarily.

"I know, baby. You're a badass. My badass." I pick her up, and she wraps her legs around my waist. Her mask is slipping. Her eyes warm to me, and I am so fucking sorry that I wasn't with her then, but this is our time, and I don't want to concentrate on what could have been—just us moving forward.

I walk her over to the couch and drop her down. I look down at her, pull her glasses off her face, and the hair ties out of her hair. Her long blond hair falls along her shoulders. I pull back, breathless from her beauty. I tug off her pants, panties, and socks in one go. Her band hoodie still covers too much of her body, so I lift it over her head and leave it on with her arms still in the sleeves. She isn't wearing a bra underneath it; her full breasts hang deliciously on her bare body. I pull my joggers down and let them drop, showing my commando status.

Emma's eyes flare. "You went commando at work?" She seems to get upset at this.

"They have a built-in liner," I tell her, and she laughs. She laughs so hard that she twists sideways and is now snorting. Her breasts are heaving up and down as her body convulses with laughter. I move down and start to tickle her.

"What's so goddamn funny, Emma?" I am still tickling her and trying not to laugh at myself. She's wheezing, trying to stop laughing at my expense.

"Are those Lululemon lined joggers?" She is now in a fit of tears.

"I'll give you my Lululemon right here," I say, grabbing her sex. I drop to my knees and throw her legs over my shoulders, twisting her onto her back again. I drive in to nip and lick at her pussy, which effectively shuts her up. Her restricted arm goes over her face, and she moans. I twist my tongue into her pussy and begin to fuck her with it. She squeezes her legs around my neck, trying to bring me closer. I hold onto her thighs.

I drop her legs, standing up, and drag her to the side of the couch with her legs hanging off the arm's end. I wipe my mouth and bend over, licking circles around each nipple as she arches her chest to allow me better access. I suck on one nipple and hear the pop as I release it from my mouth. I drag her legs over my shoulders, lining up my cock with her dripping pussy and sinking in. I hold her one leg over my shoulder and the other I have wrapped around my waist. I drive into her, and the sound of our coupling fills the room along with the sounds of sex.

I grab her hip and plunge in over and over. My ball sack slapping her ass, and I lean over. My teeth are biting and marking her beautiful, unblemished flesh. With each mark, she moans, and I feel she is close to orgasm. She arches into me, and I smile, loving how this woman loses all control. Her lips fall open, and I lower myself, licking up her neck and fucking her mouth with my tongue like my cock is fucking her pussy. I am so horny now that I know I will not last long. I feel her walls clench around me, locking my dick in a vice grip as Emma screams out my name.

I stand up and bring her hip toward me as I fuck her hard. I come shortly after with my head thrown back. I throw myself over on the couch, and I hear Emma make a barely audible sound.

"Oof." She tries to push me off. I wiggle around and get her on top of me, bringing her up to my body to kiss her.

"Can you taste yourself on my tongue, Emma?" She sucks on my tongue, and I swear I will come again. "My dirty little thief." I kiss down her neck and suck. I am leaving yet another mark on her body. She swats at me.

"Those better go away before we go to Mexico and see my uncle and cousins," she says playfully, moving her hair to one side.

"Oh, please. You think they don't know we have sex? Are we going to be in separate rooms there too?" I ask playfully, but they better not do that to us. We are engaged, for fuck's sake.

She laughs. "I don't think so, but we might need to get everything in before we go. In case we don't have sex while we are there. It will feel weird to have sex in my uncle's house," she says poutily. I slap her on the ass and she yelps.

"Maybe I'll take that sweet ass of yours there at your uncle's house, huh, baby?" I laugh, and she shudders. "You'd like that, wouldn't you, sweetheart?" I kiss her neck and travel up until I kiss her on the mouth. I move us to get up. "Come on, let's go shower and grab something to eat. I want to hear all about the good parts of your shopping trip." I lift her, and we head to the bedroom. I feel a little better but can't help feeling like a rogue wave lurks in the heavy seas, waiting to uproot our lives any moment.

CHAPTER THIRTY-SIX

EMMA

"I know, Adrian." I roll my eyes as Eduardo looks at me in amusement. "I am so excited to see you, too."

"How long is your layover? I wanted to make sure I wasn't late to pick you up."

I hand the airline worker my phone so that she can scan my boarding pass. "We are just boarding the plane and will be there soon." Eduardo takes my bag from my hand so that I can finish up my conversation with Adrian.

"I hate that you guys had such a long layover and couldn't drive."

I pause, knowing the reason why we couldn't drive, and try to put Julian out of my mind, so that I may enjoy the holidays without him taking up space in my head.

"I know it sucks. We have to travel through Dallas and then fly from Dallas to Mexico. It is so stupid. One would think the international airport here could give us a direct flight. At least it was less than an hour's flight up to Dallas," I agree with him, and Eduardo rolls his hands in a circle, subtly telling me through hand gestures that I need to 'wrap up' the phone call as we take our seats on the plane.

"Yep, see you soon. Tell Tio I love him and will see him soon too. Bye." I hang up without allowing Adrian to reply and look at Eduardo, who is smiling at me.

"What?" I ask, and he gives me a bigger smile.

"Nothing. It's just cute watching you interact with your cousin. He seems so possessive of you. He cares." He shrugs.

"Yes, and I can't wait to see the rest of my cousins too. Are you ready for the Spanish Inquisition?"

He laughs. "Hm. I'm not sure. Do you mean unifying our families or using brutal methods to cause widespread suffering?"

He arches his eyebrows up in question.

I, on the other hand, bend over laughing. Wiping the tears from my eyes, he looks at me with his chocolate-brown eyes, humor alight in his smile. It causes the dimple that is usually hidden to make a guest appearance, and my heart melts. This is how it should always be between us. The way we fit so perfectly together—the ease of our relationship. One day, it will always be like this. I lean over and give him a chaste kiss.

"It might be a little of both. Are you up for the challenge?" I hold my hand on his cheek, and his smile displays his beautiful white teeth, showing me the tiniest of gaps that I have been fixated on since we were kids.

I remember a conversation about it when he said he would get braces to close the slight gap on his front teeth all the way, and I told him not to because I loved it so much. It was quirky and unique. He smiled bashfully at me and looked away. I kept staring at him, wondering what he was thinking of at that time. I loved him then when I didn't understand the concept at such a young age.

"Of course, baby. I wouldn't expect anything less."

My phone vibrates, pulling me away from our conversation. I notice a message from my online chat group. I've been chatting with other fans of my favorite band that are also going to the concert in a few months. Excitement builds as we all wait for the day to get here; some talk about what they are wearing, making me think about what I will wear. I want to find a blue sequined jacket to put over my tank top. While thinking about that, I can feel Eduardo looking at me.

"Who are you chatting with?" Concern is etched on his face.

"Oh." I look at him and show him my phone. "Just some people who are also attending the concert we are going to. The fan page is an excellent way to meet other people and sometimes meet up at the shows."

Eduardo raises his eyebrows at me. He disapproves of this as I notice he stiffens in his seat. I immediately feel uncomfortable and remind myself that he isn't Julian.

"Are you sure it's safe, Emma? I mean, you don't know these people, do you?" He looks down at my phone and then back up at me. I know he only wants to keep me safe. He only uses controlling behavior with me when it is in the bedroom, and there is not a complaint from me on that front.

"Well, no, but that doesn't mean it's unsafe. It's just a band fan page where we all talk about band stuff—nothing else or really personal information is given. The band has a huge fan base, and everyone here only talks about the band or gives info about the playlist for the band. Things like that." I can see the concern in his eyes. I lean in to give him a small kiss on the lips. "I won't give out information about myself. Don't worry." He brings me close to him and nuzzles into my neck.

"I love you, Emma, and just want to keep you safe. I know I say that a lot, but it's true." He always reminds me of this. It's as if he is trying to make me understand. He says the very words I repeat to myself when I become paranoid about being controlled by another person. Julian controlled me and everything I did.

I lay my head on his shoulder, breathing in the comforting smells of his body wash. The same body wash I used in the shower to have his scent with me all day.

"I know, babe. I promise. It's okay."

We are interrupted from our moment when the airline staff call out on the speaker that we will be boarding soon with a direct flight to Tamaulipas, Mexico. We get up and stretch to board the plane after the three-hour layover for a small flight over the border. We contemplated driving, but then we would have to drive through or around Brownsville. I vowed never to return, so here we are, taking the long way around to see my family in Mexico, a few miles over the Texas border.

I pull my backpack over my shoulders and follow Eduardo to board first. He extends his hand and holds onto me as we board the plane. We have the second row in first class, so only two seats exist. I place my bag underneath the seat and have my Kindle out so I can read on the plane. The flight is short, with the duration being a little under two hours. I figure it's just enough time to get through the rest of my book. Who doesn't love a good dark romance book, right?

I buckle my seat belt and begin to watch other people board the plane.

I love watching people, imagining what their lives are like. I wonder what people think when they see me or what they think of Eduardo and me. Do they know who we are? Do they know what I want to do, especially to the man who took so much from me? The girl who pretends always to be so happy but is dying on the inside. Maybe one day I can genuinely be happy, and I hope it's soon.

The flight takes off, and I start to chew on a Twizzler. It's one of my favorite candies, and I get a ton of crap for it too. Eduardo said it tastes like wax, and he'd rather not waste time eating it. I pop the rest in my mouth and open up my Kindle. Eduardo laces our fingers together, and my eyes start to get heavy. I yawn, and Eduardo kisses my head as I lay it on his shoulder.

"Why don't you take a nap, Emma? By the time you open your eyes, we'll be there." I nod in agreement and decide to take his advice. As soon as I relax into his shoulder, he wraps his arm around me, pulling me close to him in a solid embrace.

I must have fallen asleep because I hear a commotion on the plane and feel someone shaking me.

"Baby, it's time to get off the plane."

I open my eyes and see everyone standing. I immediately wipe my mouth, self-conscious that I am drooling. Eduardo catches that and smiles. He tilts his head to the side, indicating for me to look at his shoulder, and then I am mortified.

"Oh my god, no!" I bring my hand up to my face, and he chuckles.

"I couldn't bear to wake you up. You even snored a little. It was cute." He smiles at me, and I cover my face, throwing my Kindle in my bag.

"Now I know you love me because that is not sexy at all." I shake my head and he grabs his bag. His brown eyes sear into me with lust.

"You are sexy as fuck." He reaches around my neck and kisses me hard. I pull away and hit his arm. I hear a girl giggle and I look over at her. She smiles at us with hearts in her eyes as she picks up her Colleen Hoover book, tucking it under her arm.

Not exactly my type of romance book, but hey, to each his own.

"Stop, just stop." I pull away and we both laugh at my expense and join the people walking off the plane.

We walk straight out of the terminal without going to baggage claim. Eduardo and I will get everything we need and keep it at the house. I still have clothing there from when I lived with my uncle, and Eduardo said he'll grab a couple of items if he needs anything else. Everything he has is in a carry-on. It's a personal trip, not business, so he doesn't need anything fancy.

I'm on my phone and smiling when we see Adrian pull up to get us in front of the door leading into the airport departure and arrival area. He puts the car in park and jumps out, much to the airport security's displeasure.

"Prima." He picks me up and kisses me on the cheek. God, I've missed him. He clasps hands with Eduardo and does a one-sided hug. He opens my door to the back, and I jump in as he and Eduardo get into the truck.

He looks in his rearview mirror before pulling out into the airport traffic. It's a small airport but has a lot of traffic and security. Now and then, security increases depending on the amount of crime in the area. I would say that now would be one of the high crime times, especially with increased travel between families around the holidays.

We make the twenty-minute ride to my uncle's house, and as we pull in, I am glad to be back home. I consider this my only real home filled with so many great memories. Our voices echo through the house as Adrian closes the door. Soon, I hear Uncle Andrés come in through the house from the kitchen.

"Mija, how are you?" He kisses the top of my head and hugs me tightly.

"Tio, I am good." I motion with my hand for Eduardo to grab onto and bring him closer. He wraps his left arm around my waist.

"Andrés." He puts his hand out to shake hands with my uncle. "It's been a long time."

I listen to his words, but there isn't anything inhospitable about it—nothing that expresses contempt.

"Yes, it sure has, Eduardo, but I am glad you are here now." He looks at me and claps his hands together.

"Well, Emma, you guys go freshen up from your trip, and our family will be coming over this evening for a party. They are all looking forward to seeing you and catching up. Your cousins will be over to set the band up, and we will start the barbeque pit in about an hour. Please help yourself to anything that you'd like. This is your home, Emma." He squeezes my arm and walks away.

I lead Eduardo up to my room. Since they didn't specify if we would sleep in different rooms, I will let that go for now. I open the doors to the balcony, allowing the light breeze in. It's cool, and I love this time of year. I can wear my hoodie right now and be comfortable. I look out at the landscape and enjoy the view.

Eduardo comes over to me and hugs me from behind, bringing me into him. He wraps his arms around me and nuzzles into my neck. I sigh in contentment. How often did I wish he was with me when I was alone in the house after my parents died? I look back at him and see him looking out through the trees.

"What are you thinking about?"

He looks at me and waits before saying what he is thinking. The breeze blows my hair back a little, and I shiver despite it being warm for this time of year.

"I'm thinking maybe before we leave here, we can take the truck, lay in the bed like we used to, and look up at the stars." He smiles at me, and I swoon seeing the dimple pop just a little, reminding me of the innocent boy from my childhood.

"That sounds so romantic." I feel him nod.

"Yes, and then I can do all the naughty things my pubescent body wanted to do to you back then." He pulls away before I can smack him. "You are such a mood killer."

He laughs and starts to remove his clothes. "Eduardo? What are you doing?" my voice raises a few octaves. "We are at my uncle's house and it's daytime. Everyone is walking around."

He rifles through his bag. "Um, I'm getting some new clothes to shower the airport off my body?"

My face flushes. "Oh, yeah, that's a good idea." I go to grab a new outfit from my closet.

"Are you joining me?" He stops at the door. I can tell he wants to laugh.

"Go!" I point at the door as he chuckles, closing the door behind him. I hear the sound of voices carrying through the courtyard, some of them familiar. I jump off the bed and head downstairs to see the rest of my family.

CHAPTER THIRTY-SEVEN

EDUARDO

I leave the shower and enter an empty room, absent my fiancèe. Her scent still lingers, and I inhale deeply. I wasn't kidding about taking her to look at the stars like we did when we were younger, lying in the back of the pickup truck. I was inexperienced, and Emma was too young. Now, none of that is true, and I can't wait to do all the things we should have done together.

I see my erection start to tent the towel that is still wrapped around my waist. Even just thinking about her makes me hard. I'm going to need another cold shower if I continue to think about her. I dress quickly, throw my bag into her closet, and venture out looking for Emma. I head downstairs, following the sound of a party gathering in the courtyard.

I don't have to go far when I hear her laugh echoing through the inner patio. Her voice carries on the dusty air. Before I can seek out Emma, I see Andrés leaving his office. He looks behind me to see if Emma is around.

"Eduardo, before you go out there, I'd like a word with you." He holds the door open, and I walk into his office, which is full of Emma's family and some members of his security team. I also noticed that this isn't a request but an order, and I hate how he throws that in my face.

It is a bit intimidating being at the mercy of Emma's family without anyone here to have my back, but I know they won't do anything to me. They want to be sure Julian is taken care of as much as I do, and lucky for them, I am the man to get the job done. Besides, it would be poor form to take me out here. They know I love Emma fiercely and will not rest until she is safe and Julian is found. We have history. Our families have a history. Andrés sits behind his desk and motions for me to sit next to Adrian as the rest of his men stand around.

"Do you want a drink?" He already poured me one, or maybe it was for himself, but I don't ask.

"Please." I extend my hand and he nods. He advances toward me, handing me the drink, and I thank him for it. He sits in the chair behind his desk, and I wait to hear what he has to say. I can feel them all staring at me, but my focus remains on Andrés.

He clears his throat. "It has come to my attention that one of your girlfriends may be helping Julian to track down and spy on Emma?" I don't miss the tick in his jaw. I stare at him and wait for him to finish. "Explain."

This line of questioning makes my heart speed with anger. I have to control my breathing to remain calm because of this motherfucker. To say that Cherry was my girlfriend and make it seem like I have multiple girlfriends, or worse, insinuating that I am cheating on Emma, is ridiculous.

"First, just to clarify, Cherry was a waitress at my club. She was never my girlfriend. She may have wanted a relationship, but I never gave her that impression. Her boyfriend came into my club and caused an upset with the staff. He caused a fight and had to be thrown out. When I found out that Cherry was the cause of it, announcing to her boyfriend that she loved me and chose me, I set her straight and fired her with pay to leave the premises." I take a drink and down the contents of my glass, letting the alcohol soothe the anger spreading across my face.

"I was never with that girl after, nor have I seen her. I reconnected with Emma and have been with her every day after that day. I am engaged to her. I love her and will protect her until my dying day." I look at Andrés and Adrian as I say this so that they understand that I am not playing around nor entertaining any other women in my life.

I go on to tell them what happened with Emma at the boutique in uptown Houston, as well as my suspicions that Cherry may be helping

Julian with gaining information.

"Cherry wasn't wealthy but has recently come into some money. She has a fancy apartment and dresses in designer clothes. She went from begging for a shift to not working? Something is fishy, but what concerns me is that she mentioned to Emma that she, and I quote, didn't see what *'they'* saw in her."

Andrés sits up in his chair and looks over to Sergio who is already on the phone. "Do you have the address of this place?"

I nod and write it on a piece of paper for him. He looks at it and hands it over to Sergio.

"Another thing." I pause, and Adrian sits up and leans over to me. I'm glaring already, and I haven't even said anything. "I'd like to keep this between us, but as you know, Philip is a good friend and was Emma's security detail."

Adrian snorts. "So you killed him. Yeah, some friend."

I look at him, lift my lip in a half smile, and shrug. "You heard that too? Well then, my plan worked better than I thought."

Adrian cocks his eyebrow upward and looks at his father. "So Philip isn't dead?"

I shake my head. "No, he is very much alive. I never told Emma he was dead. I just made it look like I killed him for allowing Julian to get near Emma. We knew he was close, and Philip did tell me. Jameson, my frat buddy who does my security system for the club, came over and wiped the cameras when Philip was led into the basement. Obviously, there weren't any cameras in there, so he was escorted out, and the cameras were wiped clean of any evidence. He has been helping me to track Julian and see if anyone from the club is letting Cherry in to help Julian stalk Emma. She could have been taken one night at the club, and I think it's someone close by working at my club or someone who has access to it. Either way, we will find out soon and end that."

Adrian looks toward his father. Andrés rubs at his beard in concentration. I don't know what he is thinking, but I am sure he has something to contribute to helping us find Julian. He stands up, walking across the room to look out the window. I already know that he is looking at Emma down in the courtyard. "We haven't been able to track him following Emma. He has been with his family or showing up at sponsored events, but never anything suspicious. Then, he is gone on business, but there is nothing that we can find or use against him."

I nod in agreement because I have had the same findings. "We have seen him on camera twice, and he was in Emma's apartment. I have a feeling his patience is running out." They are all looking at me.

"Why do you say that?" Adrian's fists clench at his side.

"Well, he was always just watching her. Now he is coming at her. He has been close to taking her in her place. That is why she is always with me or has someone with her. Philip is finding out some more information and should have something more concrete this week. That's why my men think he is dead, and Emma doesn't think that because the men would never admit that to her."

After another drink and a consensus about coordinating information, we decide to step out and join the festivities. Although this took much longer than expected, it was needed. I would rather speak about him at the beginning of the trip than at the end. It's best to clear the air and get it out of the way.

I see Emma outside, and she is drinking a Corona with her cousin, laughing and carefree. I wish I could see her like this all the time. She picks up her cousin's son, and I walk over to her. She swings him side to side on her hip, talking to him and kissing his puffy cheeks. The boy is laughing as she blows kissy noises on his neck. He grabs her hair and laughs. I wrap my arm around her and snuggle into her neck.

"God, you look good carrying a baby," I tell her, and she laughs.

"Oh no, we are not having a baby anytime soon." She eyes me, but I see her joking with me.

"Are you sure? We could start tonight under the stars," I tell her because I am mostly kidding, but if she says yes, I would definitely put a baby in her, even if the timing isn't exactly right. With Emma, anytime is the perfect time for me.

"I'd like that, Eduardo." She kisses me on the lips, and I bite her bottom lip, sucking it into my mouth. She pulls away and hands her cousin her baby, and I take her hand, staring down at her.

"As much as I'd love to carry your baby, Eduardo, I think maybe we should wait. Maybe until..." She trails off, and I know that she is worried about Julian. I grab her face and turn it back to me.

"Soon, babe," I promise. I kiss her forehead, and her cousin's band starts to play.

They're pretty decent. I chuckle as Emma starts singing "The Best of You" by the Foo Fighters. The barbecue pit starts to smoke, and the scent of meat cooking mixes with the earthy smells of mesquite wood burning permeate the air. I take a deep breath in, and my mouth begins to water.

Emma looks at me and laughs.

"Did you miss Tio's brisket?" She leans into me, and I am salivating at the thought.

"Most definitely, yes. The man can cook some brisket." The song changes into "Warning" by Morgan Wallen. She leads me out onto the makeshift dance floor in the inner courtyard. I feel all eyes on us, but I don't care. I only see her. We hear her cousin whistle, and I chuckle.

"Was that the dinner bell?" She kisses me.

"Not soon enough. I'm starving. You?"

She looks at me. "Yes."

I bring her in and kiss her. "Then after dinner we will take that drive out to look at the stars, and I'll eat my dessert."

She swats my arm. "Come on, let's eat."

I follow her through the crowd gathered tonight and enjoy the time with my future wife and family.

The trip was over sooner than I would have liked, and we had to return to reality. Emma was sad to say good-bye to her family. The safety she felt there was soon missed, and the anxiety of returning to Houston is palpable. I give her a reassuring squeeze as Eli picks us up from the Houston airport, and we drive home. She looks out the window in contemplative silence.

"What are you thinking about?" I want to know what bothers her.

She looks over at me, smiles dimly, and then returns her gaze out the window. "I'm just worried that I might not be able to enjoy the holidays with my family anymore. I never thought I wouldn't have my parents or sister. They were taken from me one night, and I never got a chance to say good-bye. What if I don't see them again? What if that was the last holiday with them too?"

I grab her hand and bring it to my lips, giving her hand a light kiss. "I promise it won't happen. You will have us. Always."

"Don't make promises you can't keep. Evie would say the same thing, and look at what happened to her. She learned to defend herself and encouraged me to do the same thing, and look at what happened. She promised that she would never leave me."

The city whizzes by. The holiday decorations are still up, and I wonder where that fucker is hiding. Is he back already watching her? Watching us? Soon. Soon, I'll have him and make him suffer. Emma will get her revenge and be free of the blackness that shrouds her.

CHAPTER THIRTY-EIGHT

EMMA

Eduardo made me stay away from Liv for her safety as well as mine, and it seems like I haven't seen my best friend in forever. I found out Liv is having a boy and is so happy. I wish we could go shopping for baby clothes, but I understand she is in danger just hanging out with me. Learning that Julian is closer than we thought puts things into perspective. Liv is pregnant and if anything happened to her, I wouldn't be able to live with myself. I don't know what I would do if anyone else got hurt because of me.

I think about my parents and my sister, whom I miss daily. There isn't a time that goes by that I don't wish my sister was helping me plan a wedding. I see her everywhere and in certain things that I hear. Sometimes, I can even hear her talking to me through different people.

Occasionally, I pretend that one of my online friends is her, and we are excited to see each other at the Ghost concert. I know it's not healthy, but I am beyond caring about that. I want to see her so bad that I imagine her across the street looking at me just to look again, and she's gone. That's what happens when your guilt consumes you. You think you must suffer and can't forgive yourself for what happened.

After returning from Mexico and promising my family to be careful, I promised Liv I would go to the gala. This is the first time since our shopping trip that I will see her. I picked up the dress from the seamstress last week and know it will fit. I asked Dax to give me some guesstimates from her wedding dress, and I came up with something that would allow for expansion. If it is tighter, that's okay because it will still look gorgeous on Liv's tall stature and lithe body.

My knees are bouncing up and down as we round the corner to my old apartment that I shared with Liv. Eduardo agreed that if I took Eli, I could return there for a couple of hours to visit with Liv and give her the dress.

I carry the long material folded over my arm by the hanger and knock on the door before entering. I still have the key because we still have a lease. Eduardo doesn't want Julian to think I never go here, but I feel unsure since I know he has been here. When he wrote not to run from him in the mirror, I did not want to return here ever again. I feel like my personal space, my sanctuary, was violated. Did he touch my things? Go through my drawers? It's contaminated with pestilence, and I can't stay here without feeling the sense of dread creep into my subconscious, alerting me to the fact that he could get to me.

"Honey, I'm home!" I shout as I walk through the door, shutting it with my foot as I throw my tote on the table and place the dress over the sofa. I hear Liv shuffle out of the room. She's in her robe, and when she sees me, she begins to run over.

Meeting her halfway, I go over and hug her, rocking her back and forth like I never want to let her go. "Oh, Liv. I miss you so much, bestie." I pull back so I can take a look at her. "Are you even pregnant under that robe?" She releases it, and I see the baby bump. "Oh-my-god. Look at you! You are so cute."

Liv blushes and holds her belly, turning to the side so I can see her baby bump profile. "Thanks, Em. I don't look super big, do I?" She is almost self-conscious about it, and I laugh.

"Please. You are pregnant, not big. If I were pregnant, I'd be much bigger because I am so short."

Liv looks at me. "Are you...?"

I have my hand up to stop that line of questioning right away. "Nope, we are not."

Liv just smiles. "Okay. Maybe not yet."

I laugh and swat her arm. "Maybe in the future we can hang out with our kids. Right now, that is a big no for me."

Liv laughs at my quick response to no babies. "Okay, show me the dress."

I reach over and hand it to her. "Okay, Liv. Let's see how it looks."

She grabs the material, feeling the softness of the fabric moving freely through her fingers. She does a little squeal. I sigh, feeling content in this moment and knowing it won't last long.

"I'm going to pour myself some wine to see this. I know you still have some around, right?"

Liv laughs. "You know me so well." She points to the living room. "Yes, on the wine rack that sits on the dining room table."

I see my favorite wine sitting at the top of the rack with a duck on it. "Oh, yes. My favorite duckie cabbie." I open the bottle like a pro and pour myself a solid eleven ounces of wine. I sigh, welcoming the complement as the fruity overtones of blackberry, cherry, and plum assault my taste buds. I fight the urge to smack my lips. Liv just stares at me.

"I'm so envious of you right now." She looks at me and smiles. "Do you have to look like you are enjoying that wine so much?"

"I feel so much better now. Perfect. And yes, I do. You go show me how stunning you look in that dress."

Liv runs out of the room into her bedroom with the dress. I swear the girl is practically glowing. I am the one jealous of her. She looks happy now. I thought I'd never see that look on her again. It is long overdue.

While I am waiting for her, I decide to go to my old room and look around. I go to the bathroom, and when I stop to wash my hands, I stare at the mirror. Julian was standing right there when he wrote that message to me. My breathing picks up, and I think I am having a panic attack. I breathe in for a few seconds, hold it, and then blow out, repeating the process until I feel calmer.

"Fuck, I need more wine." I walk out to the dining room and top off my wine though it wasn't empty. My hands are shaking, and Liv is standing in the hall looking at me when I look up. I try my best to school my features, but I am afraid she's already seen it. My mask slipped, and all I can do is deflect and redirect her questions. That is, if they even come. She knows, after all these years, my secrets stay hidden.

When I look at her in that dress, I smile genuinely.

"Look at you!" I go over, almost skipping with giddiness at seeing my friend so radiant. "Liv, you look ravishing in this dress. Dax is going to rip this off of you after the gala."

She squares her shoulders to look at me, pointing her finger and wiggling it in my direction.

"Ha, that's where you are wrong, Emma. He'll throw the back of this dress over my head and take me from behind up against this wall instead."

I almost spit out my wine, but unfortunately, when I try to prevent that, I snort it out my nose instead. Choking, I sputter. And that's what I get for pouring so much wine in this glass.

"Why, Liv, you little minx." I manage to sputter that out in between clearing my nostrils of the wine in a coughing fit. "Now," I wheeze, finally managing to stop coughing, "that is the funniest thing I have heard. Where is my shy friend I once knew?"

We both chuckle, and I look around, noticing that Dax isn't here. "Where's Dax?"

Liv shrugs. "Oh, he went to pick up his altered tux and should be back soon. Nothing like waiting until the last minute." She starts to ask something but stops.

"Um, so how are things with Eduardo?" She pauses, and I know that she thinks I will not answer her. It reminds me of how much of a shit friend I am. I'm about to answer when she spins the question, shocking me. "You seemed happy with Jameson, and then you met Eduardo..." She trails off, not finishing the sentence. I just stare at her. Liv notices my hesitation and continues breaking the awkward silence. "I never did thank him for helping me that night when I found out I was pregnant. Fainting. Passing out at his club was not one of my finer moments."

I go over and place a hand on her arm. "Oh, Liv. Don't even worry about that. I pause, wondering if I should continue. "Yeah, I liked Jameson, but it wasn't there. When I met Eduardo... I don't know. He makes me feel." I leave it at that because that's precisely what it is. He makes me feel. After years of being numb when my parents died and I lost my sister, I didn't think I would ever recover.

My best friend died that night. A big part of me died that night.

The remaining part of me wished I would have died too, alongside them in the fire. I feel like I live in this earth-bound prison where I must watch over my shoulder and risk being captured by Julian—a worse fate than death.

Liv watches me and tries to finish my sentence. "Happy?" she asks.

I rub my lip back and forth, trying to explain without giving away too much of my story. I look over at her and hope that this at least answers her question.

"Even better. He makes me feel safe."

She looks at me in confusion. "Safe?" she questions.

I smile sadly at her and drain the entire contents of my glass. I grab my keys, effectively stopping the conversation before it even begins. "I better go. Still have to get a quick bite to eat before seeing you guys at the gala."

Defeat shines in Liv's eyes, but I can't let her know. I can't let anyone else know.

"Sure, Emma. I'll see you there. We are sitting at the same table, right?"

I start toward the door and hug her before I leave. "Of course. I'll let Eduardo know."

I sit with Eli in the car, feeling unsure about my future. Will I always have to deal with Julian? Will I ever be truly free? We drive through uptown, and I look around at people in shops and walking with friends on the sidewalks. I see a couple jogging toward a park, and I feel empty. I want that life. A normal life, but I'll never have that. In some way or another, I will always have to watch my back, but wouldn't it be nice to be rid of him finally?

My fists clench. I want him to suffer. I want him to die. I don't think I have ever really thought about it like this. I do know one thing for sure: he will pay for what he did to me and my family. I won't rest until he is gone from this earth, but not until he feels what it is like to lose it all.

I grab my Airpods and turn on Spotify. I recently played and hit "Voices in My Head" by Falling in Reverse. The song is my anthem, my battle cry. I tear myself down, and I feel all the guilt consuming me. The struggle I think about every day is that I don't have my sister.

I wonder what we will do today as I ride alone in this car. Oh, wait, not alone, but with a driver hired to keep me safe. My inner voice tells me I am to blame, but self-doubt takes over when confronted with whether or not I can continue. My sole mission is to take back my life. To break free from the confines of self-doubt I have, and it overtakes me like waves in the sea. The wind picks up, and I am tossed around with no life preserver. If I die, I will die trying. If I drown, I'll do so trying until I'm buried at sea.

CHAPTER THIRTY-NINE

EDUARDO

"What the fuck do you mean? I'll be right there. I want you to take him to the basement," I spit into the phone as I rush to go down to the nightclub.

Philip discovered that one of the bartenders was helping Cherry acquire information about me and Emma. I haul ass to the club and park sideways in the back alley, running into the building and up to my office. Jameson knocks on the door a few minutes later.

"Come in!" I shout as he walks into my office. I am pulling up the feed as he towers above the security monitors on my desk.

"May I?" he asks, and I stand from my chair and push the seat over to him. He hits a few buttons and pulls up a feed that has Gage, our long-time bartender, walking in the hallway, with Cherry leading him over to a back storage room where we keep many expensive liquors, candied Luxardo and Maraschino cherries, and various other nonperishable items. Jameson enhances the sound on the computer as I hover over him, watching the scene unfold.

"What do you have for me, baby?" She stalks toward him, and he smiles widely. She drops to her knees, unbuckles his jeans, and unzips his fly. They fall to the floor with a loud clunk as his heavy metal belt hits the tiled floor. She looks up at him, licking her lips, and he steps closer to her as she grabs his ass, digging her fingernails into his flesh as he hisses and his cock bobs. She rubs her cheek up and down his cock and looks expectantly at him. "I want to make you feel so good, and then I want you to take me any way you want, but you have to tell me what I want to know first." She turns her face sideways, licking up the underside of his shaft and sucking on the tip as she releases him, stops, and looks back up at him expectantly.

"I heard him talking about a concert he was taking her to. It was her favorite band." He stops talking as Cherry grabs his cock hard and takes it into her mouth all the way back into her throat. Gage holds onto the shelf and knocks a bottle off, hitting the floor and spilling contents all over.

"Fuck, that was a five hundred dollar bottle of Johnny Walker Blue Label. Son of a bitch."

Cherry stops and looks at the mess, frowning. She continues to look at the spilled contents while lapping at the tip of his cock. "Hm," she purrs. "Tell me more so you can bend me over and fuck me already."

He grabs her head and pushes her onto his cock again. She takes it willingly. "Let me fuck your mouth for a minute first." He backs her up to the wall and places his hand above her. She grabs his ass hard as he pounds into her mouth, stilling each time as he hits the back of her throat. Her head goes back, and he groans. She hollows out her cheeks, and he bucks forward and comes down her throat. She continues to lap at him, licking him clean as he rubs her cheek affectionately.

"You suck my cock so good, Cherry." She pulls herself up, licking her lips, and lifts her dress, showing that she isn't wearing any panties, and then pushes her tits out the front of her already low-cut dress. She grabs her tits, shoving them upward, and Gage eyes them greedily.

"Tell me more," she moans, flicking her nipples back and forth.

Gage tells her everything she wants to hear. He dives into her boobs, kneading and licking. He turns her around, and a couple more bottles fall off the shelf.

"Motherfucker!" I scream out at the monitor.

He turns her around and pushes her down on the shelf. He sticks a finger in her ass and then another, scissoring it back and forth. He takes his stiff cock and presses it against her ass and thrusts forward. I watch about another thirty seconds of him fucking her ass, until I am sure there isn't anything else said about Emma.

I get up, and Jameson follows me into the basement. Eli is still guarding Emma, so I have another few men there waiting on me. I see Gage there chained to the wall, and I walk in, hitting him in the face. I punch him over and over, until Jameson holds me back.

"Um, you might want to ask him questions before you knock him out." He grabs my arms, halting any further action.

I stand there, attempting to control my ragged breaths. "Tell me everything," I speak to him in a low growl. I smell the scent of urine and realize he pissed himself. "Alejandro, come over here." Al walks up and waits for me to give my order. I am walking out the door. "Make him speak. I have to take Emma to a function tonight. Too bad you won't be relaying information to Cherry anymore."

Al punches Gage in the ribs, and I know he's broken a couple. I look at Jameson, and he nods. I know he'll keep me posted. He is determined, just as I am determined to ensure Emma is safe.

I hear Emma enter through the door as I speak with Philip on the phone. After returning from our trip from Mexico, we have been actively trying to keep tabs on Cherry. I believe that she will lead us to Julian if we are patient enough. Patience has not always been my biggest virtue.

After extensive investigation, Philip discovered that Cherry seems to have come into some money and now lives a life of luxury in a spacious apartment in the Uptown section of Houston, nearer than we'd like. He wants to tell me more, and I know that he has been working hard to find out if there is any correlation between Cherry's newfound wealth and Julian's retaining new information to help him stalk Emma.

When I see the haunted look in Emma's eyes, I can't concentrate on anything else Philip needs to tell me. "Hey, can I call you later?" I interrupt.

"Sure, Boss, I'll keep digging and keep you posted. No worries," he says, and I end the call.

I stand up from the island barstool and drain the rest of my whiskey from the glass. I approach Emma as she puts her purse on the foyer table.

"Hey, baby. How was your day?" I bring her into me, and she softens, releasing the tension she held onto from the emotional weight bearing down on her shoulders.

"Exhausting." She lets out a long breath and pulls back from me. "I feel like such a shit friend to Liv," she says, hiding her eyes from me.

I pull her hand away from her face and tuck a loose strand of hair that fell from her messy bun behind her ear. "And why is that?" I look at her and wait for her to explain.

"She knows that I hide things from her, and every time I change the subject or deflect, I see the hurt it causes her. I want to tell her everything, but I'm scared. The last time I did that, I caused the people I love to suffer. I never want to burden anyone with that again. I'd rather be buried with my secrets."

"Emma, let me carry that burden for you. You are my partner in this life, and you no longer have to go through this alone. I am here." I hold her face in my palms and kiss her. I want to show her how much I love her in that kiss, and I understand just how much she loves me. I can feel it, and I hope she knows what I say is true. I grab her hand and lead her to the bedroom.

"Here, let me run you a bath and you can relax before the gala. You'll see your friend, and we can hang out with her and Dax."

She seems to perk up at this. "Maybe that's all we need is one good night out." She discards her clothes and walks into the bath, and I can't help but watch her as she steps into the tub.

I palm my cock through my pants and try to halt the erection tenting them. She sees that and calls me over. I lean down and kiss her.

"Later, I'll worship you. Now, you relax while I finish up on a call with Eli about security for the gala." She pouts and I laugh. "You can choke on my cock later, baby." I wink at her as I walk out.

After talking with Philip again and then Eli, I have an idea how tonight will go. We suspect Julian might be at the gala and will be watching to see if anything is suspicious. Eli understands that he is to be around in case things get out of hand and is to follow Emma everywhere. With two people on Emma, one that doesn't know about the other, I feel better about being in a crowd with eyes on her.

I walk into the room and see Emma putting on the jewelry I gave her. She wears her engagement ring and her necklace that she never goes without, as well as the tracker I had Jameson get for her. She is wearing a green dress that matches the color of her eyes. Her hair is plaited in a loosely curled braid wrapped around to the side that lands over her right chest. Pieces of hair fall from the plait at various stages, and it looks simple yet classy. She steps into her six-inch stilettos and is considerably taller than her regular five foot two inches, or at least that's what she claims her height to be. I walk to her and pick up her braid, twisting the loose pieces of the end in my finger.

"I like this," I tell her and flick it back and forth. "I think it will be fun to use later." My eyes find hers, and she smiles mischievously. She licks her lip and reaches up to gently kiss my lips. I bend, allowing her to pepper light kisses down my neck. She looks back at me and then my shirt.

"Oops, I think I got a little lipstick on your white shirt," she says sincerely.

My lip curls up in a smirk. "You don't have to mark your territory, Emma. I've been yours forever." I grab her hand and lead her out of the room before I destroy her pretty hair and makeup.

We enter the gala, which is busy with patrons begging to display their wealth and social status in the community. It's the same with all the galas. Even though this is for a good cause, they still have to be wined and dined before contributing to the community or overpaying for a silent auction item bid.

I know many people from the gym, my club, and other non-legal endeavors are here. There are a surprising number of politicians from the local area as well. They use the opportunity to network as much as possible.

I mingle, and I introduce Emma as my fiancée. She is engaging and charismatic. I hate that she gets the attention of men, and I certainly don't want her getting the attention of some of the men I see here tonight.

I receive a message from Philip saying he needed to check something suspicious, and my heart accelerates as I look around for Eli. I spot him, and he is watching us. I tip my head to the side in Emma's direction, and he nods. I want her watched now more than ever.

I see Emma looking around, no doubt to find Liv. We haven't seen her or Dax, but I am sure they must mingle and play the part just as much, since this is Dax's mother's charity.

We hear someone take the mic and see Dax's mother, Isabella, attempting to get everyone's attention. We go to our table as other people do the same thing. Just as we walk to the table, we see Liv and Dax approach from the opposite direction. Liv hurries over to Emma and hugs her.

"Geez, Liv, you'd think I didn't see you a few hours ago." She laughs, separating herself and taking a seat next to me.

I shake Dax's hand as he takes his place next to Liv. We all settle into our assigned seats, and soon, dinner is served. The silent auction follows, and we bid on a bougie charcuterie basket with a bottle of Emma's favorite wine, Caymus. When Liv's phone rings, Emma tells me she must go to the bathroom before her bladder bursts. Emma is scrutinizing Liv saying something to Dax. Liv looks at her phone, answering it as she walks off. Emma follows her, telling me she'll be right back. I send a message to Eli to let him know Emma is on the move. He makes eye contact with me and walks over to her as she disappears around the corner, following Liv. Dax is frowning and shaking his head, looking in the direction Liv went.

CHAPTER FORTY

EMMA

"I'll be right there, Liv." I head into the bathroom and quickly relieve my bladder from the extension and stretch of too much water and wine with dinner. I rush back out, looking for Liv. She looked so upset, and I know that whoever called her had terrible news. I thought I heard her say Melissa, Brodie's nurse, so that can only mean that it has to do with Brodie once again.

I am pondering all the things that could have gone wrong when I run straight into a man. I step away, muttering my apologies, and he says it's not a problem when I look up and stare into the eyes that have brought me so much agony. Eyes like his psycho son.

"Mr. Martinez," I gasp, and his eyes narrow, quickly scanning the area. He doesn't have time to act because I rush out the door searching for Liv, heading toward an outside door. I see him walk toward me as I push past it, and he hesitates. I can't worry about that. Eduardo and Eli are here somewhere; I'm safe. For once, that is the furthest thing from my mind because I can only concentrate on getting to my friend. The look on her face as she left the table concerned me.

I spot her and then see Liv drop the phone and slump to the floor.

"Liv!" I shout at her, but she doesn't respond. She doesn't even look my way.

I pick up the phone and hear Melissa crying from the other end of the line. Melissa replays the story about Brodie being rushed to the hospital on the brink of death.

"Oh god, no." I throw my head back, and the tears come to my eyes. I hang up and drop down to Liv, trying to shake her. She isn't listening. It is as if she has checked out of her body and completely shut down. After all the girl has gone through with the Brodie situation, I would, too. Why did this have to happen when things are starting to go so well?

Dax flies through the door along with Eli. I give him all the information. Dax moves, picking up Liv, and I follow them outside with Eli on my tail when a black SUV pulls around the corner. Eduardo jumps out, scanning me for any injuries. I shake my head at him, but I can't stop the look he gives me, as if he knows what happened before Liv fell onto the ground. We all drive to the hospital that Brodie was taken to not long ago.

The next few hours are the worst with how history is repeating itself, except this time, it is the end. The doctor comes in and gives us the news. Brodie didn't survive the infection that wreaked havoc on his system. Just like that, another life was lost.

I see a broken person in Liv. Broken attracts broken. I understand her and her damaged parts that are so similar to mine. Misery loves company and all that, and boy, have we both had our fair share of it. Just when they had rekindled their friendship, Brodie was no longer depressed and angry. When he began accepting his disability, this happened. It's ironic how life is sometimes. Just when you think things are better, the other shoe drops and kicks you in your ass. Eduardo holds onto me as we sit by Liv. My hand is on her shoulder as she sobs into Dax's chest.

We step out of the SUV to hear thunder cracking across the sky. It is fitting that there should be a storm approaching. It's as if the angels are weeping along with us. I am devastated for Liv. With her pregnancy, I worry about all the stress she is under. She is a shell of her former self. The priest talks about the Kingdom of God, a long speech about His son returning to be united with Him. There are a lot of people here who made the trip. I know it makes the family happy to see that their son was so well-liked by many people. He had an impact on all our lives at one point or another.

I walk to the car and see Liv alone after everyone has left, still holding on to her single rose. It's as if she doesn't want to throw it in the grave because that will be it.

The final good-bye.

She releases it, and my lips part as I see the agony on her face. She looks up at the sky as if she is talking to God. I am wracked with sobs, watching and not being able to help her. As much as I claim to want to take back my life, I haven't. Liv has faced all the obstacles thrown at her. I am afraid that this is all too much. I can't seem even to help my friend as she goes through the loss of Brodie. I haven't even told Eduardo about seeing Julian's father, Mr. Martinez, at the gala. There just hasn't been the right time, or at least that's what I tell myself. The truth is, I'm numb. I don't care.

I see Dax pick up Liv and bring her toward the car as Eduardo goes around the side to open the door for him. I witness Dax rubbing a circle with his thumb around the top of her hand, and I look away, feeling as if I am invading a private moment. I look out the window as the rain slides down against it, finding it ironic as it mimics my tears on my cheek.

We get home, and I drop my bag on the foyer table, exhausted from today's events. I kick my shoes off as I fall onto the couch. I sit there cradling my head in my hands. Eduardo comes over and starts to rub my back.

"Baby? Do you want a drink?"

I nod as he saunters over to the bar and pours us both a couple of fingers of an amber liquid. I don't ask questions, but take it as he places it into my hands while taking a seat beside me. I sit back, and he picks my feet up, placing them in his lap, and then begins rubbing them, causing me to release a moan. He stares at me, assessing the likelihood of a complete breakdown as I down the whiskey in one long pull. He takes the glass from me and places both of them on the table next to the sofa. He pulls me onto his lap, and I curl into his body as I sob.

"Baby, what's wrong? Are you okay?"

"No, I'm not. I feel so bad for Liv. I couldn't help my family, I couldn't help Liv, and I certainly can't help myself." I ugly cry into Eduardo's chest as I pull at his shirt, wiping my tears and snot away.

"Shh," he soothes. "Let it all out, Em. It's okay."

He holds me like this for what feels like hours. When I have no more tears to cry, I pull away and wipe my eyes. I shake with a sob, but no more tears fall. "Am I officially broken? No more tears to cry, and I am gutted."

Eduardo takes my hands, making me look at him.

"Emma, you are not broken. You are so strong. Resilient. What you have been through would have made weaker people crumple. You are still standing despite everything you've lost. You've always been there for Liv, and I am here to be there for you, to pick you up. I am here to make you believe in your strength and will always be there to catch you if you fall. But you are still standing, and he hasn't won."

I stand up and pace the room. "For how long, Eduardo? How long do I have to fear for my life and hope he doesn't take me or hurt someone I love?" I look at him, hoping he understands how much I feel for him. He is my world. I pause, closing my eyes as I shudder at the thought of seeing Julian's father. The way he looked at me. There is more to the story than him wanting me with Julian. The contempt he held for me was scarier than Julian's ill-treatment. I open my eyes and look at him.

"At the gala, I saw Julian's father. He knows where I am, my friends, and who I am with." I say it all and get it off my chest. "I can't help but worry that he will hurt you all."

Eduardo stiffens. "What! Why didn't you tell me? Emma, it's been a week. He could have come at you or us. I can't prepare for him if you don't tell me. I can't keep you safe if I don't have all the information. You can't hide things like that from me."

I look at him, and he looks away. I don't know why he did that, but it makes me cautious. Is there something he isn't telling me? Should I be worried?

"Fuck." He pulls on his hair and walks to his office. "Stay there. I have to make a call." I hear him on the phone, and he looks at me, shutting the door. Not caring about staying put, I walk to my bedroom and strip out of my wet funeral clothing. I put on a robe and let the hot water from the shower billow in the air. The steam rises in waves.

I stand under the hot water as I hear the door open. I see Eduardo through the frosted glass drop his clothes on the bathroom floor before he enters the shower behind me. He holds me under the hot spray, trying to stop my body from shivering. He pumps some shampoo into his hands and lathers my hair, rubbing his fingers through my scalp. I tilt my head back at how good his fingers feel massaging my scalp. He rinses off the shampoo and repeats the same actions with the conditioner, making sure to detangle my hair with his fingers as he washes it out while his strokes remain gentle and soothing. He washes my body with his shower gel, rubbing the suds over every inch in a languid caress. His hands don't linger as they usually do when we share a shower because this act isn't about sex. It's about showing how he cares for and wants to take care of me, even when I'm at my most vulnerable and cannot.

I worried him when I told him about Mr. Martinez, and he lashed out in anger. I should have told him, but my safety wasn't a priority then. He rinses me and steps out after washing the soap from his body too. He has a big fluffy towel and dries me off, slipping an oversized T-shirt over my head. We walk back to the bedroom and lie in bed. He covers me and gets into bed with me, spooning me with his body pressed against my back. Even though I can feel the hard line of his erection on my back, he doesn't try to make a move to fuck me. He just holds me and rubs his hands in a circle around my stomach while the other runs through my hair, rubbing my forehead with each pass of his thumb.

"Eduardo," I moan as he moves up and down my neck with light kisses. He nibbles on my ear, and I feel a pull from my core. I want more. I always want more from him.

"Please, Eduardo. Make me feel something."

He turns me around and looks into my eyes. "Emma, you are the most important thing in my life. You need to fight and take back your life. Only then will you be truly free. You have to continue to fight, Emma."

He gets on top of me, moving my legs apart with his knee. He positions himself with his cock lined up with my entrance. He stares down at me, hovering his body over mine. He kisses me and thrusts into me with one hard pass. He pulls my lower lip in his mouth as he balances his body on his forearms while continuing to move fluidly in and out. He buries his face in my neck and sucks on my skin, marking me all over, reminding me I am his. His thrusts become harder, as he leans into me a little more, repeatedly hitting my cervix with a delicious pounding, causing my climax to build rapidly.

I can hear my wetness and the sound of our skin smacking together. He takes my nipple into his mouth, lapping at the tender bud. His thrusts are unrelenting. I come with a gasp, shouting his name as my inner walls spasm with my climax. He comes on a groan as he spills into me. He kisses me softly on the lips. My breathing starts to regulate as I come down from my high, and my vision that blackened with my orgasm subsides as I open my eyes to bring me back into my reality.

I see Eduardo looking at me intently. "Fight, Emma. Fight for us."

His words empower me. He makes me feel again, but now I feel too much. I'll take it. It's better than not feeling anything. It means that I am alive and he hasn't won. The wave of emotions consumes me, and my rage for Julian will overpower the worst storms.

CHAPTER FORTY-ONE

EDUARDO

Things have improved over the past months. Liv has turned the corner, and she and Emma are closer than ever. After the funeral, Liv broke down, and Emma was in a constant state of worry for her mental and maternal health. All that stress wasn't healthy for the baby. Dax was always by her side, and Emma was gone a lot to stay with her when Dax couldn't. At least I knew where she was, and Eli was always close behind me.

We are sitting at the breakfast island having Mexican sweet bread and coffee—a definite Mexican food staple. We have some time to kill before the concert, and Emma could hardly sleep last night. She couldn't believe the day was actually here. I had to feel her moving back and forth all night. She even got up to pee at least a couple of times. I couldn't take it anymore, and I pulled her into me, spooning my arm over her. I held her until her breathing evened out and she finally allowed me to pass out too around two-thirty in the morning.

I look over at her and see her doing her crossword puzzle. Without looking at me she says, "I wonder when Philip is coming back."

She distracts me from my thoughts as I was looking at her and thinking about other things. She looks over at me, but I honestly have no idea how to broach that subject.

"No idea, babe. He just said maybe soon after things clear up." I shrug because my words aren't exactly untrue. She doesn't ask for further details. It's pointless. I won't give anything else away. The less she knows the better. I had people watching her, and I just hope that is enough.

"Okay, I was just curious," she continues, not really done with this conversation, "but I don't want to pry if Philip has problems with his family. I understand the need for privacy sometimes."

I reach over and squeeze her hand, returning my focus back to my computer screen on my laptop. We sit there in comfortable silence, and I think about the concert tonight, wondering if something could happen. Could tonight be the night he tries to take her?

Julian hasn't reappeared, but we are waiting for what he could do next. We also haven't heard anything from Julian's father, but I'll bet that he called his son right after he saw Emma. She mentioned that he looked at her with anger all the times he was in her sight. It was as if her presence disgusted him, and I don't understand why that is. There has to be more to the story, and I told her uncle and cousin that a few times during our visit in Mexico over the holidays.

We know Julian is in Houston, and after following Cherry, she hasn't led us to anything we consider noteworthy. After her informant at the club was placed in the ground, her well of information dried up, and she no longer had access to that source.

I had an emergency meeting with the staff and told them she was not allowed in this club. If I found out she was back in there, it would cause immediate termination or worse. When they asked about Gage, the bartender that was fucking Cherry and telling her information about me and Emma, I let them know that he wouldn't be around to cause further problems as he is no longer working at the club. I left it at that and let them come to their own conclusions about Gage's whereabouts.

Jameson and I have become closer, and I trust him to help me with Emma. I feel better that she has a button to hit in an emergency—the starburst pendant. Emma gets up from the stool and tells me she is going to start to get ready.

"Are you sure? We still have a lot of time until we leave for the concert," I inform her, but she just smiles at me.

"I have to do my makeup and costume. It might take a while." She looks at me and smiles mischievously.

"Should I be scared, baby?" I wonder what she has up her sleeves, and by the look in her eye, I can tell that she is planning something epic.

"You should always be scared, baby." She leans over and bites my lip.

"What the…?" I touch my lip, but she didn't break the skin. She smiles and winks at me, and then slowly turns around, walking off, leaving me now very turned on. I think I have met my match.

I pick up my coffee and decide to make another, but this time with a little bit of alcohol in it. I move the stool she'd been sitting on over and throw my feet up on it and relax, knowing that Emma will be in there for a while getting ready for tonight. I can make my plans with the extra security I have for us tonight without her knowing. I smile to myself as I look at our bedroom door. I am more than curious to see what she has up her sleeve tonight.

I get ready for the concert in the spare bedroom. I don't want to take away from Emma getting ready in our master bedroom. When I walked in there it was total destruction. There was makeup everywhere and I was assaulted with a hit of hairspray to the face as I approached her from behind. At least she didn't hit me in the eye. She swears that this stuff is all natural and cruelty free, but I bet it fucking hurts to get in your eye. I've been sitting on the couch answering emails from work, until I finally hear the sound of the bedroom door shut.

She walks out of the room dressed in black fitted, ripped jeans with an Eponymous Tour Ghost concert shirt. Her hair is pulled back with two inverted French braids that wrap around in a wild ponytail. Her long blond hair hits mid back, and her face is painted with ghoulish makeup. She is wearing platform black Doc Martens boots. The look is completed with a bright-blue sequined blazer she spoke about getting specifically for this concert to match Papa, the lead singer. She is a sight to behold, even in her ghoulish attire.

She sees me and smiles. Her black matte lipstick makes her teeth look even whiter and her smile wicked. I have a fitted black shirt, jeans, and boots. Nothing special. This is about Emma. It's her night, and she has been looking forward to it since I bought the tickets. She grabs her phone and a clear plastic bag that most concerts only allow into the venue. I realize that I have been staring at her when she clears her throat. I stand and put my phone away mid message as I take her arm, and we walk out of the apartment through the front lobby.

CHAPTER FORTY-TWO

EMMA

E li is there with the car, and we are soon on our way to the event. The concert is about thirty miles north of Houston, so we have a small drive ahead of us. Eli messes with the radio and hits the Spotify app.

"What do you guys want to listen to on the ride to the concert?" Eli drags his finger through the recently played section of the app.

"Oh, I made a playlist. Here, put this on." I connect my phone, and "Ghouls Night Out" by the Misfits starts to play through the car speakers. Old-school Glenn Danzig's vocals begin with the three standard power chords infamous in punk rock music—the powerful simplicity of the genre is refreshing. I also made a concert song playlist for the event tonight with every song the band planned on singing, starting with Ghost's first song, "Kaisarion."

We drive and get most of the playlist, and I sing to every song. I feel Eduardo staring at me, and I catch Eli looking in the rearview mirror, catching glimpses of him suppressing a laugh. I don't have the best voice, but I don't give a damn. This is the best music ever. When we get there, Eli comes to open the door, and Eduardo grabs my hand, helping me out. We start walking toward the venue, and I see everyone dressed in decorative attire. Eduardo looks around and then smiles down at me.

"Looks like you've found your tribe here. You should probably hit the port-a-potty before we get in there."

We go through the line, get our merch, and walk it back to the car. I don't want to lose my signed poster. We are allowed early entry and walk in to look through some of their stations in the VIP lounge. It has displays of the band and pictures. A little food spread is laid out for us, but I am too excited to eat. A lady walks in and lets us know that we will be lining up for those who have pit tickets, and my smile drops. It isn't that I am not appreciative of the chance to be here, but what I wouldn't do for pit tickets. Eduardo looks over at me.

"Let's lineup so you get a good spot."

I look over at him in shock. "What did you say?" I blink at him several times because I couldn't have heard right.

He smiles at me expectantly. "I had Helena give us her pit tickets, baby. We need to line up for the pit."

I fling myself into his arms. "Oh my god. I love you so much more right now. Let's go."

We follow the lady as she climbs on an ATV. We walk and are lined up for the concert pit entrance at the front. Once we get in there, you don't leave, so I am ready for this.

We await the beginning act, and I take my phone out and check my online chats. Her name is Genevieve, and she is in the States for the concert. I am so excited to meet her after finally chatting with this girl. She lives in New Zealand now, but was originally from Texas and still has family here. That's the great thing about online friends. You have so much in common and would have typically never met if it wasn't for modern technology.

Eduardo peers over and sees me chatting. He frowns, and I see the way he looks at me. Always so protective. He assumes everything is a threat to take me out.

The opening act was fabulous, and now it's time for the main attraction. I think I am going to burst with happiness. The Ghouls and Ghoulettes come out first on stage, and then we are blessed by Papa Emeritus IV.

Eduardo looks over at him and then at me, screaming his name, and he shakes his head.

"It's part of the lore, Eduardo. Just go with it. It's going to be amazing." And it is. Before I know it, the concert finishes with "Square Hammer," and I am losing my mind. I have gone through a series of emotions in the past couple of hours. Anticipation, excitement, happiness, and sadness that it is over all too soon.

The ghouls are out front in their masks, tossing picks, and I see Eduardo jump up in the air. He keeps his arms in as he lands back on his feet, slightly swaying. I look at him, and he holds out the contents of what is in his hand. I scream and grab it.

"A fucking pick. Yes!" I run in place and squeal with excitement. I throw myself at him and kiss him. "This is so much better than my mummy dust cash I got earlier that shot out of the cannons."

He shakes his head as tears break the corner of his eyes. He is now wheezing.

"Are you laughing at me, honey?" I poke him in the chest, and he just shakes his head, trying to control the onslaught of laughter that threatens to continue at my expense. He stops and kisses me.

"I love you Emma. Come on. Let's get out of here. I have to pee so bad."

We walk out slowly through the crowds of people, and I walk into the women's bathroom as Eduardo does the same into the men's bathroom next door. He said he will be right there when I get out. I agreed to wait for him. I see the line of people, but it goes by quickly, carefully managed by bathroom attendants.

I go to the sink to wash my hands, and a girl is putting on red lipstick in the mirror. I immediately recognize her from the other time I was shopping with Liv. I look away, and she continues to stare at me. I decide to confront her.

"What are you looking at?" I meet her eyes defiantly. She looks at me with disgust.

"Me? My name is Cherry, and I was Eduardo's girlfriend before you came along and stole him from me, so you know what? I took your boyfriend to see how you like it."

I look at her with confusion. "You were never Eduardo's girlfriend."

"Oh, honey, I know you can't keep up with the sexual needs of a man like that. The way I sucked him off or the way he bent me over his desk at work, pounding into me as I screamed his name. Hm. He doesn't love you."

The anger inside me explodes at the thought of Eduardo doing anything

303

with that girl. "Oh, he doesn't love me, huh? Is that why he wants to marry me?" I know it is a poor excuse to flaunt my ring, but I shove it right in her face, and it contorts with anger.

"I don't care anymore because now I have Julian, so you can have Eduardo."

I look at her, and she must get the reaction she wants. "You're lying," I tell her, stepping back looking around for the man who still hunts me.

"Oh no, I am perfectly serious right now." She walks closer to me.

"Cherry, you need to get away from him. He will hurt you," I plead with her, pointing at her to listen to reason. "That guy is sick." I am no longer angry with Cherry but concerned for her life, but she doesn't seem to care. She only sees me as a threat to her happiness. I grasp the top of my head, unsure of how to make her see it.

"You don't understand, Emma. He is obsessed with you, and we can't be fully together if you continue to be in the picture."

I step back again, scared when I see that crazed look in her eye, and suddenly begin to feel faint. "Stop, please just stop." I look around. I need to find Eduardo. I turn around to leave and find him when I hear a commotion outside. A fight has broken out, and that's when I feel the sharp object behind my back.

"Follow me, Emma, if you know what's good for you."

The fight is a huge distraction, and I don't see Eduardo. Cherry walks me out the side doors and out of the pavilion. We walk across the street and down an alley with an empty building. Everything is so much more amplified at night. The shadows seem to come out of everywhere, posing a threat. My sense of dread increases as Cherry brings me into an old warehouse that is in various stages of remodeling. My boots echo in the open room.

Cherry lights a candle that sits there as if she prepared for this whole thing. My mind fills with every twisted scenario, and my need to escape takes over. I see that she has a knife. I step backward and trip over a cord lying on the floor. She takes this as an opportunity to come at me. She gets on top of me, lays the knife by my head, and starts to choke me. She pins me down, straddling me with her arm around my throat.

She may be bigger, but I am stronger. I often think back to Adrian and me in the gym, and survival instincts kick in. I grab ahold of her hands, locking them against me. This causes her to become unsteady and unable to stabilize her arms upward. I twist my body, and we fall sideways. Now, I am on top of her and punch her in the face. Blood pours from her nose, and I hear her cry out. I jump off her and pick up the knife.

I see her trying to get up, holding her nose. I step back, holding onto the knife, and then I see her smile. Blood is staining her teeth, and she looks unhinged. She looks behind me, and that's when I see him—Julian. He is here, and he has finally found me. I hit the emergency star on my bracelet. I just hope it's not too late.

CHAPTER FORTY-THREE

EDUARDO

I leave the bathroom to wait for Emma, but she hasn't come out of the bathroom yet. The lines were long to get in there, but they went by quickly, and I knew I'd beat her out before she finished. I see two guys throwing insults back and forth to one another right where I am standing, and I find it fucking annoying as hell. I just want to get Emma and get out of here. I am starting to feel uneasy, and I need to find her and attach her to me ASAP.

Expectantly, blows start flying between the two guys, and I let out a frustrated sigh. A large crowd forms and people start pushing each other. One guy is drunk and is extremely obnoxious. The other has a black eye that is starting to form.

I make my way out of the commotion and look toward the bathroom. I see another girl that was close to Emma in line walk by me, and I know Emma is finished but now is nowhere to be found. I whirl around, looking for her, and hit a call to Eli. He answers on the first ring.

"Hey, Boss, are you guys headed out soon?"

My stomach drops. "Emma isn't with you? I've lost her."

"Oh, fuck," is all I get from Eli.

"Call Jameson and bring him down here. He said he would be close by in case we needed him." I look to see where Emma is on the GPS tracker and notice that she is in the area. I see the star moving toward a few buildings down the street. I run out of the pavilion and jump into Eli's car.

"Here. Look, Emma isn't far from here. We have to get to her." I see my phone ringing, and it says it's Jameson calling on the illuminated screen.

"Jameson," I answer, out of breath. "Where are you? Someone has Emma. I just know it."

"I'm at this restaurant down the street. I got stood up tonight. I'm on my way. I see her in this warehouse not far from here. Do you see it?"

I look at the star shape on my screen, nodding. "Yeah, I see her. We're on our way." Just then, we all get an SOS from the location Emma is at.

"Oh shit. Emma is in trouble." I just hope we aren't too late.

We speed to the location of the building that the SOS came from. We scan the area, and nothing looks out of the ordinary. The building is dark. I see Jameson running over from across the street, and a few of my men are walking around the park across the street, ready to intervene if necessary. Eli, Jameson, and I walk into the building, trying to be as discreet as possible. I have my gun, as does Eli, and we give one to Jameson should the situation arise for him to need it. Better to be safe than sorry.

The door is open, and we walk into almost blackness. Except, I catch sight of golden hair that shines brighter than any light. A beacon calls out from the dark of night, guiding a ship into the safety of storming waves at sea. A light shines, and I see Cherry. Her face is messed up, and I look at Emma, who is unhurt from what I can tell. She is tied to a supporting column in the middle of the room. Cherry's eyes are bruised over, and it appears her nose may be broken. I take pride in my girl; she let her have it. I wonder what caused such an exchange. Emma locks eyes with me, and Julian steps in from the corner with his gun pointed at me.

"Drop your weapons and kick them forward."

We all lower our guns and drop them, as he says. Cherry has a knife to Emma's neck, and Julian has our firearms. Emma is still staring at me. Julian steps in front of my line of sight, blocking Emma.

"Don't fucking even look at her. She's mine and for my eyes only. You remember that."

My jaw ticks, and I could murder that asshole if I knew that Emma wouldn't get hurt.

Cherry's head snaps over to Julian. Her knife leaves Emma's neck and falls at her side. She looks hurt by his words. She moves toward him, and we watch, anticipating what will happen. If she pushes him, we could get to Emma or take him down. There are three of us.

"What do you mean she's yours?" The feral, unhinged look in her eyes is scary even for me to witness, and I see Emma cringe inwardly. Cherry snaps her sights on Emma. She is defenseless as Cherry lunges for her.

"I'll fucking kill that bitch. She can't have you too. I did everything for you, Julian." She goes to attack Emma, and my girl braces for it, but Julian intercepts her and pushes Cherry onto the floor.

"No one else hurts Emma. She is only mine to hurt." The spit flies from his mouth, and he is indeed the monster Emma described him as. Cherry lies on the floor and attempts to get up. Julian walks forward to her and points his gun at her.

"I can see you are going to be a problem. I was hoping we could have some fun together, but I don't think it will work out anymore, Cherry." With that, he lifts his gun and shoots her twice in the chest.

She lands backward as red appears on the ground, pouring out from her chest wounds, making the red of her shirt even darker. She places a hand on her chest as blood comes out of her mouth in a cough that sprays blood all over the floor. Julian lifts his gun once more and shoots her in the head. Three bullets and Cherry is gone.

I stare at her dead body. Her eyes have fixed, locked on something she no longer sees. I know that she is gone. I look over at Julian, who has already lost interest in Cherry, if she ever held any interest for that man. He walks over to Emma and stands off to her side.

"I think this has gone on long enough, Emma, don't you? Why don't you tell Eduardo who you really love." He looks over at Emma expectantly. I lunge forward, praying that I can get to him, but he sees me from the corner of his eyes. He lifts his gun at Emma.

"I wouldn't do that if I were you, Eduardo." He tsks. "If you claim to love her as much as you say, it would be in your best interest not to move any closer." He moves closer to us and kicks the weapons out of the way. I look over at Jameson and Eli. We all have the same pained expression of anger and sadness in our eyes.

"Say it, Emma!" he screams at her, and she looks him in the eyes, not backing down.

"I'll never say that to you, Julian," she says low enough, but its effects are crushing to Julian. His eyes narrow, and he lifts his gun to her. Emma locks eyes with me and mouths *'I love you always.'*

EPILOGUE

EMMA

I know my time has run out. Julian has found me, and it's over. I can't say that I don't have so many regrets in my life. I can never make amends for all the lives lost at my expense. Eduardo has been the best at keeping me safe, at least up until now, but it was always going to come to this. This moment when it all changes.

I hope that he doesn't blame himself for this. It was bound to happen, and now it's over. I can't control many things, but I can manage this. If I am gone, I won't be a burden to anyone anymore. My family is all gone, and I know Eduardo might be sad for a long while, but eventually, he will move on and have the chance to be happy.

I glance over at Cherry and stare at her vacant eyes. She was so alive just a moment ago; now she is dead on the floor because she became involved with Julian.

"I think this has gone on long enough, Emma, don't you? Why don't you tell Eduardo who you really love." I hear him say this, and I just continue to stare at him. He will wait a long time if he seriously thinks I will ever say that to him. I look over to Eduardo and mouth, '*I love you always.*'

This enrages Julian, and he lifts his gun and points it right at me. I can no longer look at Eduardo and see his sad eyes looking back at me. I close my eyes, accepting my fate, and think of all the times we had recently. I see all the time spent with my sister and my family in Mexico. I see all the times spent by Eduardo and me under the stars. The time he gave me my necklace. When he proposed and worshiped my body. I smile and accept my death. I hear Julian say good-bye to me, and Eduardo screams, "No!" I hear the trigger fire, and then nothing.

I hear a loud thunk, and I open my eyes to see Julian on the floor beside me. Eduardo is running over to me, and Jameson is looking over at someone with his mouth hanging open as if he is seeing a ghost. Eduardo is rubbing my arms up and down and is holding me tight.

"Oh, my Emma." He is kissing me over and over and has a firm hold on me, getting me out of the chair and lifting me into his arms. I follow Jameson's line of sight, and if Eduardo wasn't holding on to me, I'd pass out.

She walks over to me with a smile on her face. Her hair is cut short and slicked back, but it's her—Evie, my twin sister.

"She's alive." I sob, and Eduardo holds me up.

He looks over and shakes his head. "You were always one for dramatics, Evie."

"Good to see you too, future brother-in-law." She hugs Eduardo and then grabs on to me.

"Sis, I've missed you so much." She hugs me, and we both cry. I am wracked with sobs, but it sounds odd because I am also laughing. I suppose these are tears of happiness. I swear, sometimes I don't understand myself. Eduardo walks over to Jameson, and he is staring at Evie.

"Close your mouth, James. You're drooling on the floor. It's not a good look."

I watch the exchange. He looks at me and goes to say something but stops.

"That's Emma's twin sister, huh?" he says aloud.

"Boy, you're a fast learner, aren't you?" Eduardo mocks.

"Fuck off. She's hot. I think I'm in love." He grabs his face and rubs his hands repeatedly as if trying to wake himself from a dream. In walks Philip, and Eli groans.

"What the fuck? Is everybody coming back from the dead?" Eduardo gives him a look and shakes his head.

"Too soon?" Eli says, and Eduardo snorts.

"Yeah, a bit, but I get it. It's ironic as fuck." Eduardo walks over to me and my sister.

"I'm just glad that it is all over," Eduardo says on an exhale as he hugs me from the side and brings me into a tight embrace. I feel Evie look over at me and smile. I return it and then look over to my future husband.

"Oh, Eduardo, I have a feeling that this is just the beginning," I say, remembering the words Adrian said to me not so long ago.

"Fuck, I was hoping you wouldn't say that." Evie looks over at me, winking.

"That was one sweet chokehold release that you got out of, if I do say so myself, Emma." Her eyes go wide, as do mine.

"You saw that?"

Evie nods and laughs. "Fucking epic, girlie."

"So what now, Evie?" She looks over at us and then grabs the back of her neck.

"We have a lot to talk about."

Emma snorts. "That's an understatement. I mean, what happens n-o-w?" Evie stares at me with a look that promises to wreak havoc. It's the look she would give me when we knew we would get into trouble. She takes one of her black-gloved hands and extends it to me in an invitation.

"Well, Emma, now that you are free, tell me who you wanna be."

THANK YOU FOR READING!!!

Did you enjoy reading *Black Wave?* If you did, I would be grateful if you could please consider taking a second to leave a review on one, or all of your choices below. Reviews help to make me a better writer, and I appreciate your words and constructive criticism!
Love you all,
L. Renee

Amazon:
https://a.co/d/1AiS7Nb
Goodreads:
https://www.goodreads.com/user/show/43246025-l-renee-richard
BookBub:
https://www.bookbub.com/authors/l-renee-richard

The second book, "*Twisted Tides*," in the Forged
Hearts Series—Book Two is out now!

Evie's story-
He stole their past. They'll reclaim their future.
Preorder coming soon.
Twisted Tides
Blurb:

Three of the hardest things I have ever had to do:
Not being able to protect my family from Julian.
Breaking a promise to my sister.
Pretending I was dead.

The tides turned the day Julian took everything from us.

My only regret is that I wasn't able to save my parents. My sister thinks I
died in that fire, but it was necessary to save her life.
My heart twisted, grieving at seeing her alone and at his mercy. I've been
watching from afar, waiting and biding my time. All of the secrets and
twisted lies will come to light.
The element of surprise will be his demise. But exacting revenge doesn't
come without consequences. Now it's time to finish this war we've started.
Now, reunited with my sister and our families, how far will we go
to win it all?

Enjoy an excerpt from the book:

Liv is tired of the uncertainty of their relationship.
She has a plan.
Meet Brodie at the beach.
Clarify their relationship.
What she doesn't plan on doing while working her shift in the ER is
meeting Dax, her swoon-worthy patient. They plan to meet up the next
day, celebrating the last days of Spring Break on Padre Island.
There's just one problem- Brodie, her childhood best friend, and recent
ex-boyfriend. She receives a video of him with another girl that solidifies
her thoughts of not getting back together.
One last day at the beach is the most memorable of her life—the
sparks between Liv and Dax are undeniable. The future held so many
possibilities. That is until tragedy strikes.
Pulled in two directions, Liv must choose between her new feelings for
Dax and Brodie, someone who had always been there for her.
She makes a choice, but is it the right one?

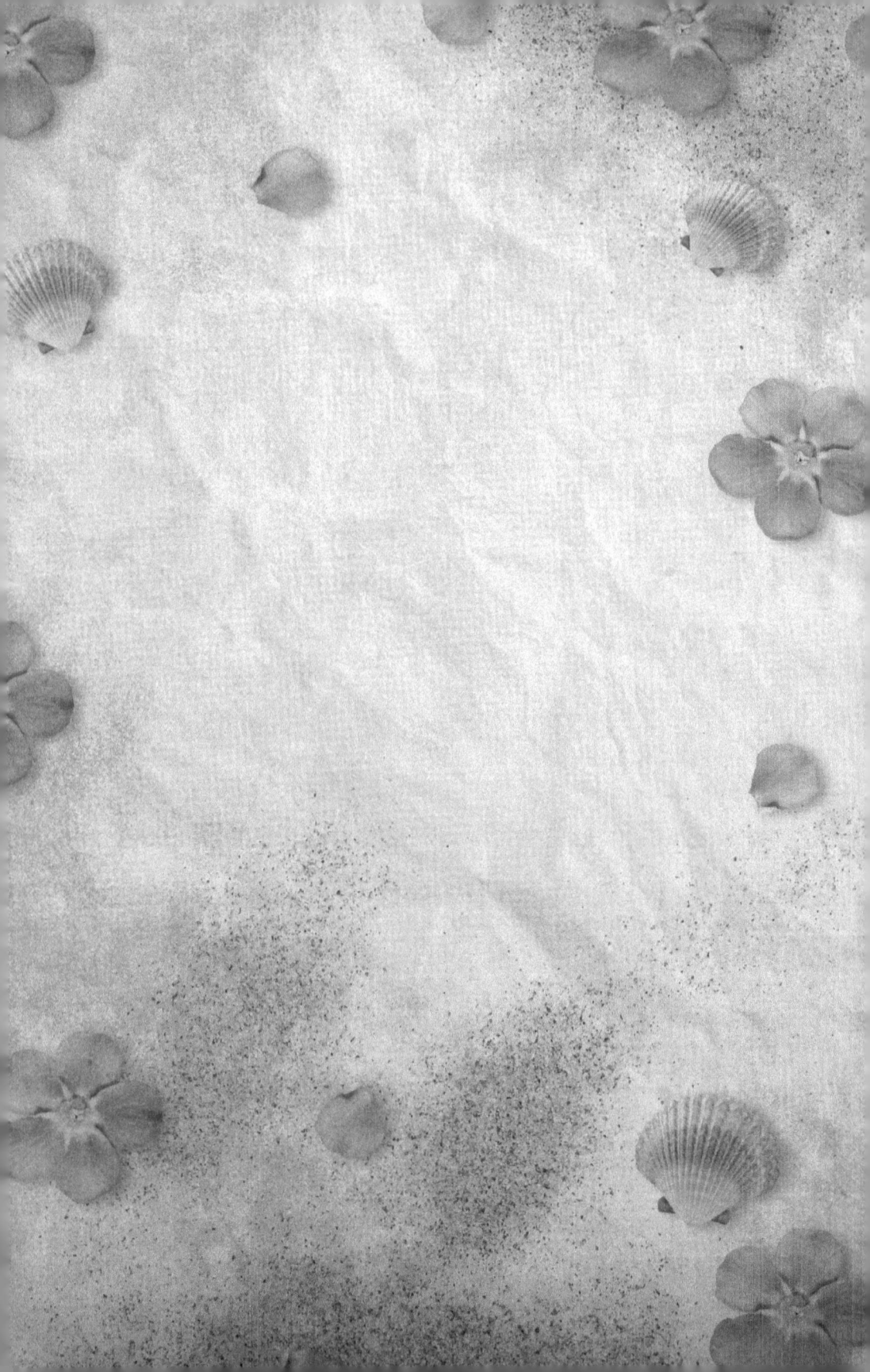

WAVES
OF
YOU

L. RENÉE RICHARD

PROLOGUE

I sit in the waiting room surrounded by my friends and Brodie's family. The hospital staff goes in and out through the operating room doors. We all look in that direction with hopes that it may be news awaiting us—an update on what happened after Brodie was rushed into the OR. Another patient is being moved down the hall on a hospital bed, an IV bag of fluids dripping in sync with the beeping monitor as he passes by. Every sound seems to be intensified, every smell much more potent. Dax is by my side. His thumb rubs circles in a continuous, soothing manner on the top of my hand. The rhythmic motion settles me as the calloused weight of his fingers offers me the stability my hand needs not to shake. The fact that he hasn't left my side speaks volumes about his character. The way he handled the situation at the beach. The authoritarian personality and calm with which he controlled the situation—the accident. If I weren't so shell-shocked, I would have been turned on witnessing him perform in such a manner. If it had not been Brodie there on the wet sand, limp and unconscious. If a million things were different.

Brodie's parents are here. It's a stressful time for all of us without dealing with the awkwardness of his parents' divorce and the bitterness between the two parties. His dad must have flown on the interstate to get here in record time.

Everyone sits in silence, waiting to hear the outcome of Brodie's surgery. Finally, after what seems like an eternity, a man wearing blue scrubs accompanied by a female in similar attire exits the operating room doors and asks for the family of Brodie. His parents stand and walk down the hall within view to receive the much-awaited results of the surgery. It's as if time stands still, and you can hear a pin drop. Except for the steps on the freshly waxed, tiled floor, no other sound exists.

The surgeon speaks, and then his mom raises her hands to her mouth, and a sob escapes, relinquishing a terrible cry of her pain. Brodie's dad just shakes his hands around, asking rapidfire questions, not allowing a moment to pause for an answer. The surgeon just shakes his head in acknowledgment. His dad puts his hands up to his eyes and lowers his head. The surgeon touches his shoulder and says something to them before walking back to our group. I rise from my chair as though I am being pulled toward this invisible force.

As I stand, the surgeon stops at our group and says, "Is there a Liv here?"

I look at him, stunned and unable to speak. I feel a nudge from my side.

The surgeon begins to speak, and I don't hear what he says. He repeats, "Brodie is awake and was asking for you specifically. He wants to see you."

I gasp–a breath let out that I didn't realize I was holding. I feel Dax bring my hand to his lips and gently kiss it. The heat of his mouth makes me shudder. He releases my hand without saying a word, telling me to go. I walk away, following the doctor without looking back. I know he won't be there when I return to the waiting room, and that this is good-bye.

CHAPTER ONE

LIV

Something about driving with the windows down while cruising over the causeway makes me smile. The second I lower the window, the familiar scent of saltwater washes through the car. The beach has always been my happy place, and I was damn lucky to find an apartment and job so close to it.

While I make my way down the highway toward work, I steal glances at the view. The waves, the people sunning themselves on the beach, the surfers in the water, and even the seagulls squawking overhead make me smile. I drink it all in for a moment… until the hot-as-fuck blast of steam assaults my face and I'm ripped back to reality.

God, it's hot as Hades today. I pull at my shirt as the sweat trickles down into my cleavage. I turn off on the next exit ramp and pull into the employee parking lot of the Bayside Hospital Emergency Department.

"Great," I mutter to myself. Quickly looking around, I see multiple ambulances parked in the designated bays. It's going to be a busy night. "What else is new?" I breathe out in a long, exasperated sigh.

This is the norm for the start of any weekend, but this isn't just any weekend. It's spring break on Padre Island—guaranteed to supply an endless amount of ER visits from sun-induced dehydration to broken bones to college kids who have one (or five) too many beers. Lucky me.

With my work bag slung over my shoulder and iced coffee in hand, I make my way to the front doors. I say a silent prayer and hope that if I hide my badge and don't make eye contact, then no one will stop and ask me anything. This is my reasoning, at least, to not be bothered with a million questions before I start my shift.

I walk past the triage desk in the emergency room and subtly scan the packed waiting room. I head to my locker, throw my bag in, and make a spot for my lunch in the fridge, gently squishing it into a packed space. Geez, I hope my leftovers from dinner last night don't fall out because that would royally suck. I had blackened catfish the previous night, and I plan on reheating it later. Nothing worse than stinky fish in the lunchroom, I chuckle to myself. Besides, there are worse smells in this place.

I keep a firm hold on my iced coffee as I leave the break room. I wish I could shoot this stuff straight into my circulatory system to get one immediate, gratifying caffeine rush. Lord knows I need it this evening. I blame the grounds crew mowing at my apartment complex for what seemed like hours, interrupting my usually death-like sleep, for my lack of energy today. Working the night shift can be challenging.

Although I'd like to blame it all on that, it isn't the real reason I had shitty sleep. I'm sure I would have tossed and turned despite the incessant noise outside my window. I've had a ton of crap on my mind lately, precisely the unpleasant subject of my current boyfriend, Brodie. Being in a perpetual state of limbo with this guy is just dragging me down. Our relationship status is something we decided to chat about this weekend. It shouldn't be this hard. We've known each other practically our whole lives. Before I go too far down that rabbit hole, I shove these thoughts to the back of my mind.

First things first, I just have to get through this shift. I walk to the nurses' station, take one last swig of my highly caffeinated drink, and reluctantly place it in the cubby. It sits among countless other beverages taking up residency there, condensation pooling all around the surface. The assignment board is already updated. I scan it quickly and begin my hunt for Emma. I need to get a report on her patients so she can get out of this place. At least one person will be having fun tonight. Why did I sign up for this shift? Oh yeah, I need the money.

I shift my gaze down one of the corridors and spot who I'm looking for. Blond hair piled on top of her head in a messy bun, Emma is not only a nurse that I happen to be relieving at shift change but also one of my best friends.

As high energy as ever, I can hear her excitedly babbling to one of our attendings. Her hand gestures raised above her head are so fast that I think she may accidentally smack him in the face. There's a reason people refer to her as the Energizer Bunny. We both took the sign-on bonus offered at the hospital after our nursing school graduation a couple of years ago. She took a job on the twelve-hour day shift, while I decided to take the opposite twelve-hour night shift. My decision to take the less-desirable shift allowed me to enroll in classes for my bachelor's degree. Classes during the day, work at night. Grueling schedule for sure, but it's getting me where I want to be, so I'm sucking it up and embracing the chaos.

My social life has taken a hit between school and work, but I'll graduate with my BSN in a couple of months and then continue to Houston, where I've been accepted into nurse practitioner school. Soon I'll be leaving this town and on to bigger and better things.

Emma catches my eye, and I nod to let her know I'm here.

As I walk toward her, she flashes me a huge smile. "Thank God you're here. It's been hell today."

I can't help but stifle a laugh. "You say that every shift."

She carefully counts the narcotics remaining in the bin and enters the correct count before closing it. "I only say it because it's true." She giggles. "I hope your night is better, but looking at the stack of pending charts..." she trails off and gives me a sympathetic frown.

Ready to brave the shift, I chuckle and head toward the nurses' station. "Judging by the waiting room, I think I'm forever and eternally fucked tonight. Let's hope nothing memorable happens."

Emma gently squeezes my shoulder before shoving some charts into my hands. "Come on, Liv, I'll give you a report on my patients. Room ten has some pain meds ordered, and I'll give her those before I leave. Can you reassess her pain in a bit?"

Thank goodness for Emma. The woman looked very uncomfortable when I peeked in as we passed her room. I do not want her to wait for her pain medication until after our shift change.

"I'll be back in a few minutes to give you a report on the rest of my patients. The sooner I do, the sooner I can get my drink on tonight." With that, she turns on her heels and prances down the hall.

Ten minutes later, she pops back up by my elbow. I'm only half-listening as she gives me the sign-out on her patients. "The labs on the patient in room eight just came back, and room two is..." She can tell by the look on my face that I'm in no mood for work. "You know we're all going to miss you tonight, right? It's the first time in a long while that we've all been able to get together."

I don't need the reminder. The fact that I am missing out on tonight is a bit of a sore spot. Our mutual high school friends are returning again for the continuous spring break beach party. The days at the beach, sea sculptures, and live entertainment are just some things that happen on the island during this carnivalesque time.

"You have no idea how jealous I am right now, Em."

She makes a melodramatic pouty face while holding both arms out for a hug. I give her a quick squeeze, feeling utterly deflated. For a second, I consider telling my manager I'm not feeling well so I can go home, but my stupid conscience won't allow it. I will only call out from my shift if I'm dead or dealing with some other near-death experience. I'm not sure even that wouldn't require a call-out. As tired (and jealous) as I am, missing work is not an option. I need every penny for graduate school; the move to Houston won't be cheap.

"I'll see them tomorrow, Em. Actually, in less than twenty-four hours, you know that." As positive as I try to sound on the outside, I'm internally cursing this shift. "Well, I want lots of pics tonight to make me feel like I am there with you guys."

"Of course," Emma quickly replies. "You know we will. I expect to meet up with the whole gang later tonight, and I will send pics of that. You better go straight to bed after your shift and get the best four hours of sleep because I am picking your ass up by noon, got it?"

I laugh. "I expect a large iced coffee and preferably a greasy breakfast burrito."

She laughs as she grabs her bags and heads toward the door. "Naturally, only the breakfast of champions for my bestie," she says over her shoulder. "I'll see you tomorrow!"

And with that, she grabs her purse and giant water bottle and heads for the door. I shuffle my feet in dramatic flair. Yup, I am definitely not ready for this shift.

As soon as she leaves, I spot Dr. Hall, the handsome thirty-eight-year-old ER physician with a reputation for flirting with the staff.

"Hi, Dr. Hall."

"Hey, Liv. Glad you're on tonight." He throws me a wink.

Typically, that little gesture would have perked me up, but even that doesn't help my mood. "Thanks," I blurt out. "I've got some updates. The labs are back on the patient in room eight, and the completed chart for review is queued first in line when you get a chance."

I am met with kind but tired eyes, almost reflecting my own. "Great," he mutters as he quickly goes to retrieve the chart.

I check on my other patients and quickly chart and update vital signs. Dr. Hall comes over and informs me that he printed out the discharge instruction for bay eight, and they can go. At least someone is getting out of here quickly tonight.

I gather all the instructions and check to see if she needs anything else before making my way over there. The drape is still closed, so I call out her name before I peek in.

Mrs. Shea replies, "Just a minute, dear. I am just pulling on my shirt."

I wait patiently for her to finish and help her to the waiting room. As I pass the discharge instructions to her, we see her husband pulling up in front of the entrance. As I watch her drive away, I can't help but think about what the next patient will bring.

I let the ED tech know that the bay is empty so they can clean up the room and prepare it for the next patient. Our department is certainly busy, but thank goodness it's efficient. I grab the following chart in the queue and look at the chief complaint—ankle pain related to a surfing injury.

"Well, that's a total surprise," I mutter as I make my way to the waiting room.

I open the door to the waiting room and call out, "Dax Johnson?"

No reply. I see two guys sitting in the chairs wearing board shorts, T-shirts, and flip-flops, chatting animatedly with each other. When they get up, I bet there will be sand all over the seats too. A quick scan of them shows one has a bruised and swollen ankle. That has to be him. But as my eyes wander up from the ankle in question, I notice the rest of him. I feel myself start to zone out a bit as they continue their conversation, and my eyes drift from his ankle up to his legs and over his lean body. He must be the most attractive man I have ever seen. Around six foot four inches, toned, tan, and totally delicious. His long, muscular legs are streaked with blond hair. His T-shirt is tight against his chest and shows off his narrow waist. His shorts sit low on his hips, just enough that I catch the shadow of a V pointing straight to where I'm trying *not* to look.

I realize both are still oblivious to my announcement and the fact that I've been so blatantly staring at them. I look away as my cheeks begin to heat. I notice a couple of patients smirking at my lack of subtlety. I give myself a mental slap and call the name again.

"Dax Johnson?" My voice comes out an octave too high, and I pray they overlooked that too. I see the pair halt their conversation, and one raises his arm.

"That's me, coming." His deep voice pierces right through me and sends a wave of butterflies straight into my stomach. He tries to get up but stumbles almost immediately, trying to avoid putting weight on his ankle.

I go to grab a wheelchair just in case he needs it. When I return, I see he's made his way across the waiting room, holding on to his friend's arm for support. It's then I notice his arms. Thick, muscular arms with every nurse's dream of pipe veins running up his forearms. If a forearm porn show were a thing, he would be the star. I lift my gaze to his face and catch him staring at me with amusement.

Am I that obvious? My face immediately flushes with embarrassment, and it becomes about a hundred degrees too hot in the room. My blood seems to have been rerouted and is collecting in my now scorching face. Taking a deep breath, I try to regain an ounce of professionalism and look up. I'm instantly met with the most exquisite pair of penetrating blue eyes. Wow, is there anything wrong with him? Oh yeah, his ankle. He stares at me with such intensity that I feel he can almost read my thoughts as his gaze also shoots to his ankle. I immediately look away in embarrassment because he knows what I am thinking.

"Do you need a wheelchair?" I state in the most squeaky-sounding voice I have ever heard myself make to further my humiliation.

He looks at the wheelchair and then back at me, smiling. As if he couldn't make me feel any giddier, a dimple appears on his left cheek, and I feel a slight warmth spread between my legs.

I try to move forward but feel my feet locked in place. It's as if my shoes are cemented to the waiting room floor. Damn, could I be any more pathetic?

I clear my throat and try again. "Do you need a wheelchair?"

He shakes his head, and I feel his unwavering stare, but I do not make eye contact this time. "No thanks, I can walk," he says while grabbing on to his friend's arm for support.

I put the wheelchair back and hit the button for the automatic door.

He begins to walk, I hear him say, "This might take me a minute."

I reply over my shoulder, "That's fine. You can take your time with me. I mean, umm, no need to rush." I immediately rush around the corner and smack my forehead. Someone just shoot me now and end my word vomit. "We don't have far to go," I add. "Just around the corner."

We make it to the empty bay, and I notice that his friend hasn't come with him. I grab a hospital gown from the cabinet and hand it to him. As he reaches out for the gown, his fingers brush my palm. The touch is soft but electric. The zap immediately shoots through my hand into my body, making me tingle all over. Jerking my hand away and wondering if he felt that too, I take a step back to close the curtain to give him privacy. But let's be honest: I just needed some space to pull myself together.

"I'll let you change and be back in a bit to check on you."

Before I can leave, I hear that deep voice say, "Miss?"

I pop my head back through the curtain.

He glances at the hospital attire with a questioning look on his face. "Do I really need to put this on? I mean, it's just my ankle, and I am wearing shorts. I'll probably just need an x-ray, right? Quick wet read by the radiologist, and I'll be on my way." He flashes me that dimple again.

I look at him dumbfounded because he is right. I was simply on autopilot, trying not to be affected by his unyielding stare and that damn dimple. "Um, yeah. That's okay. You can stay in your clothes." The words come out of my mouth, but I would genuinely like nothing more than to see a lot more of that body. I want to scramble out of the room before my traitorous blushing face gives me away.

I'm not used to people questioning instructions. Is he in the medical field? Most people simply comply and throw the damn gown on. Plus, I am surprised by his terminology. He knows the medical jargon, which makes me more curious than ever.

"Have a seat on the stretcher, and I'll get you a pillow to elevate your leg and an ice pack while you wait. My name is Liv, and I'll be your nurse this evening. You're right about the x-ray. I'll go throw the order in now, so you won't have to be here any longer than necessary. How is your pain right now?"

I'm surprised I could get out a couple of coherent sentences in a row. Autopilot phrases I commonly use seem to be taking over my thinking. He looks at me with those smoky-blue eyes, and I then notice lusciously thick lashes surrounding them.

Staring fixedly at me, he says, "Not too bad."

Why do guys have such thick eyelashes while women have to pay for that stuff? He slumps back onto the stretcher and brushes his hand through his hair, still not looking away. It makes my breath hitch, and I look down at his leg to hopefully break the tension in the room.

"Good, then I'll have one of the techs bring you that pillow and an ice pack."

As I begin to turn away again for the second time, he stops me by saying, "Liv, I thought *you* were going to bring me those items."

I glance up and see the amusement on his face. He knows that I find him attractive. Now he is just fucking with me. Cocky much? I need to get it together. With as much disinterest as I can muster, I turn back around.

Without looking back, I say, "I'll try, but otherwise, someone will be back shortly. If I cannot make it back sooner, that is." Before I close the curtain, I add more sway to my ass. I might as well play this up.

I head straight for the nurses' station. I grab a tech and ask them to bring the items over. I'd like to avoid further embarrassment if possible. I pick up my iced coffee and take a few large gulps. My mouth is dry, and my heart is hammering in my chest. I wonder if he felt the same way. Maybe it was all in my head? Either way, it's going to be a long night.

Did you enjoy the excerpt from Waves of you?
Click here to read finish reading *Waves of You*:
https://a.co/d/e2WJp5o
Free on KU

ACKNOWLEDGMENTS

To my readers–Thank you for taking a chance on my book. I know that you can read any book, but the fact that you took the time out of your busy lives to read my story means the world to me. The months I poured into writing Black Wave and finally holding a copy of this book was a journey worth taking. Your support and kind words helped to see it through.

To my family– Thank you for allowing me time to sit in my office and write. I looked ridiculous cheering at your games while talking into my headset. You're so proud of me and my accomplishment of completing another novel. I see how excited you got when I told you it was done. Instead of asking what we will do, you ask when I will finish the next one. You believe in me when I get discouraged and don't believe in myself. For that, I am so grateful for your love.

To my PA–Morgan Evans, you are by far the best, and I'd be lost without you. Your feedback, comments, and help with all author things is invaluable. I am so glad I found you and am lucky to have your reassuring words and solutions to problems that arise. I appreciate you so much.

To my close friends–my work buddies who know I write spicy books and ask me about it in hushed tones in the lounge. I am glad that I am the reason you began reading romance novels. I thoroughly enjoyed our books and giving you recs, like candy you devoured each one. My besties Jess, Kris, and Lauren: you are always around when I need you, and your support and love are unwavering. My spicy book club, The Crowned Jewels: I hope one day we can finish a book together, but I do love a good brunch punch to match our gossip and inappropriate commentary.

ABOUT THE AUTHOR

L. Renee Richard is a Hispanic author who lives in rural New England with her family. She's a born and raised South Texan girl who implements BIPOC characters into her books imbued with her cherished Hispanic culture. She is an avid reader, complete with her never-ending TBR, and a romantic at heart who appreciates a strong female main character and a good book boyfriend in the books she reads or writes. She loves summers in New England, sitting on the beach with a book, driving with the windows down through rural roads on cool autumn nights, and iced matcha lattes. Her books promise angsty romance where the journey to a happily ever after isn't always easy, but it's worth the trip.

KEEP IN
TOUCH WITH
L. RENE RICHARD

Follow me on my socials

Author page:
www.authorlreneerichard.com

Amazon:
http://www.amazon.com/author/lreneerichard

Facebook page:
https://www.facebook.com/Author-L-Renee-Richard-105887815914160

Instagram:
https://instagram.com/l.renee.richard?igshid=OGQ5ZDc2ODk2ZA==

TikTok:
TikTok @l.renee.richard

Join my hype team:
https://forms.gle/9cnsA4gSfbezY7a17

Sign up for my newsletter:
https://mailchi.mp/authorlreneerichard/signup

www.ingramcontent.com/pod-product-compliance
Lightning Source LLC
Chambersburg PA
CBHW030351120726
47901CB00007B/1977